GRAVE SECRETS

Kathy Reichs is forensic anthropologist for the Office of the Chief Medical Examiner, State of North Carolina, and for the Laboratoire de Sciences et de Médecine Légale for the province of Quebec. She is one of only fifty-six forensic anthropologists certified by the American Board of Forensic Anthropology and is on the Executive Committee of the Board of Directors of the American Academy of Forensic Sciences. A professor of anthropology at the University of North Carolina at Charlotte, Dr. Reichs is a native of Chicago, where she received her Ph.D. at Northwestern. She now divides her time between Charlotte and Montreal and is a frequent expert witness at criminal trials.

Kathy Reichs's first novel, *Déjà Dead*, shot straight to number one on the *Sunday Times* bestseller list and won the 1997 Ellis award for Best First Novel. It became an international bestseller, as did it's successors *Death du Jour*, *Deadly Décisions*, *Fatal Voyage*, *Grave Secrets*, *Bare Bones*, *Monday Mourning*, *Cross Bones* and *Break No Bones*.

Praise for Kathy Reichs

'It's becoming apparent that Reichs is not just "as good as" Cornwell, she has become the finer writer ... the ever-accelerating unfolding of the plot has all the élan of Kathy Reichs at her most adroit' *Daily Express*

Also by Kathy Reichs

Déjà Dead
Death du Jour
Deadly Décisions
Fatal Voyage
Bare Bones
Monday Mourning
Cross Bones
Break No Bones

GRAVE SECRETS

KATHY REICHS

arrow books

Published by Arrow Books in 2005

9 10

First published in the United Kingdom in 2002 by William Heinemann

Arrow Books Limited
The Random House Group Limited
20 Vauxhall Bridge Road, London, SW1V 2SA

Random House Australia (Pty) Limited
20 Alfred Street, Milsons Point, Sydney,
New South Wales 2061, Australia

Random House New Zealand Limited
18 Poland Road, Glenfield
Auckland 10, New Zealand

Random House (Pty) Limited
Isle of Houghton, Corner of Boundary Road & Carse O'Gowrie,
Houghton 2198, South Africa

Random House Publishers India Private Limited
301 World Trade Tower, Hotel Intercontinental Grand Complex,
Barakhamba Lane, New Delhi 110 001, India

The Random House Group Limited Reg. No. 954009

www.randomhouse.co.uk

A CIP catalogue record for this book
is available from the British Library

Papers used by Random House are natural, recyclable products made from wood grown in sustainable forests. The manufacturing processes conform to the environmental regulations of the country of origin

ISBN 0099307308

Typeset by SX Composing DTP, Rayleigh, Essex
Printed and bound in Great Britain by
Bookmarque Ltd, Croydon, Surrey

For the innocents:

Guatemala

1962–1996

New York, New York
Arlington, Virginia
Shanksville, Pennsylvania

September 11, 2001

I have touched their bones. I mourn for them.

Acknowledgments

As usual, this book would not have been possible without the help of others.

First and foremost, credit and recognition must go to my dear friend and colleague, Clyde Snow, Ph.D. Clyde, you started it all. I thank you. The oppressed of the world thank you.

I feel tremendous gratitude for the support and hospitality shown me by the members of the Fundación de Antropología Forense de Guatemala, especially Fredy Armando Peccerelli Monteroso, Presidente, and Claudia Rivera, Directora de Antropología Forense. The work carried out by the FAFG is unbearably difficult and tremendously important. *Muchas gracias*. I hope I can offer more help in the future.

Ron Fourney, Ph.D., Biology, Research and Development, Canadian Police Research Center, Royal Canadian Mounted Police, and Barry D. Gaudette, B.S., Manager, Canadian Police Research Center, Royal Canadian Mounted Police, explained the intricacies of animal hair analysis.

Carol Henderson, J.D., Shepard Broad Law Center, Nova Southeastern University, and William Rodriguez, Ph.D., Office of the Armed Forces Medical Examiner, Armed Forces Institute of Pathology, provided information on the construction and functioning of septic tanks.

Robert J. Rochon, Deputy High Commissioner to London, Canadian Department of Foreign Affairs and International Trade, answered many questions concerning the diplomatic world.

Diane France, Ph.D., Director, Colorado State University Human Identification Laboratory, supplied inspiration for the use of selective laser sintering in skull modeling. Allan DeWitt, P.E., furnished details on SLS technology.

Sergent-détective Stephen Rudman (retired), Police de la Communauté Urbaine de Montréal, explained the workings of internal police investigations in Quebec.

Merci to Yves St. Marie, Directeur, to André Lauzon, M.D., Chef de Service, and to all my colleagues at the Laboratoire des Sciences Judiciaires et de Médecine Légale. Thanks to James Woodward, Chancellor of the University of North Carolina-Charlotte. Your continued support is greatly appreciated.

Paul Reichs offered many valuable comments on the manuscript. And some stinkers. *Paldies*.

My daughters, Kerry Reichs and Courtney Reichs, accompanied me to Guatemala. Your presence lightened the load. *Paldies*.

My amazing editors, Susanne Kirk at Scribner and Lynne Drew at Random House–UK, took a rough manuscript and made it sing.

Last, but far from least, my agent, Jennifer Rudolph Walsh, provided a sympathetic ear, a protective firewall, and a kick in the pants when needed. You're a star, Big J!

If I have forgotten anyone, please let me know. I will buy you a beer, apologize profusely, and thank you in person. We've all had a rough year.

In the end, I wrote *Grave Secrets*. If there are errors, I made them.

GRAVE
SECRETS

1

"I am dead. They killed me as well."

The old woman's words cut straight to my heart.

"Please tell me what happened that day." Maria spoke so softly I had to strain to catch the Spanish.

"I kissed the little ones and left for market." Eyes down, voice toneless. "I did not know that I would never see them again."

K'akchiquel to Spanish, then reversing the linguistic loop, reversing again as answers followed questions. The translation did nothing to blunt the horror of the recitation.

"When did you return home, Señora Ch'i'p?"

"*A que hora regreso usted a su casa, Señora Ch'i'p?*"

"*Chike ramaj xatzalij pa awachoch, Ixoq Ch'i'p?*"

"Late afternoon. I'd sold my beans."

"The house was burning?"

"Yes."

"Your family was inside?"

A nod.

I watched the speakers. An ancient Mayan woman, her middle-aged son, the young cultural anthropologist Maria Paiz, calling up a memory too terrible for words. I felt anger and sorrow clash inside me like the thunderheads building on the horizon.

"What did you do?"

"We buried them in the well. Quickly, before the soldiers came back."

I studied the old woman. Her face was brown corduroy. Her hands were calloused, her long braids more gray than black. Fabric lay folded atop her head, bright reds, pinks, yellows, and blues, woven into patterns older than the mountains around us. One corner rose and fell with the wind.

The woman did not smile. She did not frown. Her eyes met no one's, to my relief. I knew if they lingered on mine even briefly, the transfer of pain would be brutal. Maybe she understood that and averted her gaze to avoid drawing others into the hell those eyes concealed.

Or perhaps it was distrust. Perhaps the things she had seen made her unwilling to look frankly into unknown faces.

Feeling dizzy, I upended a bucket, sat, and took in my surroundings.

I was six thousand feet up in the western highlands of Guatemala, at the bottom of a steep-sided gorge. The village of Chupan Ya. Between the

Mountains. About one hundred and twenty-five kilometers northwest of Guatemala City.

Around me flowed a wide river of green, lush forest interspersed with small fields and garden plots, like islands. Here and there rows of man-made terraces burst through the giant checker-board, cascading downward like playful waterfalls. Mist clung to the highest peaks, blurring their contours into Monet softness.

I'd rarely seen surroundings so beautiful. The Great Smoky Mountains. The Gatineau, Quebec, under northern lights. The barrier islands off the Carolina coast. Haleakula volcano at dawn. The loveliness of the backdrop made the task at hand even more heartbreaking.

As a forensic anthropologist, it is my job to unearth and study the dead. I identify the burned, the mummified, the decomposed, and the skele-tonized who might otherwise go to anonymous graves. Sometimes the identifications are generic, Caucasoid female, mid-twenties. Other times I can confirm a suspected ID. In some cases, I figure out how these people died. Or how their corpses were mutilated.

I am used to the aftermath of death. I am familiar with the smell of it, the sight of it, the idea of it. I have learned to steel myself emotionally in order to practice my profession.

But the old woman was breaking through my determined detachment.

Another wave of vertigo. The altitude, I told myself, lowering my head and breathing deeply.

Though my home bases are North Carolina and Quebec, where I serve as forensic anthropologist to both jurisdictions, I'd volunteered to come to Guatemala for one month as temporary consultant to the Fundación de Antropología Forense de Guatemala. The Guatemalan Forensic Anthropology Foundation, FAFG, was working to locate and identify the remains of those who vanished during the 1962 to 1996 civil war, one of the bloodiest conflicts in Latin American history.

I'd learned a lot since my arrival one week before. Estimates of the missing ranged from one to two hundred thousand. The bulk of the slaughter was carried out by the Guatemalan army and by paramilitary organizations affiliated with the army. Most of those killed were rural peasants. Many were women and children.

Typically, victims were shot or slashed with machetes. Villages were not always as fortunate as Chupan Ya. There they'd had time to hide their dead. More often, bodies were buried in unmarked mass graves, dumped in rivers, left under the ruins of huts or houses. Families were given no explanations, no lists of those missing, no records. A UN Commission for Historical Clarification referred to these massacres as a genocide of the Mayan people.

Families and neighbors referred to their missing members as the "*desaparecidos*." The disappeared. The FAFG was trying to find them, or, more accurately, their remains. And I had come to help.

Here in Chupan Ya, soldiers and civil patrollers

had entered on an August morning in 1982. Fearing they'd be accused of collaborating with the local guerrilla movement and punished, the men fled. The women were told to gather with their children at designated farms. Trusting, or perhaps fearing, the military, they obeyed. When the soldiers located the women where they'd been sent, they raped them for hours, then killed them along with their kids. Every house in the valley was burned to the ground.

Survivors spoke of five mass graves. Twenty-three women and children were said to lie at the bottom of the well behind Señora Ch'i'p.

The old woman continued her story. Over her shoulder I could see the structure we'd erected three days earlier to protect the well site from rain and sun. Backpacks and camera cases hung from metal uprights, and tarps covered the opening of the pit beneath. Boxes, buckets, shovels, picks, brushes, and storage containers lay as we'd left them early that morning.

Rope had been strung from pole to pole around the excavation to create a boundary between spectators and workers. Inside the restraint sat three idle members of the FAFG team. Outside it stood the villagers who came each day to observe in silence.

And the police guards who'd been told to shut us down.

We'd been close to uncovering evidence when we received the order to halt. The soil had begun yielding ash and cinders. Its color had changed from mahogany to graveyard black. We'd found a child's hair clip in the sifting screen. Fragments of cloth. A tiny sneaker.

Dear God. Did the old woman's family really lie only inches below the point at which we'd stopped?

Five daughters and nine grandchildren. Shot, macheted, and burned in their home together with neighboring women and children. How does one endure such loss? What could life offer her but endless pain?

Shifting my gaze back to the surrounding countryside, I noted half a dozen farmsteads carved out of the foliage. Adobe walls, tile roofs, smoke curling from cooking fires. Each had a dirt yard, outdoor privy, and an emaciated brown dog or two. The wealthier had chickens, a scrawny hog, a bicycle.

Two of Señora Ch'i'p's daughters had lived in the cluster of huts halfway up the eastern escarpment. Another had lived on top, where we'd parked the FAFG vehicles. These women were married; she didn't remember their ages. Their babies were three days, ten months, two, four, and five years old.

Her youngest daughters were still at home. They'd been eleven and thirteen.

Families, connected by a network of footpaths, and by a network of genes. Their world was this valley.

I imagined Señora Ch'i'p returning that day, perhaps descending the same dirt trail our team struggled down each morning and up each evening. She had sold her beans. She was probably happy.

Then horror.

Two decades is not long enough to forget. A lifetime is not long enough.

I wondered how often she thought of them. Did their phantoms walk with her as she trudged to market, following the same course she'd taken the fatal day? Did they slip past the tattered rag covering her window when darkness claimed the valley each night? Did they people her dreams? Did they come to her smiling and laughing as they'd been in life? Or bloodied and charred as she'd found them in death?

My vision blurred, and I dropped my head again, stared at the dirt. How was it possible for human beings to do that to other human beings? To helpless and unresisting women and children? In the distance, I heard the rumble of thunder.

Seconds, maybe years later, the interview stopped, an untranslated question left dangling in space. When I looked up Maria and her interpreter had shifted their attention to the hill behind me. Señora Ch'i'p remained focused on her sandals, hand to cheek, fingers curled like a newborn's.

"Mateo's back," said Elena Norvillo, an FAFG member from the El Petén region. I turned as she pushed to her feet. The rest of the team observed from under the tent.

Two men were working their way down one of the many footpaths that meandered through the gorge, the leader in blue windbreaker, faded jeans,

7

brown cap. Though I couldn't read them from where I sat, I knew the letters above his brim said FAFG. The six of us waiting wore identical caps. The man following was suited and tied and carried a collapsible chair.

We watched the pair pick their way through scraggly corn surrounded by a half-dozen subsidiary crops, careful to damage nothing. A bean seedling. A potato plant. Minor to us, but critical food or income to the family that owned it.

When they drew within twenty yards, Elena shouted.

"Did you get it?"

Mateo gave a thumbs-up.

The injunction to suspend excavation had come from a local magistrate. According to his interpretation of the exhumation order, no work was to proceed outside the presence of a judge, the Guatemalan equivalent of a district attorney. Visiting early this morning and finding no judge on site, the magistrate had ordered digging halted. Mateo had gone to Guatemala City to have this ruling overturned.

Mateo led his companion directly to the two uniformed guards, members of the National Civil Police, and produced a document. The older cop shifted the strap of his semiautomatic, took the paper and read, head down, shiny black bill reflecting the dimming afternoon light. His partner stood with foot thrust forward, a bored expression on his face.

After a brief exchange with the suited visitor, the

senior cop returned the order to Mateo and nodded.

The villagers watched, silent but curious, as Juan, Luis, and Rosa stood and exchanged high fives. Mateo and his companion joined them at the well. Elena followed.

Crossing to the tent, I glanced again at Señora Ch'i'p and her adult son. The man was scowling, hatred seeping from every pore. Hatred for whom? I wondered. For those who had butchered his family? For those who had come from a different world to disturb their bones? For distant authorities who would block even that small effort? For himself for having survived that day? His mother stood woodenly, face impassive.

Mateo introduced the suited man as Roberto Amado, a representative from the judge/district attorney's office. The Guatemala City judge had ruled that Amado's presence would satisfy the requirements of the exhumation order. Amado would be with us for the duration, observing and recording in order to validate the quality of work for the court.

Amado shook hands with each of us, moved to a corner of the covered area, unfolded his chair, and sat. Mateo began issuing orders.

"Luis, Rosa, please sift. Tempe and I will dig. Juan, haul dirt. We'll rotate as needed."

Mateo had a small, V-shaped scar on his upper lip that broadened into a U whenever he smiled. Today, the V remained narrow as a spike.

"Elena, document and photograph. Skeletal

9

inventory, artifact inventory, photo log. Every molecule goes on record."

"Where are Carlos and Molly?" asked Elena.

Carlos Menzes was a member of an Argentine human rights organization who'd been advising the FAFG since its formation in 1992. Molly Carraway was an archaeologist newly arrived from Minnesota.

"They're driving the other truck out here for transport. We'll need another vehicle when we're ready to leave with all the equipment and arti- facts."

He glanced at the sky.

"The storm is two hours off, maybe three if we're lucky. Let's find these people before there's more legal bullshit."

As I collected trowels and placed them in a bucket tied to a length of rope, Mateo zipped the court order into his pack and hung it over a crossbar. His eyes and hair were black, his body a fire hydrant, short and thick. Tubes of muscle bulged in his neck and arms as he and Luis flung back the tarps covering the mouth of the excava- tion.

Mateo placed a boot on the first of the dirt steps we'd terraced into a pit wall. Edges crumbled, sending dirt two meters to the floor below. The cascading particles made soft, ticking sounds as Mateo slowly climbed down.

When he reached bottom, I lowered the bucket, then zipped my windbreaker. Three days had taught me well. May was pleasant in the highlands, but underground the clammy cold knifed straight to your marrow. I'd left Chupan Ya each evening chilled through, my digits numb.

I descended as Mateo had done, placing my feet sideways, testing each makeshift tread. My pulse accelerated as the gloom closed around me.

Mateo held up a hand and I took it. Stepping off the last riser, I stood in a hole no more than six feet square. The walls and floor were slick, the air dank and rotten.

My heart thumped below my sternum. A bead of sweat raced down the furrow overlying my spine.

Always in narrow, dark places.

I turned from Mateo, pretended to clean my trowel. My hands trembled.

Closing my eyes, I fought past the claustrophobia. I thought of my daughter. Katy as a toddler. Katy at the University of Virginia. Katy at the beach. I pictured my cat, Birdie. My townhouse in Charlotte. My condo in Montreal.

I played the game. First song to pop into my mind. Neil Young. "Harvest Moon." I ran through the lyrics.

My breathing eased. My heart slowed.

I opened my eyes and checked my watch. Fifty-seven seconds. Not as good as yesterday. Better than Tuesday. Much better than Monday.

Mateo was already on his knees, scraping the damp earth. I moved to the opposite corner of the pit, and for the next twenty minutes we worked in silence, troweling, inspecting the ground, scooping dirt into buckets.

Objects emerged with increasing frequency. A shard of glass. A chunk of metal. Charred wood. Elena bagged and recorded each item.

Noise reached us from the world above. Banter. A request. The bark of a dog. Now and then I'd glance up, unconsciously reassuring my id.

Faces peered down. Men in gaucho hats, women in traditional Mayan weaves, toddlers clinging to their skirts. Babies stared with round, black eyes, secured to their mothers by rainbow textiles. I saw a hundred variations on high cheekbones, black hair, sienna skin.

On one upward glance I noticed a little girl, arms above her head, fingers curled around the restraining rope. Typical kid. Chubby cheeks, dirty feet, ponytails.

A stab of pain.

The child was the same age as one of Señora Ch'i'p's granddaughters. Her hair was bound with barrettes identical to the one we'd found in the screen.

I smiled. She turned her face and pressed it to her mother's legs. A brown hand reached down and stroked her head.

According to witnesses, the hole in which we worked had been intended as a cistern. Begun but never completed, it was hastily transformed into an unmarked grave on the night of the massacre.

A grave for people identical to those keeping vigil above.

Fury swirled in me as I resumed digging.

Focus, Brennan. Channel your outrage to

uncover evidence. Do that which you are able to do.

Ten minutes later my trowel touched something hard. Laying the implement aside, I cleared mud with my fingers.

The object was slender, like a pencil, with an angled neck ending in a corrugated upper surface. Above the neck, a tiny cap. Surrounding neck and cap, a circular cup.

I sat back on my heels and studied my find. A femur and pelvis. The hip of a child no older than two.

I looked up and my gaze met that of the little girl. Again she whipped away. But this time she turned back, peeked through the folds of her mother's skirt, smiled shyly.

Sweet Jesus in heaven.

Tears burned the back of my lids.

"Mateo."

I pointed at the little bones. Mateo crawled to my corner.

Along most of its length, the femur was mottled gray and black from exposure to fire and smoke. The distal end was crumbly white, suggesting more intense burning.

For a moment neither of us spoke. Then Mateo crossed himself and said in a low voice, "We've got them."

When Mateo stood and repeated the phrase, the entire team gathered at the edge of the well.

A fleeting thought. We've got whom, Mateo? We've got the victims, not the assassins. What chance is there that any of these government-sanctioned butchers will ever face charges, let alone be punished?

Elena tossed down a camera, then a plastic marker stamped with the numeral "1." I positioned the case number and took several shots.

Mateo and I went back to troweling, the others to sifting and hauling. After an hour I took my turn at the screen. Another hour, and I climbed back down into the well.

The storm held off, and the cistern told its story.

The child had been one of the last lowered into the clandestine grave. Under and around it lay the remains of others. Some badly burned, others barely singed.

By late afternoon seven case numbers had been assigned, and five skulls stared out from a tangle of bones. Three of the victims were adults, at least two were adolescents. Number one was a child. For the others, age estimation was impossible.

At dusk, I made a discovery that will stay with me the rest of my life. For over an hour I'd been working on skeleton number five. I'd exposed the skull and lower jaw and cleared dirt from the vertebrae, ribs, pelvis, and limbs. I'd traced the legs, found the foot bones mingled with those of the person beside.

Skeleton five was female. The orbits lacked heavy ridges, the cheekbones were smooth and slender, the mastoids small. The lower half of the body was enveloped in remnants of a rotted skirt identical to a dozen above my head. A coroded wedding band circled one fragile phalange.

Though the colors were faded and stained, I could make out a pattern in material adhering to the upper torso. Between the arm bones, atop the collapsed rib cage, lay a bundle with a different design. Cautiously, I separated a corner, eased my fingertips underneath, and teased back the outer layer of fabric.

Once, at my Montreal lab, I was asked to examine the contents of a burlap bag found on the shore of an inland lake. From the bag I withdrew several rocks, and bones so fragile at first I thought they were those of a bird. I was wrong. The sack held the remains of three kittens, weighted down and heaved into the water to drown. My disgust was so powerful I had to flee the lab and walk several miles before resuming work.

Inside the bundle clutched by skeleton five, I found an arch of tiny vertebral disks with a miniature rib cage curving around it. Arm and leg bones the size of matches. A minute jaw.

Señora Ch'i'p's infant grandchild.

Among the paper-thin cranial fragments, a 556 projectile, the type fired by an assault rifle.

I remembered how I'd felt at the slaughter of kittens, but this time I felt rage. There were no streets to walk here at the gravesite, no way to work off my anger. I stared at the little bones, trying to picture the man who had pulled the trigger. How could he sleep at night? How could he face people in the day?

At six Mateo gave the order to quit. Up top the air smelled of rain, and veins of lightning pulsated inside heavy, black clouds. The locals had gone.

Moving quickly, we covered the well, stored the equipment we would leave behind, and loaded up that which we would carry. As the team worked, rain began plinking in large, cold drops on the temporary roof above our heads. Amado, the DA's representative, waited with lawn chair folded, face unreadable.

Mateo signed the chain of custody book over to the police guards, then we set off through the corn, winding one behind the other like ants on a scent trail. We'd just begun our long, steep climb when the storm broke. Hard, driving rain stung my face and drenched my hair and clothes. Lightning flashed. Thunder boomed. Trees and cornstalks bent in the wind.

Within minutes, water sluiced down the hillside, turning the path into a slick, brown stream of mud. Again and again I lost my footing, hitting hard on one knee, then the other. I crawled upward, right hand clawing at vegetation, left hand dragging a bag of trowels, feet scrambling for traction. Though rain and darkness obscured my vision, I could hear others above and below me. Their hunched forms whitened each time lightning leapt across the sky. My legs trembled, my chest burned.

An eon later I crested the ridge and dragged myself onto the patch of earth where we'd left the vehicles eleven hours earlier. I was placing shovels in the bed of a pickup when Mateo's satellite phone sounded, the ring barely audible above the wind and rain.

"Can someone get that?" Mateo shouted.

Slipping and sliding toward the cab, I grabbed his pack, dug out the handset, and clicked on.

"Tempe Brennan," I shouted.

"Are you still at the site?" English. It was Molly Carraway, my colleague from Minnesota.

"We're just about to pull out. It's raining like hell," I shouted, backhanding water from my eyes.

"It's dry here."

"Where are you?"

"Just outside Sololá. We were late leaving. Listen, we think we're being followed."

"Followed?"

"A black sedan's been on our ass since Guatemala City. Carlos tried a couple of maneuvers to lose it, but the guy's hanging on like a bad cold."

"Can you tell who's driving?"

"Not really. The glass is tinted an—"

I heard a loud thump, a scream, then static, as though the phone had been dropped and was rolling around.

"Jesus Christ!" Carlos's voice was muted by distance.

"Molly?"

I heard agitated words that I couldn't make out.

"Molly, what is it?"

Shouts. Another thump. Scraping. A car horn. A loud crunch. Male voices.

"What's happening?" Alarm raised my voice an octave.

No response.

A shouted command.

"Fuck you!" Carlos.

"Molly! Tell me what's going on!" I was almost screaming. The others had stopped loading to stare at me.

"No!" Molly Carraway spoke from a distant galaxy, her voice small and tinny and filled with panic. "Please. No!"

Two muted pops.

Another scream.

Two more pops.

Dead air.

2

We found Carlos and Molly about eight kilometers outside of Sololá, more than ninety kilometers from Guatemala City, but thirty short of the site.

It had rained steadily as our convoy lurched and heaved across the narrow dirt and rock trail that connected the rim of the valley with the paved road. First one vehicle then another became mired, requiring team effort to free the wheels. After shouldering and straining in an ocean of mud we'd resume our seats and push on, looking like New Guinea tribesmen daubed for mourning.

It was normally twenty minutes to the blacktop. That night the trip took more than an hour. I clung to the truck's armrest, body pitching from side to side, stomach knotted with anxiety. Though we didn't voice them, Mateo and I contemplated the same questions. What had happened to Molly and Carlos? What would we find? Why had they been so late? What had delayed them? Had they actually been followed? By whom? Where were their pursuers now?

At the juncture of the valley road with the highway, Señor Amado alighted from the Jeep, hurried to his car, and drove off into the night. It was evident that the DA's representative had no desire to linger in our company a moment longer than necessary.

The rain had followed us out of the valley, and even the blacktop was hazardous. Within fifteen minutes we spotted the FAFG pickup in a ditch on the opposite side of the road, headlights burning at a cockeyed angle, driver's door ajar. Mateo made a razor U-turn and skidded onto the shoulder. I flew from the cab before he had fully braked, fear tightening the knot in my gut to a hard, cold fist.

Despite rain and darkness, I could see dark splatter covering the exterior panel on the driver's side. The scene on the interior turned my blood to ice.

Carlos lay doubled over behind the wheel, feet and head toward the open door, as though shoved in from the outside. The back of his hair and shirt were the color of cheap wine. Blood oozed across the top and down the front of the seat, adding to that pooled around the gas and brake pedals, and to the hideous stains on his jeans and boots.

Molly was on the passenger side, one hand on the door handle, the other palm up in her lap. She was slumped like a rag doll, with legs splayed and head at an odd angle against the seatback. Two mushrooms darkened the front of her nylon jacket.

Racing across the shoulder, I pressed trembling fingers to Carlos's throat. Nothing. I moved my hand, testing for signs of life. Nothing. I tried his wrist. Nothing.

Please, God! My heart pounded wildly below my sternum.

Mateo ran up beside me, indicated I should check Molly. I scrambled to her, reached through the open window, and felt for a pulse. Nothing. Again and again I positioned my fingers against the pale flesh of her throat. Opposite me Mateo shouted into his phone as he mimicked my desperate moves.

On my fourth try I felt a beat, low and weak and uncertain. It was barely a tremor, but it was there.

"She's alive," I shouted.

Elena was beside me, eyes wide and glistening. As she opened the door, I bent in and took Molly in my arms. Holding her upright, rain stinging my neck, I unzipped her jacket, raised her sweatshirt, and located the two sources of bleeding. Spreading my feet for balance, I placed pressure on the wounds, and prayed that help would arrive in time.

My own blood hammered in my ears. A hundred beats. A thousand.

I spoke softly into Molly's ear, reassuring her, cajoling her to stay with me. My arms grew numb. My legs cramped. My back screamed under the strain of standing off balance.

The others huddled for mutual support, exchanging an occasional word or embrace. Cars flashed by with faces pointed in our direction, curious but unwilling to be drawn into whatever drama was unfolding on the road to Sololá.

Molly's face looked ghostly. Her lips were blue around the edges. I noticed that she wore a gold chain, a tiny cross, a wristwatch. The hands said eight twenty-one. I looked for the cell phone, but didn't see it.

As suddenly as it started, the rain stopped. A dog howled and another answered. A night bird gave a tentative peep, repeated itself.

At long last I spotted a red light far up the highway.

"They're here," I crooned into Molly's ear. "Stay tough, girl. You're going to be fine." Blood and sweat felt slick between my fingers and her skin.

The red light drew nearer and separated into two. Minutes later an ambulance and police cruiser screamed onto the shoulder, blasting us with gravel and hot air. Red pulsed off glistening blacktop, rain-glazed vehicles, pale faces.

Molly and Carlos were administered emergency care by the paramedics, transferred to the ambulance, and raced toward the hospital in Sololá. Elena and Luis followed to oversee their admittance. After giving brief statements, the rest of us were permitted to return to Panajachel, where we were staying, while Mateo made the trip to police headquarters in Sololá.

The team was quartered at the Hospedaje Santa Rosa, a budget hotel hidden in an alleyway off

Avenida el Frutal. Upon entering my room I stripped, heaped my filthy clothes in a corner, and showered, thankful that the FAFG had paid the extra quetzals for hot water. Though I'd eaten nothing since a cheese sandwich and apple at noon, fear and exhaustion squelched all desire for food. I fell into bed, despondent over the victims in the well at Chupan Ya, terrified for Molly and Carlos.

I slept badly that night, troubled by ugly dreams. Shards of infant skull. Sightless sockets. Arm bones sheathed in a rotting *güipil*. A tissue-spattered truck.

It seemed there was no escape from violent death, day or night, past or present.

I awoke to screeching parrots and soft, gray dawn seeping through my shutters. Something was terribly wrong. What?

Memories of the previous night hit me like a cold, numbing wave. I drew knees to chest and lay several minutes, dreading the news but needing to know.

Flinging back the quilt, I went through my abbreviated morning ritual, then threw on jeans, T-shirt, sweatshirt, jacket, and cap.

Mateo and Elena were sipping coffee at a courtyard table, their figures backlit by salmon-pink walls. I joined them, and Señora Samines placed coffee in front of me, and served plates of *huevos rancheros*, black beans, potatoes, and cheese to the others.

"*¿Desayuno?*" she asked. Breakfast?

"*Sí, gracias.*"

I added cream, looked at Mateo.

He spoke in English.

"Carlos took a bullet in the head, another in the neck. He's dead."

The coffee turned to acid in my mouth.

"Molly was hit twice in the chest. She survived the surgery, but she's in a coma."

I glanced at Elena. Her eyes were rimmed by lavender circles, the whites watery red.

"How?" I asked, turning back to Mateo.

"They think Carlos resisted. He was shot at close range outside the truck."

"Will an autopsy be performed?"

Mateo's eyes met mine, but he said nothing.

"Motive?"

"Robbery."

"Robbery?"

"Bandits are a problem along that stretch."

"Molly told me they'd been followed from Guatemala City."

"I pointed that out."

"And?"

"Molly has light brown hair, fair skin. She's clearly gringo. The cops think they were probably targeted as a tourist couple in G City, then tailed until the truck hit a suitable ambush site."

"In plain view along a major highway?"

Mateo said nothing.

"Molly was still wearing jewelry and a wristwatch," I said.

"The police couldn't find their passports or wallets."

"Let me get this straight. Thieves followed them for over two hours, then took their wallets and left their jewelry?"

"*Sí.*" He lapsed into Spanish.

"Is that typical for highway robbery?"

He hesitated before responding.

"They might have been scared off."

Señora Samines arrived with my eggs. I poked at them, speared a potato. Carlos and Molly had been shot for money?

I had come to Guatemala fearing government bureaucracy, intestinal bacteria, dishonest taxi drivers, pickpockets. Why was I shocked at the thought of armed robbery?

America is the leading producer of gunshot homicides. Our streets and workplaces are killing fields. Teens are shot for their Air Jordans, wives for serving the pot roast late, students for eating lunch in the high school cafeteria.

Annually, over thirty thousand Americans are killed by bullets. Seventy percent of all murders are committed with firearms. Each year the NRA spoons up propaganda, and America swallows it. Guns proliferate, and the slaughter goes on. Law enforcement no longer has an advantage in carrying arms. It only brings the officers up to even.

But Guatemala?

The potato tasted like pressed wood. I laid down my fork and reached for my coffee.

"They think Carlos got out?" I asked.

Mateo nodded.

"Why take the trouble to shove him back into the truck?"

"A disabled vehicle would draw less interest than a body on the ground."

"Does a robbery scenario sound reasonable to you?"

Mateo's jaw muscles bulged, relaxed, bulged again.

"It happens."

Elena made a sound in her throat, but said nothing.

"Now what?"

"Today Elena will keep watch at the hospital while we continue at Chupan Ya." He tossed coffee dregs onto the grass. "And we all pray."

My grandmother used to say that God's tonic for sorrow was physical labor. She also felt toads caused infertility, but that was another issue.

For the next six days the team ingested megadoses of Gran's elixir. We worked at the well from sunrise until sunset, hauling equipment up and down the valley, troweling, hoisting buckets, shaking screens.

In the evenings we dragged ourselves from our *hospedaje* to one of the restaurants lining Lake Atitlán. I enjoyed these brief respites from death. Though darkness obscured the water and the ancient volcanoes on the far shore, I could smell fish and kelp and hear waves lapping against rickety wooden piers. Tourists and locals wandered the shore. Mayan women passed with impossible bundles on their heads. Notes drifted from distant xylophones. Life continued.

Some nights we ate in silence, too exhausted for conversation. On others we talked of the project, of Molly and Carlos, of the town in which we were temporary residents.

The history of Panajachel is as colorful as the textiles sold on its streets. In another age, the place was a K'akchiquel Mayan village settled by ancestors of the current citizens when a force of rival Tzutujil warriors was defeated by the Spanish. Later, the Franciscans established a church and monastery at "Pana," and used the village as a base for missionary operations.

Darwin was right. Life is opportunity. One group's loss is another's gain.

In the sixties and seventies the town became a haven for gringo gurus, hippies, and dropouts. Rumors that Lake Atitlán was one of the world's few "vortex energy fields" led to an influx of cosmic healers and crystal watchers.

Today Panajachel is a blend of traditional Mayan, contemporary Guatemalan, and non-descript Western. It is luxury hotels and *hospedajes*; European cafés and *comedores*; ATMs and outdoor markets; *güipils* and tank tops; mariachis and Madonna; Mayan *brujos* and Catholic priests.

By late Wednesday we'd finished our excavation at Chupan Ya. In all, we'd removed twenty-three souls from the well. Among the skeletons we'd found thirteen projectiles and cartridge casings and two broken machete blades. Every bone and object had been recorded, photographed, packaged, and sealed for transport to the FAFG lab in Guatemala City. The cultural anthropologist had recorded twenty-seven stories, and taken DNA samples from sixteen family members.

Carlos's body had been transported to the Guatemala City morgue, where an autopsy confirmed the impression of the local police. Death was due to gunshot wounding at close range.

Molly remained comatose. Each day one of us made the drive to the San Juan de Dios Hospital in Sololá, sat by her bedside, reported back. That report was always the same. No change.

The police found no prints or physical evidence, located no witnesses, identified no suspects. The investigation continued.

After dinner on Wednesday, I went by myself to visit Molly. For two hours I held her hand and stroked her head, hoping that the fact of my presence would penetrate to wherever it was her spirit had gone. Sometimes I talked to her, recalling shared times and acquaintances from our years before Guatemala brought us back together. I told her of the progress at Chupan Ya and spoke of her role in the work ahead. Otherwise, I sat silent, listening to the muted hum of her cardiac monitor, and praying for her recovery.

On Thursday morning we loaded the trucks and Jeep under the indifferent eye of Señor Amado and set out for the capital, winding our way up the precipitous road from Panajachel. The sky was flawless, the lake blue satin. Sunlight speared the trees, turning leaves translucent and glistening in the spiderwebs overhead.

As we made the hairpin turn high above Lake Atitlán, I gazed at the peaks on her far side.

Vulcan San Pedro. Vulcan Tolimán. Vulcan Atitlán.

Closing my eyes, I said one more silent prayer to whatever god might be willing to listen.

Let Molly live.

The FAFG is headquartered in Guatemala City's Zone 2. Built on a spit of land between steep ravines, or *barrancas,* the lovely, tree-shaded neighborhood was once an enclave for the well-to-do. But the grand old quarter had seen better times.

Today, businesses and public offices sit cheek to jowl with residences hanging on by suction cups. The National Baseball Stadium looms over the far end of Calle Siméon Cañas, and multicolored buses stop at graffiti-covered shelters along both curbs. Vendors hawk fast food from pushcarts and metal huts with slide-up windows. From one, Pepsi. From another, Coke. Tamales. *Chuchitos.* Hot dogs plain. Hot dogs *shuco.* Dirty. With avocado and cabbage.

The FAFG labs and administrative offices are located in what was once a private family home on Siméon Cañas. The two-story house, complete with pool and walled patio, sits across four lanes of traffic from a similar domicile now housing the

Kidnapping and Organized Crime Unit of the Public Ministry.

Arriving at the compound, Mateo pulled into the drive and sounded the horn. Within seconds a young woman with an owl face and long dark braids swung the gate wide. We entered and parked on a patch of gravel to the right of the front door. The other truck and Jeep followed, and the woman closed and locked the gate.

The team spilled out and began unloading equipment and cardboard boxes, each coded to indicate site, exhumation date, and burial number. In the weeks to come we'd examine every bone, tooth, and artifact to establish identity and cause of death for the Chupan Ya victims. I hoped we'd finish before professional commitments required my return home in June.

I was going back for my third box when Mateo pulled me aside.

"I have a favor to ask."

"Of course."

"The *Chicago Tribune* plans to do a feature on Clyde."

Clyde Snow is one of the grand old men of my profession, the founder of the subspecialty of forensic anthropology.

"Yes?"

"Some reporter wants to interview me about the old man's involvement in our work down here. I invited him weeks ago, then completely forgot."

"And?" Normally reluctant to deal with the press, I didn't like where this was going.

"The guy's in my office. He's very excited that you're here."

"How does he know that I'm in Guatemala?"

"I might have mentioned it."

"Mateo?"

"All right, I told him. Sometimes my English is not so good."

"You grew up in the Bronx. Your English is perfect."

"Yours is better. Will you talk to him?"

"What does he want?"

"The usual. If you'll talk to the guy I can start logging and assigning the Chupan Ya cases."

"O.K."

I would have preferred measles to an afternoon of baby-sitting an "excited" reporter, but I was here to do what I could to help.

"I owe you." Mateo squeezed my arm.

"You owe me."

"*Gracias.*"

"*De nada.*"

But the interview was not to be.

I found the reporter working on a nostril in Mateo's second-floor office. He stopped trolling when I entered, and feigned scratching the scraggly trail of hair tinting his upper lip. Pretending to notice me for the first time, he shot to his feet and stuck out a hand.

"Ollie Nordstern. Olaf, actually. Friends call me Ollie."

I held palms to chest, wanting no part of Ollie's nasal booty.

"I've been unloading the trucks." I smiled apologetically.

"Dirty job." Nordstern dropped his hand.

"Yes." I gestured him back into his chair.

Nordstern was dressed in polyester from his gel-slicked hair to his Kmart hiking boots. His head turtled forward on a neck the size of my upper arm. I guessed his age at around twenty-two.

"So," we began simultaneously.

I indicated to Nordstern that he had the floor.

"It is an absolute thrill to meet you, Dr. Brennan. I've heard so much about you and your work in Canada. And I read about your testimony in Rwanda."

"The court actually sits in Arusha, Tanzania."

Nordstern was referring to my appearance before the United Nations International Criminal Tribunal for Rwanda.

"Yes, yes, of course. And those cases you did with the Montreal Hells Angels. We followed that very closely in Chicago. The Windy City has its own biker boys, you know." He winked and pinched his nose. I hoped he wasn't going back in.

"I'm not the reason you're here," I said, glancing at my watch.

"Forgive me. I digress."

Nordstern pulled a notepad from one of the four zillion pockets on his camouflage vest, flipped the cover, and poised pen above paper.

"I want to learn all I can about Dr. Snow and the FAFG."

Before I could respond, a man appeared at the

open door. He was dark-skinned, with a face that looked as if it had taken some hits. The brows were prominent, the nose humped and slightly off angle. A scar cut a tiny white swath through his left eyebrow. Though not tall, the man was muscular and carried not an ounce of fat. The phrase Thugs Are Us popped to mind.

"Dr. Brennan?"

"*Sí.*"

The man held out a badge. SICA. Special Crimes Investigative Unit, Guatemala National Civil Police. My stomach went into free fall.

"Mateo Reyes directed me here." The man spoke in unaccented English. His tone suggested the call was not social.

"Yes?"

"Sergeant-detective Bartolomé Galiano."

Oh, God. Was Molly dead?

"Does this have to do with the shooting near Sololá?"

"No."

"What is it?"

Galiano's eyes shifted to Nordstern, returned to me.

"The subject is sensitive."

Not good, Brennan. What interest could SICA have in me?

"Could it wait a few minutes?"

His dead gaze gave me the answer.

33

3

Sergeant-Detective Galiano took the chair reluctantly vacated by Ollie Nordstern, crossed ankle over knee, and impaled me with a stare.

"What is this about, Detective?" I forced my voice steady, scenes from *Midnight Express* rolling through my head.

Galiano's eyes held me like a bug on a pin.

"We at the National Civil Police are aware of your activities, Dr. Brennan."

I said nothing, lowered hands to lap, leaving two sweaty palm prints on the plastic blotter.

"I am largely responsible for that." A small oscillating fan ruffled a half dozen hairs on the crown of his head. Otherwise, the man was motionless.

"You are."

"Yes."

"Why is that?"

"Part of my youth was spent in Canada, and I still follow the news up there. Your exploits do not go unnoticed."

"My exploits?"

"The press loves you."

"The press loves to sell papers." He may have heard my irritation. "Why have you come to see me, Detective Galiano?"

Galiano withdrew a brown envelope from his pocket and placed it in front of me. Hand-printed on the outside was a police or coroner dossier number. I looked at but did not reach for it.

"Take a look." Galiano resumed his seat.

The envelope contained a series of five-by-seven color photographs. The first showed a bundle on an autopsy table, liquid oozing from the edges to form a brown puddle on the perforated stainless steel.

The second showed the bundle untangled into a pair of jeans, the lower end of a long bone protruding from one ragged cuff. The third featured a watch, and what were probably pocket contents: a comb, an elastic hair binder, two coins. The last photo was a close-up of a tibia and two metatarsals.

I looked at Galiano.

"That was discovered yesterday."

I studied the skeletal elements. Though everything was stained a deep chocolate brown, I could see flesh clinging to the bones.

"A week ago toilets began backing up at the Pensión Paraíso, a small hotel in Zone One.

Though the place ain't the Ritz, guests grumbled, and the owners went poking in the septic tank. They found the Levi's blocking the exit drain."

"When was the system last inspected?"

"Seems the owners are a bit lax on upkeep. But minor maintenance was done last August, so the body probably went in after that."

I agreed but said nothing.

"The victim may be a young woman."

"I couldn't possibly express an opinion based on these photographs."

"I wouldn't ask you to."

We stared at each other in the stuffy heat of the room. Galiano's eyes were extraordinary, brown with a luminous red cast, like amber caught in sunlight. The lashes might have landed him a Maybelline contract, had he been of the female gender.

"Over the past ten months, four young women have gone missing in this city. The families are frantic. We suspect the disappearances may be linked."

Down the corridor, a phone sounded.

"If so, the situation is urgent."

"Lots of people go missing in Guatemala City."

I pictured Parque Concordia, where orphans gathered each night to sniff glue and sleep. I remembered stories of children being rounded up and killed. In 1990, witnesses reported armed men snatching eight street kids. Their bodies were found a few days later.

"This is different." Galiano's voice brought me

back. "These four young women stand out. They don't fit the usual pattern."

"What does this have to do with me?" I had a pretty good idea.

"I described your work to my superiors, told them you were in Guatemala."

"May I ask how you knew that?"

"Let's just say SICA is kept apprised of foreign nationals entering Guatemala to dig up our dead."

"I see."

Galiano pointed at the photos. "I've been authorized to request your help."

"I have other commitments.

"Excavation is finished at Chupan Ya."

"Analysis is just beginning.'

"Señor Reyes has agreed to the loan of your services."

First the reporter, now this. Mateo had been busy since our return to the city.

"Señor Reyes can examine these bones for you."

"Señor Reyes's experience and training don't compare to yours."

It was true. While Mateo and his team had worked on hundreds of massacre victims, they'd had little involvement with recent homicide cases.

"You coauthored an article on septic tank burial."

Galiano had done his homework.

Three years back, a small-time drug dealer was busted in Montreal for supplying product to the wrong buyer. Not fancying a long separation from his medicine chest, the man offered the story of an associate floating in a septic tank. The provincial police turned to my boss, Dr. Pierre LaManche, and LaManche turned to me. I learned more than I ever wanted to know about human waste disposal, and LaManche and I spent days directing the recovery. We'd written an article for the *Journal of Forensic Sciences*.

"This is a local problem," I said. "It should be handled by local experts."

The fan hummed. Galiano's cowlick did pliés and pirouettes.

"Ever hear of a man named André Specter?"

I shook my head.

"He's the Canadian ambassador to Guatemala."

The name rang a very distant bell.

"Specter's daughter, Chantale, is one of those missing."

"Why isn't this being handled through diplomatic channels?"

"Specter has demanded absolute discretion."

"Sometimes publicity can be helpful."

"There are" – Galiano groped for a word – "extenuating circumstances."

I waited for him to elaborate. He didn't. Outside, a truck door slammed.

"If there's a Canadian link, liaison between jurisdictions will be useful."

"And I've spent time in septic tanks."

"A rare claim. And you've done cases for Canadian Foreign Affairs."

"Yes." He really had done his homework.

It was then Galiano played his trump card.

"My department has taken the liberty of contacting your ministry in Quebec, requesting permission to engage you as special consultant."

A second item emerged from Galiano's pocket, this one a fax with a familiar fleur-de-lis logo. The paper came across the desk.

M. Serge Martineau, Ministère de la Sécurité Publique, and Dr. Pierre LaManche, Chef de Service, Laboratoire de Sciences Judiciaires et de Médecine Légale, had granted permission, pending agreement on my part, for my temporary assignment to the Special Crimes Investigative Unit of the Guatemala National Civil Police.

My bosses in Montreal were part of the ambush. There would be no end run around this.

I looked up at Galiano.

"You have a reputation for finding the truth, Dr. Brennan." The Maybelline eyes were relentless. "Parents are in agony not knowing the truth about their missing kids."

I thought of Katy and knew the fear I'd experience should my daughter disappear, the absolute terror that would grip me should she vanish in a place with unknown language, laws, and procedures, peopled by unfamiliar authorities who might or might not exert genuine effort to find her.

"All right, Detective. I'm listening."

Zone 1 is the oldest part of Guatemala City, a claustrophobic hive of rundown shops, cheap hotels, bus terminals, and car parks, with a sprinkling of modern chain outlets. Wimpy's and McDonald's share the narrow streets with German delis, sports bars, Chinese restaurants, shoe stores, cinemas, electrical shops, strip joints, and taverns.

Like many ecozones, the sector follows a diurnal rhythm. Come dark, the vendors and pedestrians clogging its streets yield to cigarette sellers and hookers. The shoeshine boys, taxi drivers, buskers, and preachers vanish from Parque Concordia, and homeless children gather to bed down for the night.

Zone 1 is broken pavement, neon, fumes, and noise. But the quarter also has a grander side. It is home to the Palacio Nacional, the Biblioteca Nacional, the Mercado Central, Parque Central, Parque del Centenario, museums, a cathedral, and a spectacular Moorish post office. Police headquarters is located in an outlandish castle at the intersection of Calle 14 and Avenida 6, one block south of the Iglesia de San Francisco, famous for its carving of the sacred heart and for the banned books discovered in a roof cavity, hidden decades earlier by rebellious clergy.

Ninety minutes later Galiano and I were seated at a battered wooden table in a conference room on the castle's third floor. With us were his partner, Sergeant-detective Pascual Hernández, and Juan-Carlos Xicay, head of the evidence recovery team that would process the septic tank.

The room was a cheerless gray, last painted about the time the padres were stashing their books. Putty-colored stuffing sprouted from my chair, and I wondered how many nervous, bored, or frightened buttocks had squirmed in that same seat.

A fly buzzed against the room's single window. I felt empathy, and I shared the insect's desire for escape. Beyond the window, through filthy blinds, I could see one of the castle's battlements.

At least there was an upside. I was safe from attack by medieval knights.

Sighing, I shifted for the billionth time, picked up a paper clip, and began tapping the table. We'd been waiting twenty minutes for a representative from the DA's office. I was hot, tired, and disappointed to be pulled from my FAFG work. And I was not hiding it well.

"Shouldn't be long." Galiano looked at his watch.

"Couldn't I outline the procedure?" I asked. "It may take Señor Xicay some time to line up the equipment."

Xicay scratched an eyebrow, said nothing. Hernández gestured his powerlessness by raising a hand and dropping it onto the tabletop. He was a heavy man, with black wavy hair that crawled down his neck. His forearms and hands were also layered with dark, wiry hair.

"I'll check again." Galiano strode from the room, his gait indicating annoyance.

With whom? I wondered. Me? The tardy DA? Some higher-up?

Almost immediately, I heard Galiano arguing in

the corridor. Though the Spanish was rapid fire, and I missed many words, the animosity was clear. I caught my name at least twice.

Moments later the voices stopped, and Galiano rejoined us, followed by a tall, thin man in rose-pink glasses. The man was slightly stooped, with a soft belly that pooched over his belt.

Galiano made introductions.

"Dr. Brennan, may I present Señor Antonio Díaz. Señor Díaz heads up the criminal investigative section of the office of the district attorney."

I rose and held out a hand. Ignoring it, Díaz crossed to the window and spun toward me. Though colored lenses obscured his eyes, the hostility was palpable.

"I have been a prosecutor for almost twenty years, Dr. Brennan. In all that time, I have never required, nor have I requested, outside help in a death investigation." Though heavily accented, Díaz's English was precise.

Stunned, I dropped my hand.

"While you may view our forensic doctors as inadequately trained hacks laboring in a Third World medico-legal system, or as mere cogs in an antiquated and ineffective judicial bureaucracy, let me assure you they are professionals who hold themselves to the highest standards."

I looked to Galiano, cheeks burning with humiliation. Or anger.

"As I explained, Señor Díaz, Dr. Brennan is here at our request." Galiano's voice was tempered steel.

"Why exactly *are* you in Guatemala, Dr. Brennan?" From Díaz.

Anger makes me feisty.

"I'm thinking of opening a spa."

"Dr. Brennan is here on other business," Galiano jumped in. "She is a forensic anthrop—"

"I know who she is," Díaz cut him off.

"Dr. Brennan has experience with septic tank recovery, and she's offered to help."

Offered? How did Galiano come up with "offered"?

"We'd be foolish not to avail ourselves of her expertise."

Díaz glared at Galiano, his face concrete. Hernández and Xicay said nothing.

"We shall see." Díaz looked hard at me, then stomped from the room.

Only the fly broke the silence. Galiano spoke first.

"I apologize, Dr. Brennan."

Anger also goads me to action.

"Can we begin?" I asked.

"I'll handle Díaz," Galiano said, pulling out a chair.

"One other thing."

"Name it."

"Call me Tempe."

For the next hour I explained the glories of septic disposal. Galiano and his partner listened closely, interrupting now and then to comment or to ask for clarification. Xicay sat in silence, eyes lowered, face devoid of expression.

"Septic tanks can be made of rock, brick, concrete, or fiberglass, and come in a number of designs. They can be round, square, or rectangular. They can have one, two, or three compartments, separated by partial baffles or by full walls."

"How do they work?" Galiano.

"Basically, a septic tank is a watertight chamber that acts as an incubator for anaerobic bacteria, fungi, and actinomycetes that digest organic solids that fall to the bottom."

"Sounds like Galiano's kitchen." Hernández.

"What can we expect?" Galiano ignored his partner.

"The digestion process creates heat, and gases bubble to the surface. Those gases combine with particles of grease, soap, oils, hair, and other junk to produce a foamy scum. That's the first thing we're going to see when we open the tank."

"Bring a little sunshine into your day." Hernández.

"With time, if left undisturbed, a floating semisolid mat can form."

"Shit pudding." Hernández was covering his repugnance with macho humour.

"Tanks should be pumped out every two to three years, but if the owners are as lax as you say they are, that isn't likely to have happened, so we'll probably encounter this type of sediment."

"So you've got this soup kitchen for microbes. Where does everything go from there?" Galiano asked.

"Once a tank fills to a certain level, the altered waste products flow out through an exit drain to a series of pipes, usually laid out in parallel rows, called a drain field."

"What kind of pipes?"

"Typically, clay or perforated plastic."

"This system dates to the Preclassic, so I'm sure we're talking clay. What goes on there?"

"The drain field rests on a bed of gravel, usually covered by soil and vegetation. While some aerobic breakdown occurs there, the drain field primarily functions as a biological filter."

"Fine or coarse drip. Now we're talking Mr. Coffee."

Hernández was starting to get on my nerves.

"As the final step in treatment, the waste water leaks from the pipes and percolates through the gravel bed. Bacteria, viruses, and other pollutants are absorbed by the soil or taken up by the root systems of the overlying plants."

"So the grass really is greener over the septic tank." Galiano.

"And a lot happier. What else do we know about this setup?"

Galiano pulled out a small spiral pad and flipped through his notes.

"The tank is located approximately seven feet from the south wall of the *pension*. It's about ten feet long, five feet wide, and six feet deep, made of concrete, and covered by eight rectangular concrete lids."

"How many chambers?"

"The owner, one Señor Serano, has no idea what's down there. By the way, Serano'll never be holding his breath when the Nobels are announced."

"Noted."

"Serano and his son, Jorge, remembered workers near the east end last summer, so that's the lid they lifted. They found the tank nearly full, the jeans jamming the exit drain."

"The entrance drain will be on the west."

"That's what we figured."

"O.K., gentlemen. We're going to need a backhoe to lift the concrete lids."

"All eight?" Xicay spoke for the first time.

"Yes. Since we don't know what we're dealing with, we'll uncap the whole thing. If there are multiple chambers, parts of the skeleton could be anywhere."

Xicay pulled out his own pad and began making a list.

"A commercial septic service vacuum truck to pump out the scum and liquid layers, and a fire truck to dilute the bottom sediment," I went on.

Xicay added them to the list.

"There's going to be a lot of ammonia and methane gas down there, so I want an oxygen pack respiration device."

Xicay looked a question at me.

"A standard full-face air mask with a single strap over the back O_2 tank. The type firemen wear. We should also have a couple of small pressurized spray tanks."

46

"The kind used to spray weed killer?"

"Exactly. Fill one with water, the other with a ten-percent bleach solution."

"Do I want to know?" asked Hernández.

"To spray me when I climb out of the tank."

Xicay noted the items.

"And quarter-inch mesh screens. Everything else should be standard equipment."

I stood.

"Seven A.M.?"

"Seven A.M."

It was to be one of the worst days of my life.

4

The last red streaks were yielding to a hazy, bronze dawn when Galiano arrived at my hotel the next day.

"*Buenos días.*"

"*Buenos días,*" I mumbled, sliding into the passenger seat. "Nice shades."

He was wearing aviator lenses blacker than a hole in space.

"*Gracias.*"

Galiano indicated a paper cup in the central holder, then swung into traffic. Grateful, I reached for the coffee.

We spoke little driving across town then inching our way through Zone 1. I read the city as it slid past the windshield. Though not the highest form of Guatemalteca conversation, the billboards and placards, even the graffiti on service station walls, allowed me to improve my Spanish.

And to block out thoughts of what lay ahead.

Within twenty minutes Galiano pulled up to a pair of police cruisers sealing off a small alley. Beyond the checkpoint the pavement was clogged with squad cars, an ambulance, a fire engine, a septic tank vacuum service truck, and other vehicles I assumed to be official. Gawkers were already gathering.

Galiano showed ID, and a uniformed cop waved us through. He added his car to the others, and we got out and walked up the street.

The Pensión Paraíso squatted at mid-block, opposite an abandoned warehouse. Galiano and I crossed to its side and proceeded past liquor and underwear merchants, a barbershop, and a Chinese takeout, each establishment barred and padlocked. As we walked, I glanced at sun-bleached items in the shop windows. The barber featured big-haired models with dos that hadn't been stylish since Eisenhower left office. The Long Fu had a menu, a Pepsi ad, a peacock embroidered on glittery fabric.

The Pensión Paraíso was a decrepit two-story bunker made of plaster-covered brick, once white, but long since aged to the color of cigar smoke. Broken roof tiles, dirty windows, off-angle shutters, retractable metal grille on the front door. Paradise.

Another guard. More ID.

The hotel interior was exactly as promised by its exterior. Threadbare carpet with yellowed plastic runner, linoleum-covered counter, wooden grid for keys and letters, cracked plaster walls. The air smelled of mold, dust, and years of cigarette smoke and sweat.

I followed Galiano across a deserted lobby, down a narrow corridor, and out a rear door to a yard that saw little sunlight and even less care. Ceramic pots with withered vegetation. Rusted kitchen chairs with split vinyl seats. Plastic lawn furniture, green with mold. An upended wheelbarrow. Bare earth. A lone tree.

An upholstered sofa missing one leg leaned against the back of the pension, and shards of plaster, fallen bricks, dead leaves, cellophane wrappers, and aluminum pop-tops littered its foundation. The bright yellow backhoe was the only spot of color in the dreary setting. Beside the shovel I could see freshly turned soil, and the concrete lid removed, then hastily replaced by Señor Serano and his son.

I took account of those present. Juan-Carlos Xicay was conversing with a man in a dark blue jumpsuit identical to his own. A driver sat behind the wheel of the backhoe. A uniformed policeman guarded the back entrance to the property. Antonio Díaz hovered alone on its far side, rose-tinted glasses hiding his eyes.

I smiled and raised a hand. The DA did not reply, did not look away.

Happy day.

Pascual Hernández stood with a wiry, rat-faced man wearing sandals, jeans, and a Dallas Cowboys sweatshirt. A sturdy woman flanked the rat, plastic

50

bracelets on her wrists, breasts hanging heavy inside an embroidered black dress.

Galiano and I crossed to his partner, and Hernández introduced the innkeepers. Up close I noticed that Señora Serano had one brown eye and one blue one, giving her face an odd, unbalanced look. When she gazed at me I found it hard to decide into which eye I should look.

I also noticed that Señora Serano's lower lip was swollen and cracked, and I wondered if the rat had struck her.

"And these folks are going to be as helpful as Scouts at a jamboree." Hernández drilled the rat with a look. "Even with the hard stuff."

"I have no secrets." Serano held his hands palms up, fingers splayed. He was so agitated I could barely follow the Spanish. "I know nothing."

"You just happen to have a body in your tank."

"I don't know how it got there." Serano's eyes flicked from face to face.

Galiano turned the shades on Serano.

"What else don't you know, señor?"

"*Nada.*" Nothing. The rat eyes darted like a sparrow seeking a safe perch.

Galiano drew a bored breath. "I have no time for games, Señor Serano. But take this to the bank." He tapped a finger on the big blue "C" in Cowboys. "When we're finished here, you and I are gonna have a real heart-to-heart."

Serano shook his head but said nothing.

The Darth Vader lenses shifted to the backhoe. "All set?" Galiano shouted.

Xicay spoke to the driver, gave a thumbs-up. He pointed to me, then to a jumble of equipment near the uniformed guard. A zipping gesture on his chest indicated that I should suit up. I raised my thumb.

Galiano turned back to the Seranos.

"Your job today is to do nothing," he said levelly. "You will do it seated there." He jabbed a finger at the lopsided sofa. "And you will do it without comment."

Galiano made a circular gesture in the air above his head.

"*Vámonos.*"

I hurried to the equipment locker. Behind me, the backhoe rumbled to life.

As I pulled on a Tyvek jumpsuit and knee-high rubber boots, the driver shifted gears and maneuvered into position. Metal squawked, the bucket dropped with a thunk, scraped the ground, scooped the exposed lid, swung left, and laid it aside. The smell of wet soil drifted on the morning air.

Digging a recorder from my pack, I walked to the edge of the tank.

One look, and my stomach rolled in on itself.

The chambers were brimming with a hideous dark liquid topped by a layer of organic scum. A million cockroaches scuttled across the gelatinous mass.

Galiano and Hernández joined me.

"*Cerote.*" Hernández backhanded his mouth.

Galiano said nothing.

Swallowing hard, I began to dictate. Date. Time. Location. Persons present.

The bucket rattled, dropped again. Serrated teeth bit into the ground, swung free, returned. A second concrete lid appeared, was displaced. A third. A fifth. The odor of putrefaction overpowered the smell of damp earth.

As items were revealed, I dictated description and location. Xicay shot pictures.

By mid-morning eight concrete lids lay in a heap, and the tank was fully exposed. I'd spotted an arm bone lodged against the entrance drain on the west side, fabric in the southeast corner, and a blue plastic object and several hand bones embedded in the scum.

"Cue the truck?" Galiano asked when I'd finished my last entry.

"Have it driven into position. But first I have to remove what's visible and search the top layer."

Turning to Xicay, I indicated that I was ready for a body bag. Then I crossed to the equipment locker and dug out the respirator mask and heavy rubber gloves. Using duct tape, I sealed the top of the boots to the legs of my jumpsuit.

"How?" asked Galiano when I returned to the tank.

I pulled the gloves to my elbows and handed him the duct tape.

"*Dios mío.*" Hernández.

"Need help?" Galiano asked without enthusiasm as he sealed the gloves to my sleeves.

I looked at his suit, tie, and crisp white shirt.

"You're underdressed."

"Shout when you need me." Hernández walked to the equipment locker, removed his jacket, and draped it over the open lid. Though the day wasn't hot, his shirt was damp against his chest. I could see the outline of a sleeveless T-shirt through the thin cotton.

Galiano and I circled to the west end of the tank.

Señor Serano watched from the sofa, rat eyes bright and intent. His wife sucked on a strand of hair.

Xicay's assistant joined us, body bag in hand. I asked his name. Mario Colom. I told Mario to lay the bag on the ground behind me, opened and lined with a clean white sheet. Then I told him to glove and mask.

Handing Galiano my Dictaphone, I secured my own mask over my face. When I squatted and leaned into the tank, my stomach went into a granny knot. I tasted bile and felt a tremor below my tongue.

Breathing shallowly, I plunged in a hand and drew the arm bone from the decomposing waste. Two roaches scuttled up my glove. Inside the rubber, I felt furtive legs, feathery antennae. My arm jerked and I let out a squeal. Behind me, Galiano shifted.

Stop it, Brennan. You're gloved.

Swallowing, I flicked the insects, watched them right themselves and scurry away.

Swallowing again, I curled my fingers and slid the ulna through them. Muck peeled off its surface

54

and dropped to the ground in slimy globs. I laid the bone on the sheet.

Working my way around the tank, I collected everything I could see. Xicay shot stills. When I'd finished, the ulna, two hand bones, one foot bone, three ribs, and the bow from a pair of glasses lay on the sheet.

After instructing Mario, I returned to the southeast corner and began working my way down the south side of the tank, systematically palpating every millimeter of floating scum as far out as I could reach. Opposite me, Mario mirrored my efforts.

In forty minutes we'd searched the entire top layer. Two ribs and one kneecap had been added to the sheet.

The sun was straight up in the sky when Mario and I finished. Consensus: no one wanted lunch. Xicay went for the vacuum truck, and in moments it pulled through the opening in the back fence.

As the operator arranged equipment, I glanced over my shoulder at Díaz. The DA maintained his vigil, lenses pink diamonds in the mottled sunlight. He did not approach.

Five minutes later Xicay shouted.

"Ready?"

"Go."

Another motor sputtered to life. I heard sucking, saw bubbles in the murky, black liquid.

Galiano stood at my side, arms crossed, gaze fixed on the tank. Hernández observed from the safety of the locker. The Seranos watched from their couch, faces the color of oatmeal.

Slowly, the liquid subsided. One inch, three, seven.

Approximately two feet from the tank's bottom, a layer of sludge appeared, its surface lumpy with debris. The pump fell silent and the operator looked at me.

I showed Mario how to work a long-handled net. Scoop by scoop, he dredged muck and laid muddy globs at my feet. I swabbed and untangled the booty from each.

A floral shirt containing ribs, vertebrae, a sternum. Foot bones inside socks inside shoes. Femora. A humerus. A radius. A pelvis. Every bone was covered with putrid tissue and organic waste.

Fighting back nausea, I scraped and arranged everything on the sheet. Xicay recorded the process on film. Feeling too ill for close inspection, I simply entered the bones into a skeletal inventory. I would conduct a full evaluation after cleaning.

When Mario had netted what he could, I walked to the edge of the tank and sat. Galiano came up behind me.

"You're going in there?" It wasn't really a question.

I nodded.

"Can't we just blast the remaining crap with a pressure hose and suck everything up?"

I pushed aside my mask to speak.

"After I find the skull."

I repositioned the mask, rolled to my stomach, and lowered myself over the side. My soles hit the muck with a soft slap. Slime crept up my shins. Odor enveloped me.

Moving felt like slogging through exactly what it was, a stew of human feces and microbial dung. I felt more tremors under my tongue, again tasted bile.

At the southeast corner, I reached up and Mario handed me a long, slender pole. Breathing as shallowly as possible, I began a systematic survey of the tank, inching sideways, probing, inching, probing. Four sets of eyes followed my progress.

On the fourth sweep, I tapped something lodged in the same drain that had held the jeans. Handing up the pole, I swallowed, took a deep breath, and slid my hands into the muck.

The object was roughly the size and shape of a volleyball. It rested on the tanks' bottom, its top one foot below the surface of the sludge. Despite the queasiness, my pulse ratcheted up a notch.

Gingerly, I explored my find, gloved fingers reading the anatomical Braille.

Ovoid globe. Hollows separated by a tented bridge. Rigid bands winging outward beside an oblong aperture.

The skull!

Careful, Brennan.

Ignoring my roiling innards, I bent at the waist, grasped the brain case in both hands, and tugged. The muck refused to yield its booty.

Frustrated, I scooped away handfuls of slime.

When I could see a patch of parietal, I rewrapped my fingers around the cranium and applied alternating pressure.

Nothing budged.

Damn!

Barely resisting the urge to yank, I continued the gentle twisting motion. Clockwise. Counterclockwise. Clockwise. Inside my jumpsuit, I felt hot perspiration roll down my sides.

Two more twists. The seal broke, and the skull shifted.

I cleared what path the sludge would allow, repositioned my fingers, and teased the skull upward. It rose slowly, emerged with a soft sucking sound. Heart thudding, I cradled it in both hands. Slick brown goo filled the orbits and coated the features.

But I saw enough.

Wordlessly, I handed the skull to Mario, accepted his gloved hand, and climbed from the tank. Mario placed the skull on the body bag, and picked up the first of the two pressure tanks. After spraying me with bleach solution, he sprayed me again with clear water.

"Ty-D-Bol called with a job offer." Galiano.

I lowered my mask.

"Whoa, nice skin tone. Bilious green."

Walking to the equipment locker for a clean jumpsuit, I realized I was trembling.

Next we did as Galiano had suggested. A pressure hose blasted the sludge into suspension, and the tanker truck evacuated the liquid. Then the pump was reversed, and we began straining 3,500 gallons of liquid through a quarter-inch screen. Mario broke up clumps and plucked out roaches. I examined every fragment and scrap of debris.

Somewhere during that process, Díaz bailed. Though I didn't see him leave, at one point I glanced up and the pink lenses were gone.

Daylight was fading to dusk as the last of the liquid poured through the screen. The blouse, shoes, socks, undergarments, and plastic bow were bagged beside the equipment locker. A skeleton lay on the white sheet, complete except for the hyoid, one tibia, some hand and foot bones, two vertebrae, and four ribs. The skull and mandible lacked eight of the front teeth.

I'd identified, sorted left from right, and recorded every bone, confirming that we had only one individual, and ascertained what was missing. I'd felt too ill to perform further analysis. Though my brief glance at the skull made me uneasy, I'd decided to say nothing to Galiano until I was certain.

I was inventorying a rib when Díaz reappeared, followed by a man in a beige suit. He had greasy blond hair, a bad complexion, and weighed less than I did.

Díaz and his companion scanned the yard, conferred, then crossed to Galiano.

The new arrival spoke.

"I am here on behalf of the district attorney."

The guy was knobby-joint skinny and looked like a kid in adult clothing.

"And you are?" Galiano removed and folded his shades.

"Dr. Hector Lucas. I am taking possession of the remains found at this site."

"Like hell you are," Galiano replied.

Lucas looked at his watch, then at Díaz.

Díaz produced a paper from a zipper case.

"This warrant says he is," said Díaz. "Pack everything for transport to the central morgue."

Not a synapse fired in any muscle in Galiano's body.

Díaz raised the warrant to eye level. Galiano ignored it.

Díaz pressed tinted glasses to nose. Everyone else remained frozen in place. Behind me I heard movement, then the pump cut off.

"Now, Detective." Díaz's voice sounded loud in the sudden stillness.

A second went by. Ten. A full minute.

Galiano was still staring when his cell phone shrilled. He clicked on after four rings, never taking his eyes from Díaz.

"Galiano."

He listened, jaw clenched, then said one thing.

"*¡Eso es una mierda!*" Bullshit.

Galiano shoved the phone into his pocket and turned to Díaz.

"Be careful, señor. Be very careful," he hissed with a low, steady venting of air from his diaphragm. "*¡No me jodas!*" Don't fuck around with me.

60

With a jerk of his hand, Galiano gestured me from the body bag. I pushed to my feet and started to step back, reversed myself, knelt next to the skeleton, and peered intently at the skull. Díaz took half a step and started to speak, then bit off whatever he had intended to say and waited until I arose again.

Lucas approached and glanced at the array in the body bag. Satisfied, he pulled gloves from his pocket, tucked the sheet inside, and ran the zipper. Then he stood, a look of uncertainty on his face.

Díaz strode from the yard, returned with two men in gray coveralls, "Morgue del Organismo Judicial" stenciled on their backs. Between them they carried a gurney, legs collapsed beneath.

Under Lucas's direction, the morgue attendants lifted the pouch by its corners, placed it on the gurney, and disappeared in the direction from which they'd come.

Díaz tried once more to deliver the warrant. Galiano's arms remained crossed on his chest.

Díaz circled to me, eyes fastidiously avoiding the tank. Sighing, he offered the document.

As I reached to accept the paper, my eyes met Galiano's. His lower lids crimped, and his chin raised almost imperceptibly. I understood.

Without another word, Díaz and Lucas hurried from the yard.

Galiano looked at his partner. Hernández was already gathering the bagged clothing.

"How much is left in there?" Galiano tipped his head at the tanker truck.

The operator shrugged, waggled a hand. "Ten, maybe twenty gallons."

"Finish it."

Nothing else showed up in the screen. I was squeezing the last of the muck through my fingers when Galiano joined me.

"Bad day for the good guys."

"Isn't the DA supposed to be a good guy?"

"Stupid little rodent didn't even think of clothing."

I felt too ill to reply.

"Does it fit the profile?"

I raised my eyebrows.

"The skeleton. Does it fit the description of one of our missing girls?"

I hesitated, furious with myself for not thoroughly examining the bones, furious with Galiano for allowing them to be taken.

"Yes and no."

"You'll know when you've examined it."

"Will I be doing that?"

"I *will* come out the winner," he said, gazing at the empty tank.

I wondered who the loser would be.

5

That night I bathed in Tahitian Vanilla bubbles for almost an hour. Then I warmed pizza slices in the microwave and dug an orange soda from the mini-fridge. Snickers and an apple for dessert. Hotel room gourmet.

As I ate, the curtains breathed in and out the window on a half-hearted breeze. The metal pull chain clicked against the frame. Three floors below, traffic honked and rumbled. Overhead, a ceiling fan whirred. On the screen inside my skull, the day's events shifted in and out of focus like a bad home movie.

After clearing wrappers, one paper plate, one plastic fork, and the empty soda can, I phoned Mateo. He told me that Molly remained comatose.

His words tipped a delicate balance. I was no longer merely exhausted. Suddenly I just wanted to lie on the bed, bury my face in the pillow, and cry. I felt overwhelmed by sorrow and worry for my friend.

Instead, I shifted topics.

Mateo was outraged when I told him about Díaz, and insisted I continue with the case. I agreed but promised to be at his lab on Saturday.

I spent the next twenty minutes jotting on paper a detailed chronology of what had happened at the Paraíso. Then I washed panties in the bathroom sink.

Teeth. Hand cream. Oil of Olay. Sit-ups.

I turned on CNN. A grim-faced commentator moved through soccer, an earthquake, the world market. Locally, a bus had crashed into a ravine, killing seventeen and hospitalizing a score of others.

It was no go. My mind looped from a septic tank, to an intensive care unit, to a well, and back again.

I pictured the skull, slick with human waste. Why hadn't I done a more thorough exam? Why did I permit people to intimidate me and prevent me from doing what I knew should be done?

I pictured Molly, tubes running from nose, mouth, and arm.

My emotional equilibrium finally collapsed as I was plugging my cell phone into its charger.

In Charlotte, Birdie would be sound asleep. In Charlottesville, Katy would be studying for finals. Or partying with friends. Or washing her hair.

My chest gave a tiny heave.

My daughter was a continent away, and I had no

idea what she was doing.

Stop sniveling. You've been alone before.

Killing the lights and TV, I slipped between the sheets.

My mind circled the same holding pattern.

In Montreal, it would be close to midnight. Ryan would be . . .

What?

I had no idea what Ryan would be doing.

Lieutenant-détective Andrew Ryan, Section des Crimes Contre la Personne, Sûreté du Québec. Tall, craggy, with all the crags in the right places. Eyes bluer than a Bahamian lagoon.

My stomach did that weird little flip.

No nausea there.

Ryan worked homicide for the provincial police, and for a decade our paths had crossed and recrossed as we investigated cases of unnatural death. Always distant, always professional. Then, two years ago, my marriage imploded, and Ryan turned his legendary charm my way.

To say our history since had been rocky would be like saying Atlantis had a water problem.

Suddenly single after a twenty-year hitch, I'd had little knowledge of the dating game, and only one maxim: no office romance. Ryan ignored it.

Though tempted, I kept him at arm's length, partly because we worked together, partly because of his reputation. I knew of Ryan's past as a wild-child turned cop, and of his present as the squad room stallion. Both personae were more than I wanted to take on.

But Détective Lothario never eased up, and a year back I'd agreed to a Chinese dinner. Before our first social outing, Ryan vanished undercover, not to resurface for many months.

Last fall, following an epiphany concerning my estranged husband, I'd decided to consider Ryan again. Though still cautious, I was finding Ryan thoughtful, funny, and one of the most annoying men I'd ever encountered.

And one of the sexiest.

Flip.

Though that runner was still in the blocks, the gun was loaded and ready to fire.

I glanced at my phone. I could be talking to Ryan in seconds.

Something in my brain said "bad idea."

Why?

You'd look like a wimp, the something answered.

I'd look like I care.

You'd look like a grade-B heroine mooning for a shoulder to cry on.

I'd look like I miss him.

Suit yourself.

"What the hell," I said aloud.

Throwing back the quilt, I grabbed the phone and hit autodial 5. The miracle of modern communication.

A hundred miles north of the forty-ninth parallel, a phone rang.

And rang.

And rang.

I was about to disconnect when a machine answered. Ryan's voice invited a message in French then English.

Satisfied? The cerebral something smirked.

My thumb moved toward the "end" button, hesitated.

What the hell.

"Hi. It's Temp—"

"*Bonsoir, Madame la Docteure,*" Ryan's voice cut in.

"Did I wake you?"

"I screen all calls."

"Oh?"

"Cruise and Kidman split. It's just a matter of time until Nicole starts ringing."

"You wish, Ryan."

"How's it going on the mudflats?"

"We were in the highlands."

"Were?"

"We've finished digging. Everything's at the lab in Guatemala City."

"How many?"

"Twenty-three. Looks like mostly women and kids."

"Rough."

"It gets rougher."

"I'm listening."

I told him about Carlos and Molly.

"Jesus, Brennan. Watch your butt down there."

"It gets rougher still."

"Go on." I heard the sound of a match, then exhaled air.

"The local gendarmerie think they have a serial operating in Guatemala City. They requested my help with a recovery."

"There's no local talent?"

"The remains were in a septic tank."

"*La spécialité du chef.*"

"I've done one or two."

"How did that pearl float to Central America?"

"I am *not* unknown on the world stage, Ryan."

"Curriculum vitae posted on the Web?"

Could I tell him about the ambassador's missing daughter? No. I'd promised Galiano full confidentiality.

"A detective saw one of my *JFS* articles. This may come as a surprise to you, but some cops do read publications unadorned by pictures that fold in the middle."

A long exhalation. I pictured smoke blasting from his nostrils like steam from a fun-house dragon.

"Besides, there's the possibility of a Canadian connection."

As usual, I felt I was justifying my actions to Ryan. As usual it was making me churlish.

"And?"

"And today we recovered a skeleton."

"And?"

"I'm not sure."

He picked up on something in my voice.

"What's eating you?"

"I'm not sure."

"Does the vic fit their profile?"

68

"I'm not sure."

"Didn't you do a prelim on site?"

How could I explain? My tummy was upset?

"No." Again, the burning guilt. "And I probably never will."

"Oh?"

"The DA confiscated the bones."

"Let me get this straight. These yokels ask you to do the leprous slog, then the DA lays paper and boogies with the goods?"

"The cops were given no choice."

"Didn't they have their own paper?"

"It's a different legal system. I didn't inquire." My voice dripped icicles.

"It's probably a minor glitch. The coroner will be calling you first thing tomorrow."

"Doubtful."

"Why?"

I searched for a tactful way to explain Díaz. "Let's just say there's resistance to the idea of outside help."

"What about the Canadian connection?"

I pictured the skull.

"Dubious. But I'm not certain."

"Jesus, Brennan—"

"Don't say it."

He did.

"How do you get yourself into these things?"

"They asked me to recover bones from a tank," I spat. "I did that."

"What moron was in charge?"

"What difference does it make?"

"I may nominate the guy for dumb-ass of the year."

"Sergeant-detective Bartolomé Galiano."

"SICA?"

"Yes."

"Holy shit."

"What?"

"Face like a bulldog, eyes like a Guernsey?"

"They're brown."

"The Bat." It was almost a whoop.

"What bat?"

"I haven't thought of the Bat in years."

"You're making no sense, Ryan."

"Bat Galiano."

Galiano said he'd spent time in Canada.

"You know Galiano?"

"I went to school with him."

"Galiano went to St-F.X.?"

St-Francis Xavier, Antigonish, Nova Scotia. The small university town was the scene of many of Ryan's more colorful performances. Then a cokehead biker opened his carotid with the shattered neck of a twelve-ounce Bud. Following serious stitching and introspection, Ryan changed sides. His allegiance shifted from booze and bars to the boys in blue, and he never looked back.

"Bat lived across the hall my senior year. I graduated, joined the SQ. He wrapped up a semester later, returned to Guatemala to become a cop. I haven't spoken to him in ages.

"Why 'Bat?'"

"Never mind. But clear your calendar. You'll be

looking at bones before the week is out."

"I should have refused to hand them over."

"A gringo intermeddler bucking local authority in a system known for massacring dissidents. There's good thinking."

"I should have examined them on site."

"Wasn't everything coated in shit?"

"I could have cleaned it."

"And possibly done more damage than good. I wouldn't lose sleep over this one. Besides, you're down there for another reason."

But lose sleep I did, tossing and turning, captive to uninvited images from the day. Downstairs, traffic receded to a hum, then to the sound of individual cars. Next door, a TV went from the muted cadence of baseball, to a talk show, to silence.

Over and over I chastised myself for failing to examine the bones. Was my initial impression of the skull correct? Would Xicay's photos be adequate for establishing a biological profile? Would I ever see the bones again? What was behind Díaz's hostility?

I was troubled by thoughts of how far from home I was, geographically and culturally. While I had some understanding of the Guatemalan legal system, I knew nothing of the jurisdictional rivalries and personal histories that can impede an investigation. I knew the stage, but not the players.

My misgivings went beyond the complications of policework. I was an outsider in Guatemala, with a superficial grasp of its inner soul. I knew little of the people, their preferences in cars, jobs, neighborhoods, toothpaste. Their views toward law and authority. I was a stranger to their likes, their dislikes, their trusts, their lusts. Their reasons for murder.

Their nicknames.

Bat? Bartolomé Galiano? Bat Galiano? Bat Guano?

On that note I finally drifted off.

Saturday morning began as a replay of the day before. Galiano picked me up, shaded and bearing coffee, and we drove in silence to police headquarters. This time he led me to a second-floor office. Though larger, it was decorated in the same style as Thursday's conference room. Mucous-gray walls. Bile-green floor. Fluorescent lighting. Engraved wooden desks. Duct-taped pipes. Institutional folding tables. *Nouveau cop*.

Hernández was removing boxes from stacks at the back of the room and placing them on a dolly. Two men were stapling items onto bulletin boards on the left-hand wall. One was slight, with curly black hair that shone with oil. The other stood six foot six and had a shoulder span the size of Belize. Both turned when we entered.

Galiano introduced the pair.

Two faces scanned me, as though worked by one puppeteer. Neither looked thrilled with what it saw.

What *did* they see? An outsider cop? An American? A woman?

Screw it. I would make no effort to win them over.

I nodded.

They nodded.

"Pics here yet?" Galiano asked.

"Xicay says they'll be ready by ten," Hernández said, tipping the dolly and pushing it toward us.

"Taking these to the basement," he puffed, steadying the load with his right hand. "You want the bags?"

"Yeah."

Hernández wheeled past us, face raspberry, shirt damp as at the septic tank.

"The space was being used for storage," Galiano said to me. "I'm having it cleared."

"Task force?"

"Not exactly." He gestured to one of the desks. "What do you need?"

"The skeleton," I said, tossing my pack onto the blotter.

"Right."

The men finished at the first board, shifted to the next. Galiano and I moved in. In front of us was a map of Guatemala City. Galiano touched a point in the southeastern quadrant.

"Number one. Claudia de la Alda lived here."

He shook a red-tipped pin from a box on the board's ledge, pushed it into the map, and added a yellow pin beside it.

"De la Alda was eighteen. No police record, no history of drugs, doesn't profile as a runaway. Spent a lot of time working with handicapped kids and helping out at her church. She left the family home for work last July fourteenth, and hasn't been seen since."

"Boyfriend?" I asked.

"Alibis out. Not a suspect."

He pushed a blue pin into the map.

"Claudia worked at the Museo Ixchel."

The Ixchel is a privately owned museum dedicated to Mayan culture. I'd been there, remembered it looked vaguely like a Mayan temple.

"Number two. Lucy Gerardi, age seventeen, was a student at San Carlos University."

He added a second blue pin.

"Gerardi also had no prior arrests, also lived with her family. Good student. Aside from a lousy social life, she appears to have been a normal college kid."

"Why no friends?"

"Father kept a tight rein."

His finger moved to a small street halfway between the Ixchel and the American embassy.

"Lucy lived here."

He added a second red pin.

"She was last seen in the Botanical Gardens—"

He inserted a yellow pin in a green-shaded space at the intersection of Ruta 6 and Avenida la Reforma.

"—on January fifth."

Galiano's finger hopped to Calle 10 at Avenida la Reforma 3.

"Familiar with the Zona Viva?"

A stab of pain. Molly and I had eaten at a café in the Zona Viva the day before I left for Chupan Ya.

Focus, Brennan.

"It's a small enclave of upmarket hotels, restaurants, and night clubs."

"Right. Number three. Patricia Eduardo, age nineteen, lived just a few blocks away."

Red pin number three.

"Eduardo left friends at the Café San Felipe on the night of October twenty-ninth, never made it home."

Yellow pin.

"She worked at the Hospital Centro Médico."

A blue pin went in at Avenida 6 and Calle 9, just a few blocks from the Ixchel Museum.

"Same story, clean liver, boyfriend a candidate for canonization. Spent most of her free time with her horses. Was quite an equestrian."

Galiano pointed to a spot equidistant between the Lucy Gerardi and Patricia Eduardo residences.

"Missing person number four, Chantale Specter, lived here."

Red pin.

"Chantale went to a private girls' school—"

Blue pin.

"—but she'd just returned from an extended stay in Canada."

"What was she doing?"

He hesitated a moment. "Some sort of special course. Chantale was last seen at home."

"By?"

"The mother."

"Both parents check out?"

He took a long breath through his nostrils, let it out slowly.

"Hard to investigate a foreign diplomat."

"Any reason for suspicion?"

"None that we've found. So. We know where each young woman lived."

Galiano tapped the red pins.

"We know where each worked or went to school."

Blue pins.

"We know where each was last seen."

Yellow pins.

I stared at the pattern, realizing the answer to at least one question. I knew Guatemala City well enough to know that Claudia de la Alda, Lucy Gerardi, Patricia Eduardo, and Chantale Specter came from the affluent side of the tracks. Theirs was a world of quiet streets and mowed lawns, not one of drugs and peddled flesh. Unlike the poor and homeless, unlike the victims at Chupan Ya or the addict orphans in Parque Concordia, these women were not without power. They were missed by families that had a voice, and everything possible was being done to find them.

But why such interest in remains uncovered at a slum hotel?

"Why the Paraíso?" I asked.

Again, that hitch of hesitation. Then, "No stone unturned."

I turned from the map to Galiano. His face was expressionless. I waited. He offered nothing.

"Are you going to level with me, or do we have to go through some elaborate pas de deux?"

"What do you mean?"

"Suit yourself, Bat." I turned to go.

Galiano looked at me sharply but said nothing. Then his hand closed around my upper arm.

"All right. But nothing leaves this room."

"Normally I like to float my cases in a chat room, get a consensus of who's thinking what."

He released his grip and ran a hand backward through his hair. Then the Guernsey eyes locked onto mine.

"Eighteen months ago Chantale Specter was arrested for cocaine possession."

"Was she using?"

"That was unclear. She dropped a dime and was released without testing. But her buddies came up positive."

"Selling?"

"Probably not. Last summer she was busted again. Same story. Police raided a candy party in a low-rent hotel. Chantale turned up in the net. Shortly after, Papa shipped her off to rehab – that spell in Canada. She reappeared at Christmas, started school in January, vanished a week into the term. The ambassador tried searching on his own, finally gave up and reported her missing."

His finger moved to the maze of streets making up the old city.

"Both of Chantale's arrests took place in Zone One."

"Some kids go through a rebellious phase," I

said. "She probably got back home, went at it with Daddy, and took off."

"For four months?"

"It's probably coincidence. Chantale doesn't fit the pattern."

"Lucy Gerardi disappeared January fifth. Ten days later, it was Chantale Specter."

Galiano turned to me.

"According to some, Lucy and Chantale were close friends."

6

Crime scene pictures provide a cheap peek into the secrets of strangers. Unlike photographic art in which lighting and subjects are chosen or positioned to enhance moments of beauty, scene photos are shot to capture stark, unadorned reality in vivid detail. Viewing them is a jarring and dispiriting task.

A shattered window. A blood-spattered kitchen. A woman spreadeagled in bed, torn panties covering her face. The bloated body of a child in a trunk. Horror revisited, moments, hours, or days later.

Or even months.

At nine-forty Xicay delivered the Paraíso prints. With no bones to examine, these shots offered my only hope of constructing an accurate victim profile, of perhaps linking the septic tank skeleton to one of the missing girls.

I opened the first envelope, afraid, but anxious to know how much anatomical detail had been saved.

Or lost.

The alley.

The Paraíso.

The dilapidated little oasis out back.

I studied multiple views of the septic tank before and after uncapping, before, during, and after draining. In the last, shadows crossed the empty chambers like long, bony fingers.

I replaced the first set and switched to another envelope.

The top print featured my ass pointed skyward at the edge of the tank. The second showed a lower arm bone lying on a sheet in a body bag. Even with my magnifier, I could make out no detail. I laid down the lens and continued.

Seven shots down I found a close-up of the ulna. Inching my glass along the shaft, I scrutinized every bump and crest. I was about to give up when I spotted a hair-thin line at the wrist end.

"Look at this."

Galiano took the lens and bent over the print. I pointed with the tip of a pen.

"That's a remnant epiphyseal line."

"*Ay, Dios.*" He spoke without raising his eyes. "And that means?"

"The growth cap is fusing to the end of the shaft."

"And that means?"

"It means young."

"How young?"

"Probably late teens."

He straightened.

"*Muy bueno, Dr. Brennan.*"

The cranial series began halfway down the third stack. As I viewed image after image, my gut curled tighter than it had in the septic tank. Xicay had shot down on the skull from at least six feet away. Mud, shadow, and distance obscured every feature. Even the magnifier didn't help.

Discouraged, I finished envelope three and moved on. One by one, body parts spread across the sheet. Fusing growth caps on several long bones supported the age range suggested by the ulna.

Xicay had taken at least a half dozen shots of the pelvis. Soft tissue held the three parts together, allowing me to note a heart-shaped inlet. The pubic bones were long, and met above an obtuse sub-pubic angle.

I flipped to the side views.

Broad, shallow sciatic notch.

"Female," I said to no one in particular.

"Show me." Galiano returned to my desk.

Spreading the photos, I explained each feature. Galiano listened in silence.

As I was gathering the prints, my eye picked out several odd-shaped flecks on the belly side of the right iliac blade. I pulled the image to me and raised and lowered my lens above it. Galiano watched.

Tooth fragments? Vegetation? Gravel? The tiny

particles looked familiar, but try as I might, I couldn't identify them.

"What is it?" Galiano.

"I'm not sure. Maybe just debris."

I returned the photos to their envelope, and shook out another set.

Foot bones. Hand bones. Ribs.

Galiano was paged to his office. The two detectives plugged away at their boards.

Sternum. Vertebrae.

Galiano returned.

"Where the hell is Hernández?"

No answer. I imagined two shrugs behind me.

My spine ached. I raised my arms, stretched backward, then to each side.

When I resumed my perusal, a miracle.

While I was overseeing evacuation of the tank, Xicay had returned to the skull. The last series of photographs showed top, bottom, side, and front views, taken from approximately one foot away. Despite the muck, I could see plenty.

"These are good."

Galiano was immediately at my elbow. I pointed out features on the facial view.

"Rounded orbits, broad cheeks."

I shifted to a shot of the skull base, and indicated the zygomatics.

"See how the cheekbones flare out?"

Galiano nodded.

"The skull is short from front to back, broad from side to side."

"Sort of globular."

"Well put." I tapped the upper palate. "Parabolic shape. Too bad the front teeth are missing."

"Why?"

"Shoveled incisors can indicate race."

"Shoveled?"

"Scooped-out enamel on the tongue side, with a raised border around the edge. Kind of like a shovel."

I exchanged the basal view for a side view, and noted a low nasal bridge and straight facial profile.

"What's your thinking?" Galiano asked.

"Mongoloid," I said, thinking back to my last fleeting view at the scene and correlating that impression with the photos in front of me.

He looked blank.

"Asian."

"Chinese, Japanese, Vietnamese?"

"All of the above. Or someone whose ancestors came from Asia. Native American—"

"You talking old Indian bones?"

"Definitely not. This stuff's recent."

He considered a moment, then, "Were the front teeth knocked out?"

I knew what he was thinking. Teeth are often destroyed to hamper identification. That was not the case here. I shook my head.

"Incisors have only one root. When the soft tissue decomposes, there's nothing to hold them. Most likely, hers just fell out."

"And went where?"

"They could have filtered through the septic

83

system. Or they could still be wedged in the tank."

"Would they be useful?"

"Sure. These features are only suggestive." I waved a hand at the photo.

"So who's the stranger in the septic tank?"

"Female, probably late teens, possibly Mongoloid ancestry."

I could sense neurons firing behind the Guernsey eyes.

"Most Guatemalans would have Mongoloid traits?"

"Many would," I agreed.

"And mighty few Canadians."

"Native peoples, Asian immigrants, their descendants."

Galiano said nothing for a long time. Then, "Odds are we're not looking at Chantale Specter."

I was about to answer when Hernández rolled his dolly into the room. The large boxes had been replaced by two trash bags and a black canvas case.

"Where the hell have you been?" Galiano asked his partner.

"Assholes didn't want to loan out their precious light. Acted like it's the crown jewels." Hernández's voice sounded like a jammed garbage disposal. "Where do you want this stuff?"

Galiano indicated two folding tables by the right-hand wall. Hernández offloaded his cargo, then parked the dolly by the remaining boxes.

"Next stuff gets moved, it won't be me." Pulling a swatch of yellow from his pocket, he wiped his face. "Goddamn stuff's heavy."

Hernández shoved the hankie into his back pocket. I watched a corner of yellow swatch storm from the room.

"Let's have a look at the photos," Galiano said to me. "Most are from the families. One from the embassy."

I followed, though I had no need to see the display. I'd worked serial homicides, and knew exactly what was there. Faces: hostile, happy, puzzled, sleepy. Young or old, male or female, stylish or frumpy, pretty or homely, each caught at a moment in time, oblivious to future calamity.

My first glance made me think of Ted Bundy and his taste in victims. All four women had long straight hair, parted down the crown. There the resemblance ended.

Claudia de la Alda was not blessed with beauty. She was an angular young woman with a broad nose and wide-set eyes no larger than olives. In each of three snapshots, she wore a black skirt and a pastel blouse, buttoned to the chin. A silver crucifix rested on her ample chest.

Lucy Gerardi had shiny black hair, blue eyes, a delicate nose and chin. A school portrait showed her in a bright blue blazer and starched white blouse. In a home pic she wore a yellow sundress, and held a schnauzer in her lap. A gold cross nestled in the hollow at the base of her throat.

Though the oldest of the four, Patricia Eduardo didn't look a day over fifteen. One Kodak moment captured her fiercely erect atop an Appaloosa, eyes

85

shiny black under a derby brim, one hand on the reins, one on her knee. In another she stood beside the horse, staring solemnly at the lens. Like the others, she wore a cross and no makeup.

While De la Alda, Gerardi and Eduardo seemed to be operating under the influence of Our Lady the Chaste, Chantale Specter looked like a member of the Church of the Lewd. In her mug shot, the ambassador's daughter sported a midriff tank and skin-tight jeans. Her blonde hair was streaked, her makeup vampire black.

In stark contrast was the portrait submitted through official embassy channels. Chantale posed between Mommy and Daddy on a Queen Anne couch. She wore pumps, hose, and a white cotton dress. No booking number, no streaking, no Bela Lugosi eyes.

Looking from face to face, I felt something go hollow in my chest. Was it possible that all four women were dead? Had we dredged one of them from the Paraíso tank? Was a psychopath on the prowl in Guatemala City? Was he already planning his next kill? Would more photos find their way to this display?

"Doesn't look like someone who'd hawk ass for drugs." Galiano was looking at the Specter portrait.

"None of them does."

"Anyone fit your profile?"

"They all do. Chantale Specter doesn't work for race, but that's always iffy. I'd feel more confident if I could take measurements and run them

86

through a data bank. Even then, race can be a tough call."

Behind me, the large detective transferred boxes to the dolly.

"What about timing?" I asked.

"Claudia de la Alda was LSA in July. The septic tank was serviced in August."

"Last seen alive doesn't equate to date of death."

"No," Galiano agreed.

"If she is dead."

"Patricia Eduardo vanished in October, Gerardi and Specter in January."

"Anyone LSA wearing jeans and a pink floral blouse?"

"Not according to witness accounts." He indicated a stack of folders. "The files are there."

"First, I'd like to take a look at the clothes," I said.

Galiano followed me to the table, watched as I lowered the evidence bags to the floor, pulled a plastic sheet from my pack, and spread it across the tabletop.

"I need water," I said, lifting the first bag.

Galiano shot me a questioning look.

"To clean labels."

He spoke to one of the detectives.

Pulling on latex gloves, I untied the knot, reached in, and began extracting filthy clothing. A stench filled the room as I disentangled and spread each garment.

Detective Hair Oil brought water.

"Jesus Christ, smells like sewer slime."

"Now why do you suppose that would be?" I asked as he left, closing the door behind him.

Jeans. Shirt. Mint-green bra. Mint-green panties with tiny red roses. Navy-blue socks. Penny loafers.

A cold prickle. My sister and I got penny loafers the fall I entered the fifth grade.

Slowly, a scarecrow took shape, headless, handless, flat and damp. When the bags were empty, I began a close inspection of each item.

The jeans were navy blue and bore no logo. Though the material was in good condition, the garment had separated into individual components.

I checked the pockets. Empty, as expected. I dunked the tag, scrubbed gently. The lettering was faded beyond legibility. The pant legs were rolled, but I estimated the size as similar to mine, a woman's six or eight. Galiano recorded everything in his spiral pad.

The blouse had no identifying labels. For now I left it buttoned.

"Stab wounds?" Galiano asked as I inspected one of several defects in the fabric.

"Irregular shapes, ragged edges," I said. "They're just rips."

The bra was a 34B, the panties size 5. No brand name was visible on either.

"Weird how the jeans are falling apart but everything else is almost perfect." Galiano.

"Natural fibers. Here today, gone tomorrow."

He waited for me to go on.

"The jeans were probably sewn with cotton thread. But the lady had a definite fondness for synthetics."

"Princess Polyester."

"They may not make the best-dressed lists, but polyesters and acrylics are decomp friendly."

"Longer lasting through chemistry."

Sludge oozed onto the plastic as I unrolled the right jeans leg. Aside from dead roaches, I spotted nothing.

I unrolled the left.

"Luma Lite?" I asked.

What had been grudgingly lent was an alternate light source that caused fingerprints, hairs, fibers, semen, and drug stains to fluoresce brightly.

Galiano dug a black box and two sets of tinted goggles from the case Hernández had brought. While he found an outlet and turned off the overheads, I slipped on the plastic glasses. Then I flipped the switch and moved the Luma Lite over the clothing. The beam picked up nothing until I came to the unrolled hem of the left pant leg. Filaments flared like sparklers on the Fourth of July.

"What the hell is that?" I could feel Galiano's breath on my arm.

I held the beam on the cuff, and stepped back.

"¡Puchica!" Wow!

He squinted at the jeans a full minute, then straightened.

"Hair?"

"Possibly."

"Human or animal?"

"That's one for your trace guys. But I'd start asking about family pets."

"Son of a bitch."

I dug a handful of plastic vials from my pack, labeled one, tweezed up the filaments, and sealed them inside. Then I rescanned every inch of clothing. No more fireworks.

"Lights?"

Galiano removed his goggles and hit the switch.

After marking the remaining vials with date, time, and location, I scraped muck into each, capped, taped, and initialed. Right sock, exterior. Right sock, interior. Left sock. Right pants cuff. Left pants cuff. Right shoe, interior. Right sole, shoe. Ten minutes later I was ready for the blouse.

"Overheads, please?"

Galiano killed the lights.

The buttons were standard-issue plastic. One by one, I hit them with the Luma Lite. No prints.

"O.K."

The room lit up as I slipped each button through its hole, peeled back the fabric, and exposed the blouse's interior.

The object was so small it almost escaped my notice, tangled in the recess of the right underarm seam.

I grabbed my magnifier.

Oh, no.

I took a deep breath, steadied my hands, and eased the sleeve inside out.

Another lay five inches down the sleeve.

I found another, an inch below the first.

"Sonovabitch."

"What?" Galiano was staring at me.

I went straight to the scene photos, dumped envelopes until I found the right set. Racing through the stack I pulled out the pelvic close-up and magnified the mysterious specks.

Dear God.

Barely breathing, I examined every inch of pelvic bone, then worked my way through the other shots. I spotted seven in all.

Anger rushed through my body. And sorrow. And every emotion I'd felt in the grave at Chupan Ya.

"I don't know who she is," I said. "But I may know why she died."

7

"I'm listening," Galiano said.

"She was pregnant."

"Pregnant?"

I held out the first pelvic photo.

"That speck is a fragment of fetal skull."

I shifted prints.

"So is that. And there are fetal bones in the blouse."

"Show me."

Returning to the table, I indicated three fingernail-sized fragments.

"*¡Hijo de la puta!*" Sonovabitch.

I was startled by his vehemence, and didn't respond.

"How pregnant?"

"I'm not sure. I'd like to scope these, then check a reference."

"Sonovafuckingbitch."

"Yeah."

Through the closed door I heard male voices, then laughter. The squad room banter seemed a callous intrusion.

"So who the hell is she?" Galiano's voice sounded a step lower than normal.

"A teenager with a terrifying secret."

"And Daddy wasn't looking to be a family man."

"Maybe Daddy already was one."

"Or the pregnancy could be coincidence."

"Could be. If this is a serial killer, his victims could be random."

The voices in the corridor receded, fell silent.

"Time for another visit with the innkeeper and his wife." Galiano.

"It wouldn't hurt to check out women's clinics and family planning centers in the neighborhood. She might have sought an abortion."

"This is Guatemala."

"Prenatal care."

"Right."

"Better get pictures before I collect these." I waved at the blouse.

Xicay arrived in minutes. I handed him my ABFO ruler and pointed out the bones. As Xicay filmed, Galiano shifted gears.

"What about size?"

"Size?"

"How big was she?"

"The clothing suggests average to petite. Muscle attachments are slight. What we call gracile."

I flipped through the photos until I came to the leg bones.

"I could estimate stature with the femur using the ruler for scale. But it would only be a ballpark guess. Do you know heights for the four MPs?"

"Should be in their files. If not, I'll find out."

"Got it," Xicay said.

Taking two more vials from my pack, I marked one and added the words *Fetal Remains*. Then I tweezed the bones from the armpit and sleeve, sealed the vials, and initialed the labels.

"Standard shots of the clothing?" Xicay asked.

I nodded.

Watching him move around the table, I had a sudden thought.

"Where are the tibia and foot bones that were in the jeans?" I asked Galiano.

"Díaz dropped paper on those, too."

"And left the jeans."

"The guy wouldn't know evidence if it pissed on his shoe."

"What's your take on Lucas?"

"The good doctor didn't look thrilled with his assignment."

"I got the same impression. Think Díaz is putting the screws to him?"

"I'm meeting with Mr. DA this afternoon." He unfolded and slipped on his shades. "I intend to stress the importance of candor."

An hour later I drove through the gates at FAFG headquarters. Ollie Nordstern stood on the front porch, one shoulder propped against a post, jaw working a wad of gum.

I considered reversing, but he was on me like a shark on a blood slick.

"Dr. Brennan. The woman that tops my list."

I dug my pack from the back of my rented Access.

"Let me get that for you."

"Something has come up, Mr. Nordstern." I slung a strap over one shoulder, slammed the door, and headed past him toward the house. "I won't have time for an interview today."

"Perhaps I could sweet-talk you into a few minutes."

Perhaps you could drown in a spittoon.

"Not today."

Elena Norvillo sat at one of several computers clustered in what was once the Mena family parlour. Her hair was hidden under a blue scarf knotted at the nape of her neck.

"*Buenos días, Elena.*"

"*Buenos días,*" she answered, never taking her eyes from the screen.

"*Donde está Mateo?*"

"He's out back," Nordstern answered from behind me.

I circled Elena's desk, walked down a corridor past offices and a kitchen, and exited to a walled courtyard. Nordstern trailed me like a puppy.

The courtyard was roofed around its periphery, open in the center. A swimming pool took up the left front, looking as out of place as a Jacuzzi in a homeless shelter. Sunlight shimmered off the water, tinting everything and everyone with an eerie, blue glow.

Workstations filled a covered patio at the rear of the courtyard, each with an empty box below, contents articulated above. Unopened boxes lined the stone walls. Tropical plants peeked from behind the stacks, survivors of the once lush Mena gardens.

Luis Posadas and Rosa O'Reilly were examining remains at the far end of the front row. Rosa recorded data as Luis worked calipers and called out measurements. Juan Corrales was consulting a hanging skeleton, bone fragment in his left hand. He wore a puzzled expression. The skeleton wore a porkpie hat.

When I came through the door, Mateo looked up from the lab's single microscope. He was dressed in denim coveralls and a gray T-shirt with the sleeves razored off. Moisture beaded his upper lip.

"Tempe. Glad to see you."

"How's Molly?" I asked, crossing to him.

"No change."

"Who's Molly?"

Mateo's eyes shifted past me to Nordstern, then back, and narrowed as Galiano's had done at the Paraíso. The signal was unnecessary. I intended to ignore the little twerp.

"I see you two have managed to connect," Mateo observed.

"I told Mr. Nordstern today was impossible."

"I was hoping you might persuade her other-wise," Nordstern wheedled.

"Could you excuse us?" Mateo smiled at the reporter, took my arm, and propelled me toward the house. I followed him upstairs to his office.

"Call him off, Mateo."

"A feature story can be good for us."

He gestured me to a chair and closed the door.

"The world needs to know, and the foundation needs money."

He waited for me to speak. When I didn't, he added, "Exposure can mean funding. And protection."

"Fine. You talk to him."

"I did."

"Elena can do it."

"She spent yesterday with him. Now he wants you."

"No."

"Toss him something and he'll go away."

"Why me?"

"He thinks you're cool."

I gave him a look that could freeze Death Valley at midday.

"He's impressed with the biker stuff you did."

I rolled my eyes.

"Thirty minutes?" Now Mateo was wheedling.

"What does he want?"

"Colorful quotes."

"He doesn't know about Molly and Carlos?"

"We thought it best to leave that out."

"Crack reporter." I flicked a speck from my pants leg. "The septic tank bones?"

"No."

"All right. One half hour."

"You might enjoy it."

Like ulcerating boils, I thought.

"Fill me in on the septic tank case," Mateo said.

"What about Jimmy Breslin down there?"

"He can wait."

I told him what I'd learned at police headquarters, leaving out only Chantale Specter's last name.

"André Specter, the Canadian ambassador. Heavy."

"You know?"

"Detective Galiano told me. It's why I let him ambush you the day we returned from Chupan Ya."

I couldn't be annoyed. In truth, I was relieved Mateo understood the implications of what I would be doing in the days to come.

I withdrew the vial from my pack and set it on the desk. He read the label, squinted at the contents, then looked at me.

"Fetal?"

I nodded. "I spotted cranial fragments in some of the photos."

"Age?"

"I have to check Fazekas and Kósa."

I referred to a volume titled *Forensic Fetal Osteology*, the anthropologist's bible on prenatal skeletal development. Published in Hungary in

1978 and long out of print, copies were jealously guarded by those lucky enough to possess them.

"There's one in the collection."

"Done with the scope?"

"Almost." He stood. "I should finish about the time you wrap up with Nordstern."

My eyes rolled so far back I feared they might strike my frontal lobe.

"Missed you yesterday."

"Uh huh."

"Señor Reyes said you'd be tied up until Saturday."

"We have thirty minutes, sir. What can I help you with?"

I'd swapped sides of Mateo's desk, and Nordstern now sat where I had been.

"Right." He pulled a tiny recorder from a pocket and waggled it. "Do you mind?"

I looked at my watch while he played with buttons.

"O.K.," he said, leaning back. "Tell me what went on down here."

The question surprised me.

"Didn't you cover that with Elena?"

"I like to get different points of view."

"It's historic record."

He raised shoulders, palms, and eyebrows.

"How far back do you want to go?"

He gave the same annoying shrug.

O.K., asshole. Human Rights Abuses 101.

"From the sixties to the nineties, many Latin

American countries were gripped by periods of violence and repression. Human rights were trampled, with most atrocities being committed by the reigning military governments.

"The early eighties saw a shift toward democracy. With that came a need to investigate human rights violations of the recent past. In some countries those investigations led to convictions. In others various amnesty proclamations allowed the guilty to skate prosecution. It became clear that outside investigators were essential if real facts were to be unearthed."

Nordstern sat there like a student not interested in what the teacher is saying. I shifted to something more concrete.

"Argentina is a good example. When Argentina returned to democracy in eighty-three, the National Commission on the Disappearance of Persons, CONADEP, determined that close to nine thousand people had been 'disappeared' during the previous military regime, the large majority kidnapped by security forces, taken to illegal detention centers, tortured, and killed. Bodies were either dumped from airplanes into the Argentine Sea or buried in unmarked graves.

"Judges began ordering exhumations, but the doctors placed in charge had little experience with skeletal remains and no training in archaeology. Bulldozers were used, bones were broken, lost, mixed up, and left behind. Needless to say, the identification process did not go well."

I was providing the ultra-condensed version.

"In addition, many of these doctors had themselves been complicit in the slaughter, either by omission or commission."

An image of Díaz flashed into my mind. Then Díaz and Dr. Lucas at the Paraíso.

"Anyway, for all these reasons, it was deemed necessary to establish a more rigorous scientific protocol and to utilize experts not subject to the influence of suspected perpetrators."

"That's where Clyde Snow came in."

"Yes. In eighty-four, the American Association for the Advancement of Science, AAAS, sent a delegation, which included Clyde Snow, to Argentina. The Argentine Forensic Anthropology Team, EAAF, was founded that year, and has been active ever since."

"Not just in Argentina."

"Hardly. The EAAF has worked with human rights organizations in Bosnia, East Timor, El Salvador, Guatemala, Paraguay, South Africa, Zimbabw—"

"Who picks up the tab?"

"Team members are paid from the EAAF's general budget. In most of these countries human rights institutions have very limited resources."

Knowing Mateo's goal, I pursued the topic.

"Money is a chronic problem in human rights work. In addition to worker salaries, there are expenses for travel and local arrangements. Funding for a mission may come entirely from the EAAF, or in Guatemala, the FAFG, or from a local or international organization."

"Let's talk Guatemala."

So much for the funding pitch.

"During the civil war here – which lasted from 1962 until 1996 – one to two hundred thousand people were killed or 'disappeared.' It's estimated that another million were displaced."

"Most being civilians."

"Yes. The UN Guatemalan Commission for Historical Clarification concluded that ninety percent of all human rights violations were committed by the Guatemalan army and its allied paramilitary organizations."

"The Mayans really took it in the pants."

The man was revolting.

"Most victims were Mayan peasants, many with no involvement in the conflict. The military swept through the countryside killing anyone they even suspected of being a guerrilla supporter. The highland provinces of El Quiché, and Huehuetenango contain hundreds of unmarked graves."

"Strictly scorched earth."

"Yes."

"And then they played innocent."

"For years successive Guatemalan governments denied that these massacres ever occurred. The current government has abandoned that charade, but it's unlikely anyone will go to jail. In 1996, a peace accord was signed between the Guatemalan government and a coalition of the main guerrilla groups, formally ending the conflict. That same year immunity was granted to persons accused of committing human rights violations during the war."

"So why this?" Nordstern waved a hand around the office.

"Survivors and relatives began to speak out, demanding an investigation. Even if they couldn't expect prosecution, they wanted to cast light on what had taken place."

I thought of the little girl at Chupan Ya. I felt like an apologist for the offenders to speak of their crimes in such a sterile and detached way. The victims deserved a more impassioned recitation.

"But even before that, in the early nineties, Guatemalan groups representing families of the victims began inviting foreign organizations, including the Argentines, to carry out exhumations. The Argentines, along with scientists from the U.S., trained local Guatemalans. That led to the operation you see here. Over the past decade Mateo and his team have conducted scores of forensic investigations and have established a degree of independence from the organs of government."

"Like Chupan Ya."

"Yes."

"Tell me about Chupan Ya."

"In August 1982, soldiers and civil patrollers entered the village—"

"Under the command of Alejandro Bastos," Nordstern cut in.

"I don't know that."

"Go on."

103

"You seem to know more about this than I do."

Again the shrug.

What the hell. I'd had enough of this man. The massacres were just a story to him. To me they were more. So much more.

I stood.

"It's getting late, Mr. Nordstern. I have work to do."

"Chupan Ya or the septic tank?"

I quietly left the room.

8

Baby building is a complex operation, run with military precision. The chromosomes form command central, with squads of grunt genes taking orders from control genes, which answer to more control genes higher up the chain.

At first the embryo is an undifferentiated mass. An order is issued.

Vertebrate!

Segmented bones form around a spinal cord, jointed limbs with five digits each. A skull. A real jaw.

The embryo is a perch. A wood frog. A gecko.

The double-helix generals up the ante.

Mammal!

Homeothermy, viviparity, heterodonty.

The embryo is a platypus. A kangaroo. A snow leopard. Elvis.

The generals push harder.

Primate!

Opposable thumbs – 3-D vision.

Harder.

Homo sapiens!

Gray matter to die for. Bipedality.

The human skeleton begins to ossify around the seventh week. Between the ninth and twelfth, tiny tooth buds appear.

I identified four cranial elements in the crime scene photos.

The sphenoid is a butterfly-shaped bone that contributes to the orbits and to the cranial base. The large wings arise during the eighth fetal week, the small pair follows a week later.

Using the scope and a calibrating grid, I measured length and breadth. Using the ABFO ruler for scale, I calculated actual size. Greater wing: fifteen by seven millimeters. Lesser wing: six by five millimeters.

The temporal bone also comes with some assembly required. The flat portion forming the temple and the most lateral part of the cheekbone appears during the eighth fetal week. This one measured ten by eighteen millimeters.

The tympanic ring begins life at approximately week nine, grows to three bony slivers during the next twenty-one days. The slivers join to form a ring around week sixteen. Just before baby checks out of the uterine hotel, the ring attaches to the ear opening.

That first puzzling speck I'd seen in the pelvic photo was a tiny tympanic ring. Though lines of fusion were still evident, the three segments were firmly attached. The ABFO ruler indicated I was viewing the ring dead on. I measured diameter, corrected, added the figure to my list. Eight millimeters.

I turned my attention to the vial.

A miniature half jaw, with sockets that would never hold teeth. Twenty-five millimeters.

One collarbone. Twenty-one millimeters.

Moving through tables in the fetal osteology book, I checked each measurement. Sphenoid greater wing. Sphenoid lesser wing. Temporal squamous. Tympanic ring. Mandible. Clavicle.

According to Fazekas and Kósa, the girl in the tank had been five months pregnant.

I closed my eyes. The baby had been six to nine inches long and weighed around eight ounces when its mother was killed. It could blink, grasp, make sucking motions. It had eyelashes and finger-prints, could hear and recognize Mom's voice. If it was a girl, she had six million eggs in her tiny ovaries.

I was feeling overwhelmed by sadness when Elena called out from the doorway.

"There's a call for you."

I didn't want to talk to anyone.

"A Detective Galiano. You can take it in Mateo's office."

I thanked Elena, resealed the evidence in its vial, and climbed back to the second floor.

"Five months," I said, skipping preliminaries.

He needed no explanation.

"About the time she might have been leveling with Papa."

"Her own, or the donor of the lucky sperm?"

"Or nondonor."

"Jealous boyfriend?" I threw out.

"Angry pimp?"

"Psycho stranger? The possibilities are endless. That's why the world needs detectives."

"I did some detecting this morning."

I waited.

"The Eduardos are the proud owners of two boxers and a cat. Lucy Gerardi's family has a cat and a schnauzer. The De la Aldas are not animal lovers. Nor are the ambassador and his clan."

"Patricia Eduardo's boyfriend?"

"A ferret named Julio."

"Claudia de la Alda's?"

"Allergies."

"When will your trace guys be done viewing the samples?"

"Monday."

"What did the DA have to say?"

I heard Galiano draw a long breath through his nostrils.

"His office will not be releasing the skeleton."

"Can we have access at the morgue?"

"No."

"Why not?"

"The guy really wanted to be my best friend, was devastated he couldn't discuss the case."

"Is this typical?"

"I've never been stonewalled by a DA, but I've never tangled with this one."

I pointed my thoughts at that for a while.

"What do you think is going on?"

"Either the guy's got a hard-on for protocol, or someone's putting the screws to him."

"Who?"

Galiano didn't answer.

"The embassy?" I asked.

"What are you doing?" There was a dark guardedness to his voice.

"Now?"

"For the junior prom."

I could see why Ryan and Galiano had hit it off.

I looked at my watch. Five-forty. A Saturday evening calm had settled over the lab.

"It's too late to start anything here. I'll head back to my hotel."

"I'll pick you up in an hour."

"For?"

"*Caldos.*"

I started to object, pictured the gathering of one I'd attend in my room.

What the hell.

"My dress is blue."

"O.K." Puzzled.

"I prefer a wrist corsage."

"Donated by a citizen with a horticultural bent." Galiano proffered two pansies stapled to a blue rubber band.

"Donated?"

109

"The band is sold separately."

"Broccoli?"

"Asparagus."

"They're lovely."

Cars honked and jockeyed as we walked toward the Café Gucumatz. An early evening shower had come and gone, and the air smelled of wet cement, diesel fuel, earth, and flowers. Now and then the soggy maize scent of *tamal* or *chuchito* drifted by as we passed a vendor's cart.

We shared the sidewalk with throngs of others. Couples heading out for dinner or drinks. Young professionals returning home from work. Shoppers. Saturday-evening strollers. A breeze tossed ties over shoulders and molded skirts to legs and hips. Overhead, palm fronds rose and fell with soft clicking sounds.

The Gucumatz was done in techno-Mayan, with dark wooden beams, plastic flora, and an artificial pond with arching bridge. Murals decorated every wall, most depicting the fifteenth-century Quiché king who'd lent his name to the place. I wondered how Feathered Serpent felt about the implied endorsement, but kept it to myself.

Lighting was by torch and candle, and entering was like passing into a Mayan tomb. As my pupils dilated, a parrot shrilled greetings in Spanish and English. So did a man in white shirt, black pants, and apron.

"*Hola, Detective Galiano.* Hello. *¿Cómo está?*"

"*Muy bien, Señor Velásquez.*"

110

"Such a long time since we've seen you."

An enormous mustache handle-barred over Velásquez's mouth, plunged south at the sides, then curled back north as though reaching for his nostrils. I thought of an emperor tamarin.

"Working my tail off, señor."

Velásquez wagged his head in understanding.

"Crime is so terrible today. Everywhere. Everywhere. The citizens of this city are privileged to have you on the job."

Another sad head shake, then Velásquez took my hand and pressed it to his lips. The facial hair felt like steel wool.

"*Bienvenido, señorita.* A friend of Detective Galiano is always a friend of Velásquez."

Releasing my fingers, he flashed both eyebrows at Galiano and winked theatrically.

"*Por favor.* My best table. Come. Come."

Velásquez led us to his prize pond-side seating, turned and beamed at Galiano. The detective tipped his head toward the restaurant's interior.

"*Sí, señor.* Of course."

Velásquez hurried us to an alcove constructed around a back corner, and gave Galiano a questioning look. My companion nodded. We entered the cave and sat. Another Groucho display for the great crime fighter, and our host withdrew.

"That was as subtle as a baboon's ass," I said.

"I apologize for the *machismo* of my brothers."

Within seconds a waitress appeared with menus.

"Libation?" Galiano asked me.

Oh, yeah.

111

"Can't do it."

"Oh?"

"Over quota."

Galiano did not question that.

He ordered a Grey Goose martini neat. I asked for Perrier with lime.

When the drinks arrived, we opened our menus. The lighting had gone from low to nonexistent with our relocation to the underworld, and I could hardly make out the handwritten text. I wondered about Galiano's motive for the move, but didn't ask.

"If you haven't had *caldos*, I recommend it."

"*Caldos* being . . .?"

"Traditional Mayan stew. Tonight they have duck, beef, and chicken."

"Chicken." I closed my menu. I couldn't read it anyway.

Galiano chose beef.

The waitress brought tortillas. Galiano took one, offered the basket.

"*Gracias*," I said.

"When?" He settled back into his chair.

I'd missed a bridge somewhere.

"When?" I repeated his question.

"When did you burn your allotment?"

I made the connection, but had no intention of discussing my love affair with alcohol.

"A few years back."

"Friend of Bill Wilson?"

"I'm not a joiner."

"A lot of people rely on AA."

"It's a wonderful program." I reached for my

glass. The bubbles made soft fizzing sounds as the ice settled. "Was there something you wanted to tell me about the case?"

"Yes."

He smiled, sipped his martini.

"You have a daughter, correct?"

"Yes."

Pause.

"I have a son. He's seventeen."

I said nothing.

"Alejandro, but he prefers Al."

Galiano continued, unconcerned by the lack of feedback.

"Bright kid. He'll start college next year. Probably ship him up to Canada."

"St-FX?" I hoped to blow a hole in his unassailable self-confidence.

Galiano grinned.

"That's where you scored the Bat tidbit."

So he *had* caught my use of his nickname at headquarters.

"Who?" he asked.

"Andrew Ryan."

"*Ay, Dios.*"

He threw back his head and laughed.

"What the hell's Ryan up to these days?"

"He's a detective with the provincial police."

"Using his Spanish?"

"Ryan speaks Spanish?"

Galiano nodded. "We used to discuss passing members of the opposite sex and no one knew what we were saying."

"Commenting on their intelligence, no doubt."

"Sewing skills."

I drilled him with a look.

"It was a different time."

The waitress arrived, and we both set to seasoning stew. Then we ate in silence, Galiano's eyes roving the restaurant. Had someone been watching, they'd have thought us a couple grown bored with each other. Finally, "How well do you understand the Guatemalan justice system?"

"Obviously, I'm an outsider."

"You know you're not working in Kansas here."

Jesus. This guy was just like Ryan.

"I know about the torture and assassination, Detective Galiano. That's why I'm in Guatemala."

Galiano took a bite of stew, pointed his fork at mine.

"It's better hot."

I resumed eating, waited for him to go on. He didn't. Across from our catacomb, an old woman cooked tortillas on a *comal*. I watched her toss dough, lay it on the flat clay pan, and place it over the fire. Over and over her hands moved through the motions, her face a wooden mask.

"Tell me how the system works." It came out sharper than I intended, but Galiano's evasiveness was starting to irritate.

"We don't have jury trials in Guatemala. Criminal matters are investigated by judges of the first instance, *primera instancia*, occasionally by magistrates appointed by the Supreme Court. These judges, you'd call them DAs, are supposed to seek both exculpatory and incriminating evidence."

"Meaning they act as both defense and prosecution."

"Exactly. Once the investigating judge decides that there's a case against an accused, he passes the matter on to a sentencing judge."

"Who has the power to order an autopsy?" I asked.

"The judge of the first instance. An autopsy is mandatory in a violent or suspicious death. But if cause can be determined by external exam, there's no Y incision."

"Who's in charge of the morgues?"

"They're directly under the authority of the president of the Supreme Court."

"So forensic doctors really work for the courts."

"Or for the national social security institute, the Instituto Guatemalteco de Seguridad Social, IGSS. But yes, forensic doctors are under the authority of the judiciary. It's not like Brazil, for example, where the state-run medico-legal institutes work for the police. Here forensic doctors have very little interaction with the police."

"How many are there?"

"Around thirty. Seven or eight work at the judicial morgue here in G City, the rest are spread out across the country."

"Are they well trained?"

He ticked points off on his fingers. It took only three.

"You must be a Guatemalan citizen by birth, a

medical doctor, and a member of the medico-legal association."

"That's it?"

"That's it. Hell, USAC doesn't even have a residency program in forensic medicine."

He referred to the University of San Carlos, Guatemala's only public university.

"Frankly, I don't know why anyone does it. The status is zip and the pay sucks. Have you been to the G City morgue?"

I shook my head.

"It's like something out of the dark ages."

He used a torn tortilla to sponge sauce, then pushed his bowl aside.

"Are forensic doctors full-time employees?"

"Some are. Some work for the courts just to supplement their earnings. Especially in rural areas."

Galiano's eyes darted left as the waitress entered. She cleared dishes, asked about dessert and coffee, left.

"What's the drill when a body is found?"

"You'll love this. Until about ten years ago, stiffs were collected by the fire department. They'd arrive on scene, examine the body, take pics, then call it in. Central dispatch would notify the police, and we'd notify the judge. Police investigators would then gather evidence and take statements. Eventually the judge would show up, release the body, and the firemen would take it to the morgue. Today police vehicles are used for transport."

"Why the policy change?"

"Fireman Friendly and his colleagues were helping themselves to money and jewelry."

"So forensic doctors don't usually go to the scene?"

"No."

"Why Lucas?"

"Díaz probably gave him no choice."

The coffee arrived, and we sipped in silence for a few moments. When I looked out at the old woman, Galiano's eyes followed mine.

"Here's something else you'll find appalling. In Guatemala, forensic doctors are only required to determine cause, not manner."

Galiano referred to the four terms used to categorize the circumstances of death: homicide, suicide, accident, natural. A body is found in a lake, and an autopsy determines that sufficient water filled the lungs to have halted breathing. Cause of death is drowning. But did the deceased fall, jump, or was he pushed? Those are issues of manner.

"Who determines manner?"

"The judge. DA."

Galiano observed a couple being seated on the far side of the room. Then he turned his chair slightly, leaned in, and lowered his voice.

"Are you aware that many of those who were involved in atrocities remain in command of the military?"

He spoke in a voice that sent goose bumps crawling up my arms.

"Do you know that many of those performing

investigative work today were or are direct participants in extrajudicial executions?"

"Are?"

His eyes held steady on mine.

"The police?"

Not a flicker.

"How can that be?"

"Although nominally under the jurisdiction of the Interior Ministry, the police here remain effectively under army control. The criminal justice system is permeated by fear."

"Who's afraid?"

Another visual sweep. Not a movement was going unnoticed. When Galiano turned back to me his face was a harder version of the one it had been.

"Everyone's afraid. Witnesses and relatives won't swear out complaints, won't testify for fear of retribution. When evidence leads to the army, a prosecutor or judge has to worry about what will happen to his family."

"Aren't monitors watching out for human rights violations?" My voice was barely above a whisper. Galiano was getting to me.

He blew air through his lips, glanced over my shoulder.

"More monitors have been killed or disappeared in Guatemala than anywhere else on the planet. That's not my stat, it's official."

I'd read that in a recent *Human Rights Watch*.

"And we're not talking ancient history. All but four of those murders have taken place since the civilian government was established in eighty-six."

I felt a tingle of fear in the pit of my stomach.

"What is your point?"

"Death investigation here ain't day care work." His eyes were dark with bitterness. "Produce an autopsy finding or a police report that implicates the wrong people, life's no longer clean and easy. Reporting results can be hazardous if the recipient of your report happens to be affiliated with the bad guys even though he's holding a prosecutorial office."

"Meaning?"

He started to say something, then his eyes backed away.

The tingle coalesced into a cold, hard knot.

9

It was my day for flowers. Back in my room I found an arrangement the size of a Volkswagen Beetle. The card was classic Ryan.

Tanks for the memories. Bone jour.
                                     AR

I laughed for the first time in over a week.

After showering, I studied myself in the bathroom mirror, much as I would a stranger on the street. What I saw was a middle-aged woman with a delicate nose and cheekbones, starburst wrinkling at the corners of the eyes, jawline holding firm. Chicken pox scar above the left brow. Asymmetric dimples.

I brushed bangs from my forehead and did a two-handed tuck behind my ears. My hair was fine, blonde turned brown now galloping toward gray.

I'd always coveted my younger sister's thick blonde hair. Sprays and volumizing gels never entered Harry's thoughts, while I'd spent thousands on mousse alone.

For a moment I stared directly at myself. Tired green eyes stared back, each underbrushed with pale violet. A new furrow winged down at the inner edge of my left eyebrow. Lighting? I shifted to my right, back a half step. The line was real. Great. One week in Guatemala and I'd aged a decade.

Or was it worry over Galiano's warning? *Was* it a warning? I squeezed Crest onto the toothbrush, began on my upper molars.

What *was* the point of the conversation in the Gucumatz? Just a prompt to be alert? To be careful where I went and with whom? Walking back we'd talked mostly about the septic tank case. Galiano had little to report.

A visit to the Zone 1 family planning or APROFAM clinic had produced zilch. Ditto for a private clinic, Mujeres por Mujeres. Though reluctant, the doctor on call, Maria Zuckerman, had agreed to check her patient database. She found two Eduardos, Margarita and Clara, both in their thirties. No Lucy Gerardi, Claudia de la Alda, or Chantale Specter. If any of the missing women had made an appointment or been examined by a doctor, she'd done so using a false name.

Big surprise.

Galiano also learned that nonappearances at the clinic raised no flags. Many patients booked, then failed to show up. Some came once or twice, then vanished. Many were in the age range of the lady in the tank. Many were pregnant. With no picture or descriptive information, Dr. Zuckerman refused to allow her staff to be "bothered" with questioning.

Galiano had requested a list of everyone who'd phoned or been seen over the past year. As expected, Zuckerman had refused, citing patient confidentiality. Galiano intended to pursue a court order when more descriptors were available.

I swished and spat, feeling another wave of guilt. If I'd done a better prelim at the tank, we'd *have* more descriptors.

I'd asked Galiano about the attack on Carlos and Molly. He'd heard about the shooting, but knew little since the investigation was being handled in Sololá. He'd promised to find out what he could.

I pumped cream onto my palm and spread it over my face.

We'd also talked about Andrew Ryan. I'd told Galiano about Ryan's work with the SQ. He'd shared new tales from their bad-boy years together.

As he was leaving, Galiano told me that his partner would be visiting the Eduardos and De la Aldas in the morning, and he'd be calling on the Gerardis and Specters. Given the discovery at the Paraíso, they felt Sunday visits were warranted. I asked to be included. Wouldn't be dangerous, I argued, and an outsider's eye might even be useful. Though skeptical, he agreed.

I clicked off the light, opened the windows as far

as they would go, set the alarm, and climbed into bed.

It seemed hours that I listened to traffic and hotel noises and watched the curtains fill and deflate. I finally fell asleep with my head under the pillow. I dreamed of Ryan and Galiano partying in the Maritimes.

Galiano picked me up at eight. Same greeting. Same shades.

Over a quick breakfast, he told me he intended to put pressure on Mario Gerardi, Lucy's older brother.

"Why Mario?" I asked.

"Bad vibes."

"Groovy." I hadn't heard about vibes since the Beach Boys faded.

"Something about the kid bothers me."

"His socks?"

"Sometimes you go with your gut."

I couldn't disagree with that.

"What does Mario do?"

"As little as he can."

"Is he a student?"

"Physics degree, Princeton." Galiano scooped the last of his eggs and beans onto a tortilla.

"So the boy's no dummy. What's he doing now?"

"Probably working out alternatives to Planck's Constant."

"Detective Galiano knows quantum theory. Impressive."

"Mario is rich, good-looking, a regular Gatsby with the ladies."

"Detective Galiano knows literature. Next category. How about 'Why doesn't Bat like young Mario?'"

"It's his socks."

"Curious that Lucy and Chantale Specter disappeared at virtually the same time."

"More than curious."

Ignoring my protest, Galiano snatched and paid the check, then we headed toward Zone 10.

Creeping with the slowly moving log jam on Avenida la Reforma, we sat for a full ten minutes by the Botanical Gardens of San Carlos University. In my mind's eye I saw Lucy Gerardi walking down that sidewalk, long dark hair framing her face. I wondered about that day.

Why did she go to the gardens? To meet someone? To study? To dream girl dreams she'd never realize?

Were hers the bones Díaz had taken from me? I turned from the window, feeling guilty again.

"Why are we seeing the Gerardis first?"

"Señora Specter is not an early riser."

I must have looked surprised.

"I believe in holding firm on the big issues and letting the little ones slide. If her ladyship likes to sleep, let her. Besides, I want to get to the Gerardis while Papa's still there."

Just past the American embassy, Galiano turned onto a narrow, tree-shaded street and pulled to the curb. I got out and waited while he answered a call.

The May sun felt warm on my head.

Had Lucy gone to the gardens because it was a sunny day? To feed the squirrels? To watch birds? To wander without purpose and observe what was there? To be alone with all the possibilities of youth?

The Gerardi residence was centered within manicured hedges surrounding a manicured lawn. A flagstone path led from the sidewalk to the front door. Brightly colored flowers lined both edges of the walkway, and crowded gardens wrapped around the house foundation.

A driveway, complete with Mercedes 500 S and Jeep Grand Cherokee, ran along the right side of the property. Chain-link fencing formed a small enclosure on the left. Inside the fence, a schnauzer the size of a woodchuck raced from end to end, barking frantically.

"I guess that would pass for the dog," Galiano said, pressing the bell.

The door was answered by a tall, gaunt man with silver hair and black-rimmed glasses. He wore a dark suit, blazing white shirt, and yellow silk tie. I wondered what calling required such formality on a Sunday morning.

"*Buenos días Señor Gerardi.*" Galiano.

Gerardi's chin raised slightly, then his eyes shifted to me.

"Dr. Brennan is the anthropologist helping on your daughter's case."

Gerardi stepped back, indicating that we could enter, and led us down a polished tile corridor to a paneled study. Beshir carpet. Burled walnut desk. Big-ticket collectibles aesthetically positioned on mahogany shelves. Whatever Gerardi did, it paid well.

We'd hardly crossed the threshold when a woman appeared in the doorway. She was overweight, with hair the color of dead leaves.

"*Buenos días, Señora Gerardi*," Galiano greeted her.

Señora Gerardi regarded him with fear and revulsion, as she might a scorpion in the bathroom sink.

Gerardi spoke to his wife in full-throttle Spanish that was lost on me. When she started to reply, he cut her off.

"*Por favor, Edwina!*"

Señora Gerardi clutched one hand with the other, reversed grip, reversed again, knuckles bulging white under flaky, pink skin. Indecision battled in her eyes, and for a moment, I thought she would object. Instead, she bit down on her lower lip and withdrew.

Señor Gerardi gestured at two leather chairs facing the desk.

"Please."

I sat. The leather had the smell of a new Jag. Or what I imagined the scent of a new Jag would be, having never ridden in one.

Galiano remained standing. So did Gerardi.

"Unless you have news, this session is pointless." Gerardi held both arms rigid at his sides.

"How 'bout a skeleton?" The tone told me Galiano was coiled.

Our host showed no reaction.

"Would Lucy have had reason to be in Zone One?" Galiano asked.

"I made clear in my statements that my daughter did not frequent public places. She went—" His lips pursed, relaxed. "She goes to school, to church, and to our club."

"Have you remembered the names of any friends she might have mentioned? Fellow students?"

"I have already answered that question. My daughter is not a frivolous young woman."

"Was Lucy close to Chantale Specter?"

"They saw each other occasionally."

"What did they do together?"

"This is all in my statement."

"Humor me."

"They studied, watched movies, swam, played tennis. The ambassador and I belong to the same private club."

"Where is your son, Señor Gerardi?"

"Mario is taking a golf lesson."

"Uh. Huh. Did Chantale Specter spend time in your home?"

"Let me clarify something for you. Regardless of her father's position, I did not encourage my daughter's relationship with the Specter girl."

"Why was that?"

Gerardi hesitated a moment.

"Chantale Specter is a confused young woman."

"Confused?"

"I do not feel she is a good influence for my daughter."

"What about boys?"

"I do not allow my daughter to date."

"I imagine she was ecstatic about that."

"My daughter does not question my rules."

I folded my hands in my lap, looked at them. Lucy, I thought. Your daughter's name is Lucy, you cold, arrogant prick.

"Yes." Galiano grinned cynically. "Anything else you might have remembered since our last conversation?"

"I know nothing more than what you know. I made that clear on the phone."

"And I made clear that I wanted to talk to Mario today."

"These lessons are scheduled weeks in advance."

"Wouldn't want to compromise the boy's chip shot."

Gerardi fought to suppress a twitch of anger.

"Frankly, Detective, I had hoped for progress by now. This affair has been dragging on for over four months. The strain is unbearably difficult for my wife and son. This recent attack on our pets was barbarous." Allusion to hair sample collection by the police, I presumed.

Galiano made a clicking sound with his mouth. "I'll talk to the schnauzer."

"Don't patronize me, Detective."

Galiano leaned across the desk and brought his face to within inches of Gerardi's.

"Don't underestimate me, señor."

Galiano stepped back.

"I will find Lucy," he said, regarding our host coolly. "With or without your cooperation."

"I have cooperated fully, Detective, and I resent your implication. No one is more concerned about my daughter than I."

A clock bonged somewhere outside the room. For the full ten count no one spoke. Galiano broke the silence.

"I keep getting caught up in one thought this morning."

Gerardi's face was a closed door.

"I tell you a skeleton surfaced and you show about as much interest as you would in a weather report."

"I assume that if this skeleton has relevance to my daughter's disappearance you will say that." A red wash was spreading upward from Gerardi's perfectly white collar.

"Seems you've also assumed a lot about your daughter's life."

"*Is* this person you've found my daughter?" Gerardi's upper lip was white with anger.

Galiano did not reply.

"Obviously you do not know."

My face felt hot with embarrassment. Correct, Mr. Gerardi. Because I was queasy and intimidated by pink spectacles.

Gerardi aligned his vertebrae even straighter than they had been. "I think it's time you leave my home."

"*Buenos días, Señor Gerardi.*" Galiano nodded to me "*Regresaré.*" I'll be back.

He strode toward the door.

I rose and followed.

"*¡Hijo de la gran puta!*" Galiano reached out and twisted a knob on the police scanner. The static receded to a sputter.

"Tell me what you really think of him."

"He's a pompous, overbearing, self-righteous ass."

"Don't hold back."

"What sort of parent sees adolescent friendship as frivolity?" Galiano's voice dripped disdain.

"My thought exactly. What does Daddy do to afford the Mercedes and Beshir?"

"Gerardi and his brother own the largest auto dealership in Guatemala."

We were in the car, heading toward the ambassador's residence.

"But he is right." I made a print on the dashboard with my index finger, wiped it away with the heel of my hand. "We don't know dick about that skeleton."

"We will."

I made another print.

"Think Lucy was as compliant as her father believes?"

Galiano turned one palm up and raised shoulders and eyebrows, a very French gesture for a Guatemalan cop.

"Who knows? Experience tells us they almost never are."

Two more prints. Trees flashed by outside the window. Several turns, then we pulled onto a street of large homes set far back on spacious and professionally tended lots. In most cases, the only thing visible was a tile roof.

"Gerardi may have been right about one thing, though."

"What's that?" I asked.

"Chantale Specter."

The ambassador and his family lived behind hedges identical to those surrounding the Gerardi place. They also lived behind an electrified fence with enormous scrolled wrought-iron gates and a matched set of uniformed guards.

Galiano angled onto the drive and held his badge to the window for guard number one. The man leaned close, then stepped to a control booth. Seconds later the gates swung in.

We made a wide sweep to the front of the house, where guard number two examined ID. Satisfied, he rang. The door opened, and the guard handed us off to a house servant.

"Mrs. Specter is expecting you." The man looked at us without looking at us. "Please follow me."

The setting was a repeat of the Gerardi home. Paneled study, expensive tile, furniture, and objets d'art. This time the carpet was Bakhtiari.

The encounter couldn't have been more different.

Mrs. Specter's hair was copper, her lips and

nails Chinese red. She wore a three-piece silk pants suit the color of sunflower petals, and matching strap sandals on her feet. The filmy material flowed around her as she crossed to greet us. So did a cloud of Issey Miyaki.

"Detective Galiano, it's always a pleasure to see you." French accent. "Though I'd rather it were under different circumstances, of course."

"How are you today, Mrs. Specter?" Her fingers looked ghostly enveloped in Galiano's brown hand.

"I'm well." She turned her smile on me. A practiced smile. "Is this the young woman of whom you spoke?"

"Tempe Brennan," I introduced myself.

The Chinese-red nails shot out. Her skin was so soft, her bones so delicate, it felt like shaking the hand of a child.

"Thank you so much for making yourself available to the local authorities. This means a great deal to my husband and me."

"I hope I can help."

"Please, forgive my beastly manners." She placed one hand on her chest, gestured with the other. "Please. Let's sit down."

She led us to a conversational grouping tucked into a bay on the right of the room. Each window was covered by three-inch wooden shutters, slats closed to the morning sun.

"Would you like tea or coffee?" She looked from Galiano to me.

We both declined.

"So, Detective. Please tell me that you have good news."

"I'm afraid not." Galiano's voice was gentle.

All color drained from her face. The smile quivered, but held.

"But no bad news," he added quickly. "I just wanted to touch base, check a few facts, and see if anything has occurred to you since our last conversation."

She dropped the chest hand to the armrest, allowed her spine to curve into the chair back.

"I've tried, really I have, but other than what I've told you, I've come up blank."

Despite her best efforts, the smile collapsed. She began pulling at one of several loose threads in the upholstery by her knee.

"I lie awake nights going over and over the past year. I – it's difficult to say this. But I obviously missed a lot that was happening in front of me."

"Chantale was riding out a rough patch." His tone was a galaxy from where it had been with Gerardi. "As you've said, she was being less than open with you and your husband."

"I should have been more observant. More perceptive."

Her face looked dead white within its halo of orange hair. One lacquered nail worked the threads, as though commanded by an independent source.

My heart ached for her, and I groped for comforting words.

"Don't blame yourself, Mrs. Specter. None of us can entirely control our children."

Her eyes shifted from Galiano to me. Even in the dim light I could see they were the brilliant green of colored contacts.

"Do you have children, Dr. Brennan?"

"My daughter is a university student. I know how difficult teenagers can be."

"Yes."

"Could we go back over a few things, Mrs. Specter?" Galiano.

"If it will help."

He produced a notebook and began clarifying names and dates. Throughout the exchange, Mrs. Specter unconsciously worried the threads, alternating between twisting and smoothing. Now and then a nail would flick the fabric, sending filaments hurtling into space.

"Chantale's first arrest was one year ago this past November."

"Yes." Flat.

"The Hotel Santa Lucía in Zone One."

"Yes."

"Her second arrest was last July."

"Yes."

"The Hotel Bella Vista."

"Yes."

"Chantale was in Canada from August until December of last year for treatment of drug dependence."

"Yes."

"Where?"

"A rehab center near Chibougamau."

Watching the downward drift of a liberated fiber, I felt a sudden jolt of neural electricity. I looked at Galiano. He gave no indication he'd noticed.

"That's in Quebec?"

"It's a camp, really, several hundred miles north of Montreal."

I'd once flown to Chibougamau for an exhumation. The region was so heavily forested the view from the plane had reminded me of broccoli.

"The program teaches young people to assume personal responsibility for their drug abuse. The encounters can be harsh, but my husband and I decided the 'tough love' approach was best." She gave a wan version of the diplomat's smile. "The remote location ensures that participants complete the entire course of therapy."

Galiano's questioning continued for several minutes. I focused on the red nails, verifying. Finally, "Do you have any questions for me, Mrs. Specter?"

"What do you know of these bones that were found?"

Galiano showed no surprise at her knowledge of the Paraíso skeleton. Undoubtedly, her husband's connections kept them well informed.

"I was about to mention that, but there's little to report until Dr. Brennan finishes her analysis."

"Can you tell me anything?" Her gaze shifted to me.

I hesitated, not wanting to comment on the basis of photos and a cursory tank-side inspection.

"*Anything?*" Pleading.

My mother's heart battled with my scientist's brain. What if Katy were missing instead of Chantale? What if I were the one twisting threads on a tapestry chair?

"I doubt the skeleton is your daughter."

"Why is that?" The voice was calm, but the fingers were moving towards Mach 1.

"I suspect the individual is non-Caucasian."

She stared at me, thought working behind the electric-green eyes.

"Guatemalan?"

"Probably. But until I've completed my examination, that's little more than an impression."

"When will that be?"

I looked to Galiano.

"We've run into a jurisdictional hitch," he said.

"Which is?"

Galiano told her about Díaz.

"Why has the judge done this?"

"That's unclear."

"I will explain the situation to my husband."

She turned back to me.

"You are a kind woman, Dr. Brennan. I can tell by your face. *Merci.*"

She smiled, the ambassador's wife once again.

"You're sure I can't get either of you a drink? Lemonade, perhaps?"

Galiano declined.

"May I trouble you for a little water?"

"Of course."

When she'd gone I bolted for the desk, tore a strip of adhesive tape from the dispenser, raced back to Mrs. Specter's chair, and pressed the sticky side to the upholstery. Galiano watched without comment.

Mrs. Specter rejoined us carrying a crystal glass filled with ice water, a lemon slice stuck onto the rim. As I drank, she spoke to Galiano.

"I'm sorry I have nothing else for you, Detective. I am trying. Truly, I am."

In the foyer, she surprised me with a request.

"Have you a card, Dr. Brennan?"

I dug one out.

"Thank you." She waved off a servant who was bearing down. "Can you be reached locally?"

Surprised, I scribbled the number of my rented cellular.

"Please, please, Detective. Find my baby."

The heavy oak door clicked shut at our backs.

Galiano didn't speak until we were in the car.

"What's with the upholstery-cleaning routine?"

"Did you see her chair?"

He fastened his seat belt and started the engine.

"Aubusson. Pricey."

I held up the tape. "That Aubusson has a fur coat."

He turned to me, hand on the key.

"The Specters reported no pets."

10

I spent the rest of Sunday examining skeletons from Chupan Ya. Elena and Mateo were also working, and updated me on developments in the Sololá investigation. It took five minutes.

Carlos's body had been released. His brother had flown in to accompany it to Buenos Aires for burial. Mateo was arranging a memorial service in Guatemala City.

Elena had been to the hospital on Friday. Molly remained comatose. The police had no leads.

That was it.

They also gave me news from Chupan Ya. Thursday night, Señora Ch'i'p's son had become a grandfather for the fourth time. The old lady now had seven great-grandchildren. I hoped those new lives would bring joy into hers.

The lab was weekend quiet. No chatter. No radios. No microwave whirs and beeps.

No Ollie Nordstern pressing for a quote.

Nevertheless, I found it hard to concentrate. My feelings were like wheels inside wheels inside wheels. Loneliness for home, for Katy, for Ryan. Sadness for the dead lying in boxes around me. Worry for Molly. Guilt for my lack of backbone at the Paraíso.

The guilt prevailed. Vowing to do more for the Chupan Ya victims than I had for the girl in the septic tank, I worked long after Elena and Mateo called it quits.

Burial fourteen was a female in her late teens, with multiple fractures of the jaw and right arm, and machete slashes to the back of the head. The mutants who had done this liked working up close and personal.

As I examined the delicate bones my thoughts swung again and again to the Paraíso victim. Two young women killed decades apart. Does anything ever change? My sadness felt like a palpable thing.

Burial fifteen was a five-year-old child. Tell me again about turning the other cheek.

Galiano called in the late afternoon. Hernández had learned little from the parents of Patricia Eduardo and Claudia de la Alda. Señora Eduardo's one recollection was that her daughter disliked a supervisor at the hospital, and Patricia and the supervisor had argued shortly before Patricia disappeared. She couldn't recall the person's name, gender, or position.

Señor De la Alda thought his daughter had begun losing weight shortly before she went missing. Señora De la Alda disagreed. The museum had called to inform them that they could no longer hold Claudia's position for her. They would be hiring a permanent replacement.

By Monday I'd moved on to burial sixteen, a pubescent girl with second molars in eruption. I estimated her height at three foot nine. She'd been shot and decapitated by a machete blow.

At noon I drove to police headquarters and Galiano and I proceeded to the trace evidence section of the forensic lab. We entered to find a small, balding man hunched over a dissecting scope. When Galiano called out, the man swiveled to face us, hooking gold-rimmed glasses behind chimpanzee ears.

The chimp introduced himself as Fredi Minos, one of two specialists in hair and fiber analysis. Minos had been provided samples from the septic tank jeans, from the Gerardi and Eduardo homes, and from Mrs. Specter's chair.

"It's wookie, right?" Galiano.

Minos looked puzzled.

"Chewbacca?"

No glint.

"*Star Wars*?"

"Oh yes. The American movie."

In Minos's defense, the joke sounded lame in Spanish.

"Never mind. What did you come up with?"

"Your unknown sample is cat hair."

"How can you be sure?"

"That it's hair, or that it's cat?"

"That it's cat," I jumped in, seeing Galiano's expression.

Minos rolled his chair to the right, and selected a slide case from a stack on the counter. Then he rolled back to the scope and slipped one specimen under the eyepiece. After adjusting focus, he got up, and indicated that I should sit.

"Take a look."

I glanced at Galiano. He waved me into the chair.

"Would you prefer that I speak English?" Minos asked.

"If you don't mind." I felt like a dunce, but my Spanish was shaky, and I wanted to fully understand his explanation.

"What do you see?"

"It looks like a wire with a pointed end."

"You're looking at an uncut hair. It is one of twenty-seven included in the sample marked 'Paraíso.'"

Minos's English had an odd up-and-down cadence, like a calliope.

"Notice that the hair has no distinctive shape."

"Distinctive?"

"With some species shape is a good identifier. Horse hair is coarse, with a sharp bend near the root. Deer hair is crinkly, with a very narrow root. Very distinctive. The Paraíso hairs are nothing like that." He readjusted his glasses. "Now check the pigment distribution. See anything distinctive?"

Minos was fond of the word *distinctive*.

141

"Seems pretty homogenous," I said.

"It is. May I?"

Withdrawing the slide, he moved to an optical slope, inserted it, and adjusted the focus. I rolled my chair down the counter and peered through the eyepiece. The hair now looked like a thick pipe with a narrow core.

"Describe the medulla," Minos directed.

I focused on the hollow center, the region analogous to the marrow cavity in a long bone.

"Resembles a ladder."

"Excellent. Medullar form is extremely variable. Some species have bipartite, or even multipartite medulla. The llama group is a good example of that. Very distinctive. Llamas also tend to have large pigment aggregates. When I see that combination, I immediately think llama."

Llama?

"Your samples have a single-ladder medulla. That's what you're seeing."

"Which means cat?"

"Not necessarily. Cattle, goats, chinchilla, mink, muskrat, badger, fox, beaver, dog, indeed many forms can have a single-ladder medulla in the fine hairs. Muskrat has a chevron-scale pattern, so I knew it wasn't muskrat."

"Scales?" Galiano asked. "Like fish?"

"Actually, yes. I'll explain scales shortly. Cattle hairs frequently have a streaky pigment distribution, often with large aggregates, so I eliminated cattle. The scales didn't look right for goat."

Minos seemed to be talking more to himself

than to us, reviewing verbally the thought process he'd used in his analysis.

"I also excluded badger because of the pigment distribution. I ruled out—"

"What could you *not* rule out, Señor Minos?" Galiano broke in.

"Dog." Minos sounded wounded by Galiano's lack of interest in mammalian hair.

"*Ay, Dios.*" Galiano puffed air out of his lips. "How often would dog hair turn up on clothing?"

"Oh, it's very, very common." Minos missed Galiano's sarcasm. "So I decided to double-check myself."

He walked to a desk and pulled a manila folder from a slotted shelf.

"Once I'd eliminated everything but cat and dog, I took measurements and did what I call a medullary percentage analysis."

He withdrew a printout and laid it on the counter beside me.

"Since cat and dog hair is so frequently encountered at crime scenes, I've done a bit of research on discriminating between the two. I've measured hundreds of dog and cat hairs and set up a database."

He flipped a page and pointed to a scatter graph bisected by a diagonal slash. The line divided dozens of triangles above from dozens of circles below. Only a handful of symbols crossed the metric Rubicon.

"I calculate medullary percentage by dividing medullar width by hair width. This graph plots that

143

figure, expressed as a percentage, against simple hair width, expressed in microns. As you can see, with few exceptions, cat values cluster above a certain threshold, while dog values lie below."

"Meaning that the medulla is relatively wider in cat hairs."

"Yes." He beamed at me, a teacher pleased with a bright student. Then he pointed to a clump of asterisks in the swarm of triangles above the line.

"Those points represent values for randomly selected hairs from the Paraíso sample. Every one falls squarely with the cats."

Minos fished in the folder and withdrew several color prints.

"But you asked about scales, Detective. I wanted a good look at surface architecture, so I popped hairs from the Paraíso sample into the scanning electron microscope."

Minos handed me a five-by-seven glossy. I felt Galiano lean over my shoulder.

"That's the root end of a Paraíso hair magnified four hundred times. Look at the outer surface."

"Looks like a bathroom floor." Galiano.

Minos produced another photo. "That's farther up the shaft."

"Flower petals."

"Good, Detective." This time Galiano was the recipient of the proud smile. "What you've so aptly described is what we call scale pattern progression. In this case the scale pattern goes from what we call irregular mosaic to what we call petal."

Minos was what we call a jargon meister. But the guy knew his hair.

Print number three. The scales now looked more honeycombed, their margins rougher.

"That's the tip end of a hair. The scale pattern is what we call regular mosaic. The borders have become more ragged."

"How is this relevant to cats and dogs?" Galiano.

"Dogs show wide variation in scale pattern progression, but, in my opinion, this progression is unique to cats."

"So the hairs on the jeans came from a cat." Galiano straightened.

"Yes."

"Are they all from the same cat?" I asked.

"I've seen nothing to suggest otherwise."

"What about the Specter sample?"

Minos leafed through his folder.

"That would be sample number four." He smiled at me. "Cat."

"So everything comes up feline." I thought a moment. "Is the Paraíso sample consistent with any of the other three?"

"That's where it gets interesting."

Minos selected another page, scanned the text.

"In sample number two, the average length of the hairs was greater than in any of the other three samples." He looked up. "Over five centimeters, which is quite long." Back to the report. "Also, the hairs were more consistently of the fine variety." He looked up again. "As opposed to coarse." Back to the report. "And the surface architecture of each hair showed a mixture of smooth-edged regular mosaic and smooth-edged coronal scale types."

Minos closed the folder, but offered no explanation.

"What does that mean, Señor Minos?" I asked.

"Sample two derives from a different cat than the other three samples. My guess, and it's only a guess, won't go into my report, is that cat number two is Persian."

"And the other samples are not from Persian cats?"

"Standard shorthairs."

"But the Paraíso sample is consistent with the other two samples?"

"Consistent, yes."

"How was sample two labeled?"

Again Minos consulted the folder.

"Eduardo."

"That would be Buttercup."

"Persian?" Minos and I asked simultaneously.

Galiano nodded.

"So Buttercup wasn't the donor of the Paraíso hairs," I said.

"A Persian cat wasn't the donor of the Paraíso hairs," Minos corrected.

"That puts Buttercup in the clear. What about the Gerardi or Specter cats?"

"Definite candidates."

I felt a sudden surge of optimism.

"Along with a million other shorthairs in Guatemala City," he added.

146

The optimism plunged like an elevator in free fall.

"Can't you determine if one of the other samples matches the hairs from the jeans?" Galiano asked.

"Both display similar characteristics. Individualization is impossible based on hair morphology."

"What about DNA?" I asked.

"That can probably be done."

Minos tossed the folder onto the counter, removed his glasses, and began cleaning them on the hem of his lab coat.

"But not here."

"Why not?"

"There's a six-month backlog on human tissue cases. You'll have a birthday waiting for results on cat hair."

I was wrapping my mind around that when Galiano's cell phone sounded.

His face tensed as he listened.

"*¡Ay, Dios mío! Dónde?*"

He was silent a full minute, then his eyes met mine. When he spoke again he'd gone back to English.

"Why wasn't I called sooner?"

A long pause.

"Xicay's there?"

Another pause.

"We're on our way."

11

At 3 P.M. the streets were already in gridlock. Lights flashing, siren screaming, Galiano snaked forward as drivers edged over to allow us to pass. He kept his foot on the accelerator, barely slowed at intersections.

Shotgun Spanish crackled over the radio. I couldn't follow, but it didn't matter. I was thinking about Claudia de la Alda in her plain black skirts and pastel blouses. I tried to remember her expression in the photos, came up blank.

But other images flooded back from the past. Shallow graves. Putrefying bodies rolled in carpets. Skeletons covered with fallen leaves. Rotten clothing scattered by animals.

A sludge-filled skull.

My stomach knotted.

The faces of distraught parents. Their child is dead, and I am about to tell them that. They are bewildered, stricken, disbelieving, angry. Bearing that news is an awful job.

Damn! It was happening again.

My heart tangoed below my ribs.

Damn! Damn! Damn!

Señora De la Alda had received a phone call about the time I was heading out to learn more about cat hair. A male voice said Claudia was dead and told her where to find the body. Hysterical, she'd called Hernández. He'd called Xicay. The recovery team had located bones in a ravine on the far western edge of the city.

"What else did Hernández tell you?" I asked.

"The call was placed at a public phone."

"Where?"

"The Cobán bus station in Zone One."

"What did the caller say?"

"He told her the body was in Zone Seven. Gave directions. Hung up."

"Near the archaeological site?"

"On the back steps."

Zone 7 is a tentacle of the city that wraps around the ruins of Kaminaljuyú, a Mayan center that in its heyday had over three hundred mounds, thirteen ball courts, and fifty thousand residents. Unlike the lowland Maya, the builders of Kaminaljuyú preferred adobe to stone, an unwise choice in a tropical climate. Erosion and urban sprawl had taken their toll, and today the ancient metropolis is little more than a series of earth-covered knolls, a green space for lovers and Frisbee players.

"Claudia worked at the Ixchel Museum. Think there's a connection?"

"I'll definitely find out."

A stench filled the car as we sped past the dump.

"Did Señora De la Alda recognize the voice?"

"No."

As we flew through the city, the neighborhoods grew increasingly tired and run-down. Eventually, Galiano shot onto a narrow street with *comedores* and convenience stores on all four corners. We sped past ragged frame houses with clothesline laundry and sagging front stoops. Four blocks down, the street ended with a T-intersection which in turn dead-ended in both directions.

Turning left we faced a bleakly familiar scene. Patrol cars lined one side, lights flashing, radios spitting. A morgue van waited on the opposite shoulder. Beside the van, a metal guardrail; beside the rail, a steep drop into a *barranca*.

Twenty yards ahead, the pavement ended at chain linking. Yellow crime scene tape ran ten feet out, turned left, then paralleled the fence on its plunge into the ravine.

Uniformed cops moved about within the cordoned area. A handful of men watched from outside, some holding cameras, others taking notes. Behind us, I could see cars and a television truck. Media crew sat half in, half out of vehicles, smoking, talking, dozing.

When Galiano and I slammed our doors, lenses pointed in our direction. Journalists converged.

"*Señor, esta—*"

"Detective Galiano—"

"Una pregunta, por favor."

Ignoring the onslaught, we ducked under the tape and walked to the edge of the ravine. Shutters clicked at our backs. Questions rang out.

Hernández was five yards down the incline. Galiano began scrabbling toward him. I was right behind.

Though this stretch of hillside was largely grass and scrub, the grade was steep, the ground rocky. I placed my feet sideways, kept my weight low, and grasped vegetation as best I could. I didn't want to turn an ankle or stumble into a downhill slide.

Twigs snapped in my hands. Rocks broke free and skipped down the slope with sharp, cracking sounds. Birds screamed overhead, angry at the intrusion.

Adrenaline poured through my body from wherever it waited between crises. It may not be her, I told myself.

With each step the sweet, fetid stench grew stronger.

Fifteen feet down, the ground leveled off before taking one final downward plunge.

A crank call, I thought, stepping onto the small plateau. De la Alda's disappearance was reported in the press.

Mario Colom was passing a metal detector back and forth across the ground. Juan-Carlos Xicay was photographing something at Hernández's feet. As at the Paraíso, both technicians wore coveralls and caps.

Galiano and I crossed to Hernández.

The body lay in a rainwater ditch at the juncture of the slope and plateau. It was covered by mud and leaves, and lay atop torn black plastic. Though skeletonized, remnants of muscle and ligament held the bones together.

One look and I caught my breath.

Arm bones protruded like dry sticks from the sleeves of a pale blue blouse. Leg bones emerged from a rotting black skirt, disappeared into mud-stained socks and shoes.

Damn! Damn! Damn!

"The skull's farther up the gully." A sheen covered Hernández's forehead. His face was flushed, his shirt molded to his chest like the toga on a Roman sculpture.

I squatted. Flies buzzed upward, their bodies glistening green in the sunlight. Small round holes perforated the leathery tissue. Delicate grooves scored the bones. One hand was missing.

"Decapitated?" Hernández asked.

"Animals," I said.

"What sort of animals?"

"Small scavengers. Maybe raccoons."

Galiano squatted beside me. Undeterred by the smell of rotting flesh, he pulled a pen from his pocket and disentangled a chain from the neck vertebrae. Sunlight glinted off a silver cross as he raised the pen to eye level.

Returning the necklace, Galiano stood and scanned the scene.

"Probably won't find much here." His jaw muscles flexed.

"Not after ten months of ground time," Hernández agreed.

"Sweep the whole area. Hit it with everything."

"Right."

"What about neighbors?"

"We're going door to door, but I doubt we'll get much. The dump probably took place at night."

He pointed to an old man standing outside the tape at the top of the hill.

"Gramps lives one block over. Says he remembers a car prowling around back here last summer. Noticed because this is a dead end street and there's usually not much traffic. Says the driver returned two or three times, always at night, always alone. The old guy figured it might be a pervert looking for a place to jack off, so he kept his distance."

"Does he sound reliable?"

Hernández shrugged. "Probably a weenie whacker himself. Why else would he think that? Anyway, he remembers the car was old. Maybe a Toyota or Honda. He's not sure. Took this in from his front porch, so he didn't really get a good look, didn't get a plate."

"Find any personal effects?"

Hernández shook his head. "It's just like the kid in the septic tank. Clothing on the vic, but nothing else. The perp probably offloaded the body from the road, so he might have heaved something into the *barranca*. Xicay and Colom are going down when we finish here."

Galiano's eyes probed the small crowd on the bank above.

"Nothing, and I mean nothing to the media until I talk to the family."

He turned to me.

"What do you want to do here?"

What I *didn't* want to do was repeat my blunder at the Paraíso.

"I'm going to need a body bag and several hours."

"Take your time."

"But not too much," I said, self-recrimination sharpening my words.

"Take as long as you need."

I sensed from his tone that Díaz wouldn't be bothering me this time.

Taking surgical gloves from my pack, I walked to the end of the plateau, dropped to hands and knees, and began crawling the length of the ditch, sifting leaves and dirt through my fingers. As at the Paraíso, Xicay trailed me with his Nikon.

The skull lay six feet from the neck of the corpse, nudged or tugged by scavengers until they'd lost interest. Beside the skull, a mass of hair. Two feet beyond the hair, scattered phalanges led to a concentration of hand bones.

When Xicay had taken pictures and I'd recorded exact locations, I returned the displaced parts to the main body site, finished my survey of the ditch, and walked the plateau in a grid pattern. Then I walked it again, my second grid perpendicular to the first.

Nothing.

Returning to the skeleton, I dug out a flashlight and ran the beam over it. Hernández was right. After ten months, I doubted I'd find trace evidence, but hoped the plastic might have provided some protection until torn by animals.

I spotted zip.

Though trace recovery seemed hopeless, I was careful to work directly over the sheeting. If there were fragments, hairs, or fibers, we'd find them at the lab.

Laying the flashlight aside, I eased the skeleton onto its back. The odor intensified. Beetles and millipedes skittered in every direction. Xicay's shutter clicked above me.

In a climate like that of the Guatemala highlands, a body can be skeletonized in months or even weeks, depending upon access by insects and scavengers. If the cadaver is tightly wrapped, decomposition can be slowed significantly. Muscle and connective tissue may even mummify. Such was the case here. The bones held together reasonably well.

I studied the shriveled corpse, remembering the photos of eighteen-year-old Claudia de la Alda. My back teeth ground together.

Not this time, Díaz. Not this time.

Constantly shifting to find more comfortable work positions, I began at what had been the body's head and inched toward the feet, my whole being focused on my task. Time passed. Others came and went. My back and knees ached. My

155

eyes and skin itched from pollen, dust, and flying insects.

Somewhere along the way I noticed that Galiano was gone. Xicay and Colom expanded their search down into the gorge. I worked on alone, now and then hearing muffled conversation, birdsong, a shouted question from above.

Two hours later the remains, plastic sheeting, hair, and clothing lay in a body bag. The crucifix was sealed into a Ziploc baggie. My inventory form told me I was missing only five phalanges and two teeth.

This time I hadn't merely identified bones and distinguished left from right. I'd taken a long, hard look at every skeletal element.

The remains were those of a female in her late teens or early twenties. Cranio-facial features suggested she was of Mongoloid ancestry. She had a well-healed fracture of the right radius, and restorations in four of her molars.

What I couldn't tell was what had happened to her. My preliminary exam revealed no gunshot wounds, no fresh fractures, no blunt or sharp instrument trauma.

"De la Alda?"

Galiano had returned.

"Fits the profile."

"What happened to her?"

"No blows. No cuts. No bullets. No ligatures. Your guess is as good as mine."

"Hyoid?"

Galiano referred to a horseshoe-shaped bone

that floats in the soft tissue at the front of the throat. In older victims, the hyoid may crack during strangulation.

"Intact. But that means nothing with someone this young."

This young. Like the kid in the septic tank. I saw something flicker in Galiano's eyes, and knew he was sharing the same thought.

I tried to rise. My knees rebelled and I stumbled forward. Galiano caught me as I fell against him. For a heartbeat, neither of us moved. My cheek felt hot against Galiano's chest.

Surprised, I stepped back and concentrated on peeling off gloves. I sensed Guernsey eyes on my face, but didn't look up.

"Did Hernández learn anything else?" I asked.

"No one saw or heard zilch."

"Do you have De la Alda's dental records?"

"Yes."

"Should be a straightforward dental ID."

I glanced up at Galiano, back down at the gloves. Had the embrace lingered after I was safely on my feet, or had I imagined it?

"Finished here?" he asked.

"Except for digging and screening."

Galiano looked at his watch. With Pavlovian promptness, I looked at mine. Five-ten P.M.

"You're going to start that now?" he asked.

"I'm going to *finish* that now. If there's some sick bastard out there preying on young women, he could be choosing his next victim even as we speak."

"Yes."

"And the more people tramping around here, the more this scene is compromised."

The name Díaz did not need saying.

"And you've seen that mob up top. This story is going to break like a tropical thundershower."

I tucked the gloves into the body bag.

"The transport team can take the body. Be sure they strap it down."

"Yes, ma'am."

Was the bastard grinning? Was I imagining *that*?

Colom, Xicay, and I spent the next hour excavating and sifting six inches of topsoil from the portion of gully that had held the remains. The screen produced both missing teeth, three phalanges, several finger and toe nails, and one gold earring.

When Galiano returned, I showed him the stud.

"What is it?"

"It's what we call a clue." I sounded like Fredi Minos.

"De la Alda's?"

"That's a question for her family."

"She wore no jewelry in any of her photos."

"That's true."

Galiano dropped the baggie into his pocket.

Night was falling as we crested the ridge and stepped onto the road. The press trucks were gone, the obligatory body bag footage safely on tape. A few reporters lingered, hoping for a statement.

"How many, Galiano?"

"Who is it?"

"Is it a woman? Was she raped?"

"No comment."

As I got into Galiano's cruiser, a woman snapped me with one of three cameras draped around her neck.

I hit the lock, leaned back against the headrest, and closed my eyes. Galiano climbed in and started the engine. I heard a tap on my window, ignored it.

Galiano shifted into reverse. Then he draped an arm over the seat, turned his head, and shot backward. His fingers brushed my neck as he swiveled forward.

My skin tingled.

My eyes flew open.

Jesus, Brennan. A young woman is dead. A family will be devastated. You are working the case. This is not a date.

I stole a peek at Galiano. Headlights slid across his face, altering the size and shape of his features.

I thought of the pansies in the produce binder. Had Galiano felt me flinch when my cheek pressed against his chest? Had he really clasped me longer than necessary?

I thought of the Volkswagen bouquet in my hotel room.

Jesus.

"Goddamn sharks." Galiano's voice startled me. "No, they're worse than sharks. They're like hyenas circling a carcass."

He cracked his window. I reeked of mud and rotting flesh, and wondered if I was the cause.

"Did you get what you needed?" he asked.

"I did a prelim, but need to confirm."

"She's headed to the morgue."

"Does that mean I won't see the body again?"

"Not if I have anything to say."

"There are four molar restorations for the dental ID. Plus there's the old arm fracture for additional confirmation."

We drove in silence a few moments.

"Why wasn't Díaz all over this one?" I asked.

"Maybe Monday is his lawn bowling day."

Twenty minutes later Galiano pulled up at my hotel. I had the door open before the wheels stopped turning. His hand closed around my arm as I reached for my pack.

Oh, boy.

"You did a hell of a job today."

"Thanks."

"If there is some twisted psycho out there, we'll nail him."

"Yes."

He released my arm, brushed hair from my cheek with his fingertips.

More tingling.

"Get some sleep."

"Oh, yeah."

I flew from the car.

Dominique Specter had other plans.

She was waiting in the lobby, half concealed by its one rubber plant. She rose when I entered, and a copy of *Vogue* slid to the tile.

"Dr. Brennan?"

The ambassador's wife was wearing a pantsuit of pale gray silk, a black pearl choker around her neck. She looked as out of place in that hotel as a cross-dresser at a Baptist convention.

I was too stunned to answer.

"I realize this is a bit irregular."

She took in my hair, my mud-caked nails and clothes. Perhaps my scent.

"Is this absolutely too terribly inconvenient?" The practiced smile.

"No," I said warily. "Detective Galiano just dropped me off. Maybe I can catch him."

I dug for my cell phone.

"No!"

I looked up. The electric-green eyes were wide with alarm.

"I – I'd prefer talking to you."

"Detective Galia—"

"Alone. *Comprenez-vous?*"

No. I didn't understand. But I agreed.

12

Mrs. Specter returned to her *Vogue*, while I went upstairs. I wasn't sure if her patience derived from courtesy or from distaste for my state of hygiene. I didn't care. I was filthy, itchy, exhausted, and depressed from six hours of recovering a body. I needed a shower.

I took advantage of everything my toilet kit had to offer. Chamomile shampoo and conditioner, citrus bath gel, honey and almond body cream, green tea and cypress mousse.

As I dressed, I looked longingly at my bed. What I wanted was sleep. What I didn't want was an intense, prolonged conversation with a wounded and suffering mother. But I was caught by what-ifs. What if Mrs. Specter had held back and was now willing to bare herself? What if she was about to make revelations that might unlock one or more cases?

What if she knew where Chantale was?

Dream on, Brennan.

I rejoined Mrs. Specter, smelling like a Caswell-Massey shop. She suggested a park two blocks north of the hotel. I agreed.

Parque de las Flores was a small square framed by rosebushes and divided by paths cutting diagonally from corner to corner. Trees and wooden benches occupied the four triangles formed by the gravel X.

"It's a beautiful evening," said Mrs. Specter, removing a newspaper and settling onto a bench.

It's eleven o'clock, I thought.

"It reminds me of a summer night in Charlevoix. Were you aware that that's my home?"

"No, ma'am. I wasn't."

"Have you ever visited that part of Quebec?"

"It's very scenic."

"My husband and I keep a little place in Montreal, but I try to visit Charlevoix as often as I can."

A couple passed in front of us. The woman pushed a stroller, its wheels crunching softly on the gravel. The man's arm was draped around her shoulder.

I thought of Galiano. My left cheek burned where his finger had touched me. I thought of Ryan. Both cheeks burned.

"It's Chantale's birthday." Mrs. Specter's words brought me back. "She's seventeen today."

Present tense?

"She's been gone more than four months now."

It was too dark to read her expression.

"Chantale would not have allowed me to suffer as I am. If she was anywhere from where she could communicate, she would have done so."

She fidgeted with the tab on her purse. I let her go on.

"This past year has been so terribly difficult. What did Detective Galiano call it? A rough patch? *Oui*, a rough patch. But even when Chantale went *a fait une fugue* – How do you say that?"

"Ran away."

"Even when she ran away, Chantale always let me know that she was well. She might refuse to come home, refuse to tell me her whereabouts, but she'd call."

She paused, watching an old woman rummage through trash one triangle over.

"I know something dreadful has happened to her."

Her features were lit by a passing car, then receded into darkness once more. Moments later she spoke again.

"I fear it was Chantale in that septic tank."

I started to say something, but she cut me off.

"Things are not always as they seem, Dr. Brennan."

"What are you trying to tell me?"

"My husband is a wonderful man. I was very young when we married." Choppy. Throwing out thoughts as they came to her. "He is a decade older than I. In the early years there were times—"

She paused, fearful of the telling but needing to

dig something out of her heart.

"I was not ready to settle down. I had an affair."

"When?" I had my first inkling why I was here.

"In 1983. My husband was posted to Mexico City, but traveled incessantly. I was alone most of the time, started going out in the evenings. I wasn't looking for anyone, or anything, I just wanted to fill the hours." She drew a deep breath, let it out. "I met a man. We began seeing each other. Eventually, I considered leaving André to marry him."

Another pause, sorting through what to say, what to hold back.

"Before I made that decision, Miguel's wife found out. He ended it."

"You were pregnant," I guessed.

"Chantale was born the following spring."

"Your lover was Mexican?"

"Guatemalan."

I remembered Chantale's face in the photographs. She had deep brown eyes, high cheekbones, a broad jaw. The blonde hair had distracted me. Preconceived notions had colored my perception.

Jesus. What else would I bungle?

"Is there anything more?"

"Isn't that enough?"

She allowed her head to drop to one side, as though the weight of it were too much for her neck to bear.

"Many spouses cheat on their partners." I knew *that* firsthand.

"I've lived almost two decades with my secret, and it has been pure hell." The voice was tremulous and angry at the same time. "I've never been able to admit who my daughter is, Dr. Brennan. To her, to her father, to my husband, to anyone. The deception has tainted every part of my life. It has poisoned thoughts and dreams I've never even had."

I thought that an odd thing to say.

"If Chantale is dead, it's my fault."

"That's a natural reaction, Mrs. Specter. You're feeling lonely and guilty, bu—"

"Last January I told Chantale the truth."

"About her biological father?"

I sensed her nod.

"The night she disappeared?"

"She refused to believe it. She called me dreadful names. We had a terrible quarrel, and she stormed from the house. That was the last anyone has seen her."

For a full two minutes, neither of us spoke.

"Does the ambassador know?"

"No."

I envisioned the report I would write concerning the septic tank bones.

"If it was your daughter at the Paraíso, what you've told me may come out."

"I know."

Her head returned to vertical, and a hand rose to her chest. The fingers looked pale, the lacquered nails black in the night.

"I also know about the body recovered near

Kaminaljuyú today, though I'm sorry I don't remember the poor girl's name."

The Specters' sources were good.

"That victim has not been identified," I said.

"It's not Chantale. So the field now narrows to three."

"How can you know that?"

"My daughter has perfect teeth."

The Specters' sources were *very* good.

"Did Chantale see a dentist?"

"She went for cleanings and checkups. The police have her records. Unfortunately, my husband does not approve of unnecessary X rays, so the file contains none."

"The Paraíso skeleton may be none of the missing girls we are searching for," I said.

"Or it may be my daughter."

"Do you have a cat, Mrs. Specter?"

I felt more than saw her tense.

"What an odd question."

So the Specters' sources weren't infallible. She didn't know about Minos's findings.

"Cat hairs were rolled into the jeans recovered from the septic tank." I didn't mention the sample I'd collected from her home. "You told Detective Galiano that you have no pets."

"We lost our cat last Christmas."

"Lost?"

"Guimauve drowned." The black fingernails danced on the black pearls. "Chantale found his little body floating in the pool. She was heartbroken."

She fell silent a few moments, then, "It's late, and you must be very tired."

She stood, smoothed imaginary wrinkles from the perfect gray silk, and stepped onto the path. I joined her.

She spoke again when we'd reached the sidewalk. In the pale orange light of a street lamp I could see that her carefully decorated face had returned to its diplomat's wife appearance.

"My husband has made a few calls. The DA will contact you to make arrangements for your analysis of the Paraíso remains."

"I'll be allowed access?" I was stunned.

"Yes."

I started to thank her.

"No, Dr. Brennan. It is I who should thank you. Excuse me."

She drew a cell phone from her purse, and spoke a few words.

We continued in silence. Music edged from open doors as we walked past bars and bistros. A bicycle clicked by. A drunk. A granny with a shopping cart. I wondered idly if she was the old woman we'd seen in the park.

As we approached the hotel, a black Mercedes glided to the curb. A dark-suited man climbed out and opened the rear door.

"I will be praying for you."

She disappeared behind tinted glass.

At ten the next morning the Kaminaljuyú skeleton lay on stainless steel at the Morgue del Organismo

168

Judicial in Zone 3. I stood over it, Galiano at my side. Dr. Angelina Fereira was at the end of the table, flanked by an autopsy technician.

On Fereira's instructions, the remains had been photographed and X-rayed before our arrival. The clothing had been removed and spread on the counter at my back. The hair and body bag had been searched for trace evidence.

Cold tile, stainless steel table, shining instruments, fluorescent lights, masked and gloved investigators. All too familiar a scene.

As was the process about to commence. The poking and scraping, the measuring and weighing, the stripping of tissue, the sawing of bone. The relentless exposure would be a final indignity, an assault after death to exceed any she might have endured at the end of life.

A part of me wanted to cover her, to wheel her from these sterile strangers to the sanctity of those who had loved her. To allow her family to put what remained of her in a place of peace.

But the rational part of me knew better. This victim needed a name. Only then could her family bury her. Her bones deserved an opportunity to speak, to scream silently of the events of her last hours. Only then could the police hope to reconstruct what had befallen her.

So we gathered with our forms, our blades, our scales, our calipers, our notebooks, our specimen jars, our cameras.

Fereira agreed with my assessment of age, sex, and race. Like me, she found no fresh fractures or other indicators of violent attack. Together we measured and calculated stature. Together we removed bone for possible use in DNA profiling. It wasn't necessary.

Ninety minutes into the autopsy Hernández arrived with Claudia de la Alda's dental records. One look told us who lay on the table.

Shortly after Galiano and his partner left to deliver the news to the De la Alda family, the door opened again. In came a man I recognized from the Paraíso as Dr. Hector Lucas. His face was gray in the harsh light. He greeted Fereira, then asked that she leave the room.

Surprise flashed in the eyes above her mask. Or anger. Or resentment.

"Of course, Doctor."

She removed her gloves, tossed them into a biological waste receptacle, and left. Lucas waited until the door swung shut.

"You are to be allowed two hours with the Paraíso skeleton."

"That's not enough time."

"It will have to be. Four days ago seventeen people were killed in a bus accident. Three more have died since. My staff and facilities are overwhelmed."

While I felt sympathy for the crash victims and their families, I felt more for a pregnant young woman whose body had been flushed like last week's refuse.

"I don't need an autopsy room. I can work anywhere."

"No. You may not."

"By whose order am I limited to two hours?"

"The office of the district attorney. Señor Díaz remains of the opinion that an outsider is not needed."

"Outsider to what?" I asked in a rush of anger.

"What are you implying?"

I drew a deep breath, exhaled. Steady.

"I am implying nothing. I am trying to help and don't understand the DA's efforts to block me."

"I am sorry, Dr. Brennan. This is not my call." He handed me a slip of paper. "The bones will be brought to this room at a time of your choosing. Phone that number."

"This makes no sense. I am allowed full access to the Kaminaljuyú remains, but practically barred from those recovered at the Paraíso. What is Señor Díaz afraid I might find?"

"It is protocol, Dr. Brennan. And one more thing. You may not remove or photograph anything."

"That'll leave a gap in my souvenir collection," I snapped. Like Díaz, Lucas was bringing out the worst in me.

"*Buenos días.*"

Lucas walked from the room.

Seconds later Fereira reappeared, smelling of cigarette smoke and wearing a scrap of paper on her lower lip.

"An audience with Hector Lucas. Your lucky day." Though we'd stuck to Spanish throughout the autopsy, she now spoke English. It sounded Texan.

"Yeah."

Fereira rested elbows on the counter, leaned back, and crossed her ankles. She had gray hair, cut very short, Pete Sampras eyebrows over dark brown eyes, a body like a Frigidaire.

"He may look like a bird dog, but he's an excellent doctor."

I didn't reply.

"You two butting heads?"

I told her about the septic tank. She listened, face serious.

When I'd finished, Fereira took in what remained of Claudia de la Alda.

"Galiano suspects these cases are linked?"

"Yes."

"I hope to God they're not."

"Amen."

She thumbnailed the paper from her lip, inspected then flicked it.

"You think the Paraíso skeleton could be the ambassador's kid?"

"It's possible."

"Suppose that's the reason Díaz is stonewalling? Diplomatic embarrassment?"

"It doesn't make sense. Specter's the one who got me access."

"For two hours." Her voice dripped sarcasm.

Fereira was right. If Specter was powerful enough to overrule Díaz, why not obtain full clearance?

"If there's even a remote chance it is his daughter, why wouldn't Specter want to be sure?" Fereira posed the exact question that was in my mind.

"Could Díaz have other reasons for not wanting me near those bones?"

"Such as?" she asked.

I could think of no "such as."

"Lucas claims it's the bus crash," I said.

"It's been pretty crazy around here." She pushed to her feet. "If it's any comfort, it's not you. Both Lucas and Díaz abhor interference."

When I started to object, she raised a hand.

"I know you're not interfering. But that may be how they see it." She looked at her watch. "When do you plan to examine the bones?"

"This afternoon."

"Anything I can do?"

"I have an idea, but it would require help."

"Shoot."

I told her my plan. Her eyes slid to Claudia de la Alda, returned to mine.

"I can do that."

Three hours later Fereira and I had finished the De la Alda autopsy, eaten a quick lunch, and she'd moved on to one of the bus victims. Claudia de la Alda had been wheeled to a refrigerated compartment, and the Paraíso skeleton occupied the same table. The autopsy tech sat on a stool in the corner of the room, helper turned observer.

The bones were as I remembered, though clean

now of muck and debris. I inspected the ribs and pelvis, recorded the state of fusion of every crest, cap, and cranial suture, and examined the teeth.

My gender and age estimates remained unchanged. The remains were those of a female in her late teens.

I'd also been correct in my impression of Mongoloid ancestry. To confirm my visual observations, I took skull and facial measurements for computer analysis.

I searched for evidence of peri-mortem trauma, but found nothing. Nor did I spot any skeletal peculiarities that might be of use in identification. The teeth showed no anomalies or restorations.

I'd just finished recording long bone lengths for stature calculation, when a phone rang in the anteroom. The technician answered, returned, and told me my time was up.

I stepped back from the table, lowered my mask, and stripped off my gloves. No problem. I had what I needed.

Outside, the sun was dropping toward cotton candy clouds billowing from the horizon. The air smelled of smoke from a trash fire. A light breeze floated wrappers and newspaper across the sidewalk.

I took a deep breath and gazed at the cemetery next door. Shadows angled from tombstones and from dime-store vases and jelly jars holding plastic flowers. An old woman sat on a wooden crate, head veiled, withered body swathed in black. A rosary dangled from her bony fingers.

I should have felt good. Though it was incomplete, I'd scored a victory over Díaz. And my initial assessment had been right on. But all I felt was sad.

And frightened.

Three months had passed between the day Claudia de la Alda was last seen alive and the day Patricia Eduardo went missing. Just over two months had passed between the disappearances of Patricia Eduardo and Lucy Gerardi. Chantale Specter vanished ten days after Lucy Gerardi.

If one maniac was responsible, the intervals were growing shorter.

His blood lust was increasing.

I pulled out my cell and punched in Galiano's number. Before I hit send, the thing rang in my hand. It was Mateo Reyes.

Molly Carraway had regained consciousness.

13

Shortly after daybreak, Mateo and I were roller-coastering the blacktop to Sololá, shooting through pink, slanted sunshine on the ups, plunging through pockets of fog on the downs. The air was chilly, the horizon blurred by a damp morning haze. Mateo pushed the Jeep full out, face deadpan, hands tight on the wheel.

I rode in the front passenger seat, elbow out the window like a trucker in Tucson. Wind whipped my hair straight up, then forward into my face. I brushed it back absently, my thoughts focused on Molly and Carlos.

Though I'd met Carlos only once or twice, I'd known Molly a decade. Roughly my age, she'd come to anthropology late in life. A high school biology teacher grown frustrated with cafeteria duty and bathroom patrol, Molly had shifted direction at age thirty-one and returned to graduate school. Upon completion of a doctorate in bio-archaeology, she'd accepted a position in the Anthropology Department at the University of Minnesota.

Like me, Molly had been drawn into medical examiner work by cops and coroners oblivious to the distinction between physical and forensic anthropology. Like me, she donated time to the investigation of human rights abuses.

Unlike me, Molly had never abandoned her study of the ancient dead. Though she did some coroner cases, archaeology remained her main focus. She had yet to achieve certification by the American Board of Forensic Anthropology.

But you will, Molly. You will.

Mateo and I wound through the miles in silence. Traffic lightened when we drew away from Guatemala City, increased as we approached Sololá. We raced past deep green valleys, yellow pastures with scruffy brown cows grazing in clumps, villages thick with roadside vendors laying out that morning's stock.

We were ninety minutes into the drive when Mateo spoke.

"The doctor said she was agitated."

"Open your eyes to a two-week hole in your life, you'd be agitated, too."

We flew around a curve. A pair of vehicles rushed by in the opposite direction, blasting air through our open windows.

"Maybe that's it."

"Maybe?" I looked at him.

"I don't know. There was something in that doctor's voice."

He crawled up the bumper of a slow-moving truck, shifted hard, passed.

"What?"

He shrugged. "It was more the tone."

"What else did he tell you?"

"Not much."

"Is there permanent damage?"

"He doesn't know. Or won't say."

"Has anyone come down from Minnesota?"

"Her father. Isn't she married?"

"Divorced. Her kids are in high school."

Mateo drove the remaining distance in silence, wind puffing his denim shirt, reflected yellow lines clicking up the front of his dark glasses.

The Sololá hospital was a six-story maze of red brick and grimy glass. Mateo parked in one of several small lots, and we walked up a tree-shaded lane to the front entrance. In the forecourt, a cement Jesus welcomed us with outstretched arms.

People filled the lobby, wandering, praying, drinking soda, slumping or fidgeting on wooden benches. Some wore housedresses, others suits or jeans. Most were dressed in Sololá Mayan. Women swathed in striped red cloth, with burrito-wrapped babies on their bellies or backs. Men in woolen aprons, gaucho hats, and wildly embroidered trousers and shirts. Now and then a hospital worker in crisp white cut through the kaleidoscope assemblage.

I looked around, familiar with the atmosphere,

but unfamiliar with the layout. Signs routed patrons to the cafeteria, the gift shop, the business office, and to a dozen medical departments. *Radiografía. Urología. Pediatría.*

Ignoring posted instructions to check-in, Mateo led me directly to a bank of elevators. We got off on the fifth floor and headed left, our heels clicking on polished tile. As we moved up the corridor, I saw myself reflected in the small rectangular windows of a dozen closed doors.

"*¡Alto!*" Hurled from behind.

We turned. A fire-breathing nurse was bearing down, hospital chart pressed to her spotless white chest. Winged cap. Hair pulled back tight enough to cause a fault line down the center of her face.

Nurse Dragon extended her arm and the chart and circled us, the crossing guard of the fifth floor.

Mateo and I smiled winningly.

The dragon asked the reason for our presence.

Mateo told her.

She drew in the chart, eyed us as though we were Leopold and Loeb.

"*¿Familia?*"

Mateo gestured at me. "*Americana.*"

More appraisal.

"*Numero treinta y cinco.*"

"*Gracias.*"

"*Veinte minutos. Nada mas.*" Twenty minutes. No more.

"*Gracias.*"

Molly looked like a still life of cheated death. Her thin cotton gown was colorless from a million washings and clung to her body like a feathery shroud. One tube ran from her nose, another from an arm bearing little more flesh than the skeletons at the morgue.

Mateo inhaled sharply. "*Jesucristo.*"

I placed a hand on his shoulder.

Molly's eyes were lavender caverns. She opened them, recognized us, and struggled to raise herself higher on the pillows. I hurried to her side.

"*¿Qué hay de nuevo?*" Slurry.

"What's new with *you*?" I replied.

"Had one dandy siesta."

"I knew we were working you too hard." Though his words were light, Mateo's voice was not.

Molly smiled weakly, pointed to a water glass on the bedside table.

"Do you mind?"

I swung the table in front of her and tipped the straw. She closed dry lips around it, drank, and leaned back.

"Have you met my father?" One hand rose, dropped back to the gray wool blanket.

Mateo and I swiveled around.

An old man occupied a chair in the corner of the room. He had white hair, and deep lines chiseled down his cheeks and across his chin and forehead. Though the whites of his eyes had yellowed with age, the blues were as clear as a mountain lake.

Mateo went to him and held out a hand. "Mateo Reyes. I guess you'd say I'm Molly's boss down here."

180

"Jack Dayton."

They shook.

"It's nice to meet you, Mr. Dayton," I said from beside the bed.

He nodded.

"Sorry it's under these circumstances."

"Those bein'?"

"Excuse me?"

"What happened to my girl?"

"Daddy. Be nice."

I placed a hand on Molly's shoulder.

"The police are investigating."

"Been two weeks."

"These things take time," Mateo said.

"Yeah."

"Are they keeping you informed?" I asked.

"Nothin' to inform."

"I'm sure they're working on it." I wasn't certain I believed that but wanted to soothe him.

"Been two weeks." His eyes dropped to the gnarled fingers laced in his lap.

True, Jack Dayton. Very true.

I took Molly's hand in mine.

"How are you?"

"With a little time, I'll be right as rain." Another weak smile. "I've never understood that expression. Must have been coined by farmers." She rolled her head to look at her father. "Like Daddy."

The old man didn't move a muscle.

"I'm forty-two, but my parents still think I'm their little girl." Molly turned back to me. "They were against my coming to Guatemala."

The ice-blue eyes in the corner flicked up.

"Look what happened."

She gave me a conspiratorial smile.

"I could have been mugged in Mankato, Daddy."

"At home we catch lawbreakers and lock 'em up."

"You know that's not always true."

"Least the cops'd be talking a language I know."

Dayton pushed to his feet and tugged his belt upward.

"I'll be back."

He shuffled from the room, Nike Cross-Trainers squeaking on the tile.

"You'll have to excuse Daddy. He can be ornery."

"He loves you, and he's frightened and angry. It's his job to be ornery. What are your doctors saying?"

"Physical therapy, then right as rain. No need to bore you with the details."

"I'm so glad. We've all been crazy worrying. Someone's been here almost every day."

"I know. How goes Chupan Ya?"

"We're moving full-tilt boogey on the skeletal analyses," Mateo said. "Should have everyone ID'd in a couple of weeks."

"Is it as bad as the eyewitness accounts suggest?"

I nodded. "Lots of gunshot and machete wounds. Mostly women and kids."

Molly said nothing.

I looked at Mateo. He nodded. I swallowed.

"Carlos—"

"The cops told me."

"Have they questioned you?"

"Yesterday."

She sighed.

"I couldn't tell them much. I only remember fragments, like freeze-frames. Headlights in the rear window. A car forcing us off the road. Two men walking on the shoulder. Arguing. Gunshots. A figure circling to my side of the truck. Then nothing."

"Do you remember phoning me?"

She shook her head.

"Would you recognize the men?"

"It was dark. I never saw their faces."

"Do you remember anything that was said?"

"Not much. Carlos said something like '*mota, mota.*'"

I looked at Mateo.

"Bribe."

She crooked an arm across her forehead, pushed back her hair. Her underarm looked pale as a fish belly.

"One man kept telling the other to hurry."

"Anything else?" I asked.

Down the hall, the elevator bonged.

Molly's eyes flicked toward the door, back to me. When she resumed speaking, her voice was lower.

"My Spanish isn't great, but I think one cop said something about an inspector. Do you suppose they were cops?"

Again, she checked the door. I thought of Galiano in the Gucumatz.

"Or soldiers involved in the Chupan Ya massacre?"

At that moment Nurse Dragon swept in and locked Mateo in an authoritative stare.

"This patient must rest."

Mateo raised a hand to his mouth and whispered theatrically, "Abort mission. We've been discovered."

The dragon did not look amused.

"Five minutes?" I asked, smiling.

She looked at her watch.

"Five minutes. I will return." Her face said she was ready to call in backup.

Molly watched the dragon leave, then lowered her arm and raised up on her elbows.

"There was one other thing. I didn't mention it to the police. I don't know why. I just didn't."

She looked from Mateo to me.

"I—" She swallowed. "A name."

We waited.

"I could swear I heard one of the men say Brennan."

I felt like I'd been thrown against a wall. Across the room I heard Mateo curse.

"Are you certain?" I stared at Molly, stunned.

"Yes. No. Yes. Oh, God, Tempe, I think so. Everything is such a jumble." She dropped onto the pillows. The arm went back to her forehead, and tears filled her eyes.

I squeezed her hand.

"It's O.K., Molly." My mouth felt dry, the room suddenly smaller.

"What if they go after *you* now?" She was becoming agitated. "What if *you're* their next target?"

I reached out with my free hand and stroked her head.

"It was dark. You were frightened. Everything was happening so fast. You probably misunderstood."

"I couldn't stand it if anyone else got hurt. Promise me you'll be careful, Tempe!"

"Of course I'll be careful."

I smiled, but a sense of trepidation was settling over me.

After leaving the hospital, Mateo and I lunched at a *comedor* in the Hotel Paisaje, a block uphill from Sololá's central plaza. We discussed Molly's story, decided it warranted a report.

Before heading back to Guatemala City, we dropped in at the police station. The detective in charge of the investigation had nothing new to tell us. He took down our statement, but it was clear he gave little credence to Molly's recollection of hearing my name. We did not mention her suspicion about the reference to an inspector.

Throughout our return to Guatemala City, mist fell from a soft gray sky. The fog was so thick in the valleys it swallowed the world outside our Jeep. On the hilltops, it drifted across the road like sea spray.

As on the drive out, Mateo and I spoke little.

Thoughts swirled in my brain, each ending with a question mark.

Who shot Carlos and Molly? Why? Surely the police were wrong in assuming that robbery was the motive. An American passport is as good as gold. Why wasn't Molly's taken? Did the police not want to look beyond robbery? What were *their* motives?

Could Molly be correct? Was the shooting intended to hinder the Chupan Ya investigation? Did someone feel threatened by potential revelations about the massacre?

Molly was fairly certain her attackers had spoken the name Brennan. I could only think of one Brennan. What was their interest in me? Was I to be their next prey?

Who was the inspector? Were the police simply reluctant investigators, or participants in the crime?

Again and again I found myself checking the rearview mirror.

An hour into the trip, I laid my head against the seat and closed my eyes. I'd been up since five. My brain felt sluggish, my lids weighted.

The rocking of the Jeep. The wind on my face.

Despite my anxiety, I began to drift.

Inspector. What sort of inspector?

Building inspector. Agricultural inspector. Highway. Automobile emissions. Water. Sewage.

Sewage.

Septic system.

Paraíso.

I shot upright.

"What if it wasn't an inspector at all?"

Mateo glanced at me, back at the road.

"What if Molly heard more than one name?"

"Señor Inspector?"

It took Mateo a nanosecond.

"Señor Specter?"

"Exactly." I was glad Galiano had told Mateo about Chantale Specter.

"You think they were talking about André Specter?"

"Maybe the assault had something to do with the ambassador's daughter?"

"Why shoot Carlos and Molly?"

"Maybe they mistook Molly for me. We're both Americans, we're about the same size, we both have brown hair."

Jesus. This was sounding all too plausible.

"Maybe that's why my name was spoken."

"Galiano didn't bring you into the Paraíso case until a week after Carlos and Molly were shot."

"Maybe someone learned his intentions and decided to take me out of the loop."

"Who would have that information?"

Another flash of Galiano in the alcove at the Gucumatz restaurant. I felt a chill.

Minutes later, "*¡Maldición!*" Damn!

Mateo's eyes were on the rearview mirror. I checked the glass on my side.

Red pulsated in the mist to our rear. A siren, faint but unmistakable.

Mateo's attention shifted between the mirror

and the windshield. Mine remained focused on the cruiser behind us.

The light expanded, became a red whirlpool. The siren grew louder.

Mateo eased into the slow lane.

The cruiser rushed toward our bumper. Crimson swirled inside the Jeep. The siren screamed. Mateo kept his eyes straight ahead. I stared at a rust spot on the dashboard.

The cruiser pulled left, shot past, disappeared into the mist.

My heart didn't slow until we were locked inside the gate at FAFG headquarters.

Galiano was not in when I phoned his office but returned my page within minutes. He was tied up until evening, but was eager to know what I'd learned from Molly. He suggested dinner at Las Cien Puertas. Great food. Moderate prices. Good Latin music. He'd sounded like a shareholder.

I devoted the next three hours to Chupan Ya, returned to my hotel at six-fifteen thoroughly dejected over the agonizingly senseless loss of life. It seemed I would never get away from death.

As I changed clothes, I forced my mind in another direction. I thought about Galiano.

Where were his wife and young Alejandro?

I applied fresh deodorant, dabbed blusher on my cheeks.

Was I keeping Galiano from his family?

Ridiculous. Dinner was strictly professional.

Was it?

It was a scheduling issue. We were both busy during working hours.

I dug mascara from the bottom of my makeup kit. Black flakes floated to the sink as I unscrewed the applicator.

Were these dinners with Galiano justified?

Strictly business.

Then why the long lashes?

I jammed the applicator back in its place and returned the unused tube to my kit.

Galiano picked me up at seven.

The restaurant was located in an arcade typical of Zone 1. Though beautiful once, the colonial grandeur and dignity had long ago yielded to peeling paint and crude graffiti.

But Galiano was right about the food. It was excellent.

As we ate, I described my visit to Sololá. Galiano agreed with my suspicion that Molly might have been mistaken for me, insisted I take measures to protect myself. No argument there. I assured him I would stay vigilant. He suggested I carry a gun, offered to provide one. I declined, claiming trigger ineptness. I did not tell him that guns frighten me more than the thought of unknown assailants.

Galiano agreed that obstruction of the Chupan Ya investigation could well have been a motive for the shooting. If so, perhaps no further attacks would occur, since the excavation was complete. Still, he recommended that I not make trips to remote places. Recommended? Insisted.

Galiano was dubious about my Specter theory.

"It could explain why I haven't been allowed full access to the Paraíso bones."

"Why?"

"Someone's putting pressure on the DA."

"Who?"

"I don't know."

"Why?"

"I don't know."

His skepticism irritated me. Or perhaps it was my inability to provide answers.

Irrationally, my thoughts turned to the stumbling episode. Was there such a thing as tactile memory? Did my cheek *really* tingle where it had grazed his chest?

Of course not.

I listened in silence as he told me about the investigation of Claudia de la Alda's murder. Galiano's English was unaccented, but spoken with a Latin cadence. I liked his voice. I liked his crooked face.

I liked the way he looked at me. I liked the way he looked.

Business, Brennan. You're a scientist, not a schoolgirl.

When the check arrived I grabbed it, dug out my Am Ex card, and thrust it into the waiter's hand. Galiano did not object.

Back in the car, Galiano turned sideways and dropped an elbow over the seatback.

"What's bugging you?" A neon sign pulsated blue and yellow slashes across his face.

"Nothing."

"You're acting like someone who's just learned that people were trying to kill her."

"A penetrating observation." Though a misdiagnosis.

"I'm a sensitive guy."

"Really."

"I read *Venus and Mars*."

"Hm."

"*Bridges of Madison County*."

He reached out and ran a thumb around the corner of my mouth. I turned my head sideways.

"Took notes."

"Where is Mrs. Galiano this evening?"

For a moment, he looked confused. Then he laughed.

"With her husband, I presume."

"You're divorced?"

Galiano nodded. He lifted my hair and drew a finger down the side of my neck. It left a smoldering trail.

"What about Ryan?" he asked.

"A working relationship."

True. We worked together.

Galiano leaned close. I felt the warm wetness of breath on my cheek. Then his lips slid behind my ear. Onto my neck. My throat.

Oh, boy.

Galiano took my face in his hands and kissed me on the lips.

I smelled male sweat, cotton, something tangy, like citrus. The world kicked into slo-mo.

Galiano kissed my left eyelid, my right.

Galiano's cellular shrieked.

We flew apart.

He yanked the phone from his belt and clicked on, one hand lingering in my hair.

"Galiano."

Pause.

"*Ay, Dios.*"

I held my breath.

"When?"

Longer pause.

"Does the ambassador know?"

I closed my eyes, felt my fingers curl into fists.

"Where are they now?"

Please, God. Not another body.

"Yeah."

Galiano disconnected, ran his hand across my head, and dropped it onto my shoulder. For a moment, he just stared at me, the Guernsey eyes liquid in the darkness of the car.

"Chantale Specter?" I could hardly get the question out.

He nodded.

"Dead?"

"She was arrested last night in Montreal."

14

"She's alive?" I knew it was stupid as soon as I said it.

"Lucy Gerardi was with her."

"No way!"

"They were nailed shoplifting CDs at the MusiGo at Le Faubourg."

"Shoplifting?" I sounded like a moron, but this wasn't making sense.

"Cowboy Junkies."

"Why?"

"Guess they're into folk rock."

I rolled my eyes, another pointless response in the dark.

"What could have brought them to Montreal?"

"Air Canada."

Asshole. This reply I held back.

Galiano started the engine, pulled out of the lot. On the drive back I sat with feet up, knees hugged to my chest. The protective posturing was unnecessary. The news about Chantale Specter had squelched any amorous intentions either of us might have harboured.

At the hotel, I popped the door before we stopped rolling.

"Call me as soon as you know anything."

"Will do."

I flapped a hand in the air between Galiano and me.

"Will this be a problem?" My face burned.

Galiano grinned. "None at all."

Too agitated to sleep, I checked my messages in Montreal and Charlotte. Pierre LaManche had called to say that a mummified head had been found in an attic in Quebec City. Newspaper wrappings suggested it dated to the thirties. The case was not urgent. However, a putrefied human torso had drifted ashore in Lac des Deux-Montagnes, and he wanted me to examine it as soon as possible.

There were no anthropology cases in North Carolina.

Pete said both Birdie and Boyd were fine.

Katy was not in.

Ryan was not in.

I ate two doughnuts from a box I'd stashed in the kitchenette, turned on CNN.

Tropical storm Armand was threatening the Florida panhandle. Three Canadians had been arrested for a stock scam in Buenos Aires. A bomb had killed four in Tel Aviv. A train accident near Chicago had left over one hundred hurt, most with soft tissue injuries. Happy lawyers.

Next I bathed, deep-conditioned my hair, shaved my armpits and legs, plucked my eyebrows, and creamed my entire body.

Hairless and smooth, I crawled into bed.

My mind was still humming, and sleep wouldn't come.

Claudia de la Alda was a homicide victim here in Guatemala. Patricia Eduardo was still missing but she might be the girl in the septic tank. Chantale Specter and Lucy Gerardi were alive and busted in Canada.

What had drawn Chantale and Lucy to Montreal? How had they gotten there without leaving a trail? Where had they been hiding out, and why?

Was the septic tank girl linked to the murder of Claudia de la Alda, or were the cases unrelated? Was Galiano's serial killer theory evaporating? Who had phoned about Claudia's body?

Who was taking care of Claudia's family? Was someone there to help ease their unbearable heartbreak?

Where was Patricia Eduardo? Was it indeed her body in the tank? A strangely disconnected thought: who was caring for Patricia's horses?

Who had phoned Galiano about Chantale Specter? I'd been so surprised by the news, I hadn't thought to ask.

Galiano.

Mental cringe. I felt like a kid caught necking on the couch.

And what about Ryan?

What *about* Ryan?

Ryan and I were seeing each other. We'd gone to dinner, visited the Musée des Beaux-Arts, attended a few parties, played tennis. He'd even talked me into bowling.

Were we a couple?

No.

Could we be?

The jury was deadlocked.

Where did Ryan and I stand? I liked him very much, respected his integrity, enjoyed his company.

Heat rippled across my stomach.

Found him sexy as hell.

So why was I attracted to Galiano?

Another ripple.

Easy one, slut.

Ryan and I had reached an accord. Not an accord, really, an agreement. A tacit agreement. Don't ask, don't tell. The policy worked for the United States military, and so far it was working for us.

Besides, I wasn't going to get involved with Galiano.

Look on the bright side, I told myself. You haven't done the deed with Ryan or Galiano. There's nothing to tell.

That was the problem.

After thrashing about for another half an hour, my frustrated libido and I drifted off.

*

The phone woke me from a deep sleep. Dim light filtered through the curtains hanging limp across my open window.

Dominique Specter sounded wired.

"You've heard?"

"I have."

I squinted at the clock. Seven-twelve.

"*C'est magnifique.* Not the stealing, of course. But Chantale is all right." Her voice was high and taut, the accent more pronounced than I remembered.

"It's wonderful news." I sat up.

"*Oui.* My baby is alive."

"Do you know if Chantale has been charged with anything other than shoplifting?"

"No. We must go and bring her home."

I didn't point out that a judge might have different thoughts on that.

"If drugs are involved I will find a new program. A better one."

"That's a good idea."

"We will insist."

"Yes."

"She will listen to you."

"Me?"

Suddenly, I was fully awake.

"*Mais, oui.*"

"I'm not going to Montreal."

"I have booked two seats on this afternoon's flight." Mrs. Specter was a woman unaccustomed to refusal.

"I can't leave Guatemala now."

"But I need you."

"I'm committed to a project here."

"I can't do this alone."

"Where is Mr. Specter?"

"My husband is at an agricultural conference in Mexico City."

"Mrs. Spect—"

"Chantale was furious the night she left. She said terrible things. She said she never wanted to see me again."

"I'm sure—"

"She may refuse to talk with me!"

Bring on the Valium.

"May I call you back?"

"Please, don't turn your back on me. I need your help. Chantale needs your help. You are one of the only people who knows the whole situation."

"Let me see what I can do." For lack of a better remark.

I threw back the covers and swung my legs over the side of the bed.

Why wasn't the ambassador rushing to be with his wife and daughter? The woman sounded seriously distraught.

I stared at a spot where I'd nicked my knee.

Given the situation, would I be any different? Probably, but not relevant.

I shuffled to the kitchen, scooped grounds, dumped them into the coffeemaker, added water. Then I took out the doughnuts and ate one while Mr. Coffee perked.

I could see Ryan.

I mashed powdered sugar on the countertop, sucked it from my fingertip.

LaManche wanted my opinion on the Lac des Deux-Montagnes torso. Said the case was urgent.

I pictured Chupan Ya, thought of the skeletons lying on tables at the FAFG lab. That work was so important. But the victims had been dead for almost two decades. Was my need to be here as urgent as my need to help LaManche? With Carlos and Molly out of the picture, Mateo was already working shorthanded. But couldn't he get along without me for a couple of days?

I poured coffee, added milk.

I pictured the body in the ditch and felt the familiar sadness. Claudia de la Alda, age eighteen. I pictured the bones in the septic tank and was overcome by guilt.

And frustration. The harder Galiano and I worked, the farther we seemed to be from answers.

I needed to accomplish something concrete.

I wanted an opinion on cat hair.

I looked at the clock. Seven-forty.

And one other thing. But had Fereira been able to pull it off?

There were two doughnuts left in the box. How many calories would that be? One million or two? By tomorrow they'd be stale.

A trip to Montreal would take only a few days. I could get Mrs. Specter situated with Chantale, then return to the Chupan Ya victims.

I ate the doughnuts, finished my coffee, and headed for the bathroom.

At eight I dialed the lab in Montreal and asked for the DNA section. When Robert Gagné came on, I outlined the Paraíso case and explained what I wanted. He thought it could be done, agreed to give it priority if I hand-delivered the sample.

I phoned Minos. He promised to have the cat hair packaged and ready in an hour.

I phoned the Guatemala City morgue. Dr. Fereira had carried through with what I'd requested.

I phoned Susanne Jean at the RP Corporation manufacturing plant in St-Hubert and gave her the same outline I'd given Gagné. She thought my idea would work.

I phoned Mateo. He told me to take all the time I needed.

Ditto for Galiano.

I hung up and headed for the door.

O.K., Mrs. Ambassador. You've got yourself a traveling buddy. And I hope you and any companion get waved right through Guatemalan customs.

Angelina Fereira was well into another crash victim when I entered the autopsy room. A man lay on the table, head and arms badly charred, abdomen yawning like an open mouth in a Bacon painting. The pathologist was slicing a liver on a tray beside the body. She wielded a large, flat knife, and spoke without looking up.

"*Un momento.*"

Fereira peered closely at the exposed cross-

200

sections, removed three slivers, and dropped them into a specimen jar. The tissue floated to the bottom and settled among its counterparts from the lungs, stomach, spleen, kidneys, and heart.

"Are you autopsying everyone?"

"We're doing externals on the passengers. This is the driver."

"Saved him for last?"

"Most of the victims are so badly burned we couldn't be sure which one he was. Found him yesterday."

Fereira stripped off mask and gloves, washed her hands, and crossed to the swinging doors, indicating that I should follow. She led me down a dingy corridor into a small, windowless office and closed the door. Unlocking a battered metal cabinet, she withdrew a large brown envelope.

"A radiologist at the Hospital Centro Médico owed me a favor." She spoke English. "Had to call in the chit for this."

"Thank you."

"Sneaked the skull out after Lucas left on Tuesday. Wouldn't want that getting out."

"It won't come from me."

"Good thing I did."

"What do you mean?"

Fereira slid one of several films from the envelope. It contained sixteen CT scans, each representing a five-millimeter slice through the skull found in the septic tank. Raising an X ray toward the overhead light, she pointed to a small white blob in the ninth image. Through the next several images the opacity enlarged, changed shape, diminished. By the fourteenth frame it was no longer visible.

"I spotted something in the ethmoid, thought it might be useful. After your call this morning, I went for another peek at the skull. The remains were gone."

"Gone where?"

"Cremated."

"After only one week?" I was dumbfounded.

Fereira nodded.

"Is that standard procedure?"

"As you can see, we're cramped for space. Even under normal circumstances we don't have the luxury of keeping unknowns for long periods of time. This bus crash has pushed us to the edge." She lowered her voice. "But two weeks is unusual."

"Who authorized it?"

"Tried to track that down. No one seems to know."

"And the paperwork is missing," I guessed.

"The technician swears he placed the order in the filing basket after carrying out the cremation, but it's nowhere to be found."

"Any theories?"

"Yep."

She returned the film, held out the envelope.

"*Vaya con Dios.*"

At twelve fifty-seven I was belted into a first-class seat on an American Airlines flight to Miami.

Dominique Specter sat beside me, lacquered nails drumming the armrest. Dr. Fereira's CT scans were locked in a briefcase at my feet. The cat hair samples were tucked beside them.

Mrs. Specter had spoken incessantly during the limo ride and throughout the wait in the airport lounge. She described Chantale, recounted childhood anecdotes, floated theories as to the cause of her daughter's problems, wove schemes for her rehabilitation. She was like a DJ between records, terrified of silence, nonselective in the banality with which she filled it.

Recognizing the talk as tension release, I made reassuring sounds but said little. Feedback was not necessary. The verbal flow continued unabated.

Mrs. Specter finally fell silent as we thundered down the runway for takeoff. She compressed her lips, leaned her head against the seat-back, and closed her eyes. When we leveled off, she pulled a copy of *Paris Match* from her handbag and began flipping pages.

The wallpaper chatter resumed during our transfer in Miami, died again on the flight to Montreal. Suspecting my companion had a fear of flying, I continued to grant her conversational control.

Traveling with the ambassador's wife had its advantages. When our plane touched down at ten thirty-eight, we were met by suited men and whisked through customs. By eleven we were in the back of another limo.

Mrs. Specter maintained her cruising altitude

silence as we sped toward Centre-ville, exited at Guy, and turned right onto rue Ste-Catherine. Perhaps she had run out of words, or simply talked herself calm. Perhaps being home was soothing her soul. Together we listened to Robert Charlebois.

Je reviendrai à Montréal . . . I will return to Montreal . . .

Together we watched the lights of the city go by.

In minutes we pulled up at my condo. The driver got out.

As I gathered my briefcase, Mrs. Specter grabbed my hand. Her fingers felt cold and clammy, like meat from the fridge.

"Thank you," she said, almost inaudibly.

I heard the trunk squeak, thunk shut.

"I'm glad I can help."

She drew a deep breath.

"You have no idea how much."

The door on my side opened.

"Let me know when we can see Chantale. I'll go with you."

I laid my hand on Mrs. Specter's. She squeezed, then kissed it.

"Thank you." She straightened. "Shall Claude help you inside?"

"I'll be fine."

Claude accompanied me up the steps, waited as I located my key to the outer door. I thanked him. He nodded, placed my suitcase beside me, and returned to the limo.

Again, I watched Mrs. Specter glide into the night.

15

By seven the next morning I was racing through the asphalt underbelly of Montreal. Above me, the city yawned and stretched to life. Around me, the Ville-Marie Tunnel looked as gray as my mood.

Quebec was in the grip of a rare spring heat wave. When I'd arrived home near midnight, my patio thermometer still topped eighty, and the temperature inside felt like nine hundred Celsius.

The AC was indifferent to my preference for sleeping cool. Ten minutes of clicking buttons, pounding, and swearing had done nothing to coax it to life. Sweating and angry, I'd finally opened every window and fallen into bed.

The street boys had been equally unconcerned about my comfort and need for sleep. A dozen were *en fête* on the back stoop of a pizza joint ten yards from my bedroom window. Yelling did not dampen their party mood. Neither did threats. Or curses.

I had slept badly, tossing and turning under limp sheets, awakened repeatedly by laughter, song, and angry outbursts. I had greeted the dawn with a pounding headache.

The Bureau du Coroner and the Laboratoire de Sciences Judiciaires et de Médecine Légale are located in a thirteen-story glass and concrete T in a neighborhood east of Centre-ville. In deference to its principal occupant, the provincial police, or Sûreté du Québec, over the decades the structure has been dubbed the SQ building.

Several years back, the Gouvernement du Québec decided to pump millions into law enforcement and forensic science. The building was refurbished, and the LSJML was expanded and moved from the fifth to the twelfth and thirteenth floors, into space formerly occupied by a short-term jail. In an official ceremony, the tower was reborn as the Édifice Wilfrid-Derome.

Old habits die hard. To most it remains the SQ building.

Exiting the tunnel at the Molson brewery, I passed under the Jacques Cartier Bridge, shot across De Lorimier, turned right, and wound through a neighborhood where neither the streets nor the people are beautiful. Three-flats with postage-stamp yards and metal staircases spiraling up their faces. Gray stone churches with silver spires. Corner *dépanneurs*. Storefront businesses. The Wilfrid-Derome/SQ looming over all.

After ten minutes of searching, I located a spot that appeared, through some bureaucratic loophole, to be legal, without permit, during the precise period I planned to park. I rechecked the monthly, hourly, and daily restrictions, maneuvered into place, grabbed my laptop and briefcase, and headed up the block.

Children were dribbling toward a nearby school in twos and threes, like ants converging on a melting Popsicle. Early arrivals milled in the playground, kicking balls, jumping ropes, screaming, chasing. A small girl peered through the wrought-iron fence, fingers clutching the uprights like those of the child at Chupan Ya. She watched me pass, face expressionless. I did not envy her the next eight hours, trapped in a hot classroom, summer freedom still a month away.

Nor did I envy the day facing me.

I was not looking forward to a mummified head. I was not looking forward to a putrefied torso. I dreaded mediating the reunion between Chantale and her mother. It was one of those mornings I wished I'd taken a job with the telephone company.

Paid vacations. Great benefits. No corpses.

I was perspiring by the time I entered the lobby. The morning mix of smog, exhaust, and the cocktail emanating from the brewery had not helped my cranial vessels. My skull felt as though the contents had exceeded capacity and were pushing for a way out.

There'd been no coffee at the condo. As I displayed my building ID to the scanner, passed through security gates, pushed for an elevator, swiped my lab card, and exited on the twelfth floor, that single word formed on my lips.

Coffee!

One more swipe, glass doors swished open, and I entered the medico-legal wing.

Offices lined the right side of the corridor, labs lay to the left. *Microbiologie. Histologie. Pathologie. Anthropologie/Odontologie.* Windows ran from ceiling to mid-wall, designed to maximize visibility without compromising security. Through the glass I could see that every lab was empty.

I checked my watch. Seven thirty-five. Since most support, technical, and professional personnel began their day at eight, I would have almost thirty minutes to myself.

With the exception of Pierre LaManche. For the decade I'd worked at the LSJML, the director of the medico-legal section had arrived at seven and stayed long after his staff clocked out. The old man was as dependable as a Timex watch.

He was also an enigma. LaManche took three weeks off each July, one week during the Christmas holidays. During these breaks, he called in to work from home each day. He did not travel, camp, garden, fish, or golf. He had no hobbies, to anyone's knowledge. Though queried, LaManche politely refused to discuss his vacations. Friends and colleagues had quit asking.

My office is last in the row of six, directly across

from the anthropology lab. This door requires a key.

A mountain of paper covered my desk. Ignoring it, I deposited my computer and case, grabbed my mug, and set off for the staff lounge.

As expected, LaManche's was the only other door open. I poked my head in on the way back.

LaManche looked up, half-moon glasses on the end of his nose. Long nose. Long ears. Long face, with long, vertical creases. Mr. Ed in reading specs.

"Temperance." Only LaManche used my full name. In his proper, formal French, the last syllable rhymed with *sconce*. "*Comment ça va?*"

I assured him I was well.

"Please, come in." He flapped a huge, freckled hand at two chairs opposite his desk. "Sit down."

"Thanks." I balanced my coffee on the armrest.

"How was Guatemala?"

How do you summarize Chupan Ya?

"Difficult."

"On many levels."

"Yes."

"The Guatemalan police were eager to have you."

"Not everyone shared that enthusiasm."

"Oh?"

"How much do you want to know?"

He removed the half-moons, tossed them onto the desktop and leaned back.

I told him about the Paraíso investigation, and about Díaz's efforts to block my participation.

"Yet this man did not interfere with your participation in the Claudia de la Alda case?"

"Never saw him."

"Are there any suspects in that murder?"

I shook my head.

"The ambassador's daughter and her friend are here, so only one young woman remains missing?"

"Patricia Eduardo."

"And the septic tank victim."

"Yes. Though that could be Patricia."

Embarrassment must have shown on my face.

"You had no power to stop this Díaz."

"I could have done a more thorough exam while I had the chance."

We were silent for a moment.

"But I do have a couple of ideas."

I told him about the cat hair sample.

"What do you hope to accomplish?"

"A profile might prove useful if a suspect is found."

"Yes." Noncommittal.

"Dog hair nailed Wayne Williams for the Atlanta child murders."

"Don't be defensive, Temperance. I am agreeing with you."

I swirled my coffee.

"It's probably a dead end."

"But if Monsieur Gagné is willing to profile the hair, why not?"

I told him my plans for the CT scans.

"That sounds more promising."

I hoped so.

"Did you find the two requests I left on your desk?"

LaManche referred to the *Demande d'Expertise en Anthropologie*, the form I receive as entrée into every case. Filled out by the requesting pathologist, it specifies the type of exam required, lists the personnel involved, and provides a brief overview of facts.

"The skull may not be human. In any case, it does not appear to be a recent death. The torso is another story. Please begin with that."

"Any possibles?"

"Robert Clément is a small-time drug dealer in western Quebec who recently branched out on his own."

"Without paying kickback to the Angels."

LaManche nodded. "Can't allow that."

"Bad for business."

"Clément came to Montreal in early May and vanished shortly thereafter. He was reported missing ten days ago."

I raised my eyebrows. Bikers normally shunned the attention of law enforcement.

"An anonymous female caller."

"I'll get to it right away."

Back in my office, I phoned Susanne Jean. She was not in, so I left a message.

Next I took the Paraíso sample to the DNA section. Gagné listened to my request, absently clicking a ballpoint pen.

"Intriguing question."

"Yes."

"Never done a cat."

"Could be a place to make your name."

"King of the Feline Double Helix."

"Open niche."

"Could call it Project Felix Helix." The name of the cartoon cat sounded strange in French.

Gagné reached for Minos's plastic container. "Shall I hold back a subsample?"

"Run everything. The Guatemalan lab has more."

"Mind if I play around a bit, test a few techniques?"

"Knock yourself out."

We signed evidence transfer forms, and I hurried back to my office.

Before facing the head and torso, I spent several minutes sifting through the mound on my blotter. I located LaManche's request sheets, fished out the pink telephone slips, and shoved the rest aside. I was hoping for some sort of message from Ryan. *Bienvenue*. Welcome back. Glad you're here. There'd been nothing at home.

Detectives. Students. Journalists. One prosecutor had phoned four times.

Zip from Ryan.

Great. Ryan had his sources. I had no doubt Sherlock knew I was back.

The headache swirled behind my right eye.

Giving up on the desk, I grabbed the *Demande d'Expertise* forms, slipped into a lab coat, and headed for the door. I was halfway there when my phone rang.

It was Dominique Specter.

"*Il fait chaud.*"

"It's very hot," I agreed, scanning one of LaManche's forms.

"They say we may set a record today."

"Yes," I said absently. The skull had been found in a trunk. LaManche noted badly chipped teeth, and a cord laced through the tongue.

"It always seems so much hotter in the city. I do hope you have air-conditioning."

"Yes," I answered, my mind on something more macabre than the weather.

"You are busy?"

"I've been away almost three weeks."

"Of course. I do apologize for intruding on your time." She paused, indicating appropriate contrition. "We can see Chantale at one o'clock."

"Where is she?"

"At a police station on Guy near boulevard René Lévesque."

Op South. It was just blocks from my condo.

"Shall we pick you up?"

"I'll meet you there."

I'd hardly replaced the receiver when the phone rang again. It was Susanne Jean. She would be with Volvo engineers all morning, had a lunch meeting at Bombardier, but could see me in the afternoon. We agreed to meet at three.

Crossing to the lab, I prepared folders for each case, and quickly scanned the torso request. Adult male. Arms, legs, and head missing. Advanced state of decomposition. Discovered in a culvert at

Lac des Deux-Montagnes. Coroner: Leo Henry. Pathologist: Pierre LaManche. Investigating officer: Lieutenant-détective Andrew Ryan, Sûreté du Québec.

Well, well.

The remains were downstairs, so I took the secure elevator, swiped my card, and punched the lowest of the three buttons: LSJML. Coroner. Morgue.

In the basement, I entered another restricted area. On the left, doors opened into autopsy rooms, three containing single tables, the largest containing two.

Through the small window in the door of the central suite, I spotted a woman in surgical scrubs. She had long, curly hair, secured with a barrette at the back of her head. Pretty and thirty-something, with a quick smile and 36Ds, Lisa was a perennial favorite with the homicide detectives.

She was a perennial favorite with me for preferring to speak English.

Hearing the door, she turned and did that.

"Good morning. I thought you were in Guatemala."

"I'll be going back down."

"R and R?"

"Not exactly. I'd like to look at LaManche's torso."

She pulled a face.

"He's sixty-four, Dr. Brennan."

"Everyone's a comedian."

"Morgue number?"

I read it aloud from the request form.

"Room four?"

"Please."

She disappeared through double doors. Beyond lay one of five morgue bays, each divided into fourteen refrigerated compartments secured by stainless steel doors. Small white cards announced the presence of occupants. Red stickers warned of HIV-positive status. The morgue number would tell Lisa behind which door the torso lay.

I proceeded to suite four, a room specially outfitted for extra ventilation. The room for floaters and bloaters. The room for crispers. The room in which I usually worked.

I'd barely gloved and masked when Lisa rolled a gurney through swinging doors identical to those in the central suite. When I unzipped the body bag, a nauseating odor filled the air.

"I think he's done."

"And then some."

Lisa and I slid the torso onto the table. Though swollen and disfigured, the genitals were intact.

"It's a boy." Lisa Lavigne, obstetrical nurse.

"Unquestionably."

I made notes while Lisa retrieved the X rays ordered by LaManche. They revealed vertebral arthritis, and three to four inches of bone in each of the severed limbs.

Using a scalpel, I removed the soft tissue overlying the breastbone, and Lisa revved up a Stryker saw to buzz through the sternal ends of the third, fourth, and fifth ribs. We did the same for the pelvis, dissecting out then cutting free the frontal portions where the two halves meet along the midline.

All six ribs and the pubic symphyses showed porosity and lots of erratic bone. This guy looked like he was up there in years.

Sex was indicated by the genitalia. The rib ends and symphyses would allow me to estimate the man's age. Ancestry would be a tough call.

Skin color is meaningless, since a body can darken, blanch, or colorize, depending upon postmortem conditions. This gentleman had chosen a camouflage motif: mottled brown and green. I could take a few postcranial measurements, but with no head or limbs, racial assessment would be almost impossible.

Next, I detached the fifth cervical vertebra, the most superior of those remaining in the neck. I retracted soupy flesh from what was left of the arm and leg stumps, and Lisa cut a sample from the severed end of each humerus and femur.

A quick survey showed significant chipping, and deep L-shaped striations across every cut surface. I suspected I had a chain saw case.

Thanking Lisa, I took the samples to the twelfth floor and turned them over to the lab technician. Denis would soak the bones, then slowly tease off the remaining flesh and cartilage. In days I would have viewable specimens.

A McGill clock sits on my office windowsill, presented in appreciation for a guest lecture to the alumni association. Beside the clock is a framed snapshot of Katy and me, taken one summer at the Outer Banks. Entering the office my eyes fell on the photo. I felt the usual pain, followed by a rush of love so intense it hurt.

For the millionth time, I pondered why the photo triggered such emotion. Loneliness for my daughter? Guilt over being so often away? Grief for the friend with whose corpse it had lain?

I recalled finding the photo in my friend's grave, remembered the terror, the burning rage. I pictured her killer, wondered if he thought of me during his long prison days and nights.

Why did I keep the photo?

No explanation.

Why here?

I didn't have a clue.

Or did I? Didn't I understand, at some sub-conscious level? Amid the numbing madness of murder, mutilation, and self-destruction, the cracked and faded snapshot reminded me that I had feelings. It triggered emotions.

Year after year, the photo remained on my windowsill.

I shifted my gaze to the McGill clock. Twelve forty-five. I had to hurry.

16

Outside the SQ, the air felt heavy and humid. A breeze off the St. Lawrence was providing only small relief. The brewery stench had dissipated, but the smell of the river was now strong. As I walked to the car a seagull screeched overhead, protesting or celebrating the premature tickle of summer.

Policing is complicated in Quebec. The SQ is responsible for all parts of the province not under the jurisdiction of municipal forces, of which there are many in the Montreal suburbs. The island itself is protected by the Police de la Communauté Urbaine de Montréal, or CUM.

The CUM is divided into four sections: Operations North, South, East, and West. Not creative, but geographically correct. Each section has a headquarters housing investigative, intervention, and analysis divisions. Each also hosts a detention center.

Suspects arrested for crimes other than murder and sexual assault await arraignment at one of these four sectional jails. For shoplifting at the MusiGo store in Le Faubourg on rue Ste-Catherine, Chantale Specter and Lucy Gerardi were taken to Op South.

Op South, which includes my neighborhood, is as varied as a chunk of urban geography can be. Though predominantly French and English, it is also Greek, Italian, Lebanese, Chinese, Spanish, Parsi, and a dozen other dialects. It is McGill University and Wanda's strip club, the Sun Life Building and Hurley's Pub, the Cathédrale Marie-Reine-du-Monde and the Crescent Street condom shop.

Op South is home to separatists and federalists, to drug dealers and bankers, to wealthy widows and penniless students. It is a playground for hockey fans and for singles looking to mingle, a workplace for suburban commuters, a bedroom for vagrants who drink from brown bags and sleep on the walks. Over the years I've been involved in numerous murder investigations originating within its borders.

Reversing my morning route, I headed west through the tunnel, took the Atwater exit, shot north on St-Marc, turned right on Ste-Catherine, right again on Guy. At one point I was meters from home, wishing I could make that cutoff instead of continuing to my scheduled rendezvous.

As I drove, I thought about the parents of Chantale and Lucy. Señor Gerardi, arrogant and

219

overbearing. His cowed wife. Mrs. Specter, with her colorized eyes and painted nails. The absent Mr. Specter. They were the fortunate ones. Their daughters were alive.

I imagined Señora Eduardo, still frantic, wondering what had befallen Patricia. I envisioned the De la Aldas, despondent over Claudia's death, perhaps burdened with guilt that they couldn't prevent it.

I pulled into the lot and parked between two cruisers. Claude was leaning against the quarter panel of the Specter Mercedes, arms and ankles crossed. He nodded as I passed.

Entering the station at the main door, I stepped to the counter, showed ID, and explained the purpose of my visit. The guard studied the photo, checked me for a match, then ran her finger down a list. Satisfied, she looked back up.

"The lawyer and the mother have gone ahead. Leave your things."

I slipped my purse from my shoulder and handed it across the counter. The guard secured it in a locker, scribbled something in a ledger, and turned it toward me.

As I entered the time and my name, she picked up a phone and spoke a few words. In moments a second guard appeared through a green metal door to my left. Guard number two swept me with a handheld metal detector, indicated that I should follow. Our movements were tracked by overhead cameras as he led me down a fluorescent-lit corridor.

The drunk tank lay straight ahead, its occupants lounging, sleeping, or clinging to the bars. Beyond the tank, another green metal door. Beyond the door, the cell block. Across from the tank, a counter. Behind the counter, a wooden grid, hat-check station for incoming prisoners. Standard jailhouse design.

We passed several doors marked ENTREVUE DÉTENU. From previous visits I knew that each opened into a tiny cubicle with wall phone, bolted stool, counter, and window looking into a mirror-image visitor cubicle. Conversations took place across plateglass and phone line.

Conversations with detainees who were not ambassadorial offspring.

Bypassing the prisoner interview rooms, the guard stopped at a door marked ENTREVUE AVOCAT and gestured me to enter. I'd never been to the lawyers' side, and wondered what to expect. Red leather chairs? Brandy snifters? Prints of people playing golf in Scotland?

Though larger, the room was as stark as those allotted to prisoners' girlfriends and families. Aside from a phone, a metal table and chairs were the only furnishings.

Around the table sat Mrs. Specter, her daughter, and a man I assumed to be the family lawyer. He was tall, with a girth almost as great as his height. A fringe of gray hair ringed his head and curled up the collar of his two-K suit. His face and crown were high-gloss pink.

Mrs. Specter had switched to her summer color

chart. She wore an ecru linen suit, off-white panty hose, and open-toed pumps. A gold band studded with delicate seed pearls held back the copper curls. Seeing me, she gave a taut, flickery smile, then her face receded behind its perfect Estée Lauder mask.

"Dr. Brennan, I would like you to meet Ihor Lywyckij," she said.

Lywyckij half rose and extended a hand. The man's face, once muscular, had been softened by years of rich food and liquor. I smiled into it as we shook. His meaty grip registered a four.

"Tempe Brennan."

"Delighted."

"Mr. Lywyckij will be representing Chantale."

"Ooh, yeah. Don't send me to the big house." Chantale's voice oozed sarcasm.

I turned to her. The ambassador's daughter sat with legs splayed, eyes down, hands jammed into the pockets of a sleeveless denim jacket.

"You must be Chantale."

"No. I'm Snow Fucking White."

"Chantale!"

Mrs. Specter laid a hand on her daughter's head. Chantale shrugged it off.

"This is bullshit. I'm innocent."

Chantale looked as innocent as the Boston Strangler. The blonde hair was now shoe-polish black. Below the jacket she wore a pink lace bustier. A black Spandex miniskirt, black tights, black engineer boots, and black makeup completed the ensemble.

I took a chair opposite the wrongly accused.

"The security guard found five CDs in your backpack, Miss Specter." Lywyckij.

"Fuck you."

"Chantale!" This time Mrs. Specter's hand went to her own forehead.

"I'm here to help you, miss. I can't do that if you fight me." Lywyckij sounded like Mr. Rogers.

"You're here to send me to some fucking concentration camp."

When Chantale looked up, I felt as if I was gazing into pure hatred.

"And what the hell's she doing here?" She jerked an elbow in my direction.

Mrs. Specter jumped in before I could answer.

"We're all concerned, darling. If you're having a problem with drugs, we want to find the best solution for you. Dr. Brennan might be able to help with that."

"You want to lock me away somewhere so I won't embarrass you." She kicked at a table leg, and the blazing eyes went back to her boots.

"Chant—"

Lywyckij placed a hand on Mrs. Specter's shoulder, raised his other to quiet her.

"What is it you want, Chantale?"

"I want to get out of here."

"I will arrange that."

"You will?" For the first time her voice seemed to match her age.

"You have no prior convictions in Canada, and shoplifting is a minor offense. Given the circumstances, I'm sure I can persuade the judge to release you into your mother's care if you promise to abide by his, and *her*, conditions."

Chantale said nothing.

"Do you understand what that means?"

No response.

"If you disobey your mother, you'll be in violation."

Another chop to the table leg.

"Do you understand, Chantale?"

"Yeah, yeah."

"Can you comply with the conditions that will be imposed?"

"I'm not a fucking moron."

Mrs. Specter flinched but held her tongue.

"What about Lucy?"

Lywyckij lowered his palm and brushed nonexistent dust from the tabletop.

"Miss Gerardi's situation is more problematical. Your friend is here illegally. She has no papers permitting her to be in Canada. That issue will need to be addressed."

"I'm not going anywhere without Lucy."

"We will work something out."

Lywyckij laced his fingers. They looked like intertwined pink sausages.

For a few moments no one spoke. Chantale continued to whack the table leg.

"Now." Lywyckij leaned onto his forearms. "Perhaps we should talk about the drug problem."

Silence.

"Chantale, darling, you mus—"

Again Lywyckij hushed his client with a raised hand.

More silence. More table whacking.

I shifted my gaze between mother and daughter. It was like moving from *Glamour* to *Metal Edge*. Finally, another elbow in my direction.

"She some kind of social worker?"

"The lady is a friend of your moth—" Lywyckij began.

"I *asked* my mother."

"Dr. Brennan accompanied me from Guatemala City." Mrs. Specter's voice sounded small.

"She help you blow your nose on liftoff?"

I had promised myself I wouldn't let Chantale get under my skin, but by now I was fighting the urge to reach across the table and grab the little demon by the throat. The hell with kid gloves.

"I work with the police here."

Chantale didn't let that pass.

"What police?"

"All of them. And your street act won't impress anyone."

Chantale shrugged.

"Your lawyer is giving you good advice." I didn't attempt to pronounce the man's name.

"My *mother's* lawyer has the IQ of a turnip."

Lywyckij's face darkened until it looked like a large, ripe plum.

"You're riding for a fall, Chantale," I said.

"Yeah, well, it's my ticket."

"I must have full knowledge of—" Lywyckij began.

Chantale cut him off again.

"What do you mean, 'work with the police'?" My vague allusion hadn't escaped her. The ambassador's daughter wasn't stupid.

"I'm with the medico-legal lab," I said.

"The coroner?"

"That works."

"They do stiffs in G City?"

"I was invited into a murder investigation down there."

I debated leaving it at that, decided on a dose of reality.

"Both victims were women your age."

At last the vampire eyes met mine.

"Claudia de la Alda," I said.

I watched for signs of recognition. Nothing.

"Her home was not far from_yours."

"Ain't coincidence grand."

"Claudia worked at the Ixchel Museum."

Another shrug.

"The second victim hasn't been identified. We found her in a septic tank in Zone One."

"Rough neighborhood."

Chantale and I were in a stare-off now, testing wills.

"Let's try another name," I said.

"Tinkerbell?"

"Patricia Eduardo."

Corneal hardball. Her eyes didn't waver.

"Patricia worked at the Hospital Centro Médico."

"Bedpan bingo. Not my game."

"She's been missing since last October."

"People take off."

"They do."

Whack. The table jumped.

"Your name came up in the investigation."

"No way," she snorted.

Whack.

"Like, why?"

"Too many grand coincidences."

"Is this some kind of joke?"

Chantale's eyes flicked to Lywyckij. He turned his palms up. They came back to me.

"This is bullshit."

"The Guatemalan police don't think so. They want information."

"I don't care if they want a cure for the clap. I don't know what you're talking about." She was staring at me with high beams.

"You're the same age, lived blocks apart, hung out in the same neighborhoods. They find one link, one ladies' room where you and Claudia de la Alda both took a pee, they can have you hauled back down there and put through a grinder."

Not true, of course, and Lywyckij knew it. The lawyer said nothing.

"There's no way you can force me to go back to Guatemala." Chantale's voice sounded a little less confident.

"You're seventeen. That makes you a minor."

"We won't let that happen." Lywyckij jumped aboard as Nice Cop.

"You may have no choice." I continued as Mean Cop.

Chantale wasn't buying the act. She pulled her hands from her pockets and held them up, wrists pressed together.

"O.K. It was me. I killed them. And I'm dealing heroin at the junior high."

"No one is accusing you of murder," I said.

"I know. It's a reality bite for a wayward teen." She shot forward, widened her eyes, and waggled her head like a dashboard dog. "Bad things happen to bad girls."

"Something like that," I replied evenly. "You know, of course, that nothing will prevent Lucy's return to Guatemala."

Chantale stood so suddenly her chair crashed to the floor.

Mrs. Specter's hand flew to her chest.

The guard shot through the door, hand on the butt of his gun. "Everything all right?"

Lywyckij lumbered to his feet. "We're finished." He turned to Chantale. "Your mother has brought something for you to wear when you appear before the judge."

Chantale rolled her eyes. Globs of mascara clung to the lashes, like raindrops on a spiderweb.

"We should have you out of here in two or three hours," he continued. "We will deal with the drug issue later."

When the guard had escorted Chantale from the room, Lywyckij turned to Mrs. Specter.

"Do you think you can control her?"

"Of course."

"She might take off."

"These dreadful surroundings make Chantale defensive. She'll be fine once she's home with her father and me."

I could see Lywyckij had his doubts. I definitely had mine.

"When is the ambassador arriving?"

"Just as soon as he can." The plastic smile slipped into place.

Lyrics popped into my head. A song about a handy smile. We'd sung it in Brownies when I was eight years old.

I have something in my pocket that belongs across my face
I keep it very close to me in a most convenient place . . .

"What of Miss Gerardi?" Lywyckij's question snapped me back.

"What of her?" A return question from the ambassador's wife, not indicating great concern.

"Will I be representing her?"

"Chantale's difficulties probably stem from that girl's influence. Obtaining documents. Hitch-hiking with strangers. Crossing the continent on buses. My daughter would never do those things on her own."

"I'm not so sure," I said.

The emerald eyes swung to me, surprised.

"How could you know such a thing?"

"Call it gut instinct." Not backing off.

A pause by Mrs. Specter, then a pronouncement.

"In any event, it is best that we not meddle in the affairs of Guatemalan citizens. Lucy's father is a wealthy man. He will take care of her."

That wealthy man was now here in Montreal and trailing a guard as we entered the corridor. His companion was outfitted like Lywyckij in expensive suit, Italian shoes, leather briefcase.

Gerardi turned as we passed, and his eyes met mine.

I'd empathized with the little girl at the schoolyard fence. That reaction was nothing compared with the pity I now felt for Lucy Gerardi. Whatever had brought her to Canada was not about to be forgiven.

17

Forty minutes later I was passing between shoulder-high hedges on a walkway leading to double glass doors. A logo was centered in each pane, with company information printed below. French on top, English underneath in smaller font. Very québécois.

It had taken thirty minutes to drive, another thirty to find the address. The RP Corporation was one of a half dozen enterprises housed in two-story concrete boxes in a light-industrial park in St-Hubert. Each structure was gray, but expressed its individuality with a painted stripe circling the building like a gift ribbon. RP's bow was red.

The lobby had the glossiest floor I've ever tread. I crossed it to an office to the left of the main entrance. When I peeked in, an Asian woman greeted me in French. She had shiny black hair cut blunt at the ears and straight across her forehead. Her broad cheekbones reminded me of Chantale Specter, which reminded me of the girl in the septic tank. I felt the familiar cringe of self-blame.

"*Je m'appelle Tempe Brennan,*" I said.

Hearing my accent, she switched to English.

"How may I help you?"

"I have a three o'clock appointment with Susanne Jean."

"Please have a seat. It won't be a moment." She picked up and spoke into a receiver.

In less than a minute Susanne appeared and crooked a finger at me. She was about my weight, but stood a full head taller. Her skin was eggplant, her hair plaited into a trellis pattern for three inches around her face. In back it hung in long, black cornrows, bundled together with a tangerine binder. As usual, Susanne looked more like a fashion model than an industrial engineer.

I followed her back into the lobby, then through a second set of double doors opposite the main entrance. We crossed a room filled with machines. Several white-coated workers adjusted dials, studied monitors, or stood watching the technology do whatever it did. The air was packed with muted whirs, hums, and clicks.

Susanne's office was as sleek as the rest of the plant, with bare white walls and straight teak lines. A single watercolor hung behind her desk. One orchid in a crystal bud vase. One detached petal. One perfect water droplet.

Susanne liked things clean. Like me, she held

title to a messy past. Like me she'd done serious tidying up.

While my drug of choice had been alcohol, Susanne's was coke. Though neither of us belonged to the organization, we'd met through a mutual friend who was an AA zealot. That was six years ago. We'd kept in touch, periodically attending a meeting with our common link, or getting together on our own for dinner or tennis. I knew little about her world, she less about mine, but somehow we clicked.

Susanne lowered herself onto one end of an apricot couch, and crossed legs that were at least twelve yards long. I took the other end.

"What do you do for Bombardier?" I asked.

"We're prototyping plastic parts."

"Volvo?"

"Metal bearings."

Manufacturing is as mysterious to me as the Okeefenokee. Raw materials go in. Weedwhackers, Q-tips, or Buicks come out. What happens in between, I haven't a clue.

"I know you take CAD data and create solid objects, but I've never really known what kinds of objects," I said.

"Functional plastic and metal parts, casting patterns, and durable metal mold inserts."

"Oh."

"Did you bring the CT scans?"

I handed her Fereira's envelope. She withdrew the contents and began going through the films, holding them up as Fereira had done. Now and then a film bent, making a sound like distant thunder.

"This should be fun."

"Without getting technical, what will you do?"

"We'll make an STL file of your 3-D CAD data, then—"

"STL?"

"Stereolithography. Then we'll enter the STL file into our system."

"One of those machines out there?"

"Right. The machine will spread a thin layer of powdered material across a build platform. Using data from the STL file, a CO_2 laser will draw a cross-section of the object, in your case a skull, on the layer of powder, then sinter—"

"Sinter?"

"Selectively heat and fuse it. That will create a solid mass representing one cross-section of the skull. The system will spread and sinter, layer after layer, until the skull is complete."

"That's it?"

"Pretty much. When the skull is done, we'll take it out of the build chamber and blow away any loose powder. You'll be able to use it as is, or it can be sanded, annealed, coated, or painted."

I was right. Stuff in. Stuff out. In this case what would go in was information taken from Fereira's CT scan. What would come out was a cast of the Paraíso skull. I hoped.

"The technology's called SLS, Selective Laser Sintering."

"Besides metal bearings and plastic parts, what else do you make?"

"Pump impellers, electrical connectors, halogen lamp housings, automotive turbocharger housing units, brake fluid reservoir parts—"

"O-rings for the Orion nebula."

We both laughed.

"How long will it take?"

She shrugged. "Two, maybe three hours to convert the CT scan to an STL file, maybe a day to cast the skull. How about late Monday?"

"Fantastic."

"You look shocked."

I was. "I thought you'd say a week or two."

"This project sounds more interesting than hearing aid housings."

"And the Guatemalan police will be eternally grateful."

"Any cute ones down there?"

I pictured Galiano's lopsided face.

"There is one."

"What about the *caballero* you're seeing up here?"

I pictured Ryan.

"Pecos Bill's been keeping a low profile."

"Anyway, I'll do your skull myself." She held up a long, slender finger. "On one condition."

"Dinner and drinks on me." I laughed. "Tomorrow night?"

"Sounds good. Be warned, girlfriend. I'm gonna hit you up for the priciest mineral water on the menu."

★

I entered my lobby to the sight of the *caballero* supine on its leather love seat, head propped on one arm, lower legs dangling over the other.

"How did you get in here?"

"It's O.K. I'm a cop."

I set down my cases and grocery bags.

"All right. Let's go with the why."

"It's hot outside."

I waited.

Ryan sat up and swung his size twelves to the floor.

"These things aren't designed for beings over six foot two."

"It's a decorative piece."

"Would be hell for watching the Stanley Cup finals."

"It's not intended for lounging."

"What's it good for?"

"Collecting mislabeled mail, drugstore circulars, and back issues of the newspaper."

"This lobby isn't exactly visitor friendly." Ryan rubbed the back of his neck.

"There are the potted palms."

He gave me his forty-something schoolboy grin. "Missed you."

"I got in yesterday."

"I've been on a stakeout."

"Oh?"

"Drummondville."

Through the door I heard muted beeps and engine revs. Friday evening rush hour was winding down.

"Owner of a dive called Les Deux Originals decided to expand into the small-arms business. Guess the two moose made him nervous."

"You never told me you speak Spanish."

"What?"

"Never mind."

I picked up my parcels.

"It's been a long day, Ryan."

"How about dinner tomorrow night?"

"I've made plans."

"Change them."

"That would be rude."

"How about dinner tonight?"

"I just bought shrimp and veggies."

"I know a scampi recipe that's illegal in four Italian cities."

I'd bought enough food for two. Actually, I'd bought enough for twelve. I never again wanted a cupboard as bare as the one I'd faced last night.

Ryan stood, spread his hands palms out, and broke into another grin. He was tanned from hours of outdoor surveillance, and the tawny skin made his eyes appear more vivid than usual, a blue beyond the blue human cells can produce.

Normally, with time, even the most stunning beauty grows familiar. It's like watching Olympic figure skating. We grow jaded and forget how extraordinary the grace and beauty truly are. Such was the case with Susanne. I was aware of her elegance, but it no longer surprised me when she entered a room.

Not so with Ryan. His good looks still startled me on a regular basis.

And he knew it.

"Which ones?" I asked.

He looked puzzled.

"Which cities?"

"Turin, Milan, Sienna, and Florence."

"You've made this scampi?"

"I've read about it."

"This better be good."

Ryan went for beer while I changed. Then he grilled the shrimp and I mixed a salad.

During dinner we talked around things, maintaining a safe level of banality. Afterward, we cleared the table and took coffee outside to the patio.

"That really was good," I said for the second time.

Lights were blinking on in windows across the courtyard.

"Have I ever misled you?"

"Why is this repast banned under Tuscan law?"

He shrugged. "Maybe I exaggerated a little."

"I see."

"It's actually a misdemeanor."

Beyond the courtyard, the Friday night party was cranking up. Auto horns. Emergency sirens. Weekend revelers, in from their split-levels in Dorval and Pointe Claire. Pounding hip-hop, swelling then receding as cars passed by.

Ryan lit a cigarette.

"How goes Chupan Ya?"

"You remembered the name."

"The place is important to you."

"Yes."

"It must be gut-wrenching."

"It is."

"Tell me about it."

It was like speaking of some parallel universe where rotting bodies took center stage in a morality play too hideous for words. Headless mothers. Massacred infants. An old woman who lived because she had beans to sell.

Ryan listened, the periwinkle eyes rarely leaving my face. His questions were few, always germane. He did not rush or divert, allowed me to unload in my own way.

And he listened.

And I realized a truth.

Andrew Ryan is one of those rare men able to make you feel, rightly or wrongly, that yours are the only thoughts in the galaxy that interest him.

It is the most appealing trait a man can have.

And it was not going unnoticed by my libido, which seemed to be clocking a lot of overtime lately.

"More coffee?" I asked.

"Thanks."

I went to the kitchen.

Maybe having Ryan drop by wasn't such a bad thing. Maybe I'd been too harsh on the *caballero*. Maybe I should have used a little makeup.

I did a quick detour to the bathroom, ran a brush through my hair, dabbed on blusher, decided against mascara. Better lashless than hurry-up smudgy.

When I handed Ryan his mug, he reached up and touched my freshly rouged cheek. My skin burned as it had with Galiano.

Maybe it was a virus.

Ryan winked.

I looked at our shadows blended on the brick, my heart thumping on all cylinders.

Maybe it wasn't a virus.

As I resumed my seat, Ryan asked why I'd returned to Montreal.

Back to reality.

I considered what I was at liberty to say about the Paraíso case. I'd already discussed the skeleton with Ryan, but both Galiano and Mrs. Specter had requested confidentiality about the ambassadorial angle.

I decided to tell all, but refer to the Specters only as "a Quebec family."

Again, Ryan listened without interrupting. The skeleton. The four missing women, then three, then one. The cat hair. The skull cast. When I finished, there was dead silence for a full minute before he spoke.

"They dragged these girls to lockup just for pinching CDs?"

"Apparently one of them got pretty unpleasant."

"Unpleasant?"

"Resisting, screaming obscenities, spitting." Mrs. Specter had shared that little tidbit during one of our airport waits.

"Bad move. What I don't get is why Chantale Specter was held for any time at all in the Op South jail."

"You *know* about the ambassador?" I couldn't believe it. I was being so careful to respect the Specters' privacy, and Super Sleuth already had a pocketful of notes.

"Diplomats enjoy immunity," he went on.

"Diplomatic immunity," I snapped.

Closing my eyes, I fought back the irritation. Ryan had let me ramble on, knowing he already knew. And *why* did he know about the Specters?

"Jesus, Ryan. Is there any case I'm capable of working without your input?"

Ryan was intent on his line of thinking.

"Diplomatic immunity doesn't apply in your home country. Why wasn't Chantale out immediately?"

"Maybe she couldn't bear to give back the orange jumpsuit. How long have you known about this?"

"She should have been riding in a limo in less than an hour."

"Chantale gave a false name. The cops had no idea who she was. How long have you known about the Specter connection?"

Again he ignored my question.

"Who busted her cover?"

"Chantale used her allotted phone call to contact a friend." Mrs. Specter had told me that, too.

"And the playmate contacted Mommy."

I drew a deep, dramatic breath.

"Yes."

"And the men in pinstripes decided to let naughty Chantale cool her heels while Mommy burned leather getting to Quebec."

"Something like that."

Bootfalls echoed off the exterior face of the courtyard wall. A car engine turned over in a parking lot across the alley.

"A couple of hours."

"What?" I snapped again.

"I've known for a couple of hours. Galiano filled me in this afternoon." Ryan smiled and gave a little shrug. "The old Bat never changes."

When irritated, I grow testy, spit verbal missiles. When angry, red-laser-through-the-brain angry, I go deadly still inside. My mind freezes, my voice flat-lines, and every response becomes glacial.

I had been the topic of a frat boy discussion. The anger switch tripped.

"You phoned Galiano?" Even.

"He called me."

"Did Detective Galiano have questions about my competence?"

"He had questions about the Specter family."

There was a moment of arctic silence. Ryan lit a cigarette.

"Did you discuss me in Spanish?"

"What?" My reference to the old days escaped him.

"Never mind."

Ryan drew deeply, blew smoke upward into the air.

"Galiano had news about a suspect." He said it matter-of-factly, as though reading the TV listings aloud.

"So he phoned someone with no involvement in the case."

"He wanted to know what I had on the Specters, and he tried to phone you."

"Really."

"He called your cell. That's what I came by to tell you."

"You're lying."

"Have you checked your messages recently?"

I hadn't.

Wordlessly, I went inside and dug the phone from my purse. Four missed calls. All from out of area. I hit the button for my voice mail. Two messages.

The first was from Ollie Nordstern. The reporter from hell had a few questions. Could I call him back? I hit delete.

The second was from Bat Galiano.

"Thought you'd like to know. Last night we arrested the scumbag who killed Claudia de la Alda."

18

Galiano didn't return my call until late Saturday morning. When we spoke, he was in the process of interrogating the scumbag in question.

"Who is he?"

"Miguel Angel Gutiérrez."

"Go on."

"Gutiérrez was getting in touch with his roots at the Kaminaljuyú ruins last night. Gramps, our friendly neighborhood snoop, took a personal interest in the excursion and phoned the station. Gutiérrez was nailed hoisting himself over the guardrail five yards up-slope from the De la Alda dump site."

"Coincidence?"

"Like OJ's glove. Gutiérrez works as a gardener. The De la Alda home is one of his regular jobs."

"No shit."

"No shit."

"What's he saying?"

"Not much. Right now he's talking to his priest."

"And?"

"I think the Fifth Commandment might come up. In the meantime, Hernández is out tossing his trailer."

"Any link to the Paraíso or to Patricia Eduardo?"

"None we're aware of. Anything on your end?"

I told him about the cat hair sample and the skull replication.

"Not bad, Brennan."

It was exactly what Ryan would say.

"Let me know what happens."

In the afternoon, I cleaned the condo and did laundry. Then I laced up my cross-trainers and went to the gym. As I pounded out three on the treadmill, two names kept cadence in my head.

Ryan and Galiano.

Galiano and Ryan.

My anger had diminished since the night before, when I'd ushered Ryan out with an icy good-bye. But it was still registering a six-point-oh.

Why?

Because he and his college compadre had discussed me as they might last Wednesday's bowling date.

Ryan and Galiano.

Galiano and Ryan.

Had they?

Of course they had.

Was I being paranoid?

Galiano and Ryan.

What had they said?

I remembered an incident with Ryan. On a boat. I was wearing a T-shirt, cutoffs, and no underwear.

Oh, God.

Galiano and Ryan.

Ryan and Galiano.

I ran until my lungs burned and my leg muscles trembled. By the time I hit the showers my anger had eased down out of the red zone.

That evening I had dinner with Susanne Jean at Le Petit Extra on rue Ontario. She listened to my story of the Hardy Boys, a smile tugging the corners of her mouth.

"How do you know their conversation wasn't strictly professional?"

"Female intuition."

The delicate eyebrows rose. "That's it?"

"The Men Are Pigs Theory."

"*That's* not sexist?"

"Of course it is. But I have little else to go on."

"Ease back, Tempe. You're being hyper-sensitive."

Deep down, I suspected that.

"Besides, from what you've said, they have nothing to compare."

"According to The Theory, they make it up."

She laughed her full, throaty laugh.

"Girlfriend, you are losing it."

"I know. How's the skull coming?"

Susanne had converted the CT scans, and would have the model ready by four on Monday.

As we parted, she pointed a long dark finger between my eyes.

"Sister. You need a good romp in the feathers."

"I've got no romping buddy."

"Sounds like you've got one too many."

"Hm."

"How 'bout a BOB?"

"O.K., I'll bite. What's a BOB?"

"Battery Operated Boyfriend."

Susanne often presented an interesting take on life.

On Sunday, I received a call from Mateo Reyes. The FAFG leader reported good progress with the Chupan Ya victims. Only nine skeletons remained unidentified. I told him the Specter situation was under control, and that I would be returning as soon as I wrapped up my Montreal cases.

Mateo passed on an appeal from Ollie Nordstern. The reporter had been phoning daily, urgently wanted to speak with me. I was non-committal.

Mateo had good news about Molly Carraway. The archaeologist had been released from the hospital and was returning with her father to Minnesota. A full recovery was expected.

Mateo also had sad news. Señora Ch'i'p had died in her sleep on Friday night. The Chupan Ya granny was sixty-one.

"You know what I think?" Mateo's voice was unusually tight.

"What's that?"

"I think that old lady forced herself to keep breathing just long enough to see proper burial for her babies."

I agreed.

Disconnecting, I felt a warm trickle slide down each cheek.

"*Vaya con Dios, Señora Ch'i'p.*"

I backhanded a tear.

"We'll take it from here."

The torso bones were still soaking when I got to the lab on Monday. The morning meeting was surprisingly brief, the post-weekend lineup featuring only three cases: a stabbing in Laval; a tractor accident near St-Athanase; a suicide in Verdun.

I'd just placed the mummified head on my worktable when I heard a tap on the window. Ryan smiled at me from the corridor.

I pointed at the head and waved him away.

He tapped again. I ignored him.

He tapped a third time, harder. When I looked up, his badge was pressed to the glass.

Rolling my eyes, I got up and let him in.

"Feeling better?"

"I feel fine."

Ryan's gaze fell to the table.

"Jesus Christ, what happened to him?"

The thing *was* bizarre, measuring approximately six inches in diameter, with long dark hair and shriveled brown skin. The features looked like a bat imitating a human face. Pins projected from the lips, and frayed cording peeked from a hole in the tongue.

I positioned a magnifying glass so Ryan could see, moved it over the nose, cheeks, and jaws.

"What do you notice?"

"Tiny cuts."

"The skin was peeled back for removal of the muscles. The cheeks are probably stuffed with some sort of fabric."

I rotated the head.

"The base was damaged to extract the brain."

"So what the hell is it?"

"A Peruvian trophy skull."

Ryan looked at me like I'd just told him it was an alien star child.

"Most were made along the south coast between the first and sixth centuries A.D."

"A shrunken head?"

"Yes, Ryan. A shrunken head."

"How did it get from Peru to Canada?"

"Collectors love these things."

"Are they legal?"

"They've been illegal in the States since ninety-seven. I'm not sure about Canada."

"Have you ever seen one before?"

"I've looked at several fakes. Never a real one."

"This is genuine?"

"It looks authentic to me. And the dental chipping suggests the little guy's been kicking around awhile."

I laid the trophy skull on the table.

"Authentication will be up to an archaeologist. What is it you want?"

Ryan continued to study the head.

"Your thoughts on the torso."

He reached out and touched the hair, poked the cheek.

"Any septuagenarians missing upriver?"

"Oh, yeah?"

He looked up, wiped his hand on his jeans.

"I've only done a preliminary, but this guy's got a lot of miles on him."

"Probably not Clément?"

"Probably not."

I picked up my calipers, but Ryan made no move to leave.

"Is there something else?"

"Galiano asked me to have a little heart-to-heart with naughty Chantale. Save him a trip. He suggested you might like to tag along."

Tag along? A flicker of red.

Ryan pointed to the skull.

"Why the hole in the forehead?"

"Rope."

"I hate it when that happens to me."

I gave him the "spare me" face.

"The Specters are out of the picture for your septic tank case. Actually, with the Gutiérrez collar, it looks like the whole serial killer theory is sucking wind. But Galiano thought it couldn't hurt to talk to the little princess."

"Galiano phoned again?" Cool.

"This morning."

"Has Gutiérrez confessed?"

"Not yet, but Galiano's convinced he'll give it up."

"I'm glad he's keeping you informed."

"I'm here, he's there. I'm doing the interrogation as a professional courtesy."

"You're good at that."

"Yeah."

"God bless gonads."

"You're a scientist, Brennan. You look at bones. I'm a cop. I question people."

As I started to speak, Ryan's beeper sounded. He slipped it off his waistband and checked the readout.

"Gotta go. Look, you don't have to go on the Chantale visit. Galiano thought you'd like to be included."

"When is this little outing?"

"I should be back from Drummondville by six."

I shrugged. "Normally that's when I watch the Shopping Channel."

"Are you PMS, Brennan?"

"*What?*"

He feigned a self-defense maneuver with his hands.

"I'll pick you up around five forty-five."

"My heart's thumping."

"And Brennan." Ryan jerked a thumb at the table. "Take a cue from our Peruvian friend. Quit while you're a head."

★

I spent the rest of the day with our Peruvian friend. X rays verified that the skull was human, not dog or bird, the species typically used by creators of fakes. I took photographs, wrote my report, then contacted the chair of the Anthropology Department at McGill University. He promised to track down the proper expert.

At two, Robert Gagné stopped by my office to say that the profiles would be ready shortly. I was as shocked at his pace with the cat hair as I'd been with Susanne's with the cranial cast. Cops waited weeks for DNA results.

Gagné's response was identical to Susanne's. The project was out of the ordinary. It intrigued him. He'd run with it.

By three, I was on my way to St-Hubert.

By four-thirty, I was heading home, a replica of the Paraíso skull in a box on the seat beside me. The facial approximation was now up to me.

Traffic was heavy, and I moved ahead in starts and stops, alternately palming the gearshift and drumming my fingers on the steering wheel. Gradually the starts succumbed to the stops. On the Victoria Bridge, they gave out altogether, and I sat fixed in place, surrounded by a four-lane automotive showroom.

I'd been there ten minutes when my cell phone sounded. I reached for it, happy for the diversion.

It was Katy.

"Hey, Mom."

"Hi, sweetie. Where are you?"

"Charlotte. Classes are done for the year."

"Isn't this a late wrap-up?"

"I had to finish my methods class project."

Katy was a fifth-year undergraduate at the University of Virginia. Though bright, witty, attractive, and blonde, my daughter was uncertain what life was offering her, and had yet to settle on a game plan.

What *wasn't* life offering her? I agreed with my estranged husband on this one.

"What were you looking at?" I asked, shifting gears to ooze forward seventeen inches.

"The effects of Cheez Whiz on rat memory."

Katy's current major was psychology.

"And?"

"They love the stuff."

"Did you enroll for next term?"

"Yep."

"Home stretch?" Pete and I were bankrolling our daughter twelve semesters to allow her to discover the meaning of life.

"Yep."

"Are you at your dad's place?"

"Actually, I'm at yours."

"Oh?" Katy usually preferred her childhood home to my tiny townhouse.

"Boyd's with me. Hope that's O.K."

"Sure. Where's Birdie?"

I leapt forward two yards.

"On my lap. Your cat's not crazy about Boyd."

"No."

"He stays permanently fluffed."

"Is your dad out of town?"

253

"Yeah, but they're coming back today."

They?

"Oops."

"It's O.K."

"He's got a new girlfriend."

"That's nice."

"I think her bra size exceeds her IQ."

"She can't help that."

"She doesn't like dogs."

"She can help that."

"Where are you?"

"Montreal."

"Are you in a car?"

"Flashing along at the speed of light."

I was now rolling at twelve miles per hour.

"What are you doing?" she asked.

I told her.

"Why not use the real skull?"

I told her about Díaz and Lucas and the purloined skeleton.

"I had a sociology professor named Lucas. Richard Lucas."

"This one's a Hector."

I knew what was coming as soon as I said it. Katy adored one nursery rhyme the entire year she was four. She recited it now in a singsong voice.

Hector Protector was dressed all in green;
Hector Protector was sent to the queen . . .

"Hector dissector should be hung by his spleen," I cut in.

"That's bad."

"It's a first draft."

"Don't do a second. Poetry shouldn't be made to suffer because you're frustrated."

"Hector Protector is not Coleridge."

"When will you be back in Charlotte, Mom?"

"I'm not sure. I want to finish what I started in Guatemala."

"Good luck."

"Got a summer job yet?"

"I'm working on it."

"Good luck."

Gagné called as I was turning into my driveway.

"We've got a match."

His words made no sense.

"What are you talking about?"

I dived toward the underground garage.

"We're just bringing our mitochondrial technology online, so I decided to play around with that. Thought we might have better luck if the septic tank sample was badly degraded."

I depressed the button on my remote. The door rattled, rose. As I pulled into the garage, Gagné's voice grew distant, began cutting in and out.

"Two of your samples match."

"But I only gave you one."

"There were four samples in the package." I heard paper rustle. "Paraíso, Specter, Eduardo, Gerardi."

Minos must have misunderstood my request. When I'd asked for hair, I meant that taken from the septic tank jeans. He'd included samples from all four cats.

I could hardly get the question out.

"Which samples match, M. Gagné?"

Behind me, the garage door clicked, began chugging downward.

Gagné's answer was garbled. I strained to make out his words. My handset gave a series of beeps.

I was listening to silence.

19

Slinging my laptop and briefcase over my shoulders, I grabbed the package containing Susanne's cast and hurried to the elevator. The doors were barely open when I shot out.

And slammed into Andrew Ryan.

"Whoa, whoa. Where's the fire?"

As usual, my first reaction was irritation.

"Nice cliché."

"I do my best. What's in the box?"

I moved to circle him, but he stepped left, blocking my path. At that moment, a neighbor entered the lobby through the front door.

"*Bonjour.*" The old man touched cane to cap, nodded to Ryan, then to me.

"*Bonjour, Monsieur Gravel,*" I said.

M. Gravel shuffled to the mailboxes.

I stepped left. Ryan stepped right. Susanne's box filled the space between our chests.

I heard a mailbox open, shut, then a walking stick tap across marble.

"I have to make a phone call, Ryan."

"What's in the carton?"

"The head from the septic tank."

The walking stick stopped dead.

Ryan laid both hands on the box.

"Please, please don't do this," he pleaded in a loud, warbly voice.

M. Gravel inhaled so sharply it sounded like a backfire.

I glared at Ryan.

Ryan smiled at me, his back to my neighbor.

"Follow me," I said, lips barely moving.

Heading toward my hallway, I heard Ryan turn, and knew he was winking at M. Gravel. The irritation escalated.

Inside my condo, I set everything on the table and picked up the portable.

"Gagné just phoned with DNA results on feline hair I brought from Guatemala."

"It's Krazy Kat."

"He's found a match between two of the four samples."

"What four samples?"

I explained how Minos had packaged hair from the Specter, Eduardo, and Gerardi homes, along with some that I'd taken from the Paraíso jeans. Then I hit speakerphone and punched in the lab number.

"Which samples match?" Ryan asked.

When the receptionist answered, I asked for Gagné.

"That's what I'm anxious to know. The Eduardo cat's been ruled out."

"Why?"

"Persian."

"Poor Fluffy."

"Buttercup."

Gagné came on the line.

"Sorry," I said. "You caught me underground."

"You sound like you're still down there."

"I have you on speakerphone. Detective Ryan is with me."

"Ryan's on this?"

"All over it. Please repeat what you were saying."

"I was saying that I went with mitochondrial DNA. Three of the samples looked O.K., but the hairs in the packet marked 'Paraíso' had no root or sheath with an appropriate follicular tag to enable genomic DNA processing. You told me to test everything."

I had. But I'd meant Gagné could use the entire Paraíso sample, since the Guatemala forensics lab had retained hair for future testing. I had no idea Minos's package contained other samples.

"I could have looked for epithelial cells on the Paraíso shafts, but given the context I doubted I'd find much," Gagné went on.

"Cats have polymorphic regions in their mitochondrial DNA?" I asked.

"Just like humans. A feline geneticist at a cancer institute in the U.S. researches this stuff, has excellent stats on population variability."

Ryan was holding a finger to his head, mimicked pulling a trigger. Linus Pauling he's not.

"What was the match, M. Gagné?"

A paper rustled. I held my breath.

"The sample marked 'Paraíso' profiled like the sample marked 'Specter.'"

Ryan stopped blowing smoke from his fingertip and stared at the phone.

"Meaning they were consistent?"

"Meaning they were identical."

"Thank you."

I disconnected.

"You can holster your weapon."

Ryan dropped his gun pantomime and placed hands on hips.

"How can he be so sure it's a match?"

"It's his business to be sure."

"The hair's been in a friggin' septic tank." Ryan's tone oozed skepticism.

"Do you know anything about DNA?"

"What I don't know I have a feeling I'm about to learn." He raised a hand, palm out. "The five-minute version. Please."

"Do you know what a DNA molecule looks like?" I asked.

"A spiral staircase."

"Very good. Sugars and phosphates form the handrails, and bases form the steps. How can I bring this down to your level?"

Ryan opened his mouth to object, but I cut him off.

"Think of the bases as Legos that only come in

260

four colors. If there's a red Lego on one half of a step, there's always a blue Lego on the other. Green pairs with yellow."

"And not everyone has the same color pattern at a particular place."

"You're not as dumb as you look, Ryan. When multiple variations exist for a sequence of steps, it's called a polymorphism. When a position has extreme numbers of variants, maybe hundreds, it's called a hypervariable region."

"Like Manhattan."

"Did you want this in five minutes?"

Ryan held up both palms.

"Variations, or polymorphisms, can occur in the sequence of colors, or in the number of times those colors are repeated between any two specific steps. You with me?"

"A particular fragment can vary in pattern or length."

"The first technique that was adapted for forensic DNA analysis was called RFLP, Restriction Fragment Length Polymorphism. RFLP analysis determines variation in the length of a defined DNA fragment."

"Produces that thing that looks like a grocery store bar code."

"It's called an autoradiograph. Unfortunately, RFLP requires better-quality DNA than many crime scene samples provide. That's why PCR was such a breakthrough."

"Amplification."

"Exactly. Without going into details—"

"But I love it when you talk dirty." Ryan reached out and touched my nose. I brushed his hand away.

"Polymerase Chain Reaction is a technique for increasing the amount of DNA available for analysis. A defined sequence of Lego steps is copied millions of times."

"Genetic Xeroxing."

"Except that with each round the number of copies doubles, so the increase in DNA is geometric. The drawback to PCR analysis is that fewer variable regions have been identified, and each tends to show less variation."

"So you're able to use PCR with crummier DNA, but the power of discrimination is lower."

"Historically that's been the case."

"What's this mitochondrial stuff?"

"RFLP and PCR – and there are other procedures – use genomic DNA, which resides in the cell nucleus. Additional bits of genetic material are found in the mitochondria, small compartments in the cell where respiration takes place. The mitochondrial genome is smaller, slightly over sixteen thousand bases, and forms a circle, not a staircase. There are two regions on that circle that are highly variable."

"What's the advantage?"

"Mitochondrial DNA is present in hundreds to thousands of copies per cell, so it can be extracted from small or degraded samples where the genomic DNA is long gone. Researchers have found mitochondrial DNA in Egyptian mummies."

"I doubt your septic tank was built by pharaohs."

"I was trying to make this understandable."

I thought of a better example.

"Mitochondrial DNA was used to determine that skeletons recently exhumed in Russia were those of Czar Nicholas and his family."

"How?"

"Mitochondrial DNA is only passed on through maternal lines."

"The whole shooting match comes from Mommy?"

"Sorry to break that to you, Ryan."

"My gender knows grout."

"The researchers compared DNA from the Russian bones to DNA obtained from living relatives, specifically Britain's Prince Philip."

"Queen Elizabeth's hubby?"

"Prince Philip's maternal grandmother was Czarina Alexandra's sister, so Alexandra and her children, and Philip, inherited their mitochondrial DNA from the mother of both Alexandra and her sister."

"Back to the cats."

"Hair cells have no nuclei, so no genomic DNA. But mitochondrial DNA is present in hair shafts."

"Gagné referred to epithelial cells."

"Saliva, skin, buccal, vaginal. You might find saliva on cat hairs as a result of grooming – e-cells are also found in urine and feces. I appreciate Gagné's pessimism about e-cells in this case."

"Piss-poor chance of finding any."

"According to Gagné, the mitochondrial sequences from the Specter cat were identical to those from the septic tank hair."

"Meaning the Paraíso victim had contact with the Specter cat."

"Yep."

"And we know it wasn't Chantale in that tank."

"You're right, Ryan. Cops are good at this."

"The victim was someone who'd been to the Specter house, or at least been in contact with their cat."

"Before last Christmas."

He looked a question at me.

"That's when Guimauve did a dead man's float in the swimming pool."

Ryan thought a moment, then, "I think little Chantale knows more than she's letting on."

"Someone does," I agreed.

"Mrs. Specter?"

I shrugged.

Ryan and I locked eyes, each stuck on the same thought.

"I've never met the ambassador," I said.

"Where is he?"

"Discussing soybean yields in Mexico City."

"Odd, given his daughter's recent bust."

"Galiano said Specter delayed reporting Chantale's disappearance. Once the cops were brought in, he wasn't overly cooperative."

"Kitty puts things in a whole new light."

★

Lying just west of Centre-ville, Westmount flows down the mountain in a series of heavily shaded streets. Anathema to québécois separatists, the neighborhood is known for its high concentration of English speakers and its fierce federalist loyalty. Until the island of Montreal was reorganized, and many suburbs and outlying districts were incorporated under the Communauté Urbaine de Montréal umbrella, Westmount prided itself on its independence, low taxes, efficient management, and genteel good taste.

Westmount fought hard to prevent absorption into the new Super City. Upon losing, the citizenry drew their mink and cashmere coats about them, sniffed their affluent noses, and waited, confident that some resident lawyer would force a reversal on appeal.

They were still waiting.

Ryan exited the tunnel at Atwater, turned left on The Boulevard, turned right, and began climbing uphill. I watched the homes grow larger, imagined the expanding panorama of river and town as viewed from south-facing patios and sunrooms.

Westmount is like Hong Kong – the higher the elevation, the better the address. The Specter home was one of the largest in upper Westmount, a towering stone fortress, complete with turret, grille-work, and massive oak door. A cypress hedge prevented any view of the front of the property. That from the back must have been spectacular.

"Nice crib," said Ryan, sliding to the curb.

"Mrs. Specter referred to it as a 'little place.'"

"Arrogantly unpretentious. Very Westmount."

"Mrs. Specter is from Charlevoix."

Ryan thumbed the bell. Somewhere inside, chimes sounded.

"How much does an ambassador make?" he asked under his breath.

"Less than this, I'm sure. Ambassadors usually don't take the job for the money. They contribute money to get it."

We waited a full minute. Ryan rang again.

I was shocked when Mrs. Specter answered the door. Though she'd applied lipstick and rouge, her face was the color of hospital linen. The copper hair had been yanked to the top of her head, but rogue strands spiraled around her ears and down her neck.

"No, I'm sorry. Something has come up." One hand floated to her chest. "I am unable to meet with you now."

She started to close the door, but Ryan laid a palm on the outside.

"Please. I have had a migraine."

"We don't want to bother you, Mrs. Specter." He beamed his choirboy smile. "We're here to see Chantale."

"I cannot have you pestering my daughter." Her voice was jagged, her knuckles white on the doorknob.

"We will be very brief," I said.

"Chantale is sleeping."

"Please wake her."

"She is not well."

"Headache?" Ryan's voice had taken on an edge.

"I suffer from migraines, myself," I jumped in. "I know how you're feeling. Please send Chantale down, then go back to bed."

"No, thank you."

The response made no sense. I took a close look. Mrs. Specter's pupils were the size of cocktail tumblers. The ambassador's wife had knocked back some serious painkillers.

"Is Mr. Specter—"

She cut me off with a wave of her hand.

"Is your husband here, Mrs. Specter?"

"Here?"

"Is Mr. Specter in the house?"

"There's no one here."

"No one?"

Mrs. Specter shook her head, realized her mistake.

"Except Chantale."

Ryan and I exchanged glances.

"Where is she, ma'am?" I asked, placing a hand on hers.

"What?"

"Chantale has taken off, hasn't she?"

She dropped her head, nodded once.

"Did she tell you where she was going?"

"No." The foyer chandelier highlighted the tendrils obscuring her face.

"Has she contacted you?"

"No." Without looking up.

"Do you know where she is?"

"No." Her voice sounded a million miles away.

"Mrs. Specter?" I urged.

She raised her head, looked past us at the hedge.

"Chantale is out there with people who will hurt her. And she's angry. She's so very, very angry."

She drew a tremulous breath, looked from the cedars to me.

"Her father and I did this to her. My affair. His vengeful little games. How could we think this would not affect our daughter? I would do everything so very differently."

"No parent is perfect, ma'am."

"Few parents drive their children to drugs."

Hard to argue that.

"Is there anything you can think of that might help us locate your daughter?"

"What?"

I repeated my question.

Mrs. Specter searched the parts of her brain that remained functional.

"I'm sorry," she said. "I'm sorry."

"May we see her room?" Ryan asked.

She gave a half nod, turned, and led us up a carved wooden staircase to a second-floor hallway.

"Chantale's bedroom is the first on the left. I must lie down."

"We'll let ourselves out," I said.

The room was dark, but hundreds of tiny points glowed on the ceiling above Chantale's bed. I recognized them instantly. Nature Company Glow in the Dark Stars. The year Katy was fourteen we'd purchased a kit and spent an afternoon creating a stellar display. Later, she added the Solar System. Katy spent hours gazing up from her bed, dreaming of faraway worlds.

I wondered if mother or daughter had decorated Chantale's ceiling.

The stars disappeared when Ryan flipped on the light.

The room was done in yellow gingham and white eyelet. The four-poster was heaped with dolls and lacy pillows. A stuffed orangutan hung over the footboard, eyes glassy and blank. More dolls and animals lined the window seats and filled a Boston rocker.

One nightstand held a portable phone, the other a Bose clock radio and CD player. The painted armoire across from the bed looked as if it cost more than my entire collection of home furnishings.

While Ryan moved to a desktop computer, I opened the armoire doors. A poster covered the inside of each. On the right, *White Trash Two Heebs and a Bean*, scrawled across four stomachs. On the left, *Punk Rock On-Girls Kick Ass*.

The cabinet contained books, a TV, and an extensive compact disc collection. I scanned the artists. Dropkick Murphy's, Good Riddance, Buck-O-Nine, AFI, Dead Kennedys, Rancid, Saves the Day, Face to Face, The Business, Anti-Flag, The Clash, Less Than Jake, The Unseen, The Aquabats, The Vandals, NFG, Stiff Little Fingers. Lots of NOFX.

I felt old as Zeus. I hadn't heard of a single group.

The books were in French and English. Tolstoy's *Anna Karenina*. Deepak Chopra's *The Return of Merlin*. Douglas Adams's *The Hitchhiker's Guide to the Galaxy*. Guy Corneau's *Père manquant, fils manqué*. *Anne of Green Gables*. Several Harry Potters.

I felt a bit better.

"Mixed messages," said Ryan, pushing the computer's on button.

"Think the kid's having an identity crisis?"

The room was a schizoid blend of little girl whimsy, adolescent angst, and adult curiosity. I tried to picture Chantale in it. I'd experienced her punk manifestation, seen the *Father Knows Best* photo. But I had no sense of the real Chantale, had no idea who she was in this room.

I heard the CPU beep and whir as it powered up.

Did Chantale like gingham? Had she asked for the dolls? Had she spotted the orangutan in a mail-order catalog, insisted it be hers? Had she won it at a carnival? Had she fixed her eyes on the plastic stars at night, wondering what life held in store? Had she shut her lids tightly, disillusioned by what it had so far revealed?

The waterfall announced Windows. Ryan worked the mouse, typed something. Something else. Crossing to watch, I could see that he had launched AOL and was trying various passwords.

He tried another key combination.

AOL informed him his choice was invalid, and suggested he reenter.

"That could take a lifetime," I said.

"Most kids are unsophisticated."

He tried the first name of each family member, then their initials, the initials in reverse order, then in varying combinations.

No go.

"What's her birthday?"

I told him. He tried the digits forward and backward. AOL would not budge.

"How about the cat?"

"Guimauve."

"Marshmallow?"

"Don't look at me. I didn't choose it."

G-U-I-M-A-U-V-E.

AOL thought not.

E-V-U-A-M-I-U-G

The welcome screen flashed, and a melodious voice announced waiting mail.

"Damn, I'm good."

"You didn't know the cat's name."

Ryan clicked an icon, and Chantale's mailbox appeared on the screen. She had two unread e-mails. We scanned them silently. Each was from a school friend in Guatemala City.

Ryan shifted to Sent Mail. Chantale had e-mailed metalass@hotmail.com seven times since her release on Friday. Each communiqué spoke of her unhappiness, and begged for help. She'd also appealed to Dirtdoggy, Rambeau, Bedhead, Sexychaton, and Criperçant.

Chantale's Old Mail contained two entries, one dated yesterday, the other today at 3 P.M. Both

were from Metalass. Ryan opened the earlier
message.

> FUCKIN A I'M GLAD YOU'RE BACK. DIRT AND
> RAMBEAU ARE UNDERGROUND. THE HEAD'S
> GONE WEST. PHONE. YOU'VE GOTTA FRIEND.

"Terrific," said Ryan, clicking on the second e-
mail. "The guy's a closet James Taylor fan."

> CHANGE OF PLANS. TIM'S. GUY. EIGHT. IF
> HEAT, GO TO CLEM'S.

"Do you think Clem, Tim, and Guy could be
the cyber punks she e-mailed?"
Ryan was lost in thought.
I picked up Chantale's phone and hit redial.
Nothing.
I looked at the orangutan, wanted to shake it
into divulging where its mistress had gone.
Ryan shut down the computer and stood.
"Idea?" I asked.
"A dandy. Let's boogie."

20

"What's the plan?" I asked as Ryan turned onto Sherbrooke.

"Cannelloni at La Transition."

I just looked at him.

"And bread pudding. They make kick-ass bread pudding."

"I thought we were trying to find Chantale."

"Then doughnuts."

"Doughnuts?"

"I like the ones with sprinkles."

Before I could answer, he turned onto Grosvenor, parked, circled the car, and opened my door. When I joined him on the sidewalk, he took my elbow and began steering me toward a corner restaurant.

The secrecy was beginning to grate. I balked.

"What's going on?"

"Trust me."

"I don't want to spoil your Spy Versus Spy moment, Ryan, but we need to find Chantale."

"We will."

"With doughnuts and cannelloni?"

"Will you just trust me?"

"What's the problem?" I yanked my arm free. "Can't share classified police information?"

A woman with Coke-bottle glasses approached with a terrier that looked more rat than dog. Hearing my tone, she reeled in the leash, lowered her gaze, and quickened her pace.

"You're frightening the locals. Come inside and I'll explain."

My eyes narrowed, but I followed. At the door I had a sudden flashback to my dinner with Galiano at the Gucumatz. If the maître d' seated us in an alcove, I was out of there.

The restaurant was Fusion Mediterranean. Dim lights, forest-green paneling, navy and cranberry linen. A young woman led us to a table by the side windows, flashing Ryan a broad smile in the process.

Ryan grinned back, and we both sat.

"Ever hear of Patrick Feeney?"

"We don't exchange Christmas cards."

"Jesus, you can be a pain in the ass."

"I work on it."

Ryan sighed to indicate his enduring patience.

"Ever hear of Chez Tante Clémence?"

"It's a shelter for street kids."

Another young woman provided menus and

more beaming teeth, filled water glasses, asked about drinks. Ryan and I both requested Perrier.

Ryan ignored his menu.

"The cannelloni is excellent."

"So I've heard."

When the waitress returned, I chose linguine pesto Genovese. Ryan stayed true to his vision. We both ordered small Caesars.

There was little conversation as we ate bread, then salad. I stared out the window, watching the day yield to night.

Children had disappeared from the sidewalks and yards along Grosvenor, called in to supper or homework. Porch and interior lights were glowing yellow in the duplexes lining both sides of the street.

Along Sherbrooke, banks and businesses were closing, stores emptying. Neon signs were blinking on, though most night establishments had yet to come to life.

Pedestrians were quickening their steps, sensing the chill promised by the deepening twilight. I wondered about Chantale Specter. To what destination might she be hurrying in the embryonic dusk?

After the food arrived, and we'd peppered and cheesed, Ryan spoke again.

"Aunt Clémence's is run by a defrocked priest named Patrick Feeney. Feeney allows no drugs or alcohol on the premises, otherwise kids are free to come and go. He provides meals and a place to sleep. If a kid wants to talk, Feeney listens. If they ask for counselling, he steers them to it. No sermons. No curfews. No locked doors."

"Sounds pretty liberal for the Catholic Church."

"I said defrocked priest. Feeney was booted from the clergy years ago."

"Why?"

"As I remember it, the padre had a girlfriend, the Church said choose. Feeney decided to skip the ecclesiastical rehab and set off on his own."

"Who picks up the tab?"

"Clém's gets some money from the city, but most funding comes from charity events and private donations. Feeney relies a lot on volunteers."

It clicked.

"You think Clem is Aunt Clémence."

"I told you I was good at this stuff."

Another ping.

"And Tim is the Tim Hortons doughnut shop on Guy."

"You're not bad, yourself, Brennan."

"We're killing time until the rendezvous with Metalass."

We both looked at our watches. It was six fifty-eight.

Civilians think of surveillance as adrenaline-pumping, heart-pounding policework. In reality, most stakeouts are as exciting as Metamucil.

We spent two hours watching Tim Hortons, Ryan from his car, I from a park bench. I saw commuters entering and exiting the Guy métro station. I saw students leaving night classes at Concordia University. I saw geezers feeding the pigeons at the Norman Bethune statue. I saw Frisbee throwers and dog walkers. I saw businessmen, vagrants, nuns, and dandies.

What I did not see was Chantale Specter.

At ten Ryan rang my cell.

"Looks like our little darlin's a no-show."

"Could Metalass have spotted us and warned her off?"

"I suspect Metalass has the IQ of a garbanzo bean."

"He'd have to have the patience of one to wait this long."

I looked around. The only male loitering near Tim's was at least sixty-five. Several frappé drinkers at the Java U across de Maisonneuve fit the Metalass bill, but none seemed concerned about me or the doughnut shop.

"Now what?"

"Let's give her another half hour. If she doesn't show, we'll mosey to Clém's."

The tiny triangle in which I sat was an island in the middle of de Maisonneuve. Cars hummed past on all three sides. Unconsciously, I began counting. One. Seven. Ten.

Good, Brennan. Very compulsive.

I looked at my watch. Five past ten.

Why hadn't Chantale kept her date with Metalass? Had the e-mail been a setup? Had I blown our cover? Had she arrived, recognized me, and split?

An Asian family approached the shop. The woman waited outside with a toddler and a baby in a stroller while the man entered and bought doughnuts.

I looked at my watch again. Ten past ten.

Or had we missed her? Had she hidden herself until Metalass arrived, then signaled to him? Had she come disguised?

Fourteen past ten.

I glanced across the intersection. Ryan met my eyes, shook his head slowly.

Two men entered the Tim Hortons looking like billboards for Hugo Boss. Through the glass I watched them choose then purchase a dozen doughnuts. Two elderly women drank coffee in a booth. Three winos argued at an outdoor table.

Seventeen past ten.

Doughnuts for a group of students. I checked each face. Chantale's was not among them.

"Ready?"

I looked up. Halogen and neon lit the periphery of Ryan's hair, but the sky above him was dark and starless.

"Time to mosey?"

"Time to mosey."

Chez Tante Clémence was located on de Maisonneuve, two blocks east of the old Forum. The center consisted of a three-story brownstone in a trio of brownstones, each garnished with brightly painted wood. Clémence was the lavender representative in the rainbow triptych.

But her fix-up squad hadn't stopped with the trim.

Clémence's porch was mustard, her window boxes cherry red. The latter housed knots of dead vegetation, the former a subset of Feeney's flock.

Two girls painted their toenails on a second-floor fire escape. Both had short brown hair, heavy bangs, Capri pants, and enough pierced flesh to qualify for postsurgical coverage. Laverne and Shirley Go Punk. The duo suspended their pedicure to observe our approach.

The porch crew watched us from the steps, cigarettes tucked between fingers or hanging from mouths. Hairstyles included one Statue of Liberty, one Mr. T, two Sir Galahads, and a Janis Joplin. Though it was too dark to make out faces, all five looked like they were in preschool when the Berlin wall went down.

I noticed the statue nudge Mr. T. Mr. T commented, and everyone laughed.

"*Bonjour*," Ryan greeted them from the sidewalk.

No response.

"Howdy." He tried English.

From inside, I heard the intermittent blare of the Sex Pistols, as though someone were turning the music on and off.

"We're looking for Patrick Feeney."

"Why?" Mr. T wore a leather vest over a hairless, naked chest. "Pops win the lottery?"

"He's been nominated for a Nobel," said Ryan in a flat, humorless voice.

Mr. T pushed from the railing and stood with legs apart, shoulders back, thumbs hooked into the belt loops of his jeans.

"Rouse the sleeping tiger," said the statue, flicking ash onto the sidewalk. "Bad move."

While Mr. T looked like he wanted action, the statue looked desperate for attention. His hair spikes were sprayed colors I couldn't make out in the dark, and a chain looped from one nostril to its partner earlobe.

Ryan stepped forward and waggled his badge in Mr. T's face.

"Patrick Feeney?" he repeated, his voice granite.

Mr. T dropped his hands, and the fingers curled into fists. Joplin reached up and wrapped an arm around his leg.

"*À l'intérieur*," she said. Inside.

"*Merci.*"

Ryan placed a foot on the lowest tread, and the group parted a millimeter. We wove our way up, careful to avoid stepping on fingers and toes. I felt ten eyes follow our progress.

A single red bulb glowed above the front door. Though the porch sagged badly, in the crimson light I could see fresh boards sandwiched among the old. Someone had turned the soil in a window planter, and a flat of marigolds lay to the side. Though Chez Tante Clémence would never win any design awards, a caring hand was clearly at work.

Clémence's interior was in keeping with her public face. Lavender on the woodwork, crude

280

murals on the walls. Animals. Flowers. Sunsets. The colors were those I remembered from the tempera paints of my lower school art classes. The furniture was Salvation Army, the linoleum different in every room.

Ryan and I crossed a front parlor containing several futon couches, passed a wooden staircase on the left, and entered a long, narrow corridor directly opposite the front of the house. Doors opened onto bedrooms on both sides, each with battered dressers and four to six single beds or cots. From one I could see the silver-blue shaft of a TV, and hear the theme music of *Law and Order*.

Halfway down the hall, we came to a kitchen. Beyond the kitchen, I could see a dining room on the left, two more bedrooms on the right.

Feeney was on his knees in the kitchen, helping a teenage imitation of Metallica dismantle or assemble a boom box.

Like African chameleons that turn green and sway to imitate leaves, youth counselors often take on the traits of their clients. Denim, ponytails, Birkenstocks, boots. The camouflage helps them mix with the populace.

Not Feeney. With tortoiseshell glasses and thick white hair parted straight as a runway the man might have blended at a home for seniors. He wore a cable-knit cardigan, flannel shirt, and gray polyester pants hiked up to his armpits.

On hearing footsteps, Feeney turned.

"May I help you?"

Ryan flashed his badge.

"Detective Andrew Ryan."

"I'm Patrick Feeney. I run the center."

Feeney looked at me. Metallica did the same. I half expected the four of them to jam into "Die, Die My Darling" in high, cracky voices.

"Tempe Brennan." I identified myself.

Feeney nodded three times, more to himself than to us. Behind him, the boys watched with expressions ranging from curiosity to hostility.

Two girls appeared in a doorway across the hall. Both had fried blonde hair and looked like they ate a lot of potatoes. One wore jeans and a UBC sweatshirt, the other a peasant skirt that hung low on her hips. Given her poundage, it was a bad choice.

Feeney struggled to rise. As one, Metallica reached out to help him. He crossed to us, walking with feet widely spaced, as though bothered by hemorrhoids.

"How may I help you, Detective?"

"We're looking for a young woman named Chantale Specter."

"Is there a problem?"

"Is Chantale here?" Ryan said.

"Why?"

"It's a simple question, Father."

Feeney bristled slightly. Out of the corner of my eye I saw peasant skirt disappear. Moments later, the front door opened, then closed.

I slipped from the kitchen and hurried to the parlour. Through the window I could see that only Mr. T and the statue remained on the steps.

Peasant skirt was talking to them. After a brief exchange, Mr. T flicked his cigarette, and the three headed west on de Maisonneuve. I waited to allow a safety zone, then set off after them.

The Montreal Canadiens had lousy luck with their early accommodations. From the 1909 to the 1910 season, the hockey team was headquartered in Westmount Arena at the intersection of Ste-Catherine and Atwater. When that rink burned to the ground, the Habs returned to their roots on the east side of town. Following another fire, the Mont-Royal Arena was thrown together, and the boys slapped pucks there for the next four years. In 1924, the Forum was built directly across from the old home ice. Construction took just one hundred and fifty-nine days and cost $1.2 million dollars. In their opener, the Canadiens trounced the Toronto St. Pats 7–1.

Hockey is sacred in Canada. Over the years the Forum acquired the aura of a holy place. The more Stanley Cups, the holier it grew. Nevertheless, the day came. Management needed more seats. The Habs needed better locker rooms.

The team played its last game in the Forum on March 11, 1996. Four days later, fifty thousand Montrealers turned out for the "moving day" parade. On March 15, the Habs hosted their opener in the new Molson Centre, defeating the New York Rangers 4–2.

It may have been the last game the bums won, I thought as I hurried along de Maisonneuve.

The old Forum sat empty for a while, forlorn,

abandoned, an eyesore on the western edge of the city. In 1998, Canderel Management bought the project, brought Pepsi on board as title sponsor, and began a massive face-lift. Three years later, the building reopened as the Centre de divertissement du Forum Pepsi, the metaphor changed from spectator sport to food and entertainment.

Where scalpers once hawked rinkside seats, and stockbrokers and truckers jockeyed for beer, under-thirties now sip Smirnoff Ice and bowl on sonic alleys. The Pepsi Forum Entertainment Centre contains a twenty-two-screen movie megaplex, an upscale wine store, restaurants, an indoor climbing wall, and a big-screen altar paying homage to the good old days.

Mr. T, the statue, and peasant skirt turned left on rue Lambert-Closse and entered the Forum on the Ste-Catherine side. I trailed them ten yards back.

Sighting on the statue's hair spikes, I dogged the trio through a handful of bowlers and moviegoers milling about the lobby. I watched the spikes ascend the escalator to the second floor and disappear into Jillian's. I followed.

Tables and booths filled the right half of the restaurant, a bar occupied the left. Though there were few diners, every bar stool was filled, and a dozen drinkers stood in twos and threes.

When I entered, the Clémence trio was making its way toward a young woman at the far end of the bar. She wore a black lace blouse, long black beads, and fingerless black gloves. The lace securing her topknot looked like an enormous black butterfly perched on her head.

It was Chantale Specter.

On seeing her friends, Chantale smiled, jerked a thumb at a man on her left, and rolled her eyes.

I looked at the object of her disdain.

It couldn't be.

It was.

I reached for my cell phone.

21

Ryan arrived within minutes.

"Who's the goof with the hair gel?"

"A reporter from Chicago named Ollie Nordstern."

"What's he doing here?"

"Having a beer."

"What's he doing in Montreal?"

"Possibly trying to find me. Nordstern's researching a piece on human rights work. I talked to him in Guatemala City, and he's been dogging me ever since."

"Dogging you?"

"Calling my cell, leaving messages at the lab down there."

Ryan was staring at Chantale.

"Is something dripping from her eye?"

"Probably a tattoo."

"What's Nordstern's interest in the Specter kid?"

"Maybe Chantale's his quarry, not me."

"Wayward ambassador's daughter." Ryan snapped his fingers. "Ticket to a Pulitzer."

We both looked at Chantale. She was huddled with her friends now, back to Nordstern.

"Ready?"

"Let's do it."

Mr. T was in vigilante mode, thumbs belt-looped, incisors working a wad of gum. He spotted us at ten feet and tracked us like a serpent hunting a kill. The others remained focused on their conversation. Nordstern remained focused on Chantale.

Ryan circled, picked up Chantale's mug from behind, and sniffed the contents.

Everyone fell silent.

"I'm sure we all have proof of age." Ryan bestowed a fatherly smile. Officer Friendly looking out for the kids.

"Fuck off," said Mr. T. In the light he looked older than I'd estimated on the porch, probably in his early twenties.

"Metalass?" I asked.

His eyes crawled to me.

"Tempered steel. How 'bout yours?" He rapid-fire drummed on the bar with his palms. Chantale jumped slightly.

"Do you use the screen name Metalass?"

"Nice tits."

"I know you mean that in a caring way."

"Maybe we could have a cappuccino some time." Mr. T scratched his chest, and a smirk lifted one side of his mouth.

"Sure," I said. "Once you're allowed visitors, I could do it as community service."

A nervous giggle.

"The fuck you laughing at?" Mr. T swiveled toward peasant skirt.

Ryan slid behind Mr. T and levered one arm behind his back.

"What the f—"

"Let's not forget our manners." Officer Friendly's voice had chilled.

"This is fucking police harassment." A vein throbbed in Mr. T's neck. When he tried to pull free, Ryan applied upward pressure.

Chantale made a move to rise. Placing one hand on each shoulder, I eased her back onto the bar stool. Up close I could see that the tattooed tears were fake. The uppermost was curling outward along one edge.

Nordstern regarded the moment expressionless.

"My colleague asked a legitimate question," Ryan said into Mr. T's ear. "We've been calling you Mr. T, but we find it embarrassing. Makes us feel old."

No response.

Ryan tweaked Mr. T's arm.

"Fuckin' police brutality." Through clenched teeth.

"You're handling it well."

288

Nordstern began folding a napkin into smaller and smaller triangles.

Another tweak.

"Metalass." It was almost a yelp.

The couple beside Nordstern bailed with their beers.

"I doubt your mama put Metalass on your birth certificate." Ryan.

"I doubt your mama could read and write."

Another tweak.

"Fuck!"

"I'm getting impatient."

"Take a Prozac."

Ryan tweaked harder.

"Leon Hochmeister. Get the fuck off me."

Ryan released Hochmeister's arm.

Hochmeister bent and spit his gum on the floor. Then he jerked backward, rolling his shoulder and rubbing his biceps.

"You need to learn some new adjectives, Leon. Maybe try one of those thesaurus software programs."

Hochmeister placed upper incisors on lower lip, began the F word, changed his mind. His eyes simmered, Rasputin in a Mohawk.

Ryan turned to the statue.

"And you are?"

"Presley Iverson." Iverson had a look of bemused curiosity on his face.

Peasant skirt.

"Antoinette Gaudreau."

"Do I have the pleasure of addressing Dirtdoggy,

Rambeau, Bedhead, Sexychaton, or Criperçant?"

"The Crier," said Iverson, spiraling his palm in self-presentation. "*Cri perçant*. Piercing scream."

"Very poetic."

A pink bubble emerged from Iverson's mouth. When it collapsed, he began working the Bazooka for another go. Ryan looked at Gaudreau.

"I don't use e-mail that much."

"And when you do?"

Gaudreau shrugged. "Sexychaton."

"Thank you, kitten."

Gaudreau looked as sexy as a baleen whale.

"You can't just bust the fuck in and rough people up." Hochmeister was regaining his self-assurance.

"Leon, that's exactly what I *can* do. And another thing I can do is haul your skinny ass to the bag for aiding a minor in flight. Think your name might turn up some interesting reading material?"

Leon's fingers stopped massaging his arm. He looked at Chantale, then up at the ceiling. When his chin came down, sweat glistened along the line between Mohawk and forehead.

"We know nothing about that shit."

"What shit is that, Leon?"

"That shit he's talking."

Out of the corner of my eye I saw Nordstern freeze.

"Who's 'he', Leon?"

Hochmeister tilted his head in Nordstern's direction.

"Neither does Chantale." He jerked a thumb at

Nordstern. "This asshole's as psycho as you are."

"Why's that?"

"He thinks Chantale's cool to some chick got dropped in Guatemala City."

"Leon!" Chantale hissed.

"A bit off the subject of your human rights story," I said to Nordstern.

Nordstern's eyes peeled off the napkin and lifted to mine.

"Maybe."

"Where are you staying, sir?" Ryan asked.

"Please." Nordstern crumbled the napkin. "Don't waste your time or mine. My info and sources are strictly confidential."

Nordstern tossed the napkin onto the bar and looked at me.

"Unless we can find some mutually beneficial arrangement." His voice was oily as a drilling rig.

"I don't know what you're talking about."

He studied me a long time before answering.

"You don't have a clue what's really going on."

"Is that so?"

"You're so far off track you might as well be on Ganymeade." Nordstern stood. "You're not even in the right galaxy."

"Last I checked, Ganymeade was still in the Milky Way."

"That's good, Dr. Brennan." The reporter drained his glass and set it on the bar. "But I'm not talking astronomy."

"What are you talking?"

"Murder."

"Whose?"

His eyebrows rose, and he waggled an index finger like a metronome.

"Secret."

"Why?" I asked.

Again the finger.

"Grave secret."

I realized Nordstern was slightly drunk.

"Secrets of the grave."

He tried to hold his grin, but it faded, as if by its own will.

"I'm at the St. Malo," Nordstern said to Ryan.

To me, "Call when you want the answers to some very grave secrets."

I watched Nordstern cross toward the door. Halfway there, he turned and mouthed one word: "Ganymeade." Then he touched two fingers to his forehead, and disappeared through the door.

"That motherfucker is crazy," said Hochmeister. "We meet again, I'll tear him an asshole the size of Cape Breton."

"Leon, I'm going to say this just once. Go home." Ryan held up a hand. "No, I won't be that specific." He pointed one finger at Hochmeister's nose. "Go away. Go now, and you and your friends can spend the night watching Archie Bunker reruns. Stay, and you'll spend it without your shoelaces and belts."

Iverson and Gaudreau shot from their stools like they were spring-loaded. Hochmeister hesitated a beat, then brought up the rear, an alpha male in a baboon retreat. When they'd gone, Ryan turned to Chantale.

"What did Nordstern want?"

"Is that the prick's name?"

Chantale picked up her beer. Ryan took it from her and set it back down.

"Ollie Nordstern," I said. "He's a reporter with the *Chicago Tribune*."

"Really?"

Good question, I thought. I'd accepted Mateo's explanation, never questioned Nordstern's legitimacy.

"What was he asking about?"

"My plans for Sundance."

"Chantale, I don't think you realize how serious your situation is. You're in contempt. The judge can slap you right back in jail."

Chantale kept her eyes on her lap. Black wisps fell around the dead, pale face, hiding all but the tip of her nose.

"I don't hear you, Chantale."

"He wanted to know about those dead girls."

"The ones I mentioned at the jail?"

She nodded and the lace butterfly bobbed.

I remembered Nordstern's odd question at FAFG headquarters.

"During our interview, Nordstern asked about the septic tank case," I said to Ryan.

"How did he know about it?"

"Beats me."

Again, the same thought in both our minds: Did Nordstern suspect a Specter–Paraíso link?

I turned back to Chantale.

"How did Nordstern find you?"

"How the hell should I know? Probably hung around outside my house."

"And followed you to Tim Hortons."

"Isn't that how you found me?"

"Had you seen him before tonight?"

"We've been meeting secretly under the bleachers."

"Chantale?"

"No."

"What else did he ask about?"

She didn't answer.

"Chantale?"

The ambassador's daughter looked up, anger crimping her features into a cold, hard version of the little-girl face in the embassy photo.

"My father," she said in a tremulous voice. "My famous, brain-fucking, goddamn father. It's not about me. It's *never* about me."

Chantale reached into an embroidered bag slung diagonally across her chest, removed dark glasses, and slid them on. A distorted version of my face jumped onto each lens, two fun-house Tempes, each wearing the same confused look.

Ryan tossed two looneys on the bar.

"Your mother is worried. We can talk tomorrow."

Chantale allowed herself to be escorted out of the restaurant, down the escalator, and through the lobby. As we were approaching the glass doors leading to Ste-Catherine, Ryan caught my eye and gestured at the SAQ wineshop. Ollie Nordstern stood near the entrance, ostensibly studying a selection of French Chardonnays.

"What do you think?" I asked.

"A job with the CIA is definitely not in this guy's future. Let's see if he follows us."

Ryan and I hurried Chantale out the door and around the corner. She did one of her eye rolls, but said nothing.

Nordstern stepped onto the sidewalk twenty seconds behind us, looked around, and began hurrying west. At Atwater he reversed direction and doubled back.

I watched him stop at Lambert-Closse, look left toward the mountain, right toward Cabot Square. My eyes moved with his, then went past him across the intersection. It was then I saw the man in the baseball cap. He was walking toward Nordstern, a Luger nine-millimeter angling from his waistband.

What followed were ninety kaleidoscoping seconds that felt like a triple eternity.

"Ryan!" I indicated the gunman.

Ryan drew his gun. I pushed Chantale to her knees, crouched beside her.

"Police!" Ryan bellowed. "Everybody down! *Par terre!*"

The gunman drew to within five feet, extended his arm, and leveled his nine-millimeter at Nordstern's chest.

A woman screamed.

"Gun! *Arme à feu!*" The words rolled down Ste-Catherine like a balloon being bandied at a football game.

Another scream.

Two explosions ripped the air. Nordstern flew backward, a pair of red blossoms darkening his shirt.

There were maybe fifteen people on the street. Most dropped to their knees. Others scrambled to get into the Forum. A man grabbed a child, wrapped himself around her like an armadillo. Her muffled crying added to the pandemonium.

Cars pulled to the curb. Others sped up. The intersection emptied.

The shooter stood with legs spread, knees slightly bent, sweeping his Luger in wide arcs in front of him. Left to right. Right to left. He was about fifteen feet from me, but I could hear his breath, see his eyes under the navy-blue brim.

Ryan was crouched behind a taxi parked on Lambert-Closse, gun aimed at the shooter with a two-handed grip. I hadn't seen him move from my side.

"*Arrêtez!* Freeze!"

A dark barrel swung around and sighted on Ryan's head. The shooter's finger twitched against the trigger. I held my breath. Ryan hadn't shot for fear of wounding an innocent bystander. The shooter might have no such compunction.

"Drop your weapon! *Mettez votre arme par terre!*" Ryan shouted.

The shooter's face registered nothing.

One block over, a car horn sounded. Above me, the traffic signal clicked from green to yellow.

Ryan repeated his command.

Yellow to red.

In the distance, a siren. A second. A third.

The shooter tensed. Taking two steps backward, he bent toward a woman huddled on the sidewalk, never shifting the gun from Ryan's face. The woman put her head to the pavement and flung both arms over it.

"Don't kill me. I have a baby." The woman's voice was frantic with terror.

The shooter grabbed her by the jacket and dragged her across the cement.

Ryan fired.

The shooter's body jerked. He dropped the woman and grabbed his right shoulder. Blood mushroomed across his shirt.

Straightening, the shooter raised his Luger and squeezed off four rounds. Bullets pinged the wall above us. Fragments of brick rained down on our heads.

"Oh God. Oh no." Chantale's voice was high and quavery.

Ryan fired again.

The woman shrieked as the shooter fell across her. I heard a skull crack pavement, the Luger skitter then drop from the curb, the woman scrabble up the sidewalk.

The woman sobbed. The child cried. Otherwise, silence. No one spoke. No one moved.

The sirens grew louder, built into a screaming chorus. Cruisers converged from every direction, tires screeching, lights flashing, radios crackling.

Ryan rose, gun pointed at the sky. I watched him reach for his badge.

Beside me, I heard Chantale draw a series of unsteady breaths. I looked over. Her chin quivered and both cheeks glistened. I reached out and stroked her hair.

"It's over." My voice didn't sound like my own. "You're fine."

Chantale looked up. Only two tattoo tears remained on her face.

"Am I?"

I put my arm around her. She collapsed into me and wept silently.

22

As on the morning after the attack in Sololá, I awoke with an ill-formed feeling of dread. In an instant the scene flooded back to me. I relived the explosion of Nordstern's chest. Heard the crack of Ryan's gun. Saw the shooter's inert body, his blood oozing across the pavement. Though I'd been given no official word, I was certain both men were dead.

I rubbed my hands up and down on my face, then closed my eyes and pulled the blanket over my head. Would there be no end to the killing?

In my mind's eye I saw Chantale, cheeks streaked with tears, body rigid with terror. A shiver ran through me as I thought of how close she and I had come to being injured or killed. How could I ever have told her mother?

I imagined how devastated Katy would be should someone deliver news of my death. Thank God that would not be necessary.

I remembered Nordstern in Guatemala City, and in the bar at Jillian's minutes before his death. I felt a wave of remorse. I had disliked the man, had not been kind to him. But I'd never imagined him dead.

Dead.

Jesus! What had Nordstern discovered? What was so big that it had gotten him blasted on a Montreal street?

My thoughts circled back to Chantale. What impact would these events have on her? There were so many directions a troubled adolescent could take. Repentance? Flight? Escape through drugs?

Though tough on the outside, I suspected Chantale had an interior as fragile as a butterfly wing. Vowing I would stand by her, appreciated or not, I flung back the covers and headed for the shower.

The summer that had dropped in so unexpectedly had bolted during the night. I exited my garage to a steady drizzle and temperatures in the forties. *C'est la vie québécoise.*

The morning staff meeting was mercifully short and produced no anthropology cases. I spent the next hour cutting segments of eraser to proper lengths and gluing them to Susanne's replica of the Paraíso skull. Except for some shine and subtle layering, her model looked exactly like the real thing.

By 10 A.M. I was seated at a monitor in *Imagerie*, the section responsible for photography and computer imaging. Lucien, our graphics guru, was positioning the Paraíso model before a video camera when Ryan entered.

"What's sticking out all over that skull?"

"Tissue depth markers."

"Of course."

"Each marker shows how much flesh there was at a specific point on the face or skull," Lucien piped up. "Dr. Brennan cut them using standards for a Mongoloid female. Right?"

I nodded.

"We've done gobs of facial reproductions like this." He adjusted a light. "Though this is a first with a plastic skull."

Gobs?

"Let me guess. The camera captures the image, sends it to the PC, and you connect the dots."

Ryan had a way of making complex things sound kindergarten simple.

"There's a bit more to it than that. But, yes, once I've drawn facial contours using the markers, I'll choose features from the program's database, find the best fit, and paste them in."

"This the technique you used for one of the Inner Life Empowerment bodies?"

Ryan referred to a case he and I had worked several years back. A number of McGill students were recruited into a fringe sect led by a sociopath with delusions of immortality. When a skeleton turned up in a shallow grave near the group's South Carolina commune, Lucien and I did a sketch to establish that the remains were those of a missing coed.

"Yes. What's up with Chantale?"

"The judge agreed to give her another chance at home detention."

Last evening, while Ryan stayed to explain the shooting, I'd taken Chantale home. This morning he'd done a follow-up to be sure she was still there.

"Think Mommy will keep a closer watch?" I asked.

"I suspect Manuel Noriega enjoys more freedom than Chantale can hope for in the near future."

"She was pretty subdued last night," I said.

"The fuck-off-and-leave-me-alone demeanor has definitely lightened."

"How are you doing?" I asked, noticing the tension in his face.

In Montreal, an internal investigation is mandated following every police shooting. To maintain impartiality, the CUM homicide section looks into shootings by SQ officers, and the SQ investigates incidents involving the CUM. As I was leaving with Chantale, I saw Ryan hand his gun to a CUM cop.

Ryan shrugged. "Two DOAs. One was mine."

"It was a good shoot, Ryan. They know that."

"I turned Ste-Catherine into the O.K. Corral."

"The guy killed Nordstern and was about to take a hostage."

"Have you been called?"

"Not yet."

"Something to look forward to."

"I'll tell them exactly what went down. Have you got an ID on the shooter?"

"Carlos Vincente. Held a Guatemalan passport."

"The moron carried his passport to a hit?"

Ryan shook his head. "A key from the Days Inn on Guy. We tossed the room, found the passport in a carry-on bag."

"Doesn't sound like a pro."

"We also found two thousand U.S. dollars and an airline ticket to Phoenix."

"Anything else?"

"Dirty shorts."

I gave him the look.

"I phoned Galiano. Nothing popped up when he ran Vincente's name, but he's going to dig deeper."

"What about Nordstern?"

"Doesn't look good for the Pulitzer."

More of the look.

"I'm heading to the Hotel St. Malo now. Since Nordstern was your boy, I thought you might like to tag along."

"I need to finish this facial."

"I can do it, Dr. Brennan." Lucien sounded like a second-stringer on a high school football team.

I must have looked skeptical.

"Let me give it a shot." Please, Coach. Send me in.

Why not? If Lucien's sketch didn't look right, I could always do my own.

"O.K. Do a full frontal. Don't force the features. Make sure they fit the bony architecture."

"*Allons-y*," said Ryan.

"*Allons-y*." Let's go.

The St. Malo was a tiny hotel on du Fort, approximately six blocks east of the Pepsi Forum.

The proprietor was a tall, skeletal man with a wandering left eye, and skin the color of day-old tea. Though less than enthused about our visit, Ryan's badge spurred him to do the right thing.

Nordstern's room was the size of a cell, with much the same ambience. Clean, functional, no frills. I took inventory in three seconds.

Iron bed. Battered wardrobe. Battered dresser. Battered nightstand. Gideons' Bible. Not a personal item in sight. Nothing in the drawers or wardrobe.

The bathroom looked a little more lived-in. Toothbrush. Crest. Disposable razor. Gillette Cool Wave for sensitive skin. Dippity-Do Sport Gel. Hotel soap.

"No shampoo," I noted when Ryan drew the shower curtain back with his pen.

"Who needs shampoo when you've got Dippity-Do?"

We returned to the bedroom.

"Guy traveled light," said Ryan, dragging a hockey bag from under the bed.

"Crafty, though. Knew how to blend with the natives."

"It's an athletic bag."

"It's a hockey bag."

"The NHL has twenty-four franchises south of the border."

"Hockey hasn't adulterated the American sense of fashion."

"Your people wear cheese on their heads."

"Are you going to open the bag?"

I watched Ryan remove several shirts and a pair of khaki pants.

"A boxer man."

He used thumb and forefinger to extract the shorts, then reached back in and withdrew a passport.

"American."

"Let's see."

Ryan flipped it open, then handed it to me.

Nordstern was not having a good hair day when the photo was taken. Nor did he look like he'd had much sleep. His skin was pale and the flesh under his eyes looked dark and puffy.

Again, I felt a wave of remorse. While I hadn't liked Nordstern, I would never have wished him such an end. I looked at his possessions, evidence of a life interrupted. I wondered if Nordstern had a wife or girlfriend. Kids. Who would notify them of his death?

"Must have applied for the passport prior to the Dippity-Do epiphany," Ryan said.

"This was issued last year." I read further. "Nordstern was born in Chicago on July seventeenth, 1966. Jesus, I thought he was in his twenties."

"It's the gel. Shaves years."

"Get over the hair gel."

Ryan wasn't really making light of Nordstern's death. He was using cop humor to break the tension. I was doing it myself. But his flippancy was starting to annoy me.

Ryan pulled out four books. All were familiar. *Guatemala: Getting Away with Murder*; *Las Massacres en Rabinal*; *State Violence in Guatemala: 1960–1999*; *Guatemala: Never Again*.

"Maybe Nordstern really was researching human rights work," I said.

Ryan opened a zippered pocket.

"Hell-o."

He fished out a plane ticket, a key, and a spiral notebook. I waited while he checked the ticket.

"He flew to Montreal last Thursday on American."

"The twelve fifty-seven through Miami?"

"Yep."

"That's the flight Mrs. Specter and I took."

"You didn't see him?"

"We rode up front, got on last, got off first, waited in the VIP lounge between flights."

"Maybe Nordstern *was* dogging you."

"Or maybe he was following the ambassador's wife."

"Good point."

"Round-trip ticket?"

Ryan nodded. "Open return."

As Ryan inspected the key, I stared at Nordstern's belongings. Obviously the man expected to return to the St. Malo. Had he realized the danger he was in? Had he considered the possibility of sudden death?

Ryan held up the key. A plastic tag identified its owner as the Hotel Todos Santos on Calle 12 in Zone 1.

"So Nordstern was going back to Guatemala," I said.

When Ryan opened the spiral, a square white envelope fell to the floor. The sound told me what it held.

I retrieved the envelope and slid a compact disk onto my palm. It had five letters penned on a homemade label: SCELL.

"What the frig is scell?" Ryan asked.

"Punk rock?" I was still discomfited by my ignorance of the genre.

"Igneous rock?"

"Maybe it's a code in Spanish." It didn't sound right even as I said it.

"Skeleton?" Ryan suggested.

"With a 'c'?"

"Maybe the guy couldn't spell."

"He was a journalist."

"Cell phone?"

"'S'?"

We both said the name at the same time.

"Specter."

"Jesus, you think Nordstern tapped the kid's cell phone?"

I remembered Chantale's mother in migraine mode.

"Did you catch Mrs. Specter's reference to her husband's games?"

"Think hubby has a zipper problem?"

"Maybe Nordstern had no interest at all in Chantale."

"Was using her to hook a bigger fish?"

"Maybe that's what Nordstern meant when he said I was off track."

"A philandering ambassador isn't much of a scoop."

"No. It isn't," I agreed.

"Doesn't seem like enough to get a guy capped."

"How about hair from an ambassador's pet turning up in the jeans of a murder victim?"

"Fifty-pound perch."

"Holy shit."

"What?"

"I just remembered something."

Ryan gave me a "bring it on" gesture.

"I told you that two members of our team were shot while driving to Chupan Ya."

"Yes."

"Carlos died, Molly survived."

"How is she?"

"Her doctors anticipate a full recovery. She's gone back to Minnesota, but Mateo and I visited her in the hospital in Sololá before I left Guatemala. Her recall was fuzzy, but Molly thought she remembered her attackers talking about an inspector. Mateo and I speculated they might have been saying Specter."

"Moby fucking Dick."

I slid the disk back into its sleeve.

When I looked up, Ryan's eyes were on mine. They were not smiling.

"What?" I asked.

"Why was a Chicago reporter trailing people in Montreal based on a story in Guatemala? Think about that."

I had been.

"Nordstern was into something so hot it got him assassinated in a foreign country."

I'd definitely been thinking about that.

"You keep your head up, Brennan. These people were willing to burn Nordstern. They're ruthless. They won't stop there."

I felt goose bumps crimp the flesh on my arms. The moment passed. Ryan smiled, returned to cop flippant.

"I'll give Galiano a heads-up on the Todos Santos," said Ryan.

"I also suggest you get down and dirty on Specter while I finish my facial reproduction. Then we'll play the disc, read Nordstern's notebook, and get some sense of what he was up to."

Ryan's grin broadened.

"Damn. The rumors are right."

"What rumors?" I asked.

"You are the brains of the operation."

I resisted the urge to kick his ankle.

The call came as I was still shaking rain from my umbrella. The voice on the other end was the last I wanted to hear. I invited its owner to my office with an enthusiasm I reserve for IRS auditors, Klansmen, and Islamic fundamentalists.

Sergeant-détective Luc Claudel appeared within minutes, back rigid, face pinched into its usual look of disdain. I rose but remained behind my desk.

"Bonjour, Monsieur Claudel. Comment ça va?"

I did not expect a greeting. I was not disappointed.

"I must pose a few questions."

Claudel viewed me as an unfortunate necessity, a status grudgingly granted following my input into the successful resolution of a number of CUM homicide cases. Claudel's demeanor toward me was always cool, reserved, and rigidly francophone. His use of English surprised me.

"Please have a seat," I said.

Claudel sat.

I sat.

Claudel placed a tape recorder on my desk.

"This conversation will be recorded."

Of course I have no objection, you arrogant, hawk-faced prick.

"No problem," I said.

Claudel activated the recorder, gave the time and date, and identified those present at the interview.

"I am heading the inquiry into last night's shooting."

Oh happy day. I waited.

"You were present?"

"Yes."

"Did you have an unobstructed view of the events that transpired?"

"I did."

"Were you able to hear words exchanged between Lieutenant-détective Andrew Ryan and his target?"

Target?

"I was."

Claudel kept his eyes on a point halfway between us.

"Was the man armed?"

"He had a Luger nine-millimeter."

"Did the man indicate that he intended to discharge his firearm?"

"The sonovabitch shot Nordstern then turned the gun on Ryan."

"Please. Do not get ahead of me."

The air space between my molars reduced to zero.

"Following the shooting of Olaf Nordstern, did Lieutenant-détective Ryan instruct the gunman to relinquish his weapon?"

"More than once."

"Did the gunman comply?"

"He grabbed a woman cowering on the sidewalk. She asked to be excused because of parental responsibility, but I believe the request was about to be denied."

Claudel's eyebrows formed a V above his eyes.

"Dr. Brennan, I am going to ask you once again to allow me to do this in my own manner."

Steady.

"Did the gunman attempt to take a hostage?"

"Yes."

"In your opinion, was the hostage in clear and present danger?"

"Had Ryan not acted, her life expectancy would have dropped to about three minutes."

"When Lieutenant-détective Ryan discharged his weapon, did the gunman return fire?"

"He nearly spray-painted the Forum with my cerebral cortex."

Claudel's lips compressed into a hard, tight line. He inhaled, exhaled through hard, tight nostrils.

"Why were you at the Forum, Dr. Brennan?"

"I was looking for the daughter of a friend."

"Were you there in any official capacity?"

"No."

"Why was Detective Ryan at the Forum?"

What was going on? Undoubtedly Ryan had answered these questions.

"He'd come to meet me."

Finally, the hawk eyes focused on mine.

"Was Detective Ryan there in any official capacity?"

"Studmeister."

Claudel and I glared at each other like wrestlers on *Smack Down*.

"In your opinion, did Andrew Ryan act properly in the shooting of Carlos Vicente?"

"He was a peach."

Claudel stood.

"Thank you."

"That's it?"

"That is all for now."

Claudel clicked off and pocketed the recorder.

"*Bonjour, madame.*"

As usual, Claudel left me so angry I feared I might suffer an embolism. To recompense, I went to the lobby, bought a Diet Coke, and returned to my office. Resting my feet on the window ledge, I drank the soda and ate the tuna sandwich and Oreos I'd brought from home.

Twelve floors below, a barge drifted up the misty St. Lawrence. Lilliputian trucks sprayed water from the edges of the Jacques Cartier Bridge. Cars glided over shiny asphalt, wakes of street rain rising from their tires. Pedestrians scurried with heads bent, umbrellas colored bobbins in a sodden world.

My daughter and I smiled from a beach on the Carolina coast. Another place. Another time. A happy moment.

By the last Oreo, I'd convinced myself that Claudel's brevity was a good sign. Had there been any concern about Ryan's actions, the interview would have been much more protracted.

Absolutely.

Brief is good.

I looked at my watch. One-twenty. Time to check Lucien's approximation.

Arcing my wrappers into the wastebasket, I scored myself two, and headed to *Imagerie*.

Lucien was at lunch, but his composite image stared from the screen.

One look and my newfound composure shattered like a windshield in a Schwarzenegger film.

23

Patricia Eduardo wasn't smiling. Nor was she frowning or showing surprise. In one view, long dark hair framed her face. In another, the hair corkscrewed in thick, springy curls. In a third, it was cropped short.

I barely breathed as I moved through the variations Lucien had created. Glasses on, glasses off. Straight brows, arched brows. Fleshy lips, thin lips. Droopy lids, hidden lids. Though the superficial details changed, the anatomic framework remained the same.

I was returning to the second of Lucien's long-hair images when he entered the section.

"What do you think?" He set a bottle of Evian on the counter beside me.

"Can you add bangs?"

"Sure."

I moved my chair to the left. Lucien slid in and worked the keys.

Bangs. He blended the image.

"What about a hat?"

"What kind?"

"Riding derby."

He searched the database.

"Nope."

"Something with a brim."

He found a cap, sized and pasted it.

I recalled the snapshots of Patricia Eduardo, and remembered the determination in the solemn, dark eyes as she stood by her horse.

The face I was viewing was blank and empty, the programmed offspring of pixels and bits. It didn't matter. It was the face of the girl on the Appaloosa.

Other memories shot through my brain. A tank filled with sewage and human waste. A skull oozing muck from every orifice. Tiny bones trapped in a rotting sleeve. Could it be? Could this nineteen-year-old hospital worker who loved horses and went out for an evening in the Zona Viva have ended up in such a horrible last resting place?

I stared at Patricia Eduardo. I saw drowned kittens. I saw Claudia de la Alda. I saw Chupan Ya.

You bastard. You goddamn, murdering bastard.

"What do you think?"

Lucien's voice brought me back.

"It's good." I forced calm into my voice. "Much better than I could have done."

"Really?"

"Really."

316

It was. Had I created such a striking likeness, I would have questioned my own bias. Lucien had never seen or heard of Patricia Eduardo.

"Please print several copies."

"I'll bring them to your office."

"Thanks."

"*Detective Galiano.*"

"It's Tempe."

"*Ay, buenos días.* Glad you caught me. Hernández and I were just heading out."

"It was Patricia Eduardo in the septic tank."

"No doubts?"

"None."

"The facial?"

"Dead ringer."

Silence.

"I guess that was a poor choice of words," I said. "Anyway, our graphics specialist did the approximation blind. Patricia's mother couldn't distinguish the thing from her junior class portrait."

"*Dios mío.*"

"I'll fax you a copy."

Empty air rolled north from Guatemala. Then Galiano said, "We're still grilling Miguel Gutiérrez."

"The De la Alda gardener."

"*Cerote.*" Turd.

"I take it that means he's a prince among men. What's his story?"

"The *Reader's Digest* version is that he fixated on

Claudia, took to stalking her. Spent nights parked outside her bedroom window."

"Oh joy. A peeper."

"Eventually Gutiérrez made his move. Claims the vic was receptive."

"She was probably too young to know how to blow him off without hurting his feelings."

"On July fourteenth he drove to the museum and offered her a ride home. Claudia accepted. En route, he asked her to explain something about the Kaminaljuyú ruins. She agreed. Once there, he pulled onto the back road and jumped her. Claudia resisted, things got out of hand. After strangling her, he rolled the body into the *barranca*. The rest is history."

"Did Gutiérrez phone Señora De la Alda?"

"Yes. Got a late-night visit from the heavenly host."

"An angel?"

"Ariel himself. Told Gutiérrez he'd screwed up, suggested a rosary and confession."

"Jesus."

"I don't think the big guy got involved."

"Have you found anything to link Gutiérrez to Patricia Eduardo?"

"*Nada.*"

"To the Paraíso?"

"Not yet. We'll be working those angles a lot harder now."

I thought a moment.

"The hair links Patricia to the Specter cat."

"We're working that, too."

"Ryan's doing some digging on the ambassador."

"I asked him to, but I'm not optimistic."

"Diplomatic firewall?"

"Like penetrating the CIA."

After a silence, Galiano said, "Ryan's keeping us in the loop on Nordstern."

"We'll know more when we go through his notes."

"Hernández and I confiscated a laptop when we tossed his room at the Todos Santos."

"Anything useful?"

"Let you know when we crack the password."

"Ryan's pretty good at that. Listen, Galiano. I want to help."

"I would like that." I heard him draw a deep breath. When he spoke again his voice sounded huskier. "These deaths haunt me, Tempe. Claudia. Patricia. These girls were the age of my son, Alejandro. That is not an age to die."

"Díaz will be livid if he hears about the CT scans."

"We'll get him a snow cone." The melancholy was gone.

"I'm finished here. It's time to refocus on Chupan Ya. If I can also help nail Patricia Eduardo's killer, I'll die a happy woman."

"Not on my patch."

"Deal."

"Ironic, isn't it?" he asked.

"What's that?"

"The perp's full name."

It took me a moment.

"Miguel Angel Gutiérrez," I said.

"A guilt-ridden id can break your balls."

I finished my reports on the shrunken head and the dismembered torso, and informed LaManche of my plans to return to Guatemala. He told me to be safe, wished me well.

Ryan arrived as I was finalizing arrangements with Delta Airlines. He waited while I requested an aisle seat, then pried the receiver from my hand.

"*Bonjour, Mademoiselle. Comment ça va?*"

I grabbed for the phone. *My* phone. Ryan stepped back and smiled.

"*Mais, oui,*" he purred. "But I speak English."

I curled my fingers in a "gimme" gesture. Ryan reached out and wrapped his free hand around mine.

"Not really. But your job, now *that's* difficult," he said, voice oozing sympathy. "I couldn't begin to keep all those flights and timetables straight."

Unbelievable. The guy was turning the charm on a reservation agent in suburban Atlanta! My eyeballs rolled almost a full three-sixty.

"Montreal."

And the bimbo was asking his whereabouts.

"You're right. It's not that far at all."

Yanking my right hand free, I slumped back in my chair, picked up a pen, and began sliding it end to end through my fingers.

"Do you think you could squeeze me onto that same flight Dr. Brennan just booked, *chère*?"

I stopped in mid-slide.

"Lieutenant-détective Andrew Ryan."

Pause.

"Provincial police."

I heard a distant, metallic voice as Ryan shifted the phone to his other ear.

"You learn to live with the danger."

I nearly gagged.

After a pause,

"*Fantastique.*"

What was fantastic?

"That would be terrific."

What would be terrific?

"No problem at all. Dr. Brennan knows I'm a tall boy. She won't mind a middle seat."

I sat forward.

"Dr. Brennan *will* mind a middle seat."

Ryan waved a hand at me. I threw the pen. He batted it down.

"Six foot two."

Eyes of blue. I knew her reply without having to hear it.

"Yes, I guess they are." Humble laugh.

This was absurd.

"Really? I don't want you breaking rules on my account."

Long pause.

"Two A and Two B through to G City. You're amazing."

Pause.

"I owe you, Nickie Edwards."

Pause.

"You do that."

Ryan handed me the receiver. I cradled it without comment.

"No need to thank me," he said.

"Thank you?"

"We're riding up front."

"I'll send Nickie a Hallmark."

"I didn't ask for special treatment."

"I guess Nickie was overwhelmed by your French magnetism."

"I guess."

"Is Nickie going to knit you a sweater for those cool Guatemalan nights?"

"Think I can get through to her again?" Ryan leaned on the arm of my chair and reached for the phone. I held him off with a hand to the chest.

"You could have her traced," I suggested icily.

He shook his head. "Abuse of the badge."

"Not to worry. Nickie will be calling once she's finished the *Teach Yourself French* tapes."

"Think she'd FedEx the sweater ahead?"

I shoved. Ryan righted himself, but did not open the distance between us.

"Are we going to continue this little tête-à-tête, or are you going to tell me why you booked a flight to Guatemala City?"

"Quickest way to get there."

"Ryan—"

"You're not delighted at the prospect of my company? You're breaking my heart." He placed both hands over the injured organ.

"You are not going to Guatemala to please me."

322

"I would." The choirboy smile.

"Do you intend to tell me why?"

Ryan ticked off points on his fingers. "*Uno*: Olaf Nordstern was killed in Montreal shortly after arriving from Guatemala. *Dos*: Nordstern's assassin carried a Guatemalan passport. *Tres*: André Specter, Canadian ambassador to Guatemala and citizen of our fair city, is currently the subject of discreet inquiry."

"You volunteered to go to Guatemala?"

"I offered my services."

"You're being reassigned."

"Guatemala seemed preferable to central booking."

"And you speak Spanish."

"*Sí, señorita.*"

"You never told me that."

"You never asked."

"Were you able to dig up anything on Specter?"

"According to the wife, he's Albert Schweitzer."

"That's not surprising."

"According to Foreign Affairs, he's Nelson Mandela. And strictly off limits."

"Galiano said you'd run into that. Did you talk to Chantale?"

"According to Chantale, her old man's the Marquis de Sade." Ryan shook his head. "That is one angry kid."

"What did she say?"

"Plenty. None of it complimentary. Most notably, she claims Daddy's chased skirt as far back as she can remember."

"How could a child know that?"

"Says she overheard numerous arguments between her parents, once caught the ambassador having phone sex in the middle of the night."

"Could he have been talking to his wife?"

"The missus was sacked out upstairs. The ambassador was doing the deed on the phone in his study. Chantale also claims that shortly before blowing town, she and Lucy stumbled on her father exiting the Ritz Continental with a chick on his arm."

"Did Specter see them?"

"No, but Chantale recognized Daddy's companion. Says the lucky lady graduated from her high school two years back."

"Christ. Did she provide a name?"

"Aida Pera."

"Do you believe her?"

Ryan shrugged. "I definitely plan to talk to Aida."

"So the ambassador likes young girls."

"If the daughter from hell is telling it straight."

"Did you interview any of the Chez Clémence posse?"

"That pleasure was denied me. Seems the three stooges have all vanished."

"You ordered those assholes not to leave town."

"They're probably off on a geology field trip. My colleagues will round them up."

"In the meantime?"

He pulled Nordstern's disc from his pocket.

"We get acquainted with SCELL."

I slipped the disk from its envelope, inserted it into my computer, and clicked over to the D drive. One file named appeared: fullrptstem.

"It's a monster PDF file. Over twenty thousand kilobytes."

"Can you open it?" Ryan had squatted beside me.

"The contents will be gibberish without a reader."

"Do you have one?"

"Not on this machine."

"Aren't those programs available as free downloads?"

"Can't put anything on a government computer."

"God bless bureaucracy. Let's give it a shot." He gestured with his chin. "Maybe there's an imbedded reader."

I opened the file. The screen filled with letters and symbols divided by horizontal dots indicating page and column breaks.

"Damn." Ryan shifted and his knee popped.

I looked at my watch. Five forty-two.

"I have Acrobat Reader on my laptop. Why don't I take the disc home, cruise through it, and give you a synopsis during our flight tomorrow."

Ryan stood, and his knee cracked again. I knew what was coming before he said it.

"We could both—"

"I've got a lot to do tonight, Ryan. I may not get back here for a while."

"Dinner?"

"I'll grab something on the way home."

"Fast food is bad for your pancreas."

"Since when are you concerned with my pancreas?"

"Everything about you concerns me."

"Really." I pressed the button and the disc slid out.

"You get sick in the highlands, I don't want to be rinsing out your panties."

I considered flinging the disc at him. Instead, I held it out.

He raised his eyebrows. "Why don't you take that home, cruise through it, and give me a synopsis during our flight tomorrow."

"Hot damn. There's an idea." I slid the disc into my briefcase.

"Pick you up at eleven?"

"I'll pack lots of panties."

A truck had overturned in the tunnel, and the trip home took almost an hour. After dumping my briefcase and purse, I dug a frozen delight from the freezer and popped it into the microwave.

While I waited, I cranked up my laptop and opened the PDF reader. The microwave beeped as I clicked on the fullrptstem file.

When I returned, a surrealistic tableau filled the monitor. I stared at the blobs and squiggles exploding from a central mass, then scrolled upward and read the title.

It made no sense at all.

24

"Friggin' stem cells?"

Ryan had been in a rotten mood since picking me up at eleven. A forty-minute flight delay was not improving his disposition.

"Yes."

"The little buggers your moron fundamentalists are pissing their shorts to protect?"

"They are not *my* moron fundamentalists."

"That's it?"

"Two hundred and twenty-two pages' worth."

"Is it some kind of progress report?"

"And a discussion of future research directions."

Ryan was in a snit because he couldn't smoke.

"What genius prepared it?"

"The National Institutes of Health."

"How come Nordstern had the report on disk?"

"He probably downloaded it from the Net."

"Why?"

"Excellent question, Detective."

Ryan checked his watch for the billionth time. At that exact moment the digits on the screen behind the Delta agent changed again. We would now be departing an hour behind schedule.

"Sonovabitch."

"Relax. We'll make the connection."

"Thank you, Pollyanna."

I dug a journal from my briefcase and began leafing through it. Ryan got up, crossed the waiting area, recrossed it, returned to his seat.

"So what did you learn?"

"About?"

"Stem cells."

"More than I ever wanted to know. I was up until two."

A man the size of South Dakota dropped a bag on the floor and flopped into the seat to my right. A tsunami of sweat and hair oil rolled my way. Ryan's eyes met mine, then shifted toward the windows. Wordlessly, he got up and changed location. I followed a compassionate thirty seconds later.

"Stem cells are taken from embryos?" Ryan.

"Stem cells can come from embryonic, fetal, or adult tissue."

"It's the non-adult forms that have the Christian zealots in a frenzy."

"The religious right is strongly opposed to any use of embryonic stem cells."

"The usual sanctity of life crap?"

Ryan did have a way of cutting to the chase.

"That's the argument."

"And G. W. Bush bought in."

"Only partly. He's trying to sit on the fence. He's limited federal funding to research using existing stem cell lines only."

"So scientists needing government grants are only allowed to experiment with cells already growing in labs?"

"Or with stem cells derived from adult tissue."

"Will that do the job?"

"In my opinion?"

"No. Give me the thinking in the Politburo."

Nope. That's it. Back to my journal.

After a few moments, "O.K. Give me the stem cell basic course, condensed version."

"We're agreed on courteous listening as a protocol?"

"Yeah, yeah."

"Every one of the two hundred cell types in the human body arises from one of three germ layers, endoderm, mesoderm, or ectoderm."

"Inner, middle, and outer layers."

"That's excellent, Andrew."

"Thank you, Ms. Brennan."

"An embryonic stem cell, or ES cell, is what's termed pluripotent. That means it has the ability to give rise to cell types deriving from any of the three layers. Stem cells reproduce themselves through-out the life of an organism, but remain uncom-mitted until signaled to develop into something specific – pancreas, heart, bone, skin."

"Flexible little dudes."

"The term 'embryonic stem cell' really includes two types: those that come from embryos, and those that come from fetal tissue."

"The only two sources?"

"To date, yes. To be perfectly correct, embryonic *stem* cells are derived from eggs just a few days after fertilization."

"And before the egg is implanted in the mother's uterus."

"Right. At that point the embryo is a hollow sphere called a blastocyst. Embryonic stem cells are taken from the inner layer of that sphere. Embryonic *germ* cells are derived from five- to ten-week-old fetuses."

"And the grown-ups?"

"Adult stem cells are unspecialized cells that occur in specialized tissues. They have the ability to renew themselves, and to differentiate into all of the specialized cell types of the tissues in which they originate."

"Which are?"

"Bone marrow, blood, the cornea and retina of the eye, brain, skeletal muscle, dental pulp, liver, skin—"

"Don't we already use those?"

"We do. Adult stem cells isolated from bone marrow and blood have been studied extensively and are used therapeutically."

"Why not simply use the big guys and leave embryos and fetuses alone?"

I enumerated points on my fingers.

"Adult stem cells are rare. They are difficult to identify, isolate, and purify. There are way too few of them. They do not replicate indefinitely in culture the way embryonic stem and germ cells do. And, to date, there is no population of adult stem cells that is pluripotent."

"So embryonic stem and germ cells are the name of the game."

"Definitely."

Ryan fell silent for a moment. Then, "What's the potential pay-off in having lots of them available?"

"Parkinson's disease, diabetes, chronic heart disease, end-stage kidney disease, liver failure, cancer, spinal cord injury, multiple sclerosis, Alzheimer's disease—"

"The sky's the limit."

"Exactly. I can't fathom why anyone would want to block that kind of research."

The baby blues went wide, the voice went preachy, and one long finger pointed at my nose.

"It's a first step, Sister Temperance, toward a slide down the slippery slope of pregnancies conceived only for use of the embryos, resulting in an Aryan nation dedicated to the propagation of muscular, blond, blue-eyed men and slinky, long-legged women with big breasts."

With that, they called our flight.

On the way to Guatemala we talked about mutual friends, and about times and experiences we'd shared. I told Ryan about Katy's psych project with the Cheez Whiz rats, and about her quest for summer employment.

Ryan asked about my sister, Harry. We laughed as I described her latest romance with a rodeo clown from Wichita Falls. He filled me in on his niece, Danielle, who'd run off to sell jewelry on the streets of Vancouver. We agreed the two had a lot in common.

Eventually, fatigue sucked me in. I fell asleep with my head on Ryan's shoulder. Though rough on my neck, it was a warm and reassuring place to be.

By the time we collected our baggage in Guatemala City, worked our way through the throng of porters pleading to carry it, and found a taxi, it was nine-thirty. I gave the driver my destination. He turned to Ryan for directions. I provided them.

We pulled up at my hotel at ten-fifteen. While I paid the fare, Ryan unloaded the luggage. When I asked for a receipt, the driver regarded me as though I'd requested a urine sample. Muttering, he dug a scrap of paper from the seat crack, scrawled something on it, and thrust it at me.

The desk clerk greeted me by name, welcomed me back. His eyes shifted to Ryan.

"Will that be one room or two?"

"One for me. Is three fourteen still available?"

"*Sí, señora.*"

"I'll take it."

"And the señor?"

"You will have to ask the señor."

I forked over a credit card, signed in, collected my bags, and headed upstairs. I'd hung my clothes, spread out my toiletries, and started a bath when the phone rang.

"Don't start, Ryan. I'm going to bed."

"Why would I want to start Ryan?" Galiano asked.

"You invited him here."

"I also invited you here. I'd rather start you."

"I've been traveling with Detective Personality for almost twelve hours. I need sleep."

"Ryan did sound a bit edgy."

The frat brothers had already spoken. I felt a prickle of irritation.

"He shot a guy."

"Yes."

"Ryan and I are going to drop in on Aida Pera, the ambassador's little friend, tomorrow. Then I'm going to swing by for a chat with Patricia Eduardo's mother. She claims she's got some new information."

"You sound skeptical."

"She's a strange one."

"Where's the father?"

"Dead."

"Did she agree to give a saliva sample?"

I'd asked Galiano to set that in motion before my departure from Montreal. Now that we had a potential ID, it was possible to run a DNA comparison. A profile obtained from Señora Eduardo's saliva would be compared with one obtained from

333

the fetal bones found with the Paraíso skeleton. Since mitochondrial DNA is passed through maternal lines only, the baby, its mother, and its grandmother would show identical sequencing.

"Already done. And I've collected the fetal bones from Mateo's lab."

"Has Señora Eduardo seen the sketch I faxed?"

"Yes."

"Does she accept the idea that the skeleton is Patricia's?"

"Yes. As does everyone here at headquarters."

"She must be devastated."

I heard him sigh. "*Ay, Dios.* It is the saddest news a parent can receive."

For a moment neither of us spoke. I thought of Katy. I pictured Galiano thinking of Alejandro.

"So. Do you want to ride along?"

I told him I did.

"What's Pera's story?"

"She's been working as a secretary since finishing secondary school two years ago. Chantale wasn't making that part up."

"What does Pera say about Specter?"

"We haven't dropped that on her yet. Thought we'd do it in person."

"What time?"

"Eight."

"Bring coffee."

I hung up, stripped, and hopped into the bath. And flew right back out, sliding across the tile, and banging my hip on the sink. The water was cold enough to form an ice slick. Swearing, I wrapped a towel around myself and fiddled with the faucets. Both ran frigid.

Shivering and swearing some more, I slipped under the blankets.

Eventually the shivering subsided.

Ryan didn't phone.

I fell asleep uncertain if I was annoyed or relieved.

The next morning I awoke to a jackhammer loud enough to impair my hearing for life. Throwing on clothes, I stuck my head out the window. Three floors down, six men were redesigning the sidewalk. It looked like a long-term project.

Terrific.

I phoned Mateo to let him know I was back in Guatemala, and that I would be at the FAFG lab that afternoon. Ryan was already waiting when I entered the lobby.

"How did we sleep, cupcake?"

"Like a boulder."

"Mood improved?"

"*What?*"

"You must have been tired last night."

Galiano honked.

I clamped my open mouth shut, pushed through the glass doors, crossed the sidewalk, and climbed into the front seat so Ryan would have to get in back.

On the drive to Aida Pera's apartment, Galiano filled us in on developments in the Claudia de la Alda case.

"The night Patricia Eduardo disappeared, Gutiérrez was at his church preparing flowers for All Saints' Day."

"Anyone alibi him?" Ryan.

"About half a dozen parishioners, including his landlady, Señora Ajuchán. Ajuchán says she followed him home, swears Gutiérrez couldn't have gone out again, at least not driving, because she blocked him in the driveway with her car."

"An accomplice?" Ryan.

"Ajuchán insists she wakes every time Gutiérrez enters or leaves her house." Galiano made a left. "She also insists the guy's Mr. Rogers. Wouldn't hurt a flea. Also a loner. No pals."

"What did you find when you tossed his room?" I asked.

"The crazy bastard must have had forty prints of Claudia pasted to the mirror above his dresser. Arranged them like an altar. Candles and all."

"What's his story?" Ryan.

"Says he admired her virtue and piety."

"Who took the pics?"

"He's a little vague on that. But we recovered a camera from his closet shelf containing a partially exposed roll of film. You'll never guess."

"The little mistress."

"Bingo. Shot her from a distance with a telephoto lens."

"Have you had him assessed?" I asked.

Galiano made another left, then a right onto a street lined with two- and three-flats.

"Docs say he has a compulsive fixation disorder,

336

or some psychobabble like that. Erotomania? Couldn't help himself, probably never meant to hurt her."

"Lot of good that did Claudia."

Galiano pulled to the curb, shifted into park, and turned to face us.

"What about Patricia Eduardo?" Ryan asked.

"Gutiérrez says he's never met Patricia Eduardo, has never been to the Zona Viva or the Café San Felipe, and has never heard of the Pension Paraíso. He swears Claudia de la Alda is the only person he's ever loved."

"The only person he's ever killed." Ryan's voice was hard with disdain.

"Yes."

"Do you believe him?" I asked.

"*Hijo de la gran puta.* He's passed three polygraphs."

Galiano turned and chin-motioned to a beat-to-crap building on the far side of the street. Crumbling pink stucco. Bloodred door. Dozing wino. Grafitti. More clever than most. B-plus.

"Pera shares a second-floor flat with an older cousin."

"Won't she be at work?"

"When I said I'd be by, she decided to take the day off. Didn't want to upset the boss."

"Did she ask why you wanted to talk to her?" I asked.

Galiano looked surprised. "No."

We got out. At the thunk-thunk-thunk of the car doors, the wino slithered down the stucco and stretched full length across the front stoop. Stepping over him, I noticed that his pants were half zipped.

Or half unzipped. I supposed that depended on your point of view.

The lobby measured approximately six by six and smelled of disinfectant. The floor was tiled in black and white.

The names Pera and Irías had been printed on a card and inserted into the slot of one of six brass mailboxes. Galiano pushed the buzzer. A voice answered immediately. Our arrival had been monitored.

"*Sí?*"

"Detective Galiano."

The door clicked. We passed through and single-filed up a narrow staircase.

The Pera-Irías flat lay behind one of two doors opening onto a tiny second-floor hallway. As I stepped onto the landing, locks rattled, the door swung inward, and a double-take-gorgeous young woman peeked out. I felt Galiano and Ryan do the male straightening thing. I may have joined them.

"*Detective Galiano?*" A child's voice.

"*Buenos días. Señorita Pera.*"

Aida Pera nodded solemnly. Her hair was flaxen, her skin pale, her eyes brown and enormous, trusting but frightened at the same time. "Take care of me" eyes. The kind of eyes that make men stupid.

"Thank you for agreeing to see us so early." Galiano.

Another nod, then Pera looked at Ryan and me.

Galiano introduced us. A slight pucker formed above the bridge of her nose, melted.

"What is this about?" She toyed with the security chain. Though her fingers were long and slender, the nails were ragged, the cuticles raw and bloody. As far as I could see, they were her only flaw.

"May we come in?" Galiano spoke in a calming voice.

Pera stepped back, and we entered a small vestibule. A long corridor shot straight ahead toward the back of the flat. The living room lay to the front. She led us there and gestured at a grouping of couch and chairs, each outfitted with arm- and headrest doilies. I wondered how old the cousin was.

Galiano wasted no time.

"Señorita Pera, it is my understanding that you are friends with Canadian ambassador André Specter."

This time the pucker was deep and sustained.

"May I ask the nature of that relationship?"

Pera chewed a knuckle as she looked from Galiano to Ryan to me. Perhaps I appeared the least threatening. Her answer came my way.

"I can't talk about my relationship with André. I just can't. It – I – André made me promise—"

"We could do this as a formal statement at police headquarters." Galiano's voice was a wee bit harsher.

Pera did another sweep. Galiano. Ryan. Me. Again, she chose the girl.

"Promise that you will never tell?" A child, bursting with a secret.

"We will do our best to protect your confidentiality." Galiano.

The Bambi eyes cut to Galiano, came back to me.

"André and I are going to be married."

25

Galiano glanced at me. Take it away.

"How long have you been seeing the ambassador?" I asked.

"Six months."

"Are you lovers?"

She nodded, looked at the floor.

"I know you think I'm too young for André. I'm not. I love him and he loves me and nothing else matters."

"Do his wife and daughter matter?" I asked.

"André is very unhappy. He plans to leave his wife as soon as he can."

Don't they all.

"How old are you, Aida?"

"Eighteen."

My anger was building.

"When?"

She looked up. "When what?"

"When is the wedding?"

"Well, we don't have a date. But soon." She looked to Galiano and Ryan for support. "As soon as André can, you know, arrange things without jeopardizing his position."

"And then?"

"We'll go away. He'll be posted somewhere neat. Paris, maybe. Or Rome or Madrid. I'll be his wife and travel with him, and go to all the parties."

And Saddam Hussein will convert to Christianity and conduct baptisms.

"Has the ambassador ever talked about former mistresses?"

"You don't understand. André's not like that."

She looked at Galiano. She looked at Ryan. She looked at me. She had that right. We didn't understand.

"Has he ever hurt you?"

She frowned. "What do you mean?"

"Shaken you, struck you, forced you to do something you didn't want to do."

"Never." Breathy. "André's a kind, gentle, wonderful man."

"Who cheats on his wife."

"It's not what you're thinking."

It was exactly what I was thinking, the cradle-robbing bastard.

"Do you know a young woman named Patricia Eduardo?"

She gave a small shake of her head.

"Claudia de la Alda?"

"No." Her eyes were growing red around the rims.

"Will you be seeing Mr. Specter in the near future?"

"It's hard to make plans. André calls when he's able to get free."

And you wait by the phone. Bastard.

"Does he usually come here?" Galiano asked.

"If my cousin isn't home." Her nose was now as red as her eyes, and she'd begun to sniffle. "Sometimes we go out."

I dug in my purse and handed her a tissue.

Galiano handed her a card.

"Call me when you hear from him."

"Has André done something illegal?"

Galiano ignored her question.

"When he phones, agree to see him. Call me. And don't tell Specter."

Pera opened her mouth to object.

"Do it, Señorita Pera. Do it and save yourself a great deal of grief."

Galiano rose. Ryan and I did the same. Pera followed us to the door.

As we filed out she said one last thing.

"It's hard, you know. It's not like in the movies."

"No," I agreed. "It's not."

The sky was overcast when we left Pera's apartment. Anxious to begin going through Nordstern's belongings, Ryan peeled off and took a taxi to police headquarters.

It was raining by the time Galiano and I arrived

at the Eduardo home. While not as luxurious as Chez Specter or Chez Gerardi, the house was comfortable and well tended, what a Realtor might call cozy.

When Señora Eduardo opened the door one phrase stuck in my brain: ET, phone home. Our hostess had a wrinkled pie face dominated by the largest eyes I'd ever seen on a human being. Her arms and legs were scrawny, her fingers curved and knobby. She stood about four feet tall.

Señora Eduardo led us to a parlor filled with way too much floral-upholstered furniture, and indicated that we should sit. She boosted herself into a straight-back wooden chair, wrapped one ankle around the other, and made a sign of the cross. Tears glistened in the enormous eyes.

As I settled into an overstuffed armchair, I wondered if the woman had a chromosomal abnormality. I also wondered how she had produced a daughter as attractive as Patricia.

Galiano introduced me to our hostess, expressed sympathy for her loss. Señora Eduardo crossed herself again, took a deep breath.

"Have you made an arrest?" she asked in a thin, wavery voice.

"We're working on it," Galiano said.

Señora Eduardo's left eyelid did a slo-mo blink. The right lid followed a half beat behind.

"Did your daughter ever speak of a man named André Specter?"

"No."

"Miguel Gutiérrez?"

"No. Who are these men?"

"You are sure?"

Señora Eduardo reprocessed the names. Or pretended to.

"Absolutely certain. What do these men have to do with my daughter?" One tear escaped and slithered down her cheek. She swiped it away with a jerky motion.

"I just wanted to check."

"Are they suspects?"

"Not in your daughter's death."

"Whose?"

"Miguel Gutiérrez has confessed to the murder of a young woman named Claudia de la Alda."

"You think he might also have killed Patricia?"

Whatever the señora's physical condition, it clearly did not affect her intelligence.

"No."

"And Specter?" Another tear. Another swipe.

"Never mind Specter."

"Who is he?"

Or her tenacity.

"If your daughter didn't speak of him, it isn't relevant. What is this new information you have?"

The huge eyes narrowed. I detected a flicker of distrust.

"I remembered the name of Patricia's supervisor at the hospital."

"The one with whom she argued?"

She nodded and did the eyelid thing.

Galiano pulled out a notebook.

"Zuckerman."

A tiny ping.

"First name?" Galiano asked.

"Doctor."

"Gender?"

"Doctor."

"Do you know why they fought?"

"Patricia never elaborated."

At that moment Buttercup joined us, went directly to Galiano, and began rubbing back and forth on his pants legs. Señora Eduardo slid from her chair and clapped at the cat. He arched, then turned and performed another figure of eight around Galiano's ankles.

Señora Eduardo clapped louder.

"Shoo. Go on. Back with the others."

Buttercup regarded his odd mistress a very long moment, raised then flicked his tail, and strolled from the room.

"I apologize. Buttercup was my daughter's cat." Her lower lip trembled. I feared she was on the verge of crying. "Since Patricia is gone, he listens to no one."

Galiano pocketed his notebook and stood.

Señora Eduardo looked up at him. Tears now glistened on both her cheeks.

"You must find the monster who did this to my Patricia. She was all I had."

Galiano's jaw muscles bunched, and the Guernsey eyes grew moist.

"We will, Dona. I give you my promise. We will catch him."

Señora Eduardo hopped to her feet. Galiano

leaned down and took both her hands in his.

"We'll speak to Dr. Zuckerman. Again, we are so sorry for your loss. Please call if you think of anything else."

"That was one self-assured stud of a cat." Galiano finished his Pepsi and slid the can into a plastic holder hanging from the dashboard.

"We each deal with loss in a different way."

"Wouldn't want to cross ole Buttercup."

"Good call on the gray pants."

"They've seen worse."

"What's the deal with Señora Eduardo?"

"Rheumatoid arthritis at a young age. Guess she stopped growing."

We were back in the car heading to police headquarters after a brief stop at a Pollo Campero, the Guatemalan equivalent of KFC.

Galiano's cell sounded as we turned onto Avenida 6. He clicked on.

"Galiano."

He listened, then mouthed the name Aida Pera for my benefit.

"What time?"

I took a swig of my Diet Coke.

"Don't mention our visit. Don't mention this call."

Pera said something.

"Encourage her to go out."

Pera said something else.

"Uh huh."

Another pause.

"We'll deal with that."

Galiano disconnected and tossed the phone onto the seat.

"The ambassador is home and horny," I guessed.

"Dropping in on his honey at nine tonight."

"That was quick."

"Probably wants to tell her he's booked a church."

"Think you might happen to be in the neighborhood?"

"Never can tell."

"Why not just haul the bastard in and grill him?"

Galiano snorted. "Ever hear of the Vienna Conventions on diplomatic and consular relations?"

I shook my head.

"It's a piece of work that severely limits the ability of local authorities to arrest or detain diplomats."

"Diplomatic immunity."

"You got it."

"That's why New York's left with its head up its ass on a trillion parking tickets each year." I finished my Coke. "Can't immunity be waived for criminal offenses?"

"Immunity can only be waived by the sending state, in this case Canada. If Canada refuses to waive immunity, all Guatemala can do is have Specter PNG'ed."

"PNG'ed?"

"Have him declared persona non grata and expelled."

"Guatemalan authorities can't investigate anyone they want to within their own borders?"

"We can investigate up the wazoo, but we have to have permission from the Canadian government to interrogate a Canadian diplomat."

"Have you made a formal request?"

"It's in the works. If we show sufficient cause they might allow us to question Specter in the presence of Canadian officials—"

"Ryan."

"Ryan, possibly others from the diplomatic staff. But here's the kicker. Specter would have to agree to the interrogation. He would not be under oath, and evidence given could not be used to prejudice his immunity from eventual prosecution."

"The sending state decides the fate of its own."

"You bet."

Ryan was in the second-floor conference room where I'd first met Antonio Díaz, the unfortunately memorable DA. Books, journals, pamphlets, papers, notebooks, and file folders lay separated into stacks on a table in front of him.

Ryan sat with chin on palm, listening to tapes on a Dictaphone identical to the one Nordstern had used in our interview. At least a dozen cassettes lay to its right. Two lay to its left.

On seeing us, Ryan hit stop and slumped back in his chair.

"Jesus Christ, this is rugged."

We both waited.

"Our once and future Pulitzer winner spoke to a lot of angry folks."

"At Chupan Ya?" I asked.

"And other villages the army fucked over. There was a regular Gestapo down here."

"Find anything to explain why Nordstern was capped?" Galiano rested one haunch on the table edge.

"Maybe. But how the hell do I know what it is?"

I picked up a half dozen cassettes. Each had a name. Many were Mayan. Señora Ch'i'p's son. An old man from a village to the west of Chupan Ya.

Some tapes contained multiple interviews. Mateo Reyes shared space with Elena Norvillo and Maria Paiz. T. Brennan was paired with E. Sandoval.

"Who's E. Sandoval?" I asked.

Galiano shrugged.

"Nordstern must have done the interview right after yours."

Ryan took a deep breath. I turned to him. He looked drained.

"If you'd like help, I can tell Mateo I can't get away until tomorrow," I said.

Ryan looked at me like I'd just told him he'd won the lottery.

"Couldn't hurt. You know more about this stuff than I do." He jerked a thumb at a suitcase on the floor below the window. "I'll let you paw through Nordstern's motherload of undies."

"No, thanks. One dirty shorts run was enough for me."

Galiano rose.

"I've got to plan an evening outing with Hernández."

Ryan raised his eyebrows.

"Tempe can explain. Off to the war room."

"What would you like me to do?" I asked.

"Go through the books and papers while I work my way through these interview tapes."

"What am I looking for?"

"Anything."

I phoned Mateo. He had no problem with the delay. I asked him about E. Sandoval. He explained that Eugenia Sandoval worked for CEIHS, the Centro de Investigaciones de Historia Social. After hanging up, I told Ryan.

"Guess that makes sense," he said.

I gathered the books and journals and settled opposite Ryan. Some publications were in Spanish, most in English. I began a list.

The Massacre at El Mazote: A Parable of the Cold War; Massacres in the Jungle, Ixcán, Guatemala, 1975–1982; Persecution by Proxy: The Civil Patrols in Guatemala, Robert F. Kennedy Center for Human Rights. *Harvest of Violence: The Maya Indians and the Guatemala Crisis*; an Americas Watch Report dated August 1986: *Civil Patrols in Guatemala*.

"Looks like Nordstern was doing his homework."

"Till he got extra credit."

"Has anyone talked to the *Chicago Tribune*?"

"Seems Nordstern was a freelancer, didn't actually work for the paper. But the *Tribune* had commissioned him to do a piece on Clyde Snow and the FAFG."

"Why the interest in stem cells?"

"Future story?"

"Maybe."

Two hours later we caught a break.

I was leafing through a photojournal of *La Lucha Maya*, a collection of full-page color portraits. Thatched-roof houses in Santa Clara. A young boy fishing on Lake Atitlán. A baptismal ceremony in Xeputúl. Men bearing caskets from Chontalá to the cemetery in Chichicastenango.

In the early eighties, under instructions from the local army base, the Civil Patrol executed twenty-seven villages in Chontalá. A decade later, Clyde Snow exhumed the remains.

Opposite the funeral procession, a photo of young men with automatic weapons. Civil Patrollers in Huehuetenango.

The Civil Patrol system was imposed throughout rural Guatemala. Participation was obligatory. Men lost workdays. Families lost money. The patrols imposed a new set of rules and values in which weapons and force dominated. The system shattered traditional authority patterns and disrupted community life among Mayan peasants.

Ryan popped out a cassette, popped in another. I heard Nordstern's voice, then my own.

I moved through the pictures. An old man forced to leave his home in Chunimá due to death threats by the Civil Patrol. A Mayan woman with a baby on her back, tears on her cheeks.

I turned the page. Civil Patrollers at Chunimá, guns raised, misty mountains floating behind them. The caption explained that the group's former leader had assassinated two local men for refusing to serve in the "voluntary" patrol.

I stared at the young men in the photo. They could have been a soccer team. A Scout troop. A high school glee club.

I heard a mechanical version of my voice begin to explain the massacre at Chupan Ya.

"In August 1982, soldiers and civil patrollers entered the village—"

A Civil Patrol had aided the army at Chupan Ya. Together, the soldiers and patrollers had raped women and girls, then shot and macheted them, and torched their homes.

I turned the page.

Xaxaxak, a community in Sololá. Civil Patrollers marched parade style, automatic weapons held diagonally across their chests. Soldiers looked on, some in jungle fatigues, others in uniforms indicating much higher pay grades.

Nordstern had circled the names. My eyes fell on it at the precise moment Nordstern spoke it.

"Under the command of Alejandro Bastos."

"I don't know that."

"Go on."

"You seem to know more about this than I do." Rustling. *"It's getting late, Mr. Nordstern. I have work to do."*

"Chupan Ya or the septic tank?"

353

"Stop! Play that back!"

Ryan hit rewind and replayed the end of the interview.

"Look at this."

I rotated the book.

Ryan studied the photo, read the caption.

"Alejandro Bastos was in command of the local army post."

"Nordstern accused Bastos of being responsible for Chupan Ya," I said.

"Why do you suppose Nordstern circled the weasel next to him?"

Ryan handed the book back and I looked at the circle.

"Jesus Christ."

26

"It's Antonio Díaz." Though the lenses weren't pink, there was no question in my mind.

"And he would be?"

"The DA from hell."

"The guy who confiscated Patricia Eduardo's skeleton?"

"Yes."

Ryan reached for the book. I gave it to him.

"Díaz was in the army."

"Apparently."

"With Bastos."

"One picture is worth a thousand chalupas."

"The guy Nordstern accused of running the show at Chupan Ya?"

"You heard the tape."

"Who is Alejandro Bastos?"

"Search me."

Ryan started to rise.

"Down, boy."

He dropped back into his chair.

"Díaz served with this Bastos. What the hell does that mean?"

Just what I was asking myself. Were we back to Chupan Ya? Was it just that Díaz was in the army and was now a judge? Was that Nordstern's concern? Nothing unusual there. Galiano had laid that all out in our conversation at the Gucumatz. The judicial system in Guatemala was full of torturers and murderers. Everyone knew that. It wouldn't be news. Was there a link with the Paraíso? No answers were popping to mind.

"Maybe nothing," I said, not really believing it.

"Maybe something," Ryan said.

"Maybe Díaz had reasons for not wanting me on the Eduardo case."

"Such as?"

"Maybe he thought it was someone else in the Paraíso tank."

"Who?"

"Someone connected with Chupan Ya."

"A pregnant teenaged girl?"

He had me there.

"Maybe Díaz wanted me diverted from the Chupan Ya investigation."

"Why?"

"Maybe he feared revelations about his past." I was just thinking out loud. "Maybe he feared they'd cost him his job."

"Didn't the Paraíso case do just that?"

"What?"

"Divert you from working with Mateo and the team? And the more you investigated Paraíso, the more diverted you would be. If he wanted you diverted, he would not thwart the diversion."

A sudden terrible thought.

"Jesus!"

"What?"

"Maybe Díaz was behind the attack on Molly and Carlos."

"Let's not get jiggy until we have some facts. Do you know anything about this Bastos character?"

I shook my head.

"Why would Nordstern circle Díaz's picture?"

"You ask good questions, Ryan."

"About what?"

We both turned. Galiano stood in the doorway.

"Who's Alejandro Bastos?"

"Army colonel. Went on to become minister of something under Ríos Montt. Died a couple of years ago."

"Was Bastos involved in the massacres?"

"Up to his eyeballs. That prick was a perfect example of why amnesty was a lousy idea."

Ryan handed Galiano the picture.

"*Hijo de la puta.*"

Galiano looked up.

"With Díaz." This time in English. "Sonovabitch."

A fly buzzed the window. I watched it and again felt a shared frustration. I wasn't getting anywhere either.

"What's up with Specter?" I asked Galiano.

"Turns out the ambassador has an airtight alibi for the week surrounding Patricia Eduardo's disappearance."

"He and Dominique were at a nunnery renewing their vows." Ryan.

"An international trade conference in Brussels. Specter gave daily presentations, attended nightly cocktails."

"Aida Pera would have thought it was neat." Ryan.

"It's not her fault."

Both men looked at me like I'd said Eva Braun wasn't so bad.

"Specter's obviously a black-belt sleaze. Pera's a kid."

"She's eighteen."

"Exactly."

For several seconds, the only sound came from the fly.

"Patricia Eduardo had to have some contact with the Specter household for Guimauve's hair to get into her jeans," I volunteered for no particular reason.

"Maybe the hair transferred from Specter while he was getting into her jeans." Ryan.

"Eduardo disappeared on October twenty-ninth," Galiano said. "She didn't necessarily die that day."

"Did you track down Dr. Zuckerman?"

Galiano pulled out the ubiquitous notepad.

"Maria Zuckerman earned an MD at NYU, did a residency in OB/GYN at Johns Hopkins, spent a couple of years in Melbourne, Australia, at some institute of reproductive biology."

"So she's no dummy."

"The good doctor's on staff at the Hospital Centro Médico. Served as Patricia Eduardo's direct supervisor for the past two years. I talked to a few of Eduardo's coworkers. One was aware of Eduardo's run-in with Zuckerman, but didn't know the cause. Here's an interesting sidebar. Seems I've already spoken to Dr. Zuckerman."

Ping!

"Zuckerman runs the Mujeres por Mujeres clinic in Zone One!" I said.

"The very one. She's going to enjoy my next visit even less than she enjoyed my first one."

"I'd like to go along."

"Bus leaves at oh-eight-hundred."

Poor Mateo. I'd have to call him again.

"Here's another intriguing sidebar. The coworker thought Patricia was seeing someone behind her boyfriend's back. An older man."

When I look back, I recall that meeting as the beginning of the spiral. From then on details multiplied, information proliferated, and our perceptions formed and re-formed like patterns in a kaleidoscope.

Ryan and I spent another couple of hours going through Nordstern's tapes and books. Then we dragged ourselves home, grabbed a quick dinner, and went to our rooms. He didn't make a pass. I didn't care.

I'd been distracted since Galiano's report. I thought his revelation about Maria Zuckerman had been the ping I'd felt at the Eduardo home, but something else kept bothering me.

What? Something I'd seen? Something I'd heard? The feeling was like a vague itch that I couldn't quite scratch.

Ryan phoned at nine-fifteen.

"What are you doing?"

"Reading the label on my antacid."

"You do live on the edge."

"What did you think I'd be doing?"

"Thanks for your help today."

"My pleasure."

"Speaking of your pleasure—"

"Ryan."

"O.K. But I'll make it up to you when we return to the great white North."

"How?"

"I'll take you to see *Cats*."

My itch suddenly localized.

"I've got to go."

"What? What did I say?"

"I'll call you tomorrow."

I clicked off and dialed Galiano's number. He was out.

Damn.

I grabbed the phone book.

Yes.

I dialed.

Señora Eduardo answered on the first ring.

I apologized for phoning so late. She dismissed it.

"Señora Eduardo, when you shooed Buttercup, you told him to join the others. Did you mean other cats?"

"Unfortunately, yes. Two years ago, a litter of kittens turned up at the barn where my daughter boarded her horses. Patricia adopted two and found homes for the rest. She wanted to bring the kittens here, but I said Buttercup was enough. They were born at the barn, they could stay at the barn. That worked fine until Patricia stopped going."

She paused. I could picture her performing the eyelid maneuver.

"About three weeks ago the barn owner phoned and insisted I take the cats or he'd drown them. Buttercup doesn't like it, but they're here."

"Do you know who adopted the other kittens?"

"Families around here, I suppose. Patricia plastered the neighborhood with circulars. Got about a dozen calls."

I cleared my throat.

"Are the cats shorthairs?"

"Plain old barn cats."

Dominique Specter's phone rang four times, then a male voice requested a message in French and English. I left one after the tone.

I was flossing when my cell phone rang. It was Mrs. Specter.

I asked about Chantale.

Fine.

I asked about the weather in Montreal.

Warm.

Obviously, she was not in a chatty mood.

"I have just one question, Mrs. Specter."

"*Oui?*"

"Where did you get Guimauve?"

"*Mon Dieu.* I will have to think."

I waited while she did so.

"Chantale found a notice at the pharmacy. We phoned. Kittens were still available, so we drove out and chose one."

"Drove where?"

"A barn of some sort. A place with horses."

"Near Guatemala City?"

"Yes. I don't remember the exact location."

I thanked her and rang off.

Would there be no end to the mistakes I would make on this case? What a moron I was. I'd explained it to Ryan, failed to grasp it myself.

Guimauve's hair wasn't with the bones in the Paraíso tank. The hair came from Guimauve's littermate. Guimauve's sibling. An animal with identical mitochondrial DNA. Patricia Eduardo's barn cats had shed the hair I found on her jeans.

André Specter wasn't a murderer. Just a horny slimeball who deceived his family and gullible young women.

I fell asleep with a million questions swirling in my brain.

Who killed Patricia Eduardo?

Why had Díaz not wanted me to identify the body?

Why had Patricia Eduardo and Dr. Zuckerman argued?

How many people had been responsible for Chupan Ya?

Who shot Molly and Carlos?

What had Ollie Nordstern discovered that got him killed? Why couldn't we discover it?

Why the interest in stem cell research?

Always questions, never answers.

I slept fitfully.

Galiano didn't arrive until eight-thirty. By then I'd had three cups of coffee and was wired enough to put two coats on Shea Stadium. He brought cup number four.

I wasted no time describing my conversations with Señora Eduardo and Mrs. Specter. Galiano showed no surprise. Though I might not have seen it behind the Darth Vader lenses.

"One of his staff has been pretty forthcoming," Galiano said. "Looks like Specter's a lecher, but otherwise harmless."

"What happened last night?"

"Pera must have warned him. Specter never showed."

The clinic was bustling on a Friday morning. At least a dozen women sat in chairs ringing the waiting room. Several held infants. Most were pregnant. Others were there to avoid becoming so.

Four toddlers played with molded plastic toys

on the floor. Two older children colored at a child-sized table, a tub of crayons equidistant between them. The wall behind was a record of the exuberance of thousands of their predecessors. Kick marks. Food splotches. Crayon graffiti. Gouges from Tonka trucks.

Galiano stepped to the receptionist and requested an audience with Dr. Zuckerman. The young woman looked up, and light flashed off the lenses of her glasses. Her eyes widened when she saw the badge.

"Un momento, por favor."

She hurried down a corridor to the right of her desk. Time passed. The women stared at us with wide, solemn eyes. The kids colored on, faces tense with the effort of staying inside the lines.

A full five minutes later, the receptionist returned.

"I'm sorry. Dr. Zuckerman is unable to see you." She waved a nervous hand at the uterus brigade. "As you can see, we have many patients this morning."

Galiano stared directly into the lenses.

"Either Dr. Zuckerman comes out here – now – or we go in there."

"You can't go into the examining room." It was almost a wail.

Galiano unwrapped a stick of gum and put it in his mouth, never breaking eye contact.

The receptionist gave a deep sigh, threw both hands into the air, and retraced her steps.

A baby began to cry. Mama raised her blouse

and directed the infant's mouth toward a nipple. Galiano nodded and smiled. Mama turned a shoulder.

A door flew open down the hall. Zuckerman steamed into the waiting room like the little engine that could. She was a thick woman with dirty-blonde hair cut very short. At home. In poor lighting. With dull scissors.

"What the hell do you people think you're doing?" Accented English. I guessed Australian.

The receptionist crawled behind her desk and hunched over something lying on it.

"You can't come barging in here, traumatizing my patients—"

"Shall we traumatize them further, or would you prefer to take this somewhere more private?" Galiano gave the doctor an icy smile.

"You refuse to understand, sir. I do not have time for you this morning."

Galiano reached under his jacket, produced a set of handcuffs, and dangled them in front of her.

Zuckerman glared.

Galiano dangled.

"This is preposterous."

Zuckerman spun and stormed up the hall. We followed her past several examining rooms. In more than one I spotted a sheet-covered woman with her knees in the full upright and locked position. I did not envy the women their delay in the stirrups.

Zuckerman led us past an office door bearing her name to a room containing chairs and a TV-VCR setup. I imagined the instructional videos.

Tips for Examining Your Breasts. Success with the Rhythm Method. Bathing the New Baby.

Galiano wasted no time.

"You were Patricia Eduardo's supervisor at the Hospital Centro Médico."

"I was."

"Is there a reason you failed to mention that when we spoke?"

"You were inquiring about patients."

"Let me understand you, Doctor. I came here asking about three women. One of those three women was under your charge at another facility, and you failed to point that out?"

"It is a common name. I was busy. I didn't make the connection."

"I see." His tone indicated that he did not. "All right. Let's talk about her now."

"Patricia Eduardo was one of many girls under my supervision. I know nothing of their activities outside the hospital."

"You never ask about their private lives?"

"That would be improper."

"Uh huh. You and Patricia were observed arguing shortly before her disappearance."

"The girls do not always perform up to my expectations."

"Was that the case with Patricia?"

She hesitated a beat. "No."

"What is it you two fought about?"

"Fought." She blew air through her lips. "I would hardly call it a fight. Miss Eduardo disagreed with advice I was offering."

"Advice?"

"Medical advice."

"As a disinterested supervisor?"

"As a doctor."

"So Patricia *was* a patient."

Zuckerman realized her mistake right away.

"She might have visited this clinic once."

"Why?"

"I can't remember the complaint of every woman who comes to see me."

"Patricia was not every woman. She was someone you worked with every day."

Zuckerman did not reply.

"She was not listed in your records here."

"That happens."

"Tell us about her."

"You know I can't do that."

"Patient confidentiality."

"Yes."

"This is a murder investigation. Fuck patient confidentiality."

Zuckerman stiffened, and a mole on her cheek appeared to expand.

"We do it here, or we do it at headquarters." Galiano.

Zuckerman pointed at me. "This woman is not official."

"You're absolutely right," I said. "You should not compromise your oath. I'll wait in the lobby."

Before anyone could object, I left the room. The hall was deserted. Moving quietly, I hurried to

Zuckerman's office, slipped in, and closed the door.

Morning sun slanted through half-open blinds, casting neat lines across the desk and stippling it with color around a small crystal clock. Its ticking, soft and rapid like a hummingbird's heart, was the only sound breaking the silence.

Bookshelves wrapped around two walls. Filing cabinets filled a third. All were government-issue gray.

I did a quick survey of titles. Standard medical journals. *JAMA*. *Fertility*. Standard medical texts. Several volumes on cell biology. A greater number on reproductive physiology and embryology.

A door opened off the far corner of the room. Bathroom?

I held my breath and listened.

Tick. Tick. Tick. Tick. Tick.

I hurried over and turned the knob.

Whatever I was expecting, it was not what I saw. The room was dominated by two long counters crammed with microscopes, test tubes, and petri dishes. Glass-fronted cabinets held bottles and tubs. Jars of embryos and fetuses filled a set of shelves, each labeled with gestational age.

A young man was placing a container in one of three refrigerators lining the back wall. I read the label. *Fetal bovine serum.*

On hearing the door, the man turned. He wore a green T-shirt and camouflage pants tucked into black boots. His hair was slicked and bound at the neck. The initials JS hung from a gold chain around his neck. Styling commando.

His eyes shot past me into Zuckerman's office.

"The doc let you in here?"

Before I could answer Zuckerman burst through the outer door. I turned, and our eyes locked for a couple of beats.

"You don't belong here." Her face was florid to the roots of her bad hair.

"I'm sorry. I got lost."

Zuckerman circled me and closed the lab door.

"Go." Her lips were compressed, and she was breathing deeply through her nose.

Hurrying from the office, I heard the lab door open, then the sound of an angry voice. A name. I didn't linger to eavesdrop. I had to find Galiano.

Though we'd never met, I knew the name of Commando Boy.

27

"You're certain?"

"Daddy's rat face, Mama's two-tone eyes."

"One brown, one blue."

I nodded. It was hard to forget the dullard owners of the Paraíso. "And the letters JS hanging from his neck."

"Jorge Serano."

"Yes. And I heard Zuckerman say his name."

I felt a burst of elation. Then it was gone.

"What the hell are he and Zuckerman doing in that lab?"

"Did you see any rabbits?"

I looked to see if he was joking. He was.

"Look, if you're right about Jorge Serano—"

"I'm right, Galiano."

"Jorge Serano links Zuckerman to the Paraíso. Zuckerman knew Patricia Eduardo. Could be our first break at stringing some things together."

We were in Galiano's cruiser, one block east of Zuckerman's clinic.

"Zuckerman fights with Eduardo. Eduardo turns up dead at a hotel owned by the parents of one of Zuckerman's employees." I was trying but failing to keep my voice calm.

"Don't have a coronary."

"I'm showing energy and purpose."

"I'm inspired by your drive. Let's go talk to Serano."

When we reentered the clinic, Serano was gone. So was Zuckerman.

So were the women who'd been waiting for care. Score one for the Hippocratic oath.

The receptionist admitted Jorge Serano was an employee. She described him as a personal assistant to Dr. Zuckerman. The only address she had was his parents' hotel.

I suggested another peek at Zuckerman's lab. Galiano refused, preferring to wait until he had a warrant.

We drove to the Paraíso.

The senior Seranos hadn't had an infusion of brainpower since our first meeting. They had not seen their son in weeks, and knew nothing of his whereabouts. They hadn't a clue where Jorge was on October twenty-ninth. They didn't know Maria Zuckerman, hadn't heard of her clinic.

Galiano produced Patricia Eduardo's picture. They'd never laid eyes on her, had no idea how she came to be in their septic tank.

Señora Serano admired the horse.

After leaving the Paraíso, Galiano dropped me at FAFG headquarters and set off on a quest for Jorge Serano. I was laying out a Chupan Ya skeleton when Ryan called.

"I found something in Nordstern's undies."

"Skidmarks?"

"You're a laugh riot, Brennan. I need you to translate."

"Your Spanish is better than mine."

"Different type of translation. Biology-ese."

"Can't you work it out? Ever since I agreed to help Galiano I've hardly had time to look at Chupan Ya bones, and that's my day job."

"Bat told me you hadn't had lunch."

Ryan made my grandmother look like an amateur when it came to concern for eating regular meals.

"I promised Mateo—"

"Go." Mateo had materialized beside my workstation. "We'll all be here when you catch your killer."

I held the phone to my chest.

"Are you sure?"

He nodded.

I gave Ryan directions and cut off.

"Can I ask you something, Mateo?"

"Of course."

"Who is Alejandro Bastos?"

The scar on his lip went dagger-thin. He waved a hand at the skeleton lying between us.

"Army colonel. The murdering bastard responsible for this, may he rot in hell."

★

372

Next to a hot poker up the nose, my favorite thing is a mealy, overfried fish. That's what I was eating as Ryan leafed through the date book he'd found in Nordstern's suitcase.

Locating the entry, Ryan held the book out so I could read.

On May 16 Nordstern scheduled a meeting with Elias Jiménez.

I thought back.

"That was two days before his interview with me."

I chewed and swallowed. The former was a formality.

"Who's Elias Jiménez?" I asked.

"Professor of cell biology at San Carlos University."

"Was the interview taped?"

"It isn't on any of the cassettes I've been through."

"Is the professor about to enjoy the pleasure of our company?"

"As soon as Detective Galiano is free."

"Intimidated by academia?"

"I'm a visiting cop in a foreign land. No authority. No weapon. No support. I might as well be a journalist."

"And a strictly by-the-book kind of guy."

"Straight arrow."

I pushed the fish as far from me as possible.

"Jumping genomes! Another ride in the Batmobile!"

★

On the way to Ciudad University in Zone 12, Galiano updated Ryan and me on the afternoon's progress. There was little to report concerning Jorge Serano. The kid had a thick jacket, mostly minor offenses. Shoplifting. Vandalism. Drunk driving. But Jorge hadn't stuck around to discuss past indiscretions. He'd vanished like money into a wahala.

Galiano's partner had researched Antonio Díaz.

Hernández discovered that the DA had been an army lieutenant in the early eighties, served most of his hitch near Sololá. His commanding officer was Alejandro Bastos.

Terrifico.

Hernández also learned that a number of high-ranking police officials had served under Bastos.

Mucho terrifico.

Professor Jiménez's address was in Edificio M2, a blue and white rectangular affair in the center of campus. We followed the signs to Ciencias Biológias, and located his office on the second floor.

The thing I remember about Jiménez is the goiter. It was the size of a walnut and the color of a plum. Otherwise, all I retain is the impression of a very old man with intense black eyes.

Jiménez didn't rise when we appeared. He merely watched us troop through his door.

The office was approximately six by eight. The walls were covered with color photos of cells in various stages of mitosis. Or meiosis. I wasn't sure.

Jiménez didn't give Galiano a chance to speak.

"The man came asking about stem cells. I gave him a synopsis and answered his questions. That's all I know."

"Olaf Nordstern?"

"I don't remember. He said he was researching a story."

"What did he ask?"

"He wanted to know about the embryonic stem cell lines President George Bush approved for research."

"And?"

"I told him."

"*What* did you tell him?"

"According to the NIH—"

"National Institutes of Health," I translated.

"—seventy-eight lines exist."

"Where?" I asked.

Jiménez dug a printout from a stack of papers and handed it to me. As I skimmed the names and numbers, Galiano got a crash course on stem cell research.

BresaGen Inc., Athens, Georgia, 4;

CyThera Inc., San Diego, California, 9;

ES Cell International/Melbourne, Australia, 6;

Geron Corporation, Menlo Park, California, 7;

Göteborg University, Göteborg, Sweden, 19;

Karolinska Institute, Stockholm, Sweden, 6;

Maria Biotech Co. Ltd. – Maria Infertility Hospital Medical Institute, Seoul, Korea, 3;

MizMedi Hospital – Seoul National University, Seoul, Korea, 1;

National Centre for Biological Sciences / Tata

Institute of Fundamental Research, Bangalore,
India, 3;
Pochon CHA University, Seoul, Korea, 2;
Reliance Life Sciences, Mumbai, India, 7;
Technion University, Haifa, Israel, 4;
University of California, San Francisco, California,
2;
Wisconsin Alumni Research Foundation, Madison,
Wisconsin, 5.

My attention ricocheted back to the third
listing. Quietly, I showed it to Ryan. His eyes met
mine.

"Is seventy-eight enough?" Galiano asked,
having listened to ES cells 101.

"Hell, no."

Jiménez had an odd way of dropping his head to
the left when he spoke. Perhaps the goiter pressed
on his vocal cords. Perhaps he wanted to hide it.

"Some of those lines could get stale, or lose their
pluripotency, or just plain crash. Four of the six
colonies created by one U.S. biotech firm, won't
say which one, are turning out to be unstable."
Jiménez snorted. "There's already a backlog of
requests."

He pointed a bony finger at the printout in my
hand.

"And take a look at that list. Many of those lines
are in private hands."

"And private companies aren't known for
sharing." Ryan.

"You've got that right, young man."

"Is the American government doing anything to assure access?" Galiano asked.

"The NIH is creating a human embryonic stem cell registry. Still, NIH admits distribution of cell lines will be left to the discretion of those labs that birthed them."

"ES cells could become a valuable commodity." Ryan.

Jiménez's laugh sounded like a cackle.

"Stem cell stocks soared following Bush's announcement."

A very troubling conjecture was coalescing in the back of my brain.

"Dr. Jiménez, how sophisticated is the methodology for growing cultures of human ES cells?"

"You're not going to do it in your sophomore biochem class, if that's what you're asking. But it's not that complicated for someone with training."

"How does it work?"

"You get fresh or frozen embryos—"

"Where?"

"IVF labs."

"Clinics for couples undergoing treatment for infertility," I translated for my police buddies.

"You extract cells from the inner cell mass of the blastocyst. You put the cells in culture dishes with growth medium supplemented with fetal bovine serum—"

My heart rate shot to the stratosphere.

"—on feeder layers of mouse embryonic fibroblasts that have been gamma-irradiated to prevent their replication. You let the cells grow nine to fifteen days. When the inner cell masses have divided and formed clumps, you dissociate cells from the periphery, put them back in culture, and—"

I was no longer listening. I knew what Zuckerman was up to.

I caught Ryan's eye and indicated that we should go.

Jiménez droned on about an alternative technique involving the injection of ES cells into the testes of immunocompromised mice.

"Thank you, Professor," I cut in.

Ryan and Galiano looked at me like I was crazy.

"One last question. Did Nordstern ask about a woman named Maria Zuckerman?"

"Might have."

"What did you tell him?"

"Same thing I'll tell you, young lady. Never heard of her."

"Zuckerman's trying to develop a stem cell line."

We were back in the Batmobile. My face felt hot, and strange creatures were running patterns in my belly.

"Why?" Ryan asked.

"How the hell should I know? Maybe *she's* the one bucking for a prize. Or there's a black market out there."

I closed my eyes. The lunch fish played on the back of my lids. I opened them.

"But I'm certain that's what Zuckerman's doing. I saw the lab, saw the fetal bovine serum."

"There must be other uses for the stuff." Galiano.

"Six of the existing stem cell lines are at the Monash Institute of Reproductive Biology in Melbourne, Australia." I swallowed. "Zuckerman spent two years at a research institute in Melbourne. If you check, I bet Monash rings the bell."

"But why?" Ryan repeated.

"Maybe Zuckerman anticipates a growing black market now that the U.S. government has turned ES cells into a limited resource by limiting government funding." Galiano looked over at me. "Are you all right?"

"I'm fine."

"You're flushed."

"I'm fine."

"And the good doctor plans to make a bundle," Ryan said.

Galiano looked at me again, started to speak, instead picked up and keyed the radio.

"Like the hairballs that trade in illegal donor organs." Ryan was sounding less skeptical. "Holy sh—"

I cut Ryan off.

"And Jorge Serano is helping her."

I listened to Galiano put out APBs on Zuckerman and Serano. My stomach made an odd sound. Though both men glanced at me, neither commented.

We rode several miles listening to my rumbling compete with the radio.

I spoke first.

"Where does Patricia Eduardo fit in?"

"Where does Antonio Díaz fit in?" Galiano asked.

"Where does Ollie Nordstern fit in?" Ryan asked.

No one had an answer.

"Here's a plan," Ryan said. "Bat rolls out a judge to get his warrant."

"And it damn well won't be that scumbag Díaz."

"I finish the interview tapes. Brennan goes through the rest of Nordstern's papers."

"Fine," I agreed. "But I'll work at my hotel." I felt a sudden need to stay near my bathroom.

"Don't like my company?" Ryan made his hurt face.

"It's the fly," I said. "We don't get along."

By the time we swung by headquarters, picked up Nordstern's file folders, and returned to my hotel, it was after five.

The sidewalk now looked like it had been struck by a tomahawk missile. Four jackhammers were engaged in a full-throttle assault that sent vibrations through every lobe of my brain. Floodlights and lunch pails suggested the noise might continue through the night.

I muttered a particularly colorful expletive.

Ryan and Galiano asked if I'd be all right. I assured them all I needed was rest. I didn't mention the bathroom.

As they roared off I noticed the boys were laughing.

The paranoia flared.

I repeated the expletive.

Upstairs, I went straight to my med kit.

Katy always laughs at me. When traveling to foreign countries, I carry a drugstore. Eyedrops. Nasal spray. Antacid. Laxative. You never know.

Today I knew.

I downed an Imodium and a mouthful of Pepto-Bismol, stretched out on the bed.

And shot straight to the bathroom. Decades later I lay down again, shaky but better.

The jackhammers pounded.

My head joined in.

I turned on the fan. Instead of blunting the noise, the fan added to it.

I returned to the bathroom, soaked a rag in cold water, placed it on my forehead, and went supine again, questioning whether I really wanted to live.

I'd barely drifted off when my cell phone rang.

Expletive.

"Yes!"

"Ryan."

"Yes."

"Feeling better?"

"Damn you and your fish."

"I told you to have the corn dog. What's that noise?"

"Jackhammers. Why are you calling?"

"You were right-on about Melbourne.

Zuckerman spent two years there on a Reproductive Biology research fellowship or something."

"Uh huh."

I was half listening to Ryan, half listening to my stomach.

"You'll never guess who else was there."

The name got my full attention.

28

"The Lucas who confiscated the Paraíso skeleton for Antonio Díaz?"

"Hector Luis Castillo Lucas."

"But Lucas is a forensic doctor."

"Apparently he didn't start out that way."

"What's the Díaz-Lucas link?" I asked.

"Better question: What's the Zuckerman-Lucas link?"

"Any progress on netting Zuckerman or Jorge Serano?"

"Not yet. Galiano has Zuckerman's clinic and home staked out, has an APB on her car. He's also set up surveillance at the Paraíso. We should nail 'em before the ten o'clock news."

"Did Galiano get his warrant?"

"He's talking to a judge now."

I clicked off, replaced the washcloth, and lay back on the pillows.

This really didn't make sense. Or did it? Was Dr. Lucas working for Díaz? Had the doctor ordered the destruction of Patricia Eduardo's bones at the request of the DA? Or was it the other way around? Did Lucas have influence over Díaz?

Díaz could link to Chupan Ya, perhaps even to the shooting of Carlos and Molly. But why would he want the Paraíso bones confiscated? Why would he have an interest in the murder of a pregnant young girl?

Carlos and Molly! Had their attackers really spoken my name? Was I the next target? Whose?

Feeling frightened and chilled, I crawled under the blankets.

Still my head swam with questions.

Lucas must know Zuckerman. Two Guatemalan doctors at an Australian research facility at the same time could hardly fail to be aware of each other. Were they now working together? On what?

What was Nordstern's big secret? And how had he learned it?

Was there a Bastos-Díaz connection other than their time together in the army? Why did Nordstern circle the picture of Díaz with Bastos together reviewing the parade at Xaxaxak?

Did all these things tie together? Did any of them? Were these just episodes of corruption in a corrupt country?

Was I in danger?

The jackhammers obliterated the clamor of rush

hour traffic. The fan hummed. Slowly, the room dimmed, the sounds ebbed.

I wasn't sure how much time had passed when the room phone shrilled. When I bolted upright, it was dark.

Breathing. Then a dial tone.

"Goddamn inconsiderate bastard!" Must have called the wrong extension and just hung up.

I slammed the receiver.

Sitting on the edge of the bed I held my hands to my cheeks. They felt cooler. The meds were helping.

Rat-a-tat-a-tat. Rat-a-tat-taaaaat. Rat. Rat. Rat.

How much cement could there be down there?

"Enough of this."

I got a Diet Coke from the mini-fridge and tried a sip.

Oh yes.

I knocked back several swallows as a test run, and set the can on the table. Then I stripped off my clothes and showered until the bathroom was gray with steam. I closed my eyes, let the water pound my breasts, my back, my distended abdomen. I let it roll off my head, my shoulders, my hips.

After toweling off, I combed out my hair, brushed my teeth, and pulled on cotton socks and a set of FBI sweats.

Feeling like a new woman, I dug out Nordstern's files and settled at the table. In the next room I heard the TV go on, then aimless channel switching. My neighbor finally settled on a soccer match.

The first folder I picked up was labeled "Specter." It held press clippings, notes, and an assortment of photos of André Specter and his family. There were two Polaroids of the ambassador with Aida Pera.

The second folder was unlabeled. It contained restaurant and taxi receipts. Expense records. Pass.

I finished my Coke.

Outside, the jackhammers droned on.

I recognized the label on the third folder: "SCELL." I was halfway through when I found it.

Stem Cells Grown from Dead Bodies.

As I read the report, my chest tightened.

A research team at the Salk Institute in La Jolla, California, had developed a technique for sourcing stem cells from human post-mortem samples. The finding was reported in the journal *Nature*.

"Jesus Christ."

My voice sounded loud in the empty room.

I read on.

When placed in a succession of solutions, the tissues of an eleven-week-old baby and a twenty-seven-year-old man had yielded immature brain cells. The Salk team had used the technique on others of different ages, and on specimens extracted as long as two days after death.

A footer indicated that the report had been downloaded from the BBC News home page. Beside the http address, someone had written the name Zuckerman.

I felt icy-hot, and my hands were shaking.

Relapse.

Time for an Imodium hit.

Returning from the bathroom, I noticed an odd shadow falling across the carpet in front of the door. I went to check. The latch had not properly engaged.

Had I left the door open when I'd arrived and dashed to the bathroom? I was feeling lousy, but such carelessness was out of character.

I closed and locked it, a sense of trepidation joining the rest of my symptoms.

Dialing Galiano, I felt weak all over. The trembling in my hands had intensified.

Galiano and Ryan were out. I had to swallow before I could leave a message.

Damn! I couldn't be sick. I wouldn't!

I collected Nordstern's folders and stacked them beside the armchair. Stealing the quilt from the bed, I tucked my feet under my bum and wrapped myself in it. I was feeling worse by the minute.

Dramatically worse.

I opened a folder. Interview notes. I had to keep wiping my face as I read. Rivulets of perspiration rolled down the inside of my sweats.

Within minutes I felt a sharp pain in my belly, then tremors below my tongue. Heat rose from my throat to my hairline.

I raced to the bathroom, retched until my sides ached, then returned to my chair to re-cocoon. Every few minutes I repeated the journey. I felt weaker with each trip.

Collapsing into my chair for the fourth time, I

shut my eyes and pulled the quilt to my chin. I felt rough cotton against my skin. I smelled my own odor. My head spun, and I saw tiny constellations on the backs of my lids.

The jackhammers receded to a sound like popping corn. I saw locusts on a summer night. Gossamer wings. Red, bulging eyes. I felt insects buzz through my bloodstream.

Then I was with Katy. She was little, maybe three or four, and we were reading a book of nursery rhymes. Her hair was white blonde. The sun shone through it like moonlight through mist. She wore the pinafore I'd bought on a trip to Nantucket.

Let me help, sweetheart.
I can do it.
Of course you can.
I know my letters. Sometimes I just can't put them together.
That's the hard part.
Take your time.
Hector Protector was dressed all in green;
Hector Protector was sent to the queen;
The queen didn't like him, nor did the king;
So Hector Protector was sent back again.
Why didn't they like him, Mommy?
I don't know.
Was he a bad man?
I don't think so.
What was the queen's name?
Arabella.

Katy giggled.
What was the king's name?
Charlie Oliver.
More giggles.
You always say funny names, Mommy.
I like to see you laugh.
What was Hector Protector's last name?
Lucas.
Maybe he wasn't really a protector.
Maybe not.
What then, Mommy?
A collector?
Giggles.
An erecter.
A defecter.
An ejecter.
A dissector.
An inspector.

I awoke standing in the bathroom, palms and forehead pressed to the mirror.

Had that been the word Molly had overheard? Not *inspector*. Not *Specter*.

Hector.

Hector Lucas.

Did I really have it backward? Was the doctor in fact controlling the DA? Had Lucas ordered the attack on Molly and Carlos? What was his link to our work at Chupan Ya? I couldn't make sense of it. Did he have Nordstern killed when the reporter got too close to the truth? Did he have Patricia Eduardo killed? Would Lucas deal

389

with Zuckerman and Jorge Serano in the same way?

Would he try to kill Galiano and Ryan?

I lurched to the bedside table, fumbled for my cell.

Neither Ryan nor Galiano answered.

I wiped perspiration from my face with the back of an arm.

Where were they going? Zuckerman's clinic? The morgue?

Think!

I took a deep breath, opened and closed my eyes. Images swirled. Stars flashed on my lids.

What to do?

I blew out a breath. Then another.

If Lucas really was dangerous, Ryan and Galiano would have no way to know. Zuckerman may already have reached him, and Lucas might think they were coming to arrest him, and shoot.

Throwing on shoes, I grabbed my purse and headed downstairs.

It took twenty minutes to hail a taxi.

"*¿Dónde?*"

Where?

Where had Ryan and Galiano gone? Not the Paraíso or Zuckerman's clinic. Those places were staked out.

The driver drummed his fingers on the wheel.

Where would Lucas be?

Or did I want Díaz? Maybe Dr. Fereira could tell me.

I was trembling all over, my teeth clicking like a cheap party toy.

"*¿Dónde, señora?*"

Focus!

"Morgue del Organismo Judicial."

"Zona Tres?"

"*Oui.*"

That was wrong. Why?

As the taxi crossed the city I watched an ever-changing panoply of color and shape. Banners strung above the streets. Ads posted on fences, walls, and billboards. I didn't try to read them. I couldn't. My head spun as it had in my drinking days when I'd fall asleep with one foot on the floor to remain stuck to the planet.

I knew I overpaid the driver by his smile and his blast-off.

No matter.

I looked up and down the block. The neighborhood was as bleak as I remembered, the cemetery larger and darker. Galiano's car was nowhere in sight.

I stared at the morgue. Fereira. I needed to see Dr. Fereira. I followed a gravel driveway along the left side of the building. My sneakers made crunching sounds that thundered in my ears.

The drive led to a parking area containing two transport vehicles, a white Volvo, and a black station wagon. No Batmobile.

A drop of sweat rolled into my right eye. I wiped it away with my sleeve.

Now what? I hadn't thought about entering without Ryan or Galiano. Look for Fereira?

I tested the personnel entrance at the back of the building. No go. The garage door used for body intake was also locked.

I tried to be more quiet. I crossed to the first van and peered through a window. Nothing.

I scuttled to the second vehicle.

The third.

A set of keys lay on the seat!

Heart thumping, I liberated my prize and stumbled back to the building.

None of the keys worked on the personnel door.

Damn.

My hands trembled as I tried key after key at the vehicle bay.

No.

No.

No.

I dropped the cluster of keys. My legs shook as I searched on all fours in the dark. An eternity later, my hand closed around them.

Rising, I started again.

The fifth or sixth key slid into the lock and turned. I nudged the door upward an inch, and froze.

No sirens or beepers. No armed guards.

I nudged another two feet. The gears sounded louder than the jackhammers at my hotel.

No one appeared. No one called out.

Barely breathing, I crouched and crab-walked into the morgue. Why was it I wanted to be inside?

Oh yeah. Dr. Fereira, or Ryan, or Galiano.

The familiar blended odors of death and disinfectant enveloped me. It was a smell I'd know anywhere.

Keeping my back to the wall, I followed a corridor past a roll-on gurney scale, an office, and a small room with a curtained window.

My lab in Montreal has a similar chamber. The dead are wheeled to the far side of the glass. The curtains are opened. A loved one reacts with relief or sorrow. It is the most heartbreaking place in the building.

Beyond the viewing room, the corridor dead-ended into another. I looked left, right.

Another light show behind my eyes. I closed them, breathed deeply, opened them. Better.

Though it was dark in both directions, I knew where I was. To the left I recognized the autopsy rooms, to the right the hall down which Angelina Fereira had led me to her office.

How long had it been since she'd given me Eduardo's CT scans? A week? A month? A lifetime? My brain couldn't compute.

I started right. Maybe she was there. She could tell me about Lucas.

A stab to the gut doubled me over. I took quick, shallow breaths, waited for the pain to subside. When I righted myself, lightning burst behind my eyes and the top of my head exploded. Bracing against the wall, I vomited in great, heaving spasms.

Dr. Fereira? Ryan? Galiano?

A lifetime later, the contractions stopped. My mouth tasted bitter. My sides ached. My legs felt rubbery, my body hot and cold at the same time. Dr. Fereira would send someone to clean this up.

Using the wall for support, I pushed on. Her office was empty. I reversed direction toward the autopsy rooms.

Autopsy room one was dark and deserted.

Ditto for two.

I noticed violet-blue light spilling under the door of autopsy room three, the one in which I'd examined Patricia Eduardo's skeleton. She was probably there.

Gingerly, I opened the door.

There's a surreal stillness to a nighttime morgue. No sucking hoses, no whining saws, no running water, no clanking instruments. It's like no other silence I know.

The room was empty and deathly quiet.

"Dr. Fereira?"

Someone had left an X ray on an illuminator box. Fluorescence seeped around the film like the blue-white shimmer of a black-and-white TV in the dark. Metal and glass gleamed cold and steely.

A gurney sat by a stainless steel cooler at the back of the room. On it, a body bag. The bulge told me there was someone inside.

Another spasm. Black spots danced in my vision.

Lurching to the table, I dropped my head, breathed deeply.

In.

Out.

In.

Out.

The dots dissolved. The nausea backed off.

Better.

A body outside the cooler. Someone had to be working.

"Dr. Fereira?"

I reached for my cell phone. It wasn't in my pocket.

Damn!

Had I dropped it? Had I forgotten it at the hotel? When had I left the hotel?

I looked at my watch. I couldn't see the digits.

This was not working. I needed to leave. I was in no shape to help them.

Help who?

Leave where?

Where am I?

At that moment I felt more than heard movement behind me. Not a sound, more a disturbance in the air.

I whirled.

Fireworks flared in my brain. Fire shot from my groin to my throat.

Someone was standing in the doorway.

"Dr. Fereira?"

Did I speak or imagine I was speaking?

The figure held something in its hands.

"Señor Díaz?"

No answer.

"Dr. Zuckerman?"

The figure remained frozen in place.

I felt my hands slip. My cheek struck the metal lip of the gurney. Breath exploded from my lungs. The floor rushed toward my face.

Blackness.

29

I had never been so cold in my life.

I was lying on ice at the bottom of a deep, dark pond.

I wiggled my fingers to bring back feeling, fought to rise to the surface.

Too much resistance. Too far down.

I breathed in.

Dead fish. Algae. Things of the deep.

I spread my arms like a child doing a snow angel.

Contact.

I followed the contour with my hands.

A vertical rim with a rounded lip.

I explored the rim. Not ice. Metal, surrounding me like a coffin.

A tickle of recognition.

I took a deep breath.

The stench of death and disinfectant. But the

proportions were inverted. The odor of rotting flesh had the upper hand.

Refrigerated flesh.

My heart shriveled.

Oh God!

I was lying on a gurney in the morgue cooler.

With the dead!

Oh my God!

How long had I been unconscious? Who had put me on the gurney?

Was that person still there?

I opened my eyes and raised my head.

Shards of glass blasted through my brain. My insides contracted.

I listened.

Silence.

I pushed to my elbows and blinked hard.

Inky black.

I rose to a sitting position, waited. Shaky, but no nausea.

My feet were dead weight. Using my hands, I drew my ankles to me and began rubbing. Slowly, feeling returned.

I listened for signs of activity outside the cooler.

Stillness.

I swung my legs over the edge and pushed off the gurney.

My knees were liquid, and I collapsed to the floor hard. Pain shot through my left wrist.

Damn!

My right hand came down on a rubber wheel.

I crawled on all fours and pulled myself up.

Another gurney.

I was not alone.

The gurney held a bag. The bag was occupied.

I recoiled from the corpse. My mouth felt dry. My heart pounded.

I turned and stumbled in the direction I thought the door should be.

Dear God, is there a handle on the inside? Do these things have handles on the inside? Let there be a handle on the inside!

I'd opened morgue coolers a thousand times, never noticed.

Trembling, I groped in the dark.

Please!

Cold, hard metal. Smooth. I moved along it.

Please! Let there be a handle!

I could feel myself weakening by the minute. I tasted bile, fought a tremor.

Years, decades, millennia later, my hand fell on it.

Yes!

I depressed the handle, pushed on the door. It opened with a soft whoosh. I peeked out.

On the light box, smoky gray organs and opaque bones, a glow-in-the-dark portrait of a human being.

Autopsy room three, dimly lit.

Did the gurney behind me hold room three's recent occupant? Were we both put on ice by the same hand?

Leaving the door slightly ajar, I staggered to the

gurney and unzipped the pouch. A slash of light fell across pasty white feet.

I twisted the toe tag, strained to read the name. The light was dim and the letters were not large.

RAM—

They swam in and out of focus like pebbles at the bottom of a stream.

I blinked.

RAMÍR—

Fuzzy.

RAMÍREZ.

The Guatemalan equivalent of Smith or Jones.

I worked my way down the gurney, unzipping as I went. At the head end, I pulled back the flap.

Maria Zuckerman's face was ghostly, the hole in her forehead a small black dot. Smears darkened the front of her clothing.

I lifted a hand. She was fully rigorous.

Shivering uncontrollably, I backed the length of the gurney, re-zipping as I went.

Why?

Inane habit.

Opening the door with my bum, I backed into room three.

And felt cold steel pressed to the base of my skull.

"Welcome back, Dr. Brennan."

I knew the voice.

"Thank you so much for saving us a trip."

"Lucas?"

I could feel the front sight, the barrel, the hollow

tube that could send a bullet screaming through my brain.

"You were expecting someone else?"

"Díaz."

Lucas snorted.

"Díaz does what I tell him."

My addled brain cells screamed one word.

Stall!

"You killed Maria Zuckerman. Why?"

My head was heavy, my tongue thick.

"And you had Ollie Nordstern killed."

"Nordstern was a fool."

"Nordstern was smart enough to uncover your dirty cell-harvesting game."

A hitch in the breathing behind me.

Keep him talking!

"Was that also Patricia Eduardo's mistake? She learned what Zuckerman was up to?"

"You have been a busy girl."

The room was spinning.

"You're a tough one, Dr. Brennan. Tougher than I anticipated."

The gun barrel jabbed my neck.

"Back to bed."

Another jab.

"Move."

Don't get back in the cooler!

"I said move." Lucas shoved me from behind.

No!

Die from a bullet or die God knows how in the cooler? I spun around Lucas and lunged for the door.

Locked!

I whirled to face my attacker.

Lucas had a Beretta pointed at my chest.

My vision blurred.

"Go ahead, Dr. Lucas. Shoot me."

"Pointless."

We glared at each other like wary animals.

"Why Zuckerman?" I asked.

Lucas splintered into four, recongealed.

"Why Zuckerman?"

Had I said that or only imagined it?

"You're very pale, Dr. Brennan."

I blinked away a trickle of sweat.

"My distinguished colleague will keep you company."

I struggled to understand his meaning.

"Why?" I repeated.

"Dr. Zuckerman couldn't be trusted. She was weak and prone to panic. Not like you."

Why didn't Lucas shoot me?

"Did you kill your victims, Dr. Lucas? Or merely steal from their corpses?"

Lucas swallowed and his Adam's apple bounced like a kid on a bungee.

"We would have made a great contribution."

"Or a black market killing."

Lucas's lips curled in an imitation grin.

"You're even better than I thought. All right. I do love it when the gloves come off. Let's discuss science."

"Let's."

Stall.

"Your president has sent ES cell research back to the twelfth century."

"He acted out of a commitment to scientific ethics."

"Ethics?" Lucas laughed.

"Their argument has no validity?"

My thoughts were fragmenting. It was becoming harder and harder to think.

"That the retrieval of stem cells requires the killing of little babies? That stem cell researchers are no better than Mengele and his Nazi mutilators? You call that bullshit scientific ethics?"

Lucas waved his gun at a list of safety regulations taped to the wall.

"A blastocyst is no larger than the dot on that 'i.'"

"It is life." My words sounded slurry and far away.

"Throwaways from fertility treatments. The discards of aborted pregnancies."

Lucas's agitation was growing. I was doing this all wrong.

"Hundreds of thousands suffer from Parkinson's disease, diabetes, crushed spinal cords. We could have helped them."

"That was Zuckerman's goal?"

"Yes."

"And yours was to fatten your wallet."

"Why not?" Spittle glistened at the corners of his mouth. "Mechanical hearts. Pharmaceuticals. Patents on orthopedic hardware. A smart doctor can make millions."

"By killing or just stealing embryos?"

Hadn't I asked that eons earlier?

"Zuckerman would have taken forever mixing eggs and sperm in her little dishes. My way was quicker. It would have worked."

I wanted to close my eyes.

"You know it's over," I said.

"It's over when I say it is."

I wanted to stop hearing and sleep.

"Zuckerman's death will be solved. Her lab has been seized."

"You lie." The bottom rim of his eye twitched.

"Two detectives are on their way here. I was to meet them."

Lucas wet his lips.

I hammered on, barely conscious of what I was saying.

"The truth is coming out about Chupan Ya. We're putting on record what happened to those poor people." My knees began to buckle. "And the blackmail's over. Díaz's involvement in the massacre has been exposed. He won't be your patsy anymore."

Lucas's fingers tightened on the grip of the pistol.

"Jorge Serano is in custody. They'll cut him a deal and he'll give you up."

A derisive laugh. "Give me up for what, stealing a few dead embryos?"

"For murdering Patricia Eduardo."

Lucas's gaze remained level and unblinking.

"That skeleton's long gone. Its identity will always be conjecture."

"You forgot one thing, Dr. Lucas. Patricia's unborn baby. The baby you never allowed to draw breath."

In the distance I heard the sound of a siren. Lucas's head jerked to the right, returned to me.

Keep talking!

"I found that baby's bones inside its murdered mother's clothing. Those bones will provide DNA."

My voice was sounding farther away by the second.

"That DNA will match a sample provided by Patricia Eduardo's mother. That baby will reach out from death to seal your fate."

Lucas's knuckles bulged white as his eyes went hard and black. The look of a sniper, a terrorist, or a hostage taker who has been cornered. The realization there is no way out.

"In that case, I might as well settle up with you. What's one more?"

A veil fell across my vision. I couldn't speak. Couldn't move. I would die in a morgue in Guatemala.

Then, "You are skilled and resourceful, Dr. Brennan. I admit that. Consider this your luckiest year."

Through a black fog I saw Lucas take the gun from my chest, slide the barrel into his mouth, and pull the trigger.

30

The story never made headlines in Guatemala or Canada.

In Guatemala City, *La Hora* ran a blurb on the indictment of Miguel Angel Gutiérrez for first-degree homicide. Claudia de la Alda's mother was quoted expressing her satisfaction with the investigation. Two column inches. Page seventeen.

In separate articles, the Patricia Eduardo and Maria Zuckerman murders were attributed to organized crime, and Lucas's death was classified as a suicide.

Not a word about stem cells.

In Montreal, *La Presse* and the *Gazette* ran brief follow-up stories on the rue Ste-Catherine shoot-out. In addition to Carlos Vicente, a second suspect had been identified in Guatemala City. The man died before an arrest could be made. Period. No speculation as to the motive for a

Guatemalan shooting an American in Montreal.

No ink anywhere on Antonio Díaz, Alejandro Bastos, or André Specter. Díaz remained a judge. Specter remained an ambassador.

Presumably, Bastos remained dead.

I'll never really know why Hector Lucas turned the gun on himself. I believe it was arrogance combined with desperation. He saw himself as a superior being, and when he knew it was over he chose the terms. It was also arrogance, I believe, that led him to spare me. He wanted me to know that it was he who chose that I would live, and he wanted me to remember. A memorial of sorts.

Ryan was at the hospital by seven the morning after the morgue. With flowers.

"Thanks, Ryan. They're beautiful."

"Like you." Goofy grin.

"I have a black eye, my cheek's an eggplant, there's a needle in my arm, and Nurse Kevorkian just shoved a suppository up my ass."

"You look good to me."

His hair was matted, he hadn't shaved in two days, his jacket was smeared where he'd dropped ash and tried to rub it off. He looked good to me, too.

"O.K.," I said. "Give."

I was awake but weak. Whatever was in my metabolism had moved on, chased away by drugs, or simply depleted by the passage of time.

"Galiano and I phoned your cell when the judge cut paper for Zuckerman's clinic. No answer. We tried again when the cops netted Jorge Serano."

"I was either in the shower or had already left and forgotten the phone."

"We figured you'd shut the phone off to sleep. When I got back to the hotel, I knocked on your door, tried the handle."

"Hoping for?"

"Just checking on the health of a friend."

I jabbed at his stomach. He hopped back.

"That *taquería* was *your* idea."

"You chose the fish."

"I distinctly remember passing on the side order of botulism."

"Apparently it's included, no charge, though you may be falsely accusing the fish. Anyway, your door was unlocked, your room a mess," Ryan went on. "I spotted the article on stem cell retrieval from dead bodies, and wondered if you had gone detecting or done something similarly stupid."

"Thanks."

"Don't mention it. I got Galiano back out of bed to see if we could track you down."

"I'm sure he was thrilled."

"The Bat's flexible. We called FAFG. They had people working late but hadn't seen you. I mentioned that you had raised a Zuckerman-Lucas connection, and Bat decided to chat up Lucas. Lucas wasn't at home, so we thought we'd check the morgue. We spotted Zuckerman's Volvo in the morgue parking lot, then the partly open bay door."

"Where was the regular security staff?"

"Lucas had sent them home. We think he

planned to do a hurry-up post on Maria Zuckerman."

"Out of unbearable grief for his fallen colleague."

Ryan nodded. "When we hit the autopsy room, Lucas's brains were decorating the wall. You were unconscious, so we poured your pretty little butt into an ambulance, then headed back to sweat Serano."

Ryan brushed bangs from my forehead, regarded me with an expression I couldn't read.

"Lucas had ordered Serano to dispose of you. His method of choice was going to be asphyxiation. You accommodated by taking the shower of the century. The jackhammers provided sound cover. Commando boy laced your Coke, planned to wait in the closet for the big swoon, then apply your pillow. *Problemo.* A maid showed up. Serano blew out of there *muy pronto.*"

"You've spoken with housekeeping?"

Ryan nodded. "Maid thought it was me."

"What the hell did Serano slip me?"

"Who knows? Serano hasn't said. We told the paramedics you had food poisoning. They pumped your stomach, and the hotel staff had discarded the can."

"Knocked me on my ass."

"That was the idea. Docs think the Pepto and Imodium blunted some of the effect, and kept you conscious. Also, you had upchucked some."

He tickled a spot under my chin.

I batted his hand away. Winced.

"How's the wrist?"

"Just a sprain."

Ryan took my hand and kissed the fingertips.

"You had us worried, cupcake."

Embarrassed, I changed the subject.

"Lucas had Nordstern killed?"

"Looks like Nordstern came here legit to write about Clyde Snow and his human rights work. In digging up material on Chupan Ya and other massacres, Nordstern got his hands on old army records naming Alejandro Bastos and Antonio Díaz. At some point he would have exposed Díaz, and Lucas would have lost his leverage. Lucas might have had him popped for that.

"More likely it had to do with Patricia Eduardo. Seems Nordstern was an equal opportunity snoop. Once he got to Guatemala City, he either read or heard about the missing girls, and started looking into the disappearances. When he found that one of the four was an ambassador's kid, he sniffed off on that trail. When he discovered Chantale had problems and the ambassador was a sleaze, he wanted details."

"Why go to Montreal?"

"At that point he was on the same page we were. Thought he'd have the story of the decade if he could tie Specter to the body in the tank. Great stuff. Sophisticated diplomat. Naïve young girls. Sex. Murder. Mysterious death. Septic tanks. Diplomatic immunity. Foreign intrigue. I don't think he knew Patricia Eduardo was pregnant."

Ryan stroked the back of my hand as he spoke.

"God knows how he thought the ES cells fit in. We found a receipt from the Paraíso in Nordstern's expense folder."

"He actually stayed there?"

"Inquiring minds accept no limits. That's how Nordstern got to know Jorge Serano."

"Who led him to Zuckerman."

"Which led him to an interest in ES cells."

"Which is what got him killed, if the Díaz thing didn't."

We were both quiet a moment. Then, "What's happening with Chantale Specter?"

"Restitution to the MusiGo store, then rehab."

"Lucy Gerardi?"

"Parental lockdown. Without Chantale's help she can't break out."

I was almost afraid to ask.

"The internal investigation?"

"The department and I are copacetic on Señor Vicente."

"I'm glad, Ryan. It was a good shoot."

Nurse K came in to check my IV.

"Where's Galiano?" I asked when she'd left.

The flicker of a frown.

"He'll be by."

Ryan snugged an arm under my shoulders, pulled me to him, and laid his cheek on the top of my head.

I felt a comfortable warmth flood over me.

"When I saw you lying on that floor last night, next to a gun and a body, I was overcome by a great sense of loss."

I was too surprised to speak. Perhaps the best course. Whatever I said would probably be wrong.

"I realized something."

Ryan's voice sounded odd. He pressed my head to his chest.

"Or maybe I just finally admitted it to myself."

Ryan nuzzled my hair.

What? Admitted what?

"Tempe—"

His voice faltered.

Ohmygod! Was he going to use the L word?

Ryan cleared his throat.

"I've seen too much of the underside of life to have much confidence in people. I don't really believe in happy endings." I felt him swallow. "But I've come to believe in you."

He settled me back on the pillows and kissed my forehead.

"We need to rethink where we are with each other."

I wanted to talk, to pursue this line of thought. My eyelids wouldn't cooperate.

"Think about it." Cornflower eyes pierced straight to my soul.

You bet.

The next time I woke, Mateo and Elena were peering down at me. Elena's face was so wrinkled with worry she looked like a shar-pei.

"How are you?"

"Right as rain."

Mateo and I laughed. It hurt like hell.

"What's so funny?"

"Something Molly said."

They assured me the Chupan Ya work was proceeding well, told me the villagers were planning a funeral. Mateo had just spoken with Molly. She was barreling toward full recovery.

Again, hard as I tried, I couldn't stay awake.

Galiano was the next phantom to appear by my bed.

With flowers.

The place was taking on the air of a funeral parlor.

"You were right-on about the attack on your colleagues."

"Molly and Carlos?"

Galiano gave a nod. He looked as well-groomed as Ryan.

"Jorge Serano's copped to that hit."

"Why them?" I asked.

"Mistaken identity. Lucas sent Serano after you. He wanted to disrupt the recovery team by knocking off the headliner. He thought that was you."

A cold, sick feeling swirled in my chest. Guilt? Sorrow? Anger?

"Why disrupt the work at Chupan Ya?"

Galiano gave a half shrug. "Lucas didn't want to lose his firewall."

"Díaz."

Galiano nodded. "Or maybe Lucas feared Díaz knew too much, that if the DA was arrested for his role in the massacre, the little worm might begin to bargain."

"The twisted bastard."

"When Lucas found out I'd requested permission to bring you into the Paraíso investigation, he had another reason to want you out of the picture."

Galiano took my hand. His skin felt rough and cool. He kissed my fingers.

First Ryan and now Galiano. I was beginning to feel like the pope.

He kissed his lips to my palm.

O.K. Not the pope.

"I'm glad you're O.K., Tempe."

I was not O.K. I was getting less O.K. by the second. What was it with my libido and these two guys?

"Go on."

"Serano was already tied in to Lucas, since he was the one who dumped Eduardo's body in Papa's septic tank. He agreed to do the Sololá shooting."

"Why did he dispose of her so close to home?"

"I asked him that. The moron thought the body would be reduced to nothing in a matter of weeks. When the drains at the Paraíso backed up and Papa began poking around, Little Jorge nearly shit his pants."

"Who killed Patricia Eduardo?"

"Lucas."

"Why?"

"Patricia Eduardo was seeing a married man, became pregnant, and went to Zuckerman for help. Zuckerman may have seen a donor cell

414

opportunity. In the process, Eduardo somehow stumbled onto the ES cell operation.

"Eduardo and Zuckerman fought, and Eduardo might have threatened to blow the whistle. Zuckerman told Lucas. Lucas took Patricia out of the equation and enlisted Jorge Serano to get rid of the body. Now Serano is using that knowledge to cut himself a deal. He's been in transmit mode since we picked him up."

"Does he know Lucas and Zuckerman are dead?"

"We might have forgotten to mention that."

"How did Serano get involved in all this?"

"Let's just say Jorge's lifestyle exceeded his earning power in a free labor market."

"Being Lucas's gorilla paid well?"

"It beat pushing broom at the Paraíso. Lucas didn't want to dirty his hands. Jorge wanted money."

"What about Nordstern?"

"Lucas got outside help to cap Nordstern. Figured Jorge was a little green to send onto foreign shores."

"Do you think Nordstern really knew what was going on with the stem cells?"

"We found some interesting stuff on his laptop. Nordstern did a lot of digging on ES cells, and on the U.S. decision to limit funding. Most of the downloads took place either during or after Nordstern's sojourn at the Paraíso."

"After Serano unwittingly led him to Zuckerman's clinic."

"A little breaking and entering wouldn't have been beneath Nordstern. He probably crept to the lab, rifled Zuckerman's files, figured out what she and Lucas were doing. Probably guessed they were planning to make a black market fortune."

"When did all this start?"

"Years ago. Zuckerman experimented with mixing eggs and sperm to derive embryonic stem cells. You get donated eggs and sperm and mix them together until they hook up and start to grow. Then you destroy the embryos and maintain the stem cells in culture."

I waited.

"Apparently Lucas got impatient with Zuckerman's lack of progress and insisted they try another technique."

"Cadavers."

Galiano nodded. "Lucas stole tissue during routine autopsies."

"Christ."

"But the success rate is better with kids." Galiano stared into my eyes. "You don't get many kids at a morgue. Nordstern's laptop had a slew of articles on Guatemala City's street children."

"Nordstern thought Lucas was murdering orphans for their tissue?" Anger and revulsion crimped my voice.

"We've found no evidence, but we're looking."

"Sweet Jesus."

We both fell silent. A cart rumbled down the corridor. A robotic voice paged Dr. Someone.

"What about Miguel Gutiérrez?"

416

"Just a brain-fried hump who couldn't have the girl he wanted."

"Claudia de la Alda."

Galiano nodded.

"It's all so sad, isn't it?" I said.

With no forewarning he leaned over and kissed me. His lips felt soft and warm, his crooked nose rough against my skin.

"But I also met you, *corazón*."

31

By mid-June we had completed our Chupan Ya work.

Twenty-three sets of remains had been returned to their families. The village had interred its dead with great ceremony, much wailing, and an enormous sense of relief. Clyde Snow had flown down from Oklahoma, and the entire FAFG team had attended. There was the feeling of a tough job well done. We had stood up for something, had lit one match in the darkness.

But there was a lot of darkness. I thought of Señora Eduardo and Señora De la Alda, and of their daughters.

I thought of oppression, greed, psychosis. Of decent people gone forever.

Hector Lucas, Maria Zuckerman, and Carlos Vicente were dead. Jorge Serano and Miguel Angel Gutiérrez were in jail.

Mateo and Elena were compiling a full report on Chupan Ya.

Maybe there would be some account for that atrocity.

General Effraín Ríos Montt was president during 1982 and 1983 when hundreds of villages were destroyed and thousands killed. In June 2001, victims of the massacres brought a genocide case against General Montt, now head of the Guatemala congress. The suit faced considerable obstacles. Hopefully we had removed some.

Ten-fifteen. June twenty-first. The first day of summer in the northern hemisphere.

I threw the last few toiletries into my suitcase and surveyed the room. A small weaving I'd bought at the market in Chichicastenango still hung where I'd tacked it above the bed. I retrieved and studied it once more.

The Kabawil is common in Mayan textiles. *Kaba* means two. *Wil* means head. According to myth, the two-headed bird can see day and night, far and near. It is the symbol of present and future, of long- and short-range plans. It represents the alliance between humans and nature.

I tucked the Kabawil into my suitcase.

The Kabawil also represents the alliance between men and women.

I'd spent many nights pondering my alliance with men. Two men, to be precise.

Ryan never returned to the topic he'd broached at my bedside. Perhaps my recovery had assuaged his fears. Perhaps I'd hallucinated the whole exchange. But he had suggested a holiday together.

Galiano also wanted to take me away.

I knew I was beginning to resemble my passport photo. I needed a vacation.

I also knew I was pursuing a course in my personal life that had no resolution, or that I was pursuing no course at all.

I'd made a decision.

Experience is a valuable thing. It enables us to recognize mistakes when we repeat them.

Was I making a mistake?

If I didn't try, I'd never find out. I desperately wanted to rekindle happiness within me and was taking all the steps. But I feared for my success. This time more than ever my work had left me a wounded person, and recovery would not come quickly.

Each time I thought of Señora Ch'i'p, I felt a great emptiness.

The phone rang.

"I'm in the lobby."

His voice sounded lighter than it had in weeks.

"I've just finished packing," I said.

"Hope you're focused on sun and sand."

"I'm bringing everything."

"Ready?"

Oh, yeah. My hair was shiny enough to cause glare blindness. I was wearing a babe sundress and sandals. And Victoria's Secret panties and bra.

And mascara and blush.

I was ready.

Read on for an exclusive extract from

BARE BONES

available now in Arrow Books

1

As I was packaging what remained of the dead baby, the man I would kill was burning pavement north toward Charlotte.

I didn't know that at the time. I'd never heard the man's name, knew nothing of the grisly game in which he was a player.

At that moment I was focused on what I would say to Gideon Banks. How would I break the news that his grandchild was dead; his youngest daughter on the run?

My brain cells had been bickering all morning. You're a forensic anthropologist, the logic guys would say. Visiting the family is not your responsibility. The medical examiner will report your findings. The homicide detective will deliver the news. A phone call.

All valid points, the conscience guys would counter. But this case is different. You *know* Gideon Banks.

I felt deep sadness as I tucked the tiny bundle of bones into its container, fastened the lid, and wrote a file number across the plastic. So little to examine. Such a short life.

As I secured the tub in an evidence locker, the memory cells floated an image of Gideon Banks. Wrinkled brown face, fuzzy gray hair, voice like ripping duct tape.

Expand the image.

A small man in a plaid flannel shirt arcing a string mop across a tile floor.

The memory cells had been offering the same image all morning. Though I'd tried to conjure up others, this one kept reappearing.

Gideon Banks and I had worked together at the University of North Carolina at Charlotte for almost two decades until his retirement three years back. I'd periodically thanked him for keeping my office and lab clean, given him birthday cards and a small gift each Christmas. I knew he was conscientious, polite, deeply religious, and devoted to his kids.

And he kept the corridors spotless.

That was it. Beyond the workplace, our lives did not connect.

Until Tamela Banks placed her newborn in a wood stove and vanished.

Crossing to my office, I booted my laptop and spread my notes across the desktop. I'd barely begun my report when a form filled the open doorway.

"A home visit really is above and beyond."

I hit "save" and looked up.

The Mecklenburg County Medical Examiner was wearing green surgical scrubs. A stain on his right shoulder mimicked the shape of Massachusetts in dull red.

"I don't mind." Like I didn't mind suppurating boils on my buttocks.

"I'll be glad to speak to him."

Tim Larabee might have been handsome were it not for his addiction to running. The daily marathon training had wizened his body, thinned his hair, and leatherized his face. The perpetual tan seemed to gather in the hollows of his cheeks, and to pool around eyes set way too deep. Eyes that were now crimped with concern.

"Next to God and the Baptist church, family has been the cornerstone of Gideon Banks's life," I said. "This will shake him."

"Perhaps it's not as bad as it seems."

I gave Larabee The Look. We'd had this conversation an hour earlier.

"All right." He raised a sinewy hand. "It seems bad. I'm sure Mr. Banks will appreciate the personal input. Who's driving you?"

"Skinny Slidell."

"Your lucky day."

"I wanted to go alone, but Slidell refused to take no for an answer."

"Not Skinny?" Mock surprise.

"I think Skinny's hoping for some kind of lifetime achievement award."

"I think Skinny's hoping to get laid."

I pegged a pen at him. He batted it down.

"Watch yourself."

Larabee withdrew. I heard the autopsy room door click open, then shut.

I checked my watch. Three forty-two. Slidell would be here in twenty minutes. The brain cells did a collective cringe. On Skinny there was cerebral agreement.

I shut the computer down and leaned back in my chair.

What would I say to Gideon Banks?

Bad luck, Mr. Banks. Looks like your youngest gave birth, wrapped the tyke in a blanket, and used him as kindling.

Good, Brennan.

Wham-o! The visual cells sent up a new mental image. Banks pulling a Kodak print from a cracked leather wallet. Six brown faces. Close haircuts for the boys, pigtails for the girls. All with teeth too big for the smiles.

Zoom out.

The old man beaming over the photo, adamant that each child would go to college.

Did they?

No idea.

I slipped off my lab coat and hung it on the hook behind my door.

If the Banks kids had attended UNC-Charlotte while I was on the faculty, they'd shown little interest in anthropology. I'd met only one. Reggie, a son mid-range in the offspring chronology, had taken my Human Evolution course.

The memory cells offered a gangly kid in a baseball cap, brim back, connector band low over razor blade brows. Last row in the lecture hall. A intellect, C+ effort.

How long ago? Fifteen years? Eighteen?

I'd worked with a lot of students back then. In those days my research focused on the ancient dead, and I'd taught several undergraduate classes. *Bioarchaeology. Osteology. Primate Ecology.*

One morning an anthro grad showed up at my lab. A homicide detective with the Charlotte-Mecklenburg PD, she'd brought bones recovered from a shallow grave. Could her former prof determine if the remains were those of a missing child?

I could. They were.

That case was my first encounter with coroner work. Today the only seminar I teach is in forensic anthropology, and I commute between Charlotte and Montreal serving as forensic anthropologist to each jurisdiction.

The geography had been difficult when I'd taught full-time, requiring complex choreography within the academic calendar. Now, save for the duration of that single seminar, I shift as needed. A few weeks north, a few weeks south, longer when case work or court testimony requires.

North Carolina and Quebec? Long story.

My academic colleagues call what I do "applied". Using my knowledge of bones, I tease detail from cadavers and skeletons, or parts thereof, too compromised for autopsy. I give names to the skeletal, the decomposed, the mummified, the burned, and the mutilated who might otherwise go to anonymous graves. For some, I determine the manner and time of their passing.

With Tamela's baby there'd been but a cup of charred fragments. A newborn is chump change to a wood stove.

Mr. Banks, I'm so sorry to have to tell you, but –

My cell phone sounded.

"Yo, Doc. I'm parked out front." Skinny Slidell. Of the twenty-four detectives in the Charlotte-Mecklenburg PD Felony Investigative Bureau/Homicide unit, perhaps my least favorite.

"Be right there."

I'd been in Charlotte several weeks when an informant's tip led to the shocking discovery in the wood stove. The bones came to me. Slidell and his partner caught the case as a homicide. They'd tossed the scene, tracked down witnesses, taken statements. Everything led to Tamela Banks.

I shouldered my purse and laptop and headed out. In passing, I stuck my head into the autopsy room. Larabee looked up from his gunshot victim and waggled a gloved finger in warning.

My reply was an exaggerated eye roll.

The Mecklenburg County Medical Examiner facility occupies one end of a featureless brick shoebox that entered life as a Sears Garden Center. The other end of the shoebox houses satellite offices of the Charlotte-Mecklenburg Police Department. Devoid of architectural charm save a slight rounding of the edges, the building is surrounded by enough asphalt to pave Rhode Island.

As I exited the double glass doors, my nostrils drank in an olfactory cocktail of exhaust, smog, and hot pavement. Heat radiated from the building walls, and from the brick steps connecting it to a small tentacle of the parking lot.

Hot town. Summer in the city.

A black woman sat in the vacant lot across College Street, back to a sycamore, elephant legs stretched full-length on the grass. The woman was fanning herself with a newspaper, animatedly arguing some point with a non-existent adversary.

A man in a Hornets jersey was muscling a shopping cart up the sidewalk in the direction of the county services building. He stopped just past the woman, wiped his forehead with the crook of his arm, and checked his cargo of plastic bags.

Noticing my gaze, the cart man waved. I waved back.

Slidell's Ford Taurus idled at the bottom of the stairs, AC blasting, tinted windows full-up. Descending, I opened the back door, shoved aside file folders, a pair of golf shoes stuffed with audio tapes, two Burger King bags, and a squeeze tube of suntan lotion, and wedged my computer into the newly created space.

Erskine "Skinny" Slidell undoubtedly thought of himself as "old school", though God alone knew what institution would claim him. With his knock-off Ray-Bans, Camel breath, and four-letter speech, Slidell was an unwittingly self-created caricature of a Hollywood cop. People told me he was good at his job. I found it hard to believe.

At the moment of my approach Dirty Harry was checking his lower incisors in the rear view mirror, lips curled back in a monkey fear grimace.

Hearing the rear door open, Slidell jumped, and his hand shot to the mirror. As I slid into the passenger seat, he was fine-tuning the rear view with the diligence of an astronaut adjusting Hubble.

"Doc." Slidell kept his faux Ray-Bans pointed at the mirror.

"Detective." I nodded, placed my purse at my feet, and closed the door.

At last satisfied with the angle of reflection, Slidell abandoned the mirror, shifted into gear, crossed the lot, and shot across College onto Phifer.

We rode in silence. Though the temperature in the car was thirty degrees lower than that outside, the air was thick with its own blend of odors. Old Whoppers and fries. Sweat. Bain de Soleil. The bamboo mat on which Slidell parked his ample backside.

Skinny Slidell himself. The man smelled and looked like a before shot for an anti-smoking poster. During the decade and a half I'd been consulting to the Mecklenburg County ME, I'd had the pleasure of working with Slidell on several occasions. Each had been a trip to Aggravation Row. This case promised to be another.

The Banks home was in the Cherry neighborhood, just southeast of I-277, Charlotte's version of an inner beltway. Cherry, unlike many inner city *quartiers*, had not enjoyed the renaissance in recent years experienced by Dilworth and Elizabeth, its neighbors to the west and north. While those neighborhoods had integrated and yuppified, Cherry's fortunes had headed south. But the community held true to its ethnic roots. It started out black and remained so today.

Within minutes Slidell passed an Auto Bell carwash, turned left off Independence Boulevard onto a narrow street, then right onto another. Oaks and magnolias thirty, forty, a hundred years old threw shadows onto modest frame and brick houses. Laundry hung limp on clotheslines. Sprinklers ticked and whirred, or lay silent at the ends of garden hoses. Bicycles and big wheels dotted yards and walkways.

Slidell pulled to the curb halfway up the block, and jabbed a thumb at a small bungalow with dormer windows jutting from the roof. The siding was brown, the trim white.

"Beats the hell outa that rat's nest where the kid got fried. Thought I'd catch scabies tossing that dump."

"Scabies is caused by mites." My voice was chillier than the car interior.

"Exactly. You wouldn't have believed that shithole."

"You should have worn gloves."

"You got that right. And a respirator. These people –"

"What people would that be, detective?"

"Some folks live like pigs."

"Gideon Banks is a hard-working, decent man who raised six children largely on his own."

"Wife beat feet?"

"Melba Banks died of breast cancer ten years ago." There. I did know something about my co-worker.

"Bum luck."

The radio crackled some message that was lost on me.

"Still don't excuse kids dropping their shorts with no regard for consequences. Get jammed up? No-o-o-o problem. Have an abortion."

Slidell killed the engine and turned the Ray-Bans on me.

"Or worse."

"There may be some explanation for Tamela Banks's actions."

I didn't really believe that, had spent all morning taking the opposite position with Tim Larabee. But Slidell was so irritating I found myself playing devil's advocate.

"Right. And the chamber of commerce will probably name her mother of the year."

"Have you met Tamela?" I asked, forcing my voice level.

"No. Have you?"

No. I ignored Slidell's question.

"Have you met any of the Banks family?"

"No, but I took statements from folks who were snorting lines in the next room while Tamela incinerated her kid." Slidell pocketed the keys. "*Excusez-moi* if I haven't dropped in for tea with the lady and her relations."

"You've never had to deal with any of the Banks kids because they were raised with good, solid values. Gideon Banks is as straight laced as –"

"The Mutt Tamela's screwing ain't close to straight-up."

"The baby's father?"

"Unless Miss Hot Pants was entertaining while Daddy was dealing."

Easy! The man is a cockroach.

"Who is he?"

"His name is Darryl Tyree. Tamela was shacking up in Tyree's little piece of heaven out south Tryon."

"Tyree sells drugs?"

"And we're not talking the Eckerd's pharmacy." Slidell hit the door handle and got out.

I bit back a response. *One hour. It's over.*

A stab of guilt. Over for me, but what about Gideon Banks? What about Tamela and her dead baby?

I joined Slidell on the sidewalk.

"Je-zus. It's hot enough to burn a polar bear's butt."

"It's August."

"I should be at the beach."

Yes, I thought. Under four tons of sand.

I followed Slidell up a narrow walk littered with fresh mown grass, to a small cement stoop. He pressed a thumb to a rusted button beside the front door, dug a hanky from his back pocket, and wiped his face.

No response.

Slidell knocked on a wooden portion of the screen door.

Nothing.

Slidell knocked again. His forehead glistened and his hair was separating into wet clumps.

"Police, Mr. Banks."

Slidell banged with the heel of his hand. The screen door rattled in its frame.

"Gideon Banks!"

Condensation dripped from a window AC to the left of the door. A lawn mower whined in the distance. Hip-hop drifted from somewhere up the block.

Slidell banged again. A dark crescent winked from his gray polyester armpit.

"Anyone home?"

The AC's compressor kicked on. A dog barked.

Slidell yanked the screen.

Whrrrrp!

Pounded on the wooden door.

Bam! Bam! Bam!

Barked his demand.

"Police! Anyone there?"

Across the street a curtain flicked, dropped back into place.

Had I imagined it?

A drop of perspiration rolled down my back to join the others soaking my bra and waistband.

At that moment my cell phone rang.

I answered.

That call swept me into a vortex of events that ultimately led to my taking a life.

**Order further Kathy Reichs titles
from your local bookshop, or have them delivered
direct to your door by Bookpost**

☐	**Déjà Dead**	0 09 925518 9	£6.99
☐	**Death du Jour**	0 09 925519 7	£6.99
☐	**Deadly Décisions**	0 09 930710 3	£6.99
☐	**Fatal Voyage**	0 09 930720 0	£6.99
☐	**Bare Bones**	0 09 944147 0	£6.99
☐	**Monday Mourning**	0 09 944148 9	£6.99
☐	**Cross Bones**	0 09 944149 7	£6.99

Free post and packing
Overseas customers allow £2 per paperback

Phone: 01624 677237

Post: Random House Books
c/o Bookpost, PO Box 29, Douglas, Isle of Man IM99 1BQ

Fax: 01624 670923

email: bookshop@enterprise.net

Cheques (payable to Bookpost) and credit cards accepted

Prices and availability subject to change without notice.
Allow 28 days for delivery.
When placing your order, please state if you do not wish to receive any
additional information.

www.randomhouse.co.uk/arrowbooks

arrow books